WORST FEARS REALIZED

Books by Stuart Woods

FICTION

Worst Fears Realized*
Orchid Beach
Swimming to Catalina*
Dead in the Water*
Dirt*
Choke
Imperfect Strangers
Heat
Dead Eyes
L.A. Times
Sante Fe Rules
New York Dead*
Palindrome
Grass Roots
White Cargo
Under the Lake
Deep Lie
Run Before the Wind
Chiefs

TRAVEL

A Romantic's Guide to the Country Inns
of Britain and Ireland *(1978)*

MEMOIR

Blue Water, Green Skipper

*A Stone Barrington Book

WORST FEARS REALIZED

A NOVEL

STUART WOODS

HarperCollins*Publishers*

*This book is for
Elaine Kaufman*

WORST FEARS REALIZED. Copyright © 1999 by Stuart Woods. All rights reserved. Printed in the United States of America. No part of this book may be used or reproduced in any manner whatsoever without written permission except in the case of brief quotations embodied in critical articles and reviews. For information address HarperCollins Publishers, Inc., 10 East 53rd Street, New York, NY 10022-5299.

HarperCollins books may be purchased for educational, business, or sales promotional use. For information please write: Special Markets Department, HarperCollins Publishers, Inc., 10 East 53rd Street, New York, NY 10022-5299.

FIRST EDITION

Designed by Kyoko Watanabe

Library of Congress Cataloging-in-Publication Data

Woods, Stuart.
    Worst fears realized / Stuart Woods. — 1st.
       p.   cm.
    ISBN 0-06-019182-1
    I. Title.
PS3573.O642W67   1999
813' .51—ds21   98-52924

99 00 01 02 03 ❖/RRD 10 9 8 7 6 5 4 3 2 1

1

THE PAIN LAY BURIED SOMEWHERE IN THE DEPTHS OF Stone Barrington's upper body; a cross between a slipped disc and a coronary, it seemed. It had begun after a phone conversation early in the previous winter. The call, from Arrington Carter, had ended everything. Now she was the wife of another man, living in his house, rearing his son. He would never see her again, except in her husband's company, and he would never think of her again without feeling the pain.

He had never believed it would persist into the following spring, but it had. If anything, it was worse. He saw Dino a couple of times a week, always at Elaine's. Dino was his closest friend—sometimes, he felt, his only friend. Not true, of course. Elaine was his friend, and the evenings in her restaurant, with Elaine and Dino, were the only bright spots in his week. His law practice had lately been boring, a personal injury suit that dragged on and on, a bone thrown to him by Woodman & Weld, because there wasn't enough meat on it to nourish a firm with thirty partners and a hundred associates. They were ready to go to trial, and the expected settlement offer had not materialized. It was depressing. *Everything* was depressing. And the pain continued, assuaged only by bourbon, and he had done too much assuaging lately. He sat at table number five, at Elaine's, with Dino, and ordered another assuagement.

"Let's go to a party," Dino said. "Have your next one there."

"I don't feel like going to a party with a lot of cops," Stone said.

"It's not a cop party."

"You don't know anybody but cops," Stone said.

Dino caught the waiter's eye and signaled for a check. "I know lots of people," he said.

"Name three who aren't cops or Mafiosi."

"It's not a Mafia party, either," Dino said, dodging the question.

"Whose party is it?"

"It's at a deputy DA's."

"Oh. Then we get to bring our own booze."

"His name is Martin B-r-o-u-g-h-a-m," he spelled, "pronounced 'Broom,' and he's got some money, I think."

"Isn't he handling the Dante trial?" Dante was a crime boss, and his trial was the most important since Gotti's.

"He got a conviction this afternoon."

"I hadn't heard."

"Don't you watch the news anymore?"

"Not much."

"The party is to celebrate the conviction."

"How come I don't know Brougham?"

"Because he runs with a classier crowd than you're accustomed to. The only seedy lawyers he meets are in court."

"Who are you calling a seedy lawyer?"

"How many lawyers are at this table?"

"I am *not* a seedy lawyer; I just take seedy cases. There's a difference."

"Whatever you say," Dino said, standing up and reaching for his raincoat. "Let's get out of here."

"I don't want to," Stone grumbled.

"You don't want to do *anything*, you desolate fuck, and I can't stand it anymore. Now put your coat on and come with me, or I'll just shoot you here and now. Nobody would ever prosecute me; it would be justifiable homicide."

"Oh, all right," Stone said, struggling to his feet and grabbing his coat. "One drink, if the guy serves decent booze. Then I'm out of there."

The apartment was a duplex in the East Sixties, definitely not the preserve of an assistant DA.

"You're right," Stone said, as they handed their coats to a maid. "He's got money. There's at least a million dollars of art hanging in this room."

"What are you, his insurance agent?" Dino whispered. "Try and have a good time, okay?"

"Tell me more about this guy," Stone said.

"Word is, he's up for chief deputy DA, and he's going to run for DA, if the old man ever retires."

"He'll grow old waiting," Stone said.

A handsome man of about forty spotted Dino and came across the room, towing a tall blond woman in a Chanel suit.

"Dino," he said, shaking hands. "I'm glad you could make it. You remember Dana."

The woman shook Dino's hand. "Who's this?" she asked, turning her gaze on Stone.

"This is Stone Barrington, Dana. Stone, this is Martin and Dana Brougham."

"How do you do?" Stone said mechanically, shaking their hands.

"I've heard of you," Brougham said, steering Stone and Dino toward the bar. "You were Dino's partner at the Nineteenth Precinct a while back, weren't you?"

"A while back," Stone echoed. "After I left the force they had to kick him upstairs; nobody else would ride in the same car with him."

"You're over at Woodman and Weld, aren't you?"

"I'm of counsel, to them," Stone replied, "but Woodman and

Weld would probably rather you didn't know it." It was a remark he wouldn't have made if he had been entirely sober.

Brougham laughed. "What are you drinking?"

"Wild Turkey on the rocks, if you have it."

Brougham grabbed a bottle that looked like a crystal decanter and poured Stone a double. "This is Wild Turkey, but it's got a leg up on the standard stuff."

Stone tasted the whiskey. The man was right. This stuff cost thirty bucks a bottle; he was beginning to like Brougham.

A couple arrived at the front door, and Brougham went off to greet them. "Wander around," he said. "Meet some people."

Stone looked around. The room was jammed with people, and somebody was playing the piano rather well. "I see at least four cops," he said to Dino.

"So what? There are a lot of civilians here, too."

"If you consider assistant DA's civilians. Who's the tall guy by the fireplace?"

"Tom Deacon. He runs the DA's investigative division."

"I don't like him," Stone said.

"Have you ever even met him?"

"No."

"What the hell is the matter with you lately?"

"He's got shifty eyes."

"He's with the DA, isn't he?"

The party had clearly been going on for some time, because there was no food left, and everybody had had several drinks. Stone was as drunk as any of them but not as gregarious. He looked for a quiet corner. He left Dino with Dana Brougham and walked through a pair of double doors, into a handsome library. A pair of leather wing chairs faced each other before a cheerful fire, and Stone headed for one. He sat down, glad to be alone; then he saw that the other chair was occupied.

A chestnut-haired woman in a pin-striped suit sat with her legs pulled under her, reading by firelight from a leather-bound book.

She glanced at him, raised her glass a millimeter in greeting, then went back to her book.

"You'll ruin your eyes," Stone said.

She gazed at him for a moment. "You've changed, Mom."

"Sorry. What are you reading?"

"*Lady Chatterley's Lover.*"

"I haven't read that since high school," he said.

"I haven't read it at all," she replied.

"It seemed terribly erotic at sixteen, but then almost everything did."

She smiled a little but didn't look up. "I remember."

"Where were you when you were sixteen?"

"At Spence."

Spence was a very tony Manhattan private school.

"And after that?"

"Yale."

"Law?"

"Yes. I work for Martin."

"Funny, you don't look like an assistant DA."

"That's the nicest thing anybody has said to me this year."

"Then you've been seeing the wrong men."

"You're not only courtly, you're clairvoyant."

"I can't divine your name."

"Susan Bean."

"Of the L.L. Beans?"

"No, and not of the Merrill, Lynch, Pierce, Fenner, and Beans, either. Of the entirely undistinguished Beans. And you?"

"Stone Barrington."

"I believe I've heard the name. Of the Massachusetts Great Barringtons, I presume?"

Stone shook his head. "Of the Massachusetts Lesser Barringtons."

"And how did you come to be in the big city?"

"It was easy; I was born here. After my parents had bailed out of Massachusetts."

5

"Are you hungry?"

To his surprise, he was. He'd hardly touched his dinner at Elaine's. "Yes."

"The canapés were already gone when I got here. You want to get some dinner someplace?"

"I do."

She stood up, and she was taller than he had expected. Quite beautiful, too. Stone got out of his chair. "Did you have a coat?"

"Yes."

"Let's go find it."

He took her arm, and, just for a moment, he thought the pain had gone away. Not quite, but a little. He steered her toward the front door, avoiding their hosts. Dino gave him a surreptitious wink, and a moment later, they were on the sidewalk.

"It's nearly eleven," Stone said, glancing at his watch. "I wonder if anyplace is still serving around here."

"My apartment is only a couple of blocks away," she said, "and there's a good Chinese place that delivers."

"Perfect," he said.

"It's not perfect, but it delivers."

"I wasn't talking about Chinese food."

2

THEY WALKED AT A LEISURELY PACE, CHATTING IDLY. Her voice was low and musical, and Stone enjoyed listening.

"I recall that you are a lawyer, but I forget with whom," she said.

"I'm in private practice."

She laughed. "At Yale law we were taught to believe that 'private practice' meant you couldn't get a job with a good firm."

"That's probably a fair characterization, but my excuse is that I was a cop for fourteen years and came to the practice of law, as opposed to the upholding of it, late in life. I'm of counsel to Woodman and Weld, but I work out of a home office."

She wrinkled her brow. "That's kind of weird, isn't it?"

"Yes, it is, I guess."

"Oh, I get it; you do the dirty work, the stuff they don't want to be seen to handle."

"You're very quick."

"That's what they say about me down at the DA's Office," she said. "'Susan Bean is very quick.' Of course, that's not *all* they say about me."

They stopped for a traffic light. "What else do they say?"

"Some call me the conscience of the office; others call me a pain in the ass. I guess it's pretty much the same thing."

"What are you working on now?"

"I was second chair to Martin Brougham on the Dante case," she said.

"Congratulations," Stone replied. "That was a big win."

"I guess so."

"You don't sound very happy about it."

"Oh, I'm glad we won," she said. "I'm just not very happy about *how* we won."

He was about to ask her what she meant when they arrived at her apartment building. She dug for a key and let them in; they took the elevator to the top floor, which was marked PH on the button.

"The penthouse?" Stone said. "Pretty fancy for an ADA."

"It's the top floor, the twelfth. That's its only qualification as a penthouse."

They rode up, and she opened the door to the apartment. It was small—living room, a dining alcove, bedroom, and kitchen. There was a small terrace overlooking the street. Any skyline view was blocked by a taller building across the street.

She went into the kitchen, dug a menu out of a drawer, and picked up the phone. "Trust me on the selections?" she asked.

"Sure, but nothing too spicy for me."

She dialed the number and read off a list of dishes. "How long?" she asked. She listened, then covered the phone. "The delivery boy is out sick; would you mind picking it up? It's not far."

"Glad to," Stone said.

"How long?" she asked again. "Okay, twenty minutes." She hung up. "Can I get you a drink? Twenty minutes really means thirty."

"Maybe some wine?"

She dug a bottle of chardonnay out of the fridge and handed it to Stone with a corkscrew. "You open it; I'm clumsy."

Stone opened the bottle and poured them a glass. He threw his coat on a chair, and they sat on the sofa.

"That was quite a list of dishes you ordered," he said.

"I exist on leftovers from takeout," she replied. "So what fascinating dirty work are you doing for Woodman and Weld at the moment?" she asked.

"A personal injury suit," he replied. "Dirty work isn't always fascinating."

"Is it a fascinating injury?"

"Not in the least. A Woodman and Weld client's daughter was hurt in an automobile accident, and the other driver's insurance company has been recalcitrant about paying her for her pain and suffering."

"They usually are."

"What's next for you at the DA's Office, now that you've put Dante away?"

She sighed. "I don't know; I'm thinking about giving it up. It wears on me, you know?"

"I think I do, but it sounds like Brougham is on his way up. Won't he take you with him?"

"Yes, but I'm not sure I want to go. When I joined the DA's Office I was pretty idealistic, I guess. I saw it as the good guys against the bad guys, but now I'm not sure there *are* any good guys."

"Life is a gray area," Stone said.

"It's *charcoal* gray and getting darker," she said. "Did I ask you if you're married?"

"No; I'm not."

"Divorced?"

"Nope."

"A lifelong bachelor? My God! Are you gay?"

"Nope."

"Why did you never marry?"

"Just lucky, I guess." He had been using that answer for a long time. "What about you?"

"A spinster at thirty-two," she replied.

"Not for want of offers, I suspect."

"I've had my moments." She looked at him oddly. "May I kiss you?"

Stone laughed. "I've been kissed, but I've never been asked."

"May I?"

"You don't need to ask," he said.

She leaned over, put her fingertips on his face, and drew him to her.

Her lips were firm and purposeful, and her tongue lay in waiting, darting into his mouth from time to time. He snaked an arm around her and pulled her closer, but she broke off the kiss and looked at her watch.

"Uh-oh, our dinner's getting cold." She stood up and threw him his coat. "To be continued after Chinese food. I'll set the table and make some tea. Hurry."

Stone got into his coat.

"Here," she said, "take my key, so I won't have to buzz you in." She handed it to him.

Stone pocketed the key, kissed her quickly, and left the apartment. It was a block and a half to the restaurant, and he had to wait a bit for the food. It came in a large paper bag, and he paid and left, walking quickly back to the apartment house. He let himself in, went to the elevator, and pressed the button. He looked up at the lights and saw that the elevator was on the top floor. Shortly, it began to move. Elevators in short buildings moved slowly, he reflected. It stopped on the sixth floor, then began moving down again, finally reaching the ground floor. Stone pressed PH and the car crept upward.

He let himself into the apartment. Music was playing, and a loud whistling noise emanated from the kitchen. The kettle was boiling. He set the food down on the dining table, shucked off his coat, and walked toward the whistling noise. The kitchen light was off, and the single living-room lamp didn't offer much illumination. He groped for the light switch but couldn't find it. Blindly, he groped his way toward the stove, aiming at the gas flame. *Susan must be in the john*, he thought. Now that he was closer, the kettle's whistle had become a scream.

He took another step, and, suddenly, he was slipping, falling. He hit the floor with a *thump*, groaning, as his elbow took most of his weight. He put a hand on the floor to help himself up, but it was slippery, and he fell again. She had apparently spilled something on the floor. The kettle screamed on.

He grabbed hold of the kitchen counter, hoisted himself to his feet, and turned off the gas jet. Slowly, the scream died. He groped his way back toward the kitchen door, holding on to the counter, and felt again for the light switch. This time he found it and turned it on.

He looked at his hands, dumbfounded. They were covered in red paint. Slowly, still holding on to keep from slipping, he turned and looked back into the kitchen. The paint was everywhere, but it wasn't paint.

Susan Bean lay on her back next to the wall, staring at the ceiling. Her throat gaped open. He made himself move toward her, knelt at her side, and felt her wrist for a pulse. Nothing. There was no point it trying CPR, he realized. Close up, he could see that she had been very nearly decapitated.

Stone got shakily to his feet, holding on to whatever he could for support. He made it to the kitchen phone, picked it up, and started to call Dino's cell phone, then he stopped.

"No," he said aloud. He dialed 911.

"What is your emergency?" a woman's voice said.

"Is the tape rolling?" he asked.

"You're being recorded, sir; what is your emergency?"

"My name is Stone Barrington; I'm a retired police officer. I've got a homicide in the top-floor apartment at . . ." He looked around for something, found a gas bill, and gave her the address. "White female, age thirty-two, name of Susan Bean. I need homicide detectives and the coroner."

"I've got it, Mr. Barrington."

"Oh . . . tell the squad car that the perpetrator is probably a lone male, on foot, and that he's probably still in the neighborhood."

"Got it. They're on their way."

Stone hung up and dialed Dino's cell phone.

"Bacchetti," Dino's voice said. There was party noise in the background.

"It's Stone; I'm sitting on a homicide about three blocks from the party." He read the address off the gas bill again.

"Have you called nine-one-one?"

"Yes."

"I'll be there as fast as I can."

"I think the perp was in the building when I got here, and I'll bet he's still in the neighborhood."

"I'll keep an eye out. Don't start working the scene, Stone; let my people do that."

"Right."

"I'm on my way."

Stone hung up, sat on a chair at the dining table, and tried not to think about what was in the next room. He was badly shaken. He'd seen a lot of dead bodies in his years as a homicide detective, but never one that had just kissed him.

3

TWO DETECTIVES ARRIVED FIRST. STONE LET THEM IN
and pointed at the kitchen. "She's in there," he said, then sat
down at the dining table again. They went into the kitchen, then
came right out again. One was a big guy, six-three or -four; the other
was much shorter, stocky, florid-faced.

"Stand up," the shorter one said to Stone.

"What?"

"*Stand up!*"

Stone stood up.

The shorter cop swung a right and caught Stone under the ear.

Stone spun to his right and fell onto the tabletop. Before he
could move both cops were on him, handcuffing him. "What the hell
are you doing?" Stone demanded.

They sat him back in the chair, and the short cop hit him again.
"Murdering bastard!" the cop said, and then his larger partner
restrained him.

"Easy, Mick," the bigger man said. "You'll mark him, and we
don't want that."

Stone sat still, saying nothing.

"Why'd you kill her?" the short one demanded.

"I didn't kill her; I found her as she is," Stone said.

"Then why is her blood all over you?" he said, raising his fist again.

The bigger detective caught his wrist. "Mick," he said quietly, "don't make me cuff you."

The smaller cop shot him a murderous glance. "Just try it," he said.

"Stand away from him," the bigger man said.

Reluctantly, the short cop backed away.

"Sorry about that, sir," the large cop said. "I'm Detective Anderson, and this is Detective Kelly." He took out a notebook. "What is your name?"

"Stone Barrington."

Anderson looked up from his notebook and paused for a moment. "You want to tell me what happened here, Mr. Barrington?"

"I went out for Chinese food; I came back and found her as she is. I slipped on the kitchen floor and fell, that's why I'm bloody. I called nine-one-one."

"Lying fuck!" Kelly said, and started toward Stone again.

Anderson put a hand on his chest and pushed him against the wall. "I'm not going to tell you again, Mick."

There was a loud hammering on the door.

"Get that," Anderson said to his partner, shoving him toward the door.

Kelly yanked open the door and Dino Bacchetti walked in. He looked around. "Where's the corpse?" he asked.

"In there, Lieutenant," Kelly said, jerking a thumb in the direction of the kitchen.

"Stone, are you okay?" Dino asked.

"I'm cuffed," Stone replied.

"Kelly, get the cuffs off that man," Dino said.

"But Lieutenant . . ."

"Do it."

Kelly dug out his keys and took the handcuffs off.

Stone stood up, rubbing his wrists; then he hit Kelly squarely in the nose, sending him sprawling.

"All right," Dino said, "everybody calm down." Kelly was scrambling to his feet, blood streaming from his nose, heading for Stone. Dino hit him in the forehead with his open palm, knocking him down again. "I said calm down." Kelly got up more slowly this time. Dino turned to Anderson. "Did you see any of that, Andy?"

"See what?" Anderson asked.

Dino walked over to Stone and examined his jaw. "You okay?"

"I'm okay now," Stone said.

"You're covered in blood; any of it yours?"

"No."

"All right, everybody take a seat, and let's find out what happened."

The four men sat down at the table.

Kelly dabbed a handkerchief at the blood on his face. "I think he broke my fucking nose," he said to nobody in particular.

"Good," Stone said.

"Andy," Dino said.

Anderson placed his notebook on the table. "Let's start again," he said. "Can I have your address, Mr. Barrington?"

Stone gave him his address, then began at the beginning, at Martin Brougham's party, and brought everybody up-to-date. While he was talking, two uniformed cops arrived, along with two EMTs and somebody from the medical examiner's office.

Anderson reached over to the bag of Chinese food, ripped off the check stapled to the bag, and handed it to a uniform. "Go over to this restaurant, find out who ordered this food and when, who picked it up and when, and get a description," he said.

The cop left with the check.

Stone resumed his story.

Anderson waited for Stone to finish. "Is that it?" he asked.

"One other thing: I think the perp was still in the building when I got back with the food."

"Why do you think that?"

"When I rang for the elevator, it was on the top floor, and this is the only apartment on twelve. The elevator moved down to six, stopped, then continued to the ground floor. Where was it when you got here?"

"On the ground floor," Anderson said.

"Then, unless another tenant or a visitor used the elevator between the time I got to this floor and the time you arrived, the perp waited on six until the car stopped up here and I got out, then he rang for it again and rode it down to the ground floor."

"Pretty cool," Dino said.

"Yes, pretty cool," Stone agreed.

The uniformed cop returned. "A Miss Bean ordered the food by phone; the time is written on the check, right here," he said, placing the check on the table. "A man arrived to pick up the food half an hour later, waited five minutes, paid for it, and left. He was over six feet, blond hair, medium to heavy build, dressed in a raincoat."

Anderson looked at the check and did some mental calculating. "That checks with your story, Mr. Barrington," he said.

"Measure the water in the kettle," Stone said.

"What?"

"When I left, Susan said she was going to make some tea. Let's find out how long it takes for the same amount of water to boil. That might help with the time frame."

"Do it, Mick," Anderson said. Kelly got up and went into the kitchen.

They continued talking until the kettle started to whistle. Anderson looked at his watch. "I make it three and a half minutes."

"How much water was in the kettle?" Stone asked Kelly.

"A little under three cups," Kelly replied sullenly.

"Here's one scenario, then," Stone said. "The killer arrives shortly after I leave. Within three and a half minutes. He kills her, then the kettle starts whistling. He turns off the kettle."

"Why?" Kelly asked.

"Because nobody can stand around and listen to a kettle scream-ing like that," Stone said. "Let's see, five minutes for me to walk to the restaurant, I wait five minutes, and five minutes to come back, say fifteen to eighteen minutes. And when I get back, the killer is still in the apartment, maybe. So if he is, what does he do for fifteen min-utes?"

"Searches the place," Anderson said. "A robbery, maybe."

The second uniform spoke up. "I had a look in the bedroom," he said. "Neat as a pin. There's a jewelry box on the dresser with some nice-looking stuff in it."

"So it wasn't a robbery," Anderson said. "What was he looking for?"

"Something of value only to him," Dino replied, standing up and walking to a desk in the living room. He opened the drawers one at a time, including a file drawer, then came back. "Everything is neat. No way to tell if the killer found something."

Kelly spoke up. "And the killer turned on the kettle again before he left? What for?"

"To screw up our timeline," Stone said. "He wanted us to think that he killed her, then left immediately. I think he followed us from Brougham's place, or at least, picked us up on the street en route."

"Did you see anybody?" Dino asked.

"No, but it seems to me that he followed us, waited for me to leave, then went upstairs."

"How'd he get in?" Kelly asked.

"Rang the bell; maybe she thought it was me, even though she had given me the key."

"And she let him in?"

"Maybe he forced his way in, or maybe she knew him," Stone said.

"How'd he know when you were coming back?" Kelly asked.

"He didn't; he thought I'd left to go home. He got lucky. I'll bet he was getting on the elevator when I rang for it. Must have scared him."

"Maybe," Dino said. "Andy, send your patrolmen to talk to everybody in the building. Find out who came and went, and what time."

"Right, Lieutenant," Anderson said.

Dino looked at his watch. "I think it's time to wake up Martin Brougham," he said.

"The DA guy?" Kelly asked. "What for?"

"I want to take a look at her office," Dino said. "Come on, Stone; I'll drive you home; we can't have you out on the streets with blood all over you. You'd just get arrested." He turned to Kelly. "Apologize to Mr. Barrington for your behavior."

Kelly turned beet red. "I apologize," he said. "I thought you were the perp."

"Something you should know, Mick," Anderson said. "Mr. Barrington used to be a detective in the Nineteenth; he was Lieutenant Bacchetti's partner."

Kelly's face fell. "I really am sorry," he said, looking at the floor.

"Sorry about your nose," Stone said. He took care not to sound as if he meant it.

4

STONE WAS AWAKENED BY A RINGING TELEPHONE. HE rolled over, opened an eye, and looked at the bedside clock. Just past ten. He sat up on one elbow. He had been wide-awake until at least four, unable to sleep with the picture of Susan Bean's body stuck in his mind. Finally, he had drifted off and overslept. He picked up the phone.

"Hello?"

"It's Dino."

"Morning."

"You get any sleep?"

"Some. You find anything in Susan's office?"

"Everything was neat as a pin, just like the apartment; nothing missing that anybody could figure. Brougham was pretty upset. Apparently, he depended on her a lot."

"Anything on the murder?"

"Nothing yet, but whoever used the elevator when you came back was the perp. Nobody else in the building had budged from their apartments."

"Not that it does us any good."

"No. There were no prints, no evidence of any kind."

"He had to have a lot of blood on him," Stone said.

"You're right, but the patrol cars didn't come across anybody. Listen, there's something else."

"What?"

"Where's Alma?"

Alma was Stone's secretary, who had worked for him almost since the moment he had begun to practice law, after leaving the NYPD. "She should be in her office," Stone replied.

"Put me on hold and call down there," Dino said.

Stone pressed the HOLD button, then dialed Alma's extension. There was no answer. He pressed line one again. "She's not answering. She worked late last night, typing up a brief for me, so she could have overslept, I guess."

"A woman matching her description was attacked on the sidewalk in your block last night sometime after midnight, when we were at the Bean apartment. She took something like a claw hammer in the head."

Stone sat up and put his feet on the floor. "Where is she and how bad?"

"Lenox Hill, and it doesn't look good. Does she have any family?"

"A sister in Westchester, and that's it," Stone said.

"She wasn't carrying any ID, but she was wearing a Cartier watch that sounds like the one you gave her."

"I'll get up to Lenox Hill right now," Stone said.

"Let me know if it's Alma," Dino replied, then hung up.

Stone got dressed in a hurry, gave his bloody clothes from the night before to his housekeeper to take to the cleaner's, took a cab up to Lenox Hill Hospital, and presented himself at the main desk.

"My name is Stone Barrington," he told the woman behind the desk. "The police called me this morning to say that a woman answering the description of my secretary was admitted last night with a head wound. I'd like to see her right away."

"Just a minute, please," the woman said. She dialed a number and spoke for a moment, then hung up. "Dr. Thompson will be with you in just a minute," she said. "Please have a seat."

Stone paced until the doctor turned up five minutes later. They shook hands. "I'd like to see the Jane Doe brought in last night," he said. "She may be my secretary, Alma Hodges."

"Describe your secretary," the doctor said.

"Five-seven, a hundred and forty, early fifties, dark hair going gray, wearing a pin-striped suit."

The doctor nodded. "Sounds like her. I'm sorry to tell you she died twenty minutes ago."

Stone slumped.

"Her injuries were massive," the doctor said. "She was struck at least half a dozen times with a blunt object, perhaps a hammer. The police thought it was a robbery, since she had no handbag or identification."

"I'd better see her," Stone said.

"I'll walk you downstairs," the doctor replied.

They rode the elevator down to the basement, and the doctor led the way to the morgue. The tray was pulled out of the refrigerator and the sheet pulled back.

She looked utterly peaceful, Stone thought, and quite beautiful. He was glad he didn't have to look at the back of her head. He nodded. "That's Alma Hodges," he said.

"Did she have any family?" the doctor asked.

"A sister. I'll speak to her; then I'll make some arrangements."

"An autopsy is scheduled for this afternoon; I should think the body will be ready for release first thing in the morning."

Stone thanked the doctor and left the hospital. He took a cab home and went down to his office. Alma's desk was in perfect order, his brief stacked neatly on top, with a note saying, SEE YOU IN THE MORNING.

Stone sat down heavily at her desk, found her phone book and her sister's number. He broke the news as gently as he could and said he'd be glad to see to the arrangements. The woman thanked him and said that her brother-in-law was a mortician and she'd have him take care of it. Stone expressed his condolences and told the woman how loyal and valuable Alma had been to him and how much he would miss her. Finally, he was able to hang up, drained from the experience. The phone rang almost immediately.

"Stone Barrington," he said.

"Morning, Stone, it's Frank Maddox," a man's voice said. Maddox was the attorney for the insurance company Stone was suing.

"Yes, Frank?"

"My client has authorized me to offer your client half a million dollars."

"Unacceptable," Stone said. He had already thought out his strategy in responding to an offer. "I'm ready to go to trial." He was anything but ready, he thought. "I'll pass your offer on to my client, but with a strong recommendation that it be rejected."

Maddox sighed. "What's it going to take, Stone? Give me a realistic number, and I'll go back to my client."

"It's going to take a million dollars, plus a three-hundred-thousand-dollar attorney's fee, and that's bottom line, Frank. Don't bother with a counteroffer; just show up in court tomorrow."

"Hold on, Stone." Maddox punched the HOLD button.

Stone waited. Maddox was obviously with his client.

Shortly, the lawyer came back on. "Done," he said.

"I'll want your check by close of business today," Stone said. "I'm not canceling our court date until the money is in the bank."

"I think I can arrange that," Maddox said. "I'll messenger it over to your office this afternoon."

"Send it to Bill Eggers at Woodman and Weld," Stone said. "I may be out this afternoon, and my secretary isn't in today."

"Fine; I'll include the usual release." Maddox hung up.

Stone called Woodman & Weld and asked for Bill Eggers, the managing partner.

"Bill Eggers."

"Bill, it's Stone."

"Morning, Stone. You going to trial tomorrow?"

"They've just settled for a million, plus my fee. The check is coming to you this afternoon. Will you let the client know? I'd call her myself, but it's a very bad day."

"Sure, I'll call her. I think it's a hell of a settlement. What's wrong?"

"Alma was attacked on the street last night, after leaving work; she died this morning."

"Oh, Jesus, Stone, I'm so sorry. I know how close you were."

"Yeah, I'm pretty shaken. I think I'm just going to shut down the phones and take the day."

"You do that. You want me to find somebody to help you out with the work? I can speak to our personnel director."

"Thanks, I'd appreciate that," Stone said. "But don't send anybody until tomorrow."

"Fine. Again, I'm sorry, Stone. You take it easy."

"Thanks, Bill." Stone hung up. He should have been elated at the settlement and a rich fee, but he felt nothing but depression. Two women he knew, one of whom he had been very close to, had been murdered within twelve hours of each other. He switched on his answering machine and recorded a new message. "This is Stone Barrington. I won't be taking any calls today, but if you'll leave a message, I'll return your call tomorrow."

He trudged back upstairs, switched off his phone, and fell into bed, exhausted.

5

STONE GOT UP AS DARKNESS WAS FALLING. HE GOT INTO some khaki trousers, a shirt, and some moccasins, then went to the kitchenette in the master suite and made himself a cup of tea, with a large dollop of honey. He took the mug down one floor to his study and sat in one of a pair of wing chairs before the window overlooking the garden. The doorbell rang; Stone picked up the phone beside his chair. "Yes?"

"It's Dino."

"Come on in; I'm in the study." He pressed the button on the phone that opened the front door.

Dino walked into the study and threw his coat on the sofa.

"Hi. Want a cup of tea?"

"I want a cup of scotch," Dino replied.

"Help yourself."

Dino went to the little wet bar concealed behind a panel and fixed himself a scotch on the rocks, then came and sat down in the chair next to Stone's. "How about some lights?" Dino said.

"I like it this way at dusk," Stone replied. "Leave it for a few minutes."

"How are you feeling?"

"Like somebody worked me over with a baseball bat."

"You went to the hospital?"

"Yeah; it was Alma. Sorry, I forgot to call and tell you."

"A citizen found her handbag in a wastebasket a couple of blocks away. There was over a hundred bucks in it, plus her credit cards."

"Nothing at all taken?"

"Not that we can figure."

"Doesn't make any sense."

"I know."

"She was such a happy person," Stone said. "Didn't matter if I was having a grumpy day; she just took it in stride. Always managed to cheer me up."

"She was a nice lady," Dino said. "I always liked her."

They sat quietly for a while, watching the garden grow dark and the lights come on in the other houses in Turtle Bay, all of which backed up onto the same garden.

"Stone," Dino said finally.

"Yeah?"

"You see any possible connection between these two killings?"

"I thought about that; the only connection is me."

"I thought about that, too," Dino said. "Think for a minute: Is there somebody out there who hates you enough to want to kill people you know?"

"I thought about that, too; couldn't think of anybody."

"Neither could I."

"They can't be connected," Stone said. "It's just an awful coincidence."

"I think you're right; I just had to explore the other possibility."

"I know."

"When you're a cop, or when you've *been* a cop, it's always hanging over your head."

"What is?"

Dino sighed. "The other possibility. The idea that somebody you've busted and sent up will come back to haunt you, to get even. I think that, after getting killed in the line of duty, it's every cop's worst fear."

"I never thought about it until this minute."

"Stone, what did you and Susan Bean talk about last night? We never got into that."

"Just first-date chitchat," Stone said. "What do you do? Where are you from? Like that. She didn't seem to be happy in her job."

"How so?"

"She said she was thinking of leaving the DA's Office."

"From what Martin Brougham told me last night, she was on her way up."

"She said that, but it didn't seem to matter. I think she was just disillusioned with the system; she didn't like the way she had to do her job."

"What do you mean?"

"I don't know; it was just something she said. We never had time to go into it. You know how it is, Dino; a lot of idealistic people don't like an up-close view of how the justice system works. It takes a pretty thick skin to live with it every day."

"Yeah; I had a hard time with it at first, too."

"You? I'm surprised."

"What? You think I've always been the tough-but-honest, cynical cop you see before you? I had to grow a thick hide, just like you had to."

"If you say so."

Across the garden a light came on in a house directly opposite Stone's, and a woman in a business suit walked into a room framed by a large picture window.

"Watch this, Dino," Stone said.

"Watch what?"

"The woman across the way."

"What about her?"

"Just watch. I think you'll find this interesting."

The woman, who was tall with long red hair, began to undress.

"You're right," Dino said, "this is interesting."

"Just keep watching," Stone said.

The woman carefully hung up her suit, then stepped out of her half-slip, unhooked her bra, and slid out of her panty hose and panties. She dropped the underwear into a hamper. Now she was completely naked, exposing a slender but shapely body with high, firm breasts.

"Wow," Dino said softly.

"She's something, isn't she?"

Now the woman went to a closet, took out a vacuum cleaner, plugged it in, and began to vacuum the room.

"What the fuck is she doing?" Dino asked.

"She's vacuuming. She does this two or three times a week; she comes home from work, takes off her clothes, and vacuums her bedroom. Then she disappears for a while. I guess she's vacuuming her whole apartment. Then she comes back into the bedroom, puts away the vacuum, and disappears again. Sometimes she gives a little wave."

"You mean she knows you're watching her?"

"I expect half the neighborhood is watching her," Stone said.

Dino abruptly sat up straight in his chair. "Look at that," he said.

"I *am* looking at it," Stone replied.

"No; there's a guy."

"Where?"

"Standing in the bedroom door."

Stone looked. Dino was right; a shadowy figure stood in the half darkness of the doorway. "Her boyfriend, maybe?"

"No; not the way he's standing. She doesn't know he's there."

"She hasn't seen him, and she can't hear anything over the vacuum noise."

The woman continued to vacuum, turning toward the window. The man began to move toward her. He was short and slender, with bushy, dark hair—almost an afro, though he was white.

"Oh, shit," Dino said. "He's got a knife."

Stone saw that Dino was right. The man walked up behind the woman, snaked an arm around her neck, and yanked her backward, pulling her chin up.

Dino was on his feet, unlocking the window, shoving it open, grabbing the pistol at his belt. "Don't you do it, you son of a bitch!" he screamed.

Stone sat, riveted to his chair. The man was looking directly at them.

Dino raised his pistol and fired twice. Two holes appeared in the upper left-hand corner of the window.

"You've got his attention," Stone said.

It didn't seem to matter that he knew he was being watched. The man drew the knife's blade across the struggling woman's neck, and blood began to spill down her naked body. She collapsed, but he held her up with the hand under her chin, widening the wound in her neck.

"Let her go, and I'll shoot you where you stand, you bastard!" Dino screamed.

Instead, the man began to walk backward toward the door, dragging the dying woman, holding her up as a shield. Then he dropped her and left the room.

"Call nine-one-one!" Dino said, grabbing his coat. "I'm going over there; do you know the address?"

"I don't know the number; you'll have to guess," Stone replied, picking up the phone.

"Wait here and make sure he doesn't leave the house through the garden," Dino said, running for the door.

"Dino!" Stone shouted, stopping him in his tracks.

"What?"

"I know the guy," Stone said. "I know the killer."

"Later," Dino said, running down the stairs.

Stone reported the homicide, then unlocked a cabinet, took out a pistol, and stood, watching the back of the house. Maybe he could get a shot at the guy. Two minutes passed, then Dino appeared in the woman's bedroom, followed by a uniformed officer. He gave the uniform some instructions, and the officer left the room. Dino picked up the phone and dialed a number.

Stone saw the light on his phone flash. He picked it up. "Dino?"

"Get over here," Dino said, then hung up.

Stone stuck the pistol in his belt, grabbed a coat, and ran out of the house.

6

STONE JOGGED QUICKLY AROUND THE BLOCK, LOOKING at every person he passed, hoping to see the frizzy-haired perpetrator. Finding the house was easy; two black and whites were double-parked outside, their flashers working. A uniformed cop stood guard at the top of the house's steps. Stone flashed his retired officer's ID and was admitted to the house.

He could see by the mailboxes that the original town house had been divided into apartments; the door to the ground-floor unit stood open, and he walked in, breathing hard. Two uniformed patrolmen stood in the entrance hall. "Is Lieutenant Bacchetti upstairs?" Stone asked, flashing his ID.

"Yeah," one of the men said.

Stone ran up the stairs. He was met by another uniform and by the two detectives he had met at Susan Bean's, Andy Anderson and Michael Kelly.

"What are *you* doing here?" Kelly demanded.

Stone ignored him and walked toward the rear of the house. He was on the upper floor of a ground-floor duplex, handsomely decorated. He emerged from a hallway toward the woman's bedroom. Her body lay on the floor in the doorway, uncovered, her skin dead white, her throat gaping.

Dino looked up. "It's a lot like the way Susan Bean was done," he said to Stone. "Right-handed perp, knife drawn from left to right, very deep."

"Any luck on finding him?" Stone asked. "He didn't come out the back, and I didn't see him on the street on the way over here."

"No," Dino said, picking up the dead woman's handbag from a chair and stepping over the body into the hallway, taking care not to step on the blood-soaked part of the pale carpet. "Come in here for a minute," he said, leading the way down the hall and into a study. The room had bookcases on one side and was hung with good pictures on two other walls. An antique desk faced the second-story windows, looking out onto the street. "Sit down," Dino said, opening the handbag.

Stone took a seat. "What's her name?" he asked.

Dino was looking in her wallet. "Miranda Hirsch," he said, handing Stone her business card. "Executive VP in charge of loan operations at the Manhattan Bank."

"Big job," Stone said, looking at the card.

"Did you know her at all?"

"Only what I've seen of her through the window," Stone said.

"While you were playing Peeping Tom, did you ever see a man in the place?"

Stone shook his head. "Not until tonight. After the performance with the vacuum cleaner, she always closed the curtains."

"Downstairs, too?"

"Yes."

"How many times did you watch her undress?"

"A dozen, fifteen, I guess."

"You're lucky I was with you tonight," Dino said, "or Kelly and Anderson would be pulling you in, making a case for how you were overcome with passion by her performance."

"That's not a bad line to pursue," Stone said. "They should be canvassing my side of the block; the perp could be living over there, and I'll bet there were other witnesses."

"Could be, but nobody called it in. You said something before I left your house; you said you knew the perp?"

"I do, but I'm damned if I can remember where from."

"Come on, Stone, *think*."

"I *am* thinking," Stone replied testily. He looked at his feet. "We were together on it, I think."

"On what?"

"On this guy. We arrested him for something, I'm sure. A long time ago."

"Well, come on, give me a hint."

"I just can't put it together," Stone said. "Give me a minute, will you?" The two were quiet for a moment.

"Mitteldorfer," Dino said suddenly.

"What?"

"Mitteldorfer; that was his name. Accountant; killed his wife."

"Herbert Mitteldorfer!" Stone exclaimed. "How the hell did you remember that?"

"He cut her throat," Dino said. "That's how I remembered. How long ago was that?"

"Eleven, twelve years ago," Stone replied. "There was no death penalty then; he got life."

"There was no life without parole, either," Dino said. "He's been in long enough to get paroled."

"Where was he sent?"

"I don't remember. Dannemora, Attica?"

"I don't remember either. Find out."

Dino got out his cell phone and started dialing, then stopped. "Stone, are you sure it was Mitteldorfer? I'm damned if I can remember exactly what he looked like."

"He looked just like the perp, that's what he looked like."

Dino resumed dialing. "This is Bacchetti. Dig up a record on a Herbert Mitteldorfer." He spelled it. "Sent up eleven or twelve years ago for murder. I want to know what joint he was sent to and what his current status is. I'll hold." He looked up at Stone. "Two'll get you ten he was paroled last week."

"I wouldn't be surprised," Stone said.

"You remember much about this guy?" Dino asked.

"Not much. Not very big; tightly wound; borderline psycho, I'd say."

"But what the hell would he have against you?"

"I arrested him, remember?"

"Yeah, but so did I, and so far, he isn't out there killing people *I* know."

"So far," Stone said.

Dino's face fell. "Oh, Jesus," he said.

Stone muttered something.

"What did you say?"

"I said, 'worst fears realized.'"

7

DINO WAS DOING A LITTLE OVER A HUNDRED MILES AN hour on the New York State Thruway when the flashing lights appeared in his rearview mirror. Stone reflected that Dino always drove as if he'd just stolen the car.

"Well, shit," Dino said. He dug into the glove compartment for his flasher, set it on the dashboard, and plugged it into the cigarette lighter. When he saw the flashing light, the state trooper turned on his whoopers.

Dino slammed on his brakes, nearly causing a rear-end collision, then, in a spray of gravel, ground to a halt on the shoulder. He got out his badge, rolled down the window, and waited for the trooper to come to him. The man was on the radio, obviously checking Dino's plates.

"Dino," Stone said wearily, "the speed limit on the thruway is sixty-five miles an hour. Why can't you drive seventy-five or eighty, like a normal human being?"

"Like you never drive fast," Dino replied.

The beefy young trooper appeared in the driver's window.

Dino held up his ID. "And what the fuck do *you* want?" he asked pleasantly.

"I want your driver's license and your registration," the trooper said, not quite as pleasantly.

"You're looking at the only ID you're going to get from me," Dino said. "If you can read, you'll see that I'm a lieutenant in the New York City Police Department. I'm on my way to Sing Sing on official business."

"Your license and registration, and don't make me ask you again," the trooper said through gritted teeth.

Dino reached into an inside pocket for his cell phone, causing the trooper to jump back and put his hand on his pistol. "Tell you what," he said, "let's just call Colonel Joe O'Brien at the Poughkeepsie station and tell him that Trooper"—Dino squinted at the man's name tag—"*Warkowski* is impeding a triple-homicide investigation of the NYPD by acting like a rookie asshole." Dino started punching in a number.

"All right, all right," the trooper said, holding his hands out in front of him. "Just slow it down, okay?"

"Tell you what, Warkowski," Dino said. "You wait right here for a couple hours and you'll see me going south again at a hundred and twenty." Dino slammed the car into gear and left the trooper standing in a cloud of dust at the roadside.

"You really know how to make friends, Dino," Stone said. "I've always said that about you."

"Yeah, yeah, yeah," Dino said, watching the needle on the speedometer pass a hundred.

"Do you really know a Colonel O'Brien in Poughkeepsie?"

"He spoke at a dinner I went to last year. We didn't quite meet."

In Poughkeepsie they made their way to Sing Sing Prison, showed their ID at the gate, and were directed to a parking spot.

"Anybody know we're coming?" Stone asked, as they got out of the car.

"I called the warden's office before we left. We're to ask for the captain of the guard."

They entered a door marked VISITORS, presented their IDs at the desk, and asked for the captain of the guard.

"You'll have to check your weapons," the desk clerk said.

Dino handed over his pistol, and Stone opened his coat to show that he was unarmed.

A thickly built, crew-cut, uniformed man in his fifties appeared in the reception room and waved Dino and Stone through a door, locking it behind him. "And you wanted to see . . . ?" he asked, not bothering to introduce himself.

"Herbert Mitteldorfer, Captain," Dino replied, looking at Stone and shrugging at the man's coldness.

"Wait a minute," the man said, picking up a wall phone in the hallway. "Johnson?" he said. "Bring Herbie Mitteldorfer down to reception one; he's got visitors." He hung up the phone and led them on down the hallway to another locked door.

"Is Mitteldorfer a trusty?" Dino asked the man.

"Yeah."

"Was he, by any chance, out on the town last night?"

The captain stopped before a door. "He gets to shop for office supplies in the town; he's always back inside by five P.M."

"Yesterday, too?"

"Yesterday, too."

He unlocked the door, let them walk into the room, and slammed it behind them.

Dino sat down in a steel chair and rested his elbows on the table. "What's with that guy?" he asked. "Some reception for the NYPD, huh?"

"You didn't see his name tag?" Stone asked.

"No."

"His name is Warkowski," Stone said.

"War . . . ?" Dino stopped in mid-name.

"We'll be lucky to get out of here without serving time," Stone said.

Ten minutes of dead time passed before another door opened and a guard escorted a small man into the room.

"There you go, Herbie," the guard said. "Let yourself out and lock the door behind you when you're through." He handed the prisoner a key.

Herbert Mitteldorfer was five-six, 130; he had gone bald on top and gray on the sides; his hair was cut short, not the longer, frizzier hair of Stone's memory. He stared at Dino and Stone. "Well," he said, "to what do I owe *this* great pleasure?"

"Sit down," Dino said. "We want to ask you some questions."

"I think I read in the papers that you, ah, retired, Mr. Barrington," Mitteldorfer said, taking a seat. "Do you spend your time visiting prisoners now?"

"Only on special occasions," Stone said. "I understand you're a trusty here."

"Since my second year inside," Mitteldorfer replied. "I'm a trustworthy sort of fellow."

Dino spoke up. "Where were you last night, Herbert?"

Mitteldorfer burst out laughing, and Stone had to restrain himself from joining him. "I think you could say I have an iron-clad alibi," he replied.

"Yeah? Alibi for what?"

"You tell me; I've no idea why you're here."

"Tell me about your day yesterday."

"Easy question. I rose at six, showered and breakfasted, then went to work. I broke forty-five minutes for lunch, then returned to work. I finished work at four-thirty, then wrote some letters and watched TV until dinner at six. After dinner I went to the library and read for two hours, then I returned to my cell and read myself to sleep."

"Did you run any errands outside the prison yesterday?" Dino asked.

"Asked and answered," Mitteldorfer replied.

"You've been here how long?"

"Just finished my twelfth year."

"So you'll have a parole hearing coming up soon?"

"Yes."

"Well, unless you'd like me to show up at your hearing and tell the board what a dangerous little shit you still are, you'd better start answering my questions with a little more feeling."

"I apologize," Mitteldorfer replied, chastened. "I'll be happy to answer anything you'd like to ask."

"How often do you leave the prison?"

"Once or twice a week, depending on what errands have to be run."

"What sort of errands do you run?"

"I buy stationery and office supplies; I go to the computer store; sometimes I'm allowed to do some personal shopping."

"What sort of personal shopping?"

"I buy underwear and socks, batteries for my portable radio, a new toothbrush. Sometimes I'll have an ice-cream cone; they don't serve Häagen-Dazs in here."

"Do you have a son?"

"No."

"Any male relatives who are younger than you?"

"No, not in this country."

"Where else?"

"In Germany; I have a nephew, my sister's son."

"What's his age?"

"Oh, mid-thirties, I suppose. I only met him once, when he was a teenager, when I visited her."

"What's his name?"

"Ernst Hausman."

"Has he ever been to this country?"

"No. I hear from my sister several times a year; I think she'd have told me if he came here."

"Where does he live?"

"In Hamburg. I don't have his address. He works at a cigarette factory, I believe."

"Social work, huh? Helping out his fellow man."

Mitteldorfer shrugged. "He doesn't have my conscience."

"Stone, you got any questions?"

"Mr. Mitteldorfer," Stone said, "do you have any regular correspondents besides your sister?"

Mitteldorfer hesitated for a moment. "There's a woman I once worked with," he said finally. "We write from time to time."

"Anyone else?"

"No."

"Do you have any regular visitors?"

"Just the woman," he replied.

"What is her name?"

"I do hope you won't drag her into whatever this is about," Mitteldorfer said, pleading in his voice.

"What is her name?" Dino demanded.

"Eloise Enzberg," he replied softly.

"She live in the city?"

"Yes."

"Where?"

He gave Dino an address in the East Eighties. "I hope you won't find it necessary to visit her. She's a very proper sort of person, and she would be shocked if the police knocked on her door."

"What sort of work do you do here?" Stone asked.

"I'm the office manager," Mitteldorfer said. "I oversee the prison bookkeeping, and I hire and train other prisoners to do office work."

Dino broke in. "Have you cut anybody's throat lately, Herbert?"

Mitteldorfer looked horrified. "Please. I think you're aware that my crime was one of passion. I'm not the sort of person ever to repeat it."

"Does Ms. Enzberg know what you're in here for?" Dino asked.

"Yes, she does. She read about it in the papers when you arrested me, and after the trial she wrote to me."

Stone was becoming uncomfortable with this. Mitteldorfer was a mild little man, much different than Stone remembered. He seemed to have served his time well, and there was no point in persecuting him. "That's it for me, Dino," he said. "You ready to go?"

Dino ignored him. "Something I remember about you, now, Herbert," he said. "You enjoyed killing your wife, didn't you? She was fucking somebody else, and when you found out about it, you took pleasure in cutting her throat, didn't you?"

Mitteldorfer looked at the tabletop. "Please," he said.

"Let's go, Dino," Stone said.

"All right, get out of here," Dino said to Mitteldorfer.

Mitteldorfer rose and, without another word, let himself out of the room. They heard him lock the door behind him.

Stone stood up and tried the door by which they had entered. "Locked," he said. "I wonder how long it'll be before Captain War-kowski remembers to let us out of here."

It was nearly an hour before Captain Warkowski turned up and unlocked the door. Stone made a point of keeping his body between Warkowski and Dino.

Dino drove like a wild man all the way back to the city.

8

THEY WERE CROSSING THE HARLEM RIVER BRIDGE when Dino's cell phone rang. He got it out, said hello, then held it away from his ear.

Stone could hear a woman's voice, practically screaming.

"Not so loud!" Dino yelled into the phone, still holding it away from his head.

"It's me!" the woman yelled.

"Mary Ann? What's going on?"

She was still shouting, but not screaming; Stone could hear her clearly. "A man just attacked me! I shot him!"

"Are you all right?"

"I'm not hurt, if that's what you mean."

"Where did this happen?"

"On the street, outside the building."

"Where are you now?"

"I'm in the apartment."

"I'm on the West Side; I'll be there in fifteen minutes. I'll have a squad car sent. Lock the door, and don't let anybody in but cops."

"All right."

Dino hung up and dug out the flasher again. "Did you get that?" he asked Stone.

"All of it."

Dino dialed another number. "This is Bacchetti; who's got the duty?" He paused. "Anderson? Get over to my apartment right now." He gave the detective the address. "But first, get a squad car there. Somebody's attacked my wife. I'll be there in fifteen minutes." Dino hung up and concentrated on his driving, roaring down the Henry Hudson Parkway, weaving in and out of the heavy traffic.

Stone put his hands on the dashboard and braced himself. He had always thought it a good possibility that he would die in a car with Dino at the wheel, and he wondered if this was going to be the day.

Dino got off the parkway at Seventy-ninth Street and charged across the West Side. He turned down Central Park West and raced to Sixty-fifth Street, then turned into the park, driving across a traffic island to break into the traffic. "I wish the hell this thing had a siren," he said, half to himself. He overtook half a dozen cars at one go, bulling his way through the traffic from the opposite direction, miraculously not hitting another car. Two minutes after leaving the park he drove the wrong way down his block, abandoned the car in front of a fire hydrant, and ran toward his apartment building, with Stone on his heels.

The building's doorman saw them coming. "There's two uniforms up there already, Mr. Bacchetti," he shouted, as they sprinted past him for the elevator. A minute later they were in the apartment, and Dino was holding Mary Ann, who didn't seem all that flustered now.

"I'm all right," she said. "Don't make a big deal."

Dino sat her down on a sofa. "Tell me exactly what happened."

"I got out of a cab at the corner and was walking toward the building. When I was almost to the front door I saw this guy coming down the block in the opposite direction, and I could tell by the look on his face that he was coming at me. He was only a few steps away when I saw him take a knife out of his pocket—a big switchblade— and flick it open. I already had my hand in my purse." She pointed at her pocketbook, lying on a chair opposite; there was a gaping hole in the bag. "I fired before he could get to me, and the shot spun him around. He could run, though, and he did."

"Where did you hit him?"

"I didn't have much chance to aim, but I was going for his head. I think I caught an ear."

"Which ear?"

"Uh, the left. Yes, that's right, the left ear. He had his hand on it as he ran, and I saw some blood."

"You," Dino said, pointing at one of the two uniforms in the room, "go downstairs and see if you can find some blood on the sidewalk. Don't let anybody step in it; I want a sample taken."

The cop left at a run.

"You," Dino said, pointing at the other uniform, "get on the phone to the precinct and tell them I want a tech over here right now to collect a sample."

The cop went to a phone and started dialing.

"Are you all right, now?" he said to his wife.

"Perfectly," she said.

"All right enough to answer an important question?"

"Sure, I'm okay; what do you want to know?"

"What I want to know is, *where the hell did you get a gun?*" Dino demanded, his voice rising.

Mary Ann looked away petulantly. "Daddy gave it to me."

"You took a gun from your *father?*"

Stone knew that Mary Ann's father was an extremely well connected Italian gentleman of the old school with many business interests, licit and otherwise, and a wide acquaintance among people who owned guns.

"Yes, I did," she said, rounding on him. "I knew *you* wouldn't let me have one."

"Oh, swell," Dino said. "And, knowing your father, I don't suppose he bothered with the permitting process."

"As a matter of fact, he did bother," Mary Ann replied. "The permit is in my purse, if you don't believe me."

"Jesus, you're lucky you didn't shoot yourself. You've got no business with a gun."

"Listen, Dino, I go with Charlton Heston on this one, okay? And need I remind you that, if I hadn't had the gun, I'd be lying down there in the street with a very big knife in me?"

"All right, all right," Dino said, seeing that he was not going to win this one. "Can you describe the man?"

"Late thirties, early forties, small; I'd say five-seven. Wiry, and he had an Afro."

"He was black?"

"No, but he had an Afro, kind of. Kind of a Jewish Afro."

"He was Jewish? How do you know that?"

"No; I mean, that's what we used to call it in high school, when a Jewish kid had that kind of kinky hair, you know?"

"Did the guy look Jewish?"

"Not particularly. His hair was dark, though, almost black."

"How was he dressed?"

"He was wearing a raincoat, kind of new-looking, you know? Freshly pressed, no wrinkles."

"Anything else?"

"No, the raincoat covered everything. It was single-breasted, not a trench coat; I remember that."

Detectives Anderson and Kelly arrived, then, and Dino brought them up-to-date. "Andy, you get on the phone and get out an APB for this guy. Get a bulletin out to all the hospitals in Manhattan to expect a guy answering the description to come in with a gunshot wound to the head, possibly to the left ear. Be sure and tell them he's armed with a knife and to exercise extreme caution. I don't want this guy cutting up a nurse."

Anderson went to the phone, while Kelly leaned against a wall, saying nothing.

"Thank God the kid was in school," Dino said. He wrote something on a pad, ripped it off, and handed it to the idle Kelly. "Get over there and pick up my kid at his school. That's the address."

Kelly left. "Mary Ann, neither of you goes anywhere without a cop for a while."

"Oh, come on, Dino," she replied. "The guy's not coming back. No mugger is that stupid."

Dino looked at the floor. "You do like I tell you about this, you hear me?"

Stone went and sat on the sofa next to her. "Mary Ann," he said, "it's not a mugger."

"What are you talking about?"

He turned to Dino. "It's our guy," he said.

"Yeah, I know," Dino replied. "Worst fears realized."

9

KELLY RETURNED WITH DINO'S SON, BENEDETTO, A black-eyed six-year-old who looked like a tiny Sicilian prince, taking after his mother's line. Dino dismissed Kelly, then gathered up the boy, sat him on his lap, and explained what had happened that afternoon.

"Why don't you just have the guy capped?" the child asked.

Dino sighed and looked at Stone. "He spent the weekend with his grandfather." He turned back to the boy. "Because, Ben, I am a police officer, and we don't have guys capped. We arrest them and put them in jail, remember? Now you go and get washed up for dinner. Uncle Stone is going to join us." The boy got down from his father's lap and ran toward his room.

"Thanks, I'd love to," Stone said.

Mary Ann excused herself and headed for the kitchen.

"Come on into my study," Dino said. "Let's have a drink."

Stone followed Dino into the handsome little walnut-paneled room, where Dino produced Stone's favorite bourbon and a scotch for himself. It was not the study or the apartment of a New York City police lieutenant, and the books on the shelves, mostly art history, history, and biography, revealed a broader Dino than most people knew.

Stone knew that Dino's father-in-law had acquired the apartment for his daughter in circumstances that were murky, to say the least. It was in a white-shoe, East Side cooperative building that did not ordinarily entertain applications from people whose names ended in vowels, and Stone reckoned it would sell for somewhere between a million and a half and two million dollars on the open market. Stone knew that the apartment's purchaser and his daughter's ownership were protected behind a complex corporate veil, and he doubted if any other member of the NYPD had ever entered the place before today. He wondered what would happen if Dino ever became the target of some in-depth departmental investigation.

"You got any thoughts about all this?" Dino asked.

At first, Stone thought he meant the apartment, then he realized what the subject was. "Oh. Not really. Certainly, Mitteldorfer's alibi is tight. I think I'd check out the nephew in Hamburg, to see if he's really in Germany. Might be good to check out Mitteldorfer's visitors list, too?" He allowed himself a grin. "*If* you can get it out of Captain Warkowski."

Dino raised his glass in a little toast. "Fuck you," he said.

Stone lifted his glass. "Thanks. Have you got any ideas?"

Dino shook his head. "Not really. It's spooky how the perp looks like Mitteldorfer used to look, though."

"Yes, it is. I think the Hamburg nephew is not a bad bet. I wouldn't be surprised if he'd immigrated, or if he turns up on Mitteldorfer's visitors' list. I'd like to know if Mitteldorfer has any other relatives in this country, particularly any children he didn't tell us about."

"First thing tomorrow," Dino said. "Well, one good thing about all this; it's given you something else to think about besides your broken heart."

"Give me a break, Dino," Stone said wearily.

"Listen, Stone, I think you're well out of the thing with Arrington."

"I thought you *liked* Arrington."

"I did. I do. I just think that if you'd married her, she might have run off with Vance Calder later, and that would have screwed you up even worse."

"I am *not* screwed up, and, anyway, Arrington's not like that," Stone said. "*I* dropped the ball; I didn't commit when I should have, and by the time I got around to it . . ."

"And when did you get around to it?"

"I was going to ask her to marry me when we went on the sailing trip; I'd made up my mind on the way down there. Then, when the snowstorm kept her in the city, and when Calder showed up . . . well, it was a good offer, and she had no reason to think I was going to make a better one."

"So you blame yourself?"

"Yes."

"Blame her; it won't hurt as much. There's nothing like being pissed off at a woman to make her absence easier."

"I'll try and remember that," Stone said drily.

"You think there's any chance she'd leave Calder?"

"None. She's borne him a son, remember? She's locked in."

"Wouldn't be the first time people with kids got a divorce."

"Don't think it hasn't crossed my mind."

"Why don't you just go out to LA and get her?"

"I had my shot at that; she made her choice. I'll just have to learn to live with it."

"You really believe the kid is Calder's, not yours?"

"The tests were done, Dino; she wouldn't lie about that."

"Nah; women never lie."

"I'm at peace with that part of it, at least. If the child had been mine, she'd have come back to me. That was our agreement. Why are you digging through all this?"

Dino shrugged. "I figured it might do you good to talk about it."

"Well, now that you mention it, I do feel a little better having articulated the situation."

"You sound like a fucking shrink." Dino abruptly changed the subject. "I'm going to put a watch on you," he said.

"I don't think that's necessary."

"Sure it is. This guy followed you the night Susan Bean was killed, you know."

"You have a point there."

"It bothers me that he could recognize Mary Ann on the street."

"I don't blame you."

"It means he's been doing his homework, checking out our lives."

"That's pretty scary."

"And for God knows how long. He may have plans for other people we know. You been seeing any girls at all?"

"No, nobody."

"That's not like you, Stone."

"It's just as well, though, isn't it? At least I don't have to call up women and tell them there's a lunatic on the loose."

"He *is* a lunatic, isn't he?"

"This is hardly a sane thing to do, even if it is revenge."

"Has it occurred to you that one victim didn't even know you? That she just had the misfortune to live within sight of your house?"

"It has. Did anything come of checking out the residents of the buildings on my side of the block?"

Dino shook his head. "Nothing; all solid citizens."

"He had to have seen her through her rear window," Stone said. "She wasn't chosen at random."

"He wanted you to watch," Dino said. "Maybe me, too."

"It was the single worst thing I've ever seen."

"I know how you feel."

Dino picked up the phone at his side and pressed a speed-dial button. "This is Bacchetti; let me speak to Anderson. Andy? Tomorrow I want you to dig out the case file on a Herbert Mitteldorfer; killed his wife twelve, thirteen years ago. I want you to go back to the neighborhood where he used to live—in the old Germantown area, I think—the East Eighties. Talk to his neighbors, the shopkeepers, anybody who remembers him. See if any of them knows whether he had any family in this country, particularly a son or a nephew; find out who his friends were, and check with them. I want to know about everybody he knew. Check his former workplace, too. There's a woman called Eloise Enzberg who worked or maybe still works there. Talk to her nicely, and maybe she'll spill something. She's been writing to Mitteldorfer at Sing Sing. Also, call the warden's office and get a list of Mitteldorfer's visitors for the past two years. Report back to me as you find out things; I want to know it all. Hang on." Dino covered the receiver. "Can you think of anything else?" he asked Stone.

Stone furrowed his brow. "Have them find out who Mitteldorfer was friends with at Sing Sing and whether any of them has gotten out recently."

"Good idea." Dino gave the instruction to Anderson, then hung up. "I don't know of anything else we can do, do you?"

Stone shook his head. "Not apart from being very, very careful."

10

STONE WAS AWAKENED FROM A SOUND SLEEP BY THE doorbell. He rolled over, glancing at the clock—9:00 A.M. He picked up the phone and punched the intercom button. "Yes?"

"Mr. Barrington?"

"Yes."

"I'm Joan Robertson, from Woodman and Weld. Bill Eggers sent me over to do some secretarial work for you."

"Oh, yes, I'll buzz you in. Wander around until you find the kitchen, and make yourself a cup of coffee. I'll be down in twenty minutes." He pressed the button that opened the front door.

He struggled out of bed, shaved, showered, and dressed, then ran down the stairs and into the kitchen. A woman with streaked blonde hair, trim, in her forties, sat at the kitchen table, drinking coffee.

"Good morning," she said. "Join me? I made a pot."

He shook her hand. "Thanks, I will," Stone said. He got a cup and sat down. "You look a lot like . . . what's her name? The actress?"

"June Allyson?"

"That's the one."

"I get that all the time."

"You even have that husky voice. Is she your mother?"

"Not unless my parents have been lying to me for the past forty-five years."

"Did Bob tell you anything about what I need?"

"He said you needed a secretary, maybe for a few weeks. He also said that you should not get to like me too much, because he has no intention of letting you steal me."

Stone laughed. The phone rang, and he went to the wall set and picked it up. "Hello?"

"Stone? It's Sarah Buckminster."

The English accent rang like a bell, and parts of Stone were ringing, too.

"You're obviously an impostor," he said. "The real Sarah Buckminster is in Tuscany, probably treading grapes for the new Chianti."

"She was until yesterday." Sarah laughed.

"Are you really back?"

"I am."

"God, it's been, what . . ."

"Six and a half years. How the hell are you?"

"I'm extremely well."

"So am I. Buy me lunch?"

"You bet. The Four Seasons at one? We'll celebrate."

"We certainly will. See you then."

"Bye." Stone hung up and came back to the table. "Sorry about that," he said to Joan. "An old friend has turned up unexpectedly."

"You certainly sounded happy to hear from her," Joan said.

"It showed, huh? I guess I am *very* happy to hear from her. Now, I was telling you about—" The doorbell rang. "Excuse me again." He picked up the phone. "Yes?" He heard footsteps going down the front steps. "Hello?" He hung up and turned back to Joan. "Let me see who that is."

He walked through the living room to the front door. Nobody there. He looked up and down the street but saw no one who looked interested in his house. He closed the door and turned to go back to the kitchen. On the floor of the entrance hall was a small, yellow envelope. Somebody had apparently put it through the mail slot. He picked it up. A Western Union telegram. He walked back into the kitchen, tossed it onto the table, sat down, and picked up his coffee, which was getting cold. "A telegram," he said, picking up the envelope.

"That's odd," Joan replied.

"How so?" he asked, opening the envelope.

"There are no telegrams anymore. I mean, you can send a mailgram, I think, but I thought fax machines put telegrams out of business a long time ago."

Stone unfolded the single sheet of yellow paper. It was an old-fashioned telegram, with strips of message glued to the paper. It read:

SORRY I MISSED LAST NIGHT. IT WON'T HAPPEN AGAIN.

BY THE WAY, DID YOU KNOW THE POLICE ARE WATCHING

YOUR HOUSE?

YOUR WORST NIGHTMARE

Stone stared at the message, rereading it.

"Mr. Barrington," Joan said. "Are you all right? You've turned pale."

Stone realized that he felt pale. "I'm sorry," he said.

"Is it bad news?"

"I'm afraid so," he said. "Will you wait right here, Joan? Whatever you do, don't leave the house or go near the front door."

"All right," she said, looking at him curiously.

Stone went to his study and called Dino on his private line.

"Bacchetti."

"Dino, it's Stone."

"Morning. You feeling better?"

"I was until a minute ago."

Dino's voice changed. "What's happened?"

"I've had a message from our perp." Stone read the telegram. "It was pushed through the mail slot five minutes ago."

"Hang on," Dino said, putting him on hold.

Stone waited, feeling a little sick at the thought of what he might have gotten Joan Robertson into.

"You there?" Dino asked.

"Yes."

"I've put out a new APB in your neighborhood," he said. "I don't know what else I can do."

"There is something else," Stone said.

"Shoot."

"I've made a big mistake. When Alma was killed, Bill Eggers offered to send somebody over to help out until I can hire a new secretary. She arrived this morning; I had completely forgotten about it."

"Oh, shit," Dino said.

"Exactly."

"We're going to have to get her out of there," Dino said.

"What do you suggest?"

Dino thought for a minute. "Can a car get into that garage of yours?"

"Yes. I was thinking of buying a car, and I moved a lot of boxes out of the way."

"I'll send an unmarked car over there; you watch for them and open the garage. They can pull inside, then you can put your lady in the backseat, and they can drive her somewhere. I'll tell them to make sure they're not followed."

"Very good," Stone replied. "Have them call me when they turn into the block."

"Right."

Stone hung up and went back to the kitchen. "Joan, I'm afraid I'm not going to be able to use you—not for a while, anyway."

"Whatever you say," she replied, standing up.

"No, have a seat. A car is being sent to take you back to your office."

"Oh, that's not necessary, Mr. Barrington. It's not much of a walk, and it's a nice day."

"I'm afraid it *is* necessary," Stone said. "It's a police car that's coming for you."

"A *police* car? I don't understand."

"It wouldn't do any good to explain; just trust me on this."

She shrugged. "Whatever you say."

The phone rang, and Stone picked it up. "Hello?"

"It's Andy Anderson. We're coming up the street now."

"Thanks; I'll open the door." He hung up. "Please follow me," he said to Joan Robertson.

She stood up. "All right."

Stone led her down the back stairs, through his exercise room, and into the garage. He pressed the button, and the door rose noisily. Instantly, a car drove inside, with Mick Kelly at the wheel and Andy Anderson in the passenger seat. Stone opened the door and helped Joan in. "I want you to lie down on the backseat until Detective Anderson tells you it's all right to sit up."

Joan laughed. "This is the weirdest thing that's ever happened to me," she said.

"Believe me, this is for your protection. Thanks for coming over; I'll let you know when it's a better time." He closed the door and gave Anderson a thumbs-up sign. "Go," he said. The car backed into the street, and Stone closed the garage door behind them.

He was halfway back to the kitchen when it occurred to him that he had a lunch date that he didn't dare keep.

11

STONE WAITED UNTIL TWELVE-THIRTY, THEN CALLED the Four Seasons and asked for Alex von Bidder, one of the owners. "Hello, Alex, it's Stone Barrington."

"Good morning, Stone; would you like a lunch table?"

"Yes, I'm supposed to meet a young lady at one o'clock named Sarah Buckminster."

"The painter?"

"Yes."

"I have two of her pictures; she's very good."

"Yes, she is. Trouble is, I'm not going to be able to meet her, so I'd appreciate it if you'd give her a table next to somebody interesting, so she can eavesdrop . . ."

Von Bidder laughed. "Of course."

". . . and if you'd give her a phone and ask her to call me."

"Of course."

"She likes champagne; give her half a bottle of something good and charge the whole thing to my house account."

"I'll see that it's done, Stone."

Stone said goodbye and hung up. His stomach was growling, and he hated missing this lunch.

*   *   *

He was eating a ham sandwich when the phone rang.

"Hello?"

"It's Sarah; I understand you're standing me up."

"I am so very sorry; I was looking forward to seeing you, but something extremely . . . intrusive has come up."

"So, I have to drink the Veuve-Clicquot all by myself?"

"For the moment, I'm afraid."

"Shall I come to you after lunch?"

"No, we definitely can't do that."

"How about dinner?"

He hesitated. "Where are you staying?"

"I have some friends' apartment all to myself. They're in Europe." Stone thought about this.

"Are you there?" she asked after a moment.

"Yes, I'm sorry; I was thinking."

"Is this such a tough decision, Stone?"

"Of course not; I'm dying to see you, it's just . . ."

"Just what?"

"We can't be seen together."

"Stone, did you get *married* during my absence?"

"No, no, nothing like that."

"Are you living with someone?"

"No. It's just that there's a very difficult situation I'm dealing with, and I don't want you drawn into it."

"How about if I cook you some dinner? I learned a lot in Italy."

"Are you sure that won't be too much trouble?"

"Of course not." She gave him the address.

"Can I bring something?"

"You can bring the wine."

"Red or white?"

"Red. Something Italian; something robust."

"What time?"

"Eight?"

"Eight it is, and again, I apologize for the situation."

"I'll give you an opportunity to make it up to me." She hung up.

Stone called Dino.

"Bacchetti."

"Dino, it's Stone; I have an idea."

"Yeah?"

"This guy is obviously keeping tabs on me, and he's not stupid; he's already made the people you've got watching the house."

"I agree."

"You remember Sarah Buckminster?"

"The limey you used to go out with? Sure. Didn't she flee the country to get away from you?"

"She's back, and I have a dinner date with her. She's staying at a friend's apartment on Fifth Avenue in the Seventies, and I'm due up there at eight."

"I'll see that you're followed."

"No, he'll expect that. Instead, have the building covered; put a guy in the lobby and one on the street. If he follows me, he won't know what apartment I'm visiting. Maybe he'll try and talk to the doorman, or maybe he'll just lurk around, waiting for me to leave. Either way, we might get a chance to grab him."

"What's the exact address?"

Stone told him.

"Okay. Call me at home when you get there."

"How are Mary Ann and Ben?"

"They're at her father's house in Brooklyn; one of his people is driving Ben to school every day for the duration."

"They couldn't be safer, then."

"Yeah, I'd like to see the guy get past those people. Call me tonight."

Stone hung up and returned to his ham sandwich.

*　　*　　*

58

Later in the afternoon, Stone went down to the cellar. He chose a Masi Amerone '91, which filled Sarah's wine order, then he went down to the end of the racks, where he had a few very special bottles. He found a bottle of champagne—a Krug '66—that he'd been saving for an occasion, then went up to the kitchen and put the champagne on ice. At seven-thirty, he found some tissue paper, wrapped the two bottles, and put them into a small shopping bag. He dressed in some cavalry twill slacks, a cashmere turtleneck, soft kid loafers, and a light tweed jacket; then he opened his bedside drawer, took out a 9mm automatic pistol, placed it in the bag, and covered it with more tissue paper. He picked up the shopping bag and let himself out of the house.

He looked up and down the street. There were a few people in the block, and he recognized two cops in a plain sedan across the street. He walked up to Third Avenue and hailed a cab, constantly checking behind him. It was what the perp would expect him to do.

Stone got into the cab. "Here's what I want you to do," he said to the driver. "I want you to take a right on Fifty-ninth Street, go across the bridge, then make a U-turn, come back across the bridge, then take First Avenue up to Seventy-ninth, over to Fifth, and I'll direct you from there. There's an extra ten bucks in it if you don't ask me why."

The driver gave an elaborate shrug, clapped a hand over his mouth, and, miraculously, did as he was asked. When they were on Fifth Avenue, Stone asked to be let out a block before Sarah's building, tipped the driver extravagantly, and, shopping bag in hand, walked casually down the east side of Fifth Avenue. Traffic was heavy going downtown, and there were a lot of people on the street. He couldn't spot anyone following him.

Stone found the address, and the doorman opened the door for him. Inside was a desk, and two uniformed men stood behind it. The younger one, Stone noticed, was a little too large for his jacket, and there was a bulge under his left arm.

"Yes sir?" the older man asked. He looked worried.

"My name is Barrington," Stone said. "I'm here to see Miss Buckminster."

The man picked up a phone, announced Stone, then told him he could go up.

Stone recognized the elevator operator. "Evening, Andy," he said when the door was shut. "The uniform suits you."

"Thanks a lot," Anderson replied. "Maybe I should make a career change."

"Where's Mick?"

"Sitting out on the street—eating doughnuts, probably."

"I'm not surprised."

"You think the guy followed you?"

"If he did, he's good; I didn't make him."

"I hope he did; I'd like a crack at him."

"May you get your wish."

"Here we are; sixteen, top floor."

The elevator doors opened, and Stone stepped into a private foyer. "Watch yourself, Andy," he said, then he rang the doorbell.

12

THE DOOR WAS OPENED BY A BUTLER DRESSED IN A dark suit. "Good evening, Mr. Barrington," he said. "My name is William; will you follow me, please?" He led the way down a long gallery hung with very good pictures, and they emerged into a large, handsome living room. "Please have a seat, sir," William said. "Miss Buckminster will be with you in a moment; she's in the kitchen. May I get you something to drink?"

Stone handed him the shopping bag. "There's a cold bottle of champagne in there," he said, and a bottle of red wine. "If you would open the red and allow it to breathe, then bring us the champagne and a couple of glasses."

"Of course, Mr. Barrington," William replied. He took the shopping bag and left the room.

Stone walked slowly around the room, looking at the pictures; he had never seen such a collection in a private home. A Monet of water lilies covered most of one wall, and the smaller pictures were hung in rows, covering nearly every square foot of wall space. Stone recognized works by Picasso, Manet, Braque, David Hockney, and Lucian Freud. "My God," he muttered to himself. "I wouldn't want to be saddled with these people's insurance premiums." Next to the fireplace he was riveted by something that he recognized from his childhood: one of his mother's paintings, of Washington Square Park. He stood before it, taking in the brushwork and the light. "You're in good company, Mother," he said.

"Stone!"

He turned to see Sarah Buckminster walking toward him, dressed in tailored slacks and a silk blouse. She held out her arms to him, and he embraced and kissed her. She held him away from her and looked at him. "Dear God, the years have made you even more handsome."

Stone blushed. "And you are even more beautiful."

She turned and looked at the Matilda Stone. "I knew you'd find it immediately."

"I haven't seen it since I was, I don't know, eleven or twelve." He waved an arm. "Who owns all this?"

"Jack and Hillary Beacon," she replied. "He's the CEO of Celltell, the wireless-phone company. Do you know it?"

Stone nodded. "I bought some of the stock, as a matter of fact. I don't have much, but it's done well."

"This is the heart of one of the country's great private collections. The rest is scattered around the apartment, which runs to seventeen rooms, or on loan to museums."

"It's astonishing."

William appeared with a tray holding the bottle of Krug, two lovely champagne flutes, some canapés, and something wrapped in a napkin.

"Come, let's sit down," Sarah said, drawing him to the sofa before the fireplace, in which a cheerful fire burned.

William poured them both a flute of the wine and nodded at the napkin on the tray. "Yours, I believe, Mr. Barrington."

Stone winced.

"Something for me, I hope," Sarah said.

"I'm afraid not," Stone replied. "The Krug is for you."

"William," she said, "you and Martha may go, now; Mr. Barrington and I will take care of ourselves for the rest of the evening."

"If you need anything, please ring, Miss Buckminster," William said.

"I'll do no such thing. You and Martha take the rest of the evening off."

"Thank you, Miss, and good night. Good night, Mr. Barrington."

"Good night, William, and thank you for . . ." He nodded toward the napkin. William left them alone.

"All right, I'm dying to know what's in the napkin," Sarah said.

"I'm afraid it's rather embarrassing," Stone said. "I forgot that I had put it in the bag with the wine."

She slid the tray toward her and began unwrapping the napkin. "Jesus Christ!" she said, recoiling from the weapon. "You might as well have brought a rattlesnake!" She picked up the pistol by the barrel with thumb and forefinger and handed it to him. "Hide it somewhere," she said.

Stone took the weapon and tucked it into his belt at the small of his back.

"I remember that you used to go armed, Stone, but that was when you were a policeman. What's your excuse now?"

"I'm afraid I'm in a rather delicate position," Stone said.

"An angry husband?"

"Hardly. You remember Dino."

"How could I forget the 'orrible little man?"

"Some years ago, Dino and I sent someone to prison, and he's apparently decided to make us pay for it."

"Who is this person?"

"We don't know, really. We only know that he's . . . tried to harm people close to us."

"Is *that* why you didn't show up for lunch?"

"Yes, it is. I was so glad to hear from you that I completely forgot that I have to be circumspect about whom I see. This started only very recently, and I'm still getting used to the idea that I shouldn't endanger other people by associating with them."

"Well, this is really very exciting, isn't it?"

"I just don't want it to get too exciting."

"Surely, you don't think you're endangering me simply by having dinner."

"I took some precautions to see that I wasn't followed, and there are several police officers downstairs. One of them is operating your elevator."

Sarah burst out laughing. "This is hilarious," she said. "I must say, I've never had a gun served with champagne." She sipped the wine. "And Krug! It's delicious." She leaned over and kissed him. "And so are you."

"When did you get back?"

"Yesterday; I'm still not entirely over the jet lag. I came by way of London, saw my parents for a few days."

"Are you going back to Tuscany?"

"I haven't decided. I'm back for a show of my work that will open next week—all the work that I've done for the past six years."

"I can't wait to see it," Stone said.

"I'll give you a preview; I promise. Now you know that all *I* have done these past years is cloister myself in Tuscany and work; bring me up to date on you."

"I'll give you the short version. What exactly was I doing the last time we saw each other?"

"You were still on the police force, although I heard through friends that you left, and I remember that you had inherited that lovely old house from an aunt, I believe, and you were doing most of the remodeling work yourself."

"A great aunt, and yes, I couldn't afford to hire many people on my cop's salary."

"And you had gotten yourself shot and were recovering."

"Right."

"Where was it?"

"In the knee."

"Oh, yes; no place important, then."

Stone laughed. "So I retired from the force on a full-disability pension—I was nudged in that direction, if the truth be known. I was being awkward about a case I was working on, and somebody decided I shouldn't be there anymore."

"You were always the most unlikely policeman." Sarah laughed.

"That's pretty much what the NYPD thought."

"So then what did you do? Live off the fat of the land?"

"I had my law degree, so I boned up and took the bar exam. I'm of counsel to Woodman and Weld."

"I know that name; a prestigious firm, I believe. What does 'of counsel' mean?"

"It means I handle their clients' more delicate problems. I work out of an office in my home rather than from the firm's offices."

"Sounds intriguing."

"It sometimes is."

"Are you prosperous, then?"

"More so than I had ever dreamed I would be. The house is finished and furnished; I live very nearly in the lap of luxury."

"You're certainly dressing better," she said, stroking his jacket.

"I'd like to think I'm doing everything better," he said.

"That remains to be seen." She chuckled, her voice low. She stood up. "Come into the kitchen with me and watch me cook."

"I'd love to," he said. "May I make a phone call first? I promised I'd call Dino."

"Of course; there's a phone over there." She pointed.

Stone went to the phone and dialed Dino's number; he got an answering machine. "Dino, it's Stone; I'm in Sarah's apartment." He repeated the number. "Everything seems all set downstairs; Anderson is running the elevator. Don't call me unless it's important." He hung up, grabbed the champagne bottle, and followed Sarah toward the kitchen.

13

THE KITCHEN GLEAMED WITH RESTAURANT-QUALITY appliances and granite countertops. Sarah seated Stone on a stool where he could watch, then she went to the huge range, poured a generous dollop of olive oil into a skillet, and while it was heating, chopped some plum tomatoes, garlic, and fresh basil. When the oil was sizzling, she dropped half a dozen slices of Italian bread into it and fried them on both sides. She arranged a small platter with the bread slices, then spooned the mixture of tomatoes, garlic, and basil onto each slice. She picked up the platter and headed for the door.

"Follow me," she said.

Stone grabbed the bottle of Amerone and followed her through a swinging door and into a charming little corner dining room, where the table was already set for two.

"This is where the family dines," she said. "There's a much larger dining room through there, with a table that seats eighteen." She nodded at the door.

Stone lit the candles on the table, and they sat down facing the windows, which overlooked Central Park and the lights of the city to the south. He poured them both a glass of wine and raised his glass. "Happy reunions," he said.

"Hear, hear," she replied, sipping her wine. "Oh, this is *huge.* What is it?"

"An Amerone."

"Luscious. Now eat your bruscetta."

Stone sliced off a chunk of bread and put it into his mouth. "Wonderful," he said. "It's so simple, but it's really terrific."

"Glad you approve. I told you I learned a lot in Tuscany."

"Where exactly were you?"

"In the Chianti country, north of Siena and south of Florence."

"Do you know I've never been to Europe?"

Sarah looked shocked. "I don't believe it."

"When I was a cop, I couldn't afford it, and now I always seem to be too busy."

"We will cure that condition," she said. "Just as soon as my show is launched."

"That might be fun," he replied, swallowing the last of his bruscetta.

"It certainly will be, I assure you." She took away his plate. "The main course is in the oven; I'll be right back."

Stone sipped his wine and gazed out over the park. He loved his house, he thought, but it didn't have views like this.

Sarah returned with a hot crockery dish. "Cannelloni," she said, serving him the little crêpes, stuffed with ground pork. She spooned a creamy sauce over them, then served herself.

"You should give up painting for cooking," he said.

They ate slowly, then Sarah brought out cannoli for dessert. When they had finished their dinner and the wine, she drew him from the table and led him through the apartment and upstairs. "I must show you the guest room," she purred. She opened a door and led him into an elaborately decorated bedroom, then stopped and put her arms around his neck. "Now," she said. "Another dessert." She kissed him.

Stone thought he had never felt so good. The dinner had been perfection, and now, as he felt her breasts against him, felt her tongue in his mouth, he . . .

A loud buzzing noise interrupted them.

"What's that?" he asked.

"The house phone," she replied between kisses. "Ignore it."

"I think you'd better answer it," Stone said.

"Forget it."

"Sarah, this could be important."

"Oh, all right!" she said, breaking away and going to the phone. "Hello? Yes, Dan? No, I can't right now. No, it's impossible."

"What is it?" Stone asked.

She covered the receiver. "It's the desk man downstairs; he wants me to come down there and talk to the police."

"Tell him you'll be right down," Stone said.

"Are you mad?"

"Please, tell him you'll be right down."

"I'll be right down," she said, then hung up the phone. "What on earth is going on?" she asked. "Why would the police want to see me?"

"You stay here; I'm going downstairs," Stone said.

"When will you be back?" she asked plaintively.

"As soon as I possibly can. In the meantime, don't open the door to anyone except me, and I mean *anyone*."

"Stone, you're beginning to frighten me."

"Don't worry, everything will be all right. I'll be right back." He ran down the stairs, let himself out of the apartment and into the foyer, then rang for the elevator. He looked up at the lights, expecting to see it move. It remained on the ground floor. He rang again, but the car did not move. He tried a door to his left, found a staircase, and started down.

As he ran quickly down the stairs he removed the pistol from his belt, worked the action, and put the safety on. He had started at the sixteenth floor, and it took him some minutes to reach the bottom. Finally at the lobby level, he put an ear to the door and listened. Nothing.

He opened the door an inch and peered into the lobby. It was empty. No one was at the desk across the way, and he could see the elevator car, standing with the door open. He flipped the safety off the pistol and, holding it in front of him with both hands, stepped into the lobby. He looked carefully behind the furniture and found nothing, no one, then he went to the desk and looked over it.

"Good God!" he said aloud. He flipped up the desktop and opened the half door that gave access to the area behind the desk. The cop and the desk man both lay on the floor, and there was a lot of blood. He checked both for pulses; they were dead.

He stood up and noticed two things for the first time. There was a bullet hole in one of the glass doors, and outside the building and to his right, lights were flashing. He walked outside and saw an unmarked police car standing a few yards up the street, the driver's door open and a red light on the dashboard flashing. Traffic was moving unhindered down Fifth Avenue. *Where the hell are Kelly and Anderson?* He walked toward the car, passing two civilian cars on the way.

"Mr. Barrington?"

The voice spun him around. The doorman emerged from where he had been crouched between two parked cars. "Mr. Barrington, this is awful."

"What happened?" Stone demanded.

"I let a man with a parcel to deliver into the lobby. He went to the front desk and, without a word, shot the police officer, then he held the gun to Dan's head, and I saw Dan pick up the telephone. I ran outside, and then I heard a second shot."

"Then what happened?"

"About a minute passed, and I heard more shots; then the man I had let in burst out of the building, ran across the street, and vaulted over the wall into the park. A few seconds later, the police officer who was running the elevator came out, looking up and down the street. I yelled that the man had gone into the park, and the officer went after him. Then I saw the red light start flashing in that car, there, and another man, I suppose a police officer, got out of the car and ran after the other two."

"Do you know if the man in the car called for help?" Stone asked.

"No, I don't know."

Stone went to the police car, found the microphone, and punched the switch. "Dispatch?"

"Dispatch; who's calling?"

"My name is Barrington, I'm a retired police officer." He gave the address. "There's an officer down here, along with a civilian, both dead. Two other officers have pursued the perp into Central Park. Stand by." He turned to the doorman. "What did the man you let into the building look like?"

"He was small, and he was wearing a parka with the hood up. I didn't get all that good a look at him."

Stone turned back to the microphone. "The perpetrator is a white male, small of stature, wearing a parka with the hood up, and is armed and dangerous. One of the two officers in pursuit is wearing an elevator operator's uniform, and the other is in plain clothes. You want to get major backup into the park between Seventy-second and Seventy-ninth Streets and get a patrol car to the building. Also, find Lieutenant Dino Bacchetti of the Nineteenth Precinct and tell him to get over here fast."

"Where will you be?"

"I'll secure the lobby of the building and wait there."

"Got it; over and out."

Stone put down the microphone. "Come with me," he said. "You and I will wait in the lobby for the police to arrive."

"Yes, sir," the doorman said.

They went back into the building, and Stone went to the elevator. "I wonder why the killer didn't take the elevator upstairs," he said.

The doorman looked into the car. "It's locked," he said, "and the police officer must have the key."

"Is there another key?" Stone asked.

"In the top drawer of the desk," the doorman said, pointing. He clearly had no wish to go over there.

Stone retrieved the key and put it into his pocket. He could hear sirens approaching from a distance. He picked up the house phone, consulted a list of occupants, and called Sarah's apartment. The phone rang and rang, but there was no answer.

14

STONE HUNG UP, CHECKED THE NUMBER, THEN DIALED again. Still no answer. He looked up to see uniforms piling out of two police cars outside and running toward the front door with weapons drawn. He realized that they probably wouldn't know him and that to them, he was a civilian with a weapon. He put his pistol down on the desktop, moved away from the desk, dug out his ID, and held it out in front of him with one hand, while holding the other hand in the air. "I'm on the job!" he shouted, because he knew that would stop a nervous cop from shooting him. They stopped running.

"What's going on here?" a sergeant asked.

"I'm a retired police officer," Stone said. "That's my weapon on the desk. There's an officer and another man on the floor behind the desk, both shot, both dead. This man is the building's doorman."

The sergeant lowered his weapon. "Your name's Barrington, isn't it? You were in the Nineteenth with Bacchetti?"

"That's right."

The sergeant looked behind the desk. "Jesus Christ!" he said. "Who shot these two men?"

"The doorman here saw the perp run out of the building, across the street, and over the wall into the park. Detectives Anderson and

Kelly pursued him. I called it in from Kelly's car; I asked for backup in the park between Seventy-second and Seventy-ninth. I also asked the dispatcher to find Bacchetti and tell him to come here."

"So there's nothing for us to do but wait for the medical examiner?"

"That's right, except I'd like for two men to come upstairs with me. I was having dinner on the sixteenth floor when this happened, and I asked a young lady to stay there, but she's not answering the phone."

The sergeant turned to his men. "Garcia, you come with me; the rest of you stay here and secure this scene."

"Can I pick up my weapon?" Stone asked, pointing.

"Sure," the sergeant said.

Stone turned to the doorman. "Is there a passkey for sixteen?"

"In the key safe on the wall behind the desk," the man said, pointing.

Stone went behind the desk, stepped over the bodies, located the passkey, grabbed his pistol, and headed for the elevator, digging for the key. He unlocked it and pressed the button for sixteen.

"My name's McElhenny," the sergeant said.

"I remember you," Stone replied. "You were a rookie when I left the force; you've moved up."

"What the hell is going on here, Mr. Barrington?" the sergeant asked.

"Somebody's dogging Bacchetti and me; he followed me here tonight, and Anderson and Kelly were laying for him. It didn't work."

"Is this the perp who tried to harm Bacchetti's wife?"

"The same." The elevator stopped, and the men stepped into the private foyer of the apartment.

"Wow," McElhenny said softly, looking around him.

"Inside there should be one woman; she was upstairs when I left. There are also two servants, a man and a woman, who live in, but I don't know where their quarters are. I suggest the two of you search this floor, and I'll check upstairs. Follow me upstairs when you're sure there's nobody down here."

73

"Right," the sergeant said.

Stone inserted the passkey into the lock and swung the door slowly open. He walked through the gallery as quietly as possible, but the three sets of shoes made noise on the marble floor. In the living room, Stone pointed to the two men, then around the apartment; he pointed to himself, then at the stairs.

The two cops started their search, weapons drawn.

Stone flipped off the safety on his pistol and started quickly and quietly up the carpeted stairs. The door to Sarah's room stood open. He stuck his head around the doorjamb and quickly withdrew it. He had seen only the bed, which was now turned down. He stepped into the doorway in a crouch, the pistol held out before him. He took two steps into the room, and from his left came a piercing scream.

Stone swung the pistol around and found it pointed directly at Sarah Buckminster, who was entirely naked.

"Stone! What the hell are you doing?"

Stone pointed the pistol at the floor. "Are you alone? Is anybody in the house?"

"Of course, I'm alone; did you think I'd brought in another man as soon as you left?"

Stone took a deep breath and let it out. He put the pistol back on safety.

"*What* is going on?" she demanded.

"Why didn't you answer the house phone?" he asked.

"Because I was in the shower," she said. "I was a little sweaty from cooking, and I wanted to be fresh."

Stone put his arms around her and held her for a moment. "I'm sorry I frightened you. You'd better get dressed and come downstairs," he said. "The police are here." He left her to get dressed. As he reached the bottom of the stairs, the two cops were emerging from different rooms.

"All clear down here," the sergeant said. "Did you find anything?"

"The woman is all right; she's upstairs. I expect the servants are still in their quarters."

There were hurried footsteps from the direction of the gallery, and all three men swung their weapons in that direction. Dino came around the corner. "Hey, it's Bacchetti!" he cried, holding out his hands, one of which held a pistol. Everybody relaxed. "Is everything okay here?" Dino asked.

"Yes," Stone replied. "Sarah didn't answer the phone when I called from the lobby, and I was worried about her."

"What the hell happened downstairs?" Dino asked.

"Our perp showed, pretending to be delivering a package; the doorman let him into the lobby. Apparently, he walked over to the desk, shot your cop, then held the gun to the desk man's head and forced him to call up here and ask Sarah to come downstairs. I went instead and found the two men dead behind the desk. The doorman says that Anderson and Kelly pursued the perp into the park. I called for backup. That's it."

"You think he knew we were watching the place?" Dino asked.

"My guess is no. I think he shot the cop just to get the desk man's attention. I don't know where Anderson was when he came in; the elevator was locked."

"That's pretty fucking ruthless," Dino said. "Our man has moved up from knives to guns, and he's getting more dangerous."

"Looks that way."

Dino looked up at the staircase, causing Stone to turn around. Sarah was coming down the stairs.

"Sarah, you remember Dino Bacchetti," Stone said.

"Of course," she said, shaking Dino's hand.

"And this is Sergeant McElhenny."

"Sergeant," she said. "Now will someone tell me what is going on?"

"It's bad, I'm afraid," Stone said. "The man I told you about has shot a police officer and your desk man, Dan, downstairs. The police are searching the park for him now."

"Dan? That sweet man?"

"Yes, I'm sorry."

Sarah's knees seemed to go weak, and she collapsed onto a sofa.

Stone sat beside her. "Listen to me," he said. "We've got to get you out of here right now. I want you to pack your bags as quickly as possible, and we'll get Dino to drive us to my house."

"But why do I have to leave here?" she asked. "Surely I'm not in any danger."

"This is all my fault, and I apologize. I told you that this man is hurting people close to Dino and me. I'm afraid you're at risk, now; he knows where you live."

Dino spoke up. "Stone is right, Sarah; we've got to get you out of here. Is there a garage in this building?"

"Yes," she said. "The entrance is around the corner." She pointed downtown.

"I'll pull my car in there and pick up you and Stone."

"Ask the doorman for a card that opens the garage door," she said. She seemed quite calm.

"I'll be down there in ten minutes," Dino said. "I just want to make sure everything's being handled in the lobby. McElhenny, you and your man stick with them until I can get them in the car."

"Yessir, Lieutenant," the sergeant replied.

Sarah stood up. "I'll get packed," she said, then went back upstairs. Stone went up to help her with her bags.

"I'll just take a few things," Sarah said, throwing clothes into a bag. "I can come back for the rest later."

"I don't want you to come back here until this guy has been caught," Stone said. "Bring everything."

Ten minutes later, they were stepping out of the elevator into the garage, the uniforms ahead of them, weapons drawn. Dino stood by his car, the trunk open. They stowed Sarah's luggage, and a moment later were headed down to Turtle Bay.

"At least we know he's not watching the house now," Dino said. "He'll still be in the park, if they haven't already caught him."

"I hope you're right," Stone said.

15

THEY FELL EXHAUSTED INTO BED AND WENT IMMEDI-
ately to sleep. Stone hadn't felt terribly affectionate after the
events of the evening, and he assumed Sarah hadn't either. Then,
sometime before dawn, he began having an erotic dream about
Sarah. He was very nearly at climax when he realized that he wasn't
asleep, and that it wasn't a dream. He opened his eyes. Sarah's honey
brown hair spilled over his belly; he was in her mouth, and his hand
was stroking her buttocks.

"No, not yet," he said, pulling her into his arms. "There'll be
nothing left for you."

"I want a lot left for me," she whispered, kissing him and pulling
him on top of her. Stone tried to restore some calm to his body while
kissing her breasts, but soon it was obvious that he could wait no
longer. They came together, noisily, in less than a minute, then collapsed facing each other. She snuggled into his arms, mixing her
sweat with his.

"You are *so* American," she said.

"How so?"

"You're noisy, like me. Englishmen never talk in bed, never say
anything sexy."

"Wham, bam, thank you, ma'am?"

"Just wham, bam."

Stone laughed. "What about Italian men?"

"Very automotive," she said. "There's an old joke that an Italian man uses a sports car as an extension of his penis, whereas an Englishman uses it as a substitute."

"It sounds as though your best interests lie in the United States," he said. "I don't even own a car."

"That explains a lot." She laughed.

"Though I've been meaning to buy one. I do have a garage, after all."

"It would be a pity to have an empty garage," she said. She took him in her hand and began kneading gently. "Perhaps I'd better have one last go at you before you starting dissipating your energies in fast driving."

"I'm older than I used to be, you know. It might not work again quite so quickly."

"Oh, I think it will." She squeezed. "See? It's responding very nicely."

"I believe you're right," Stone said, breathing harder.

She rolled on top of him. "I'll drive," she said.

Stone regained consciousness with the doorbell ringing in his ears. He rolled over and glanced at the bedside clock: 7:15. He punched the intercom button on the phone. "Yes?" he grumbled.

"This is Detective Thomas Deacon of the Manhattan District Attorney's Office," a deep voice said.

That had a familiar ring, Stone thought. It took him a moment to remember that Dino had pointed the man out at the party at Martin Brougham's house. He'd disliked him on sight.

"I want to talk to you," Deacon said.

"Did you ever hear of business hours?" Stone asked.

"Most people are up by this time."

"Come back after nine o'clock," Stone said. He looked over at the sleeping Sarah, lying naked, her breasts exposed. "Make that after ten o'clock." He punched off the intercom.

The doorbell sounded again.

"What?" Stone growled.

"I want to talk to you right now, Barrington."

"Go fuck yourself," Stone said, switching off the intercom. He rolled over, gathered Sarah in his arms, and fell asleep again.

Next, it was the phone, and this time it was after nine.

"Hello?"

"It's Dino."

"Hi. Any luck catching our perp last night?"

"None," Dino said. "My people scoured the park half the night; he must have found some hole to crawl into. They're still watching all the exits; he might try to walk out this morning."

"Did you find out what happened to Andy Anderson last night?"

"He had locked the elevator and gone to the staff john. When he heard the shots he got himself together as quickly as he could and went into the lobby with his weapon drawn. There was an exchange of shots; Andy thought he might have nicked the guy, but he was out of the building and into the traffic and over the wall, and Andy couldn't fire again for fear of hitting somebody else. My guess is that Kelly was cooping in the car and was slow to react, then didn't call for backup. Good thing you thought of that."

"I hope this experience has rattled the perp," Stone said. "Maybe he'll think twice before trying it again."

"Especially if Andy put a bullet in him; that's twice he'd have been shot, after Mary Ann fired at him. It's a shame nobody got him in the center of the chest."

"You remember that guy Deacon you pointed out to me at Martin Brougham's house?"

"Yeah."

"Well, he rang my doorbell at the crack of dawn this morning."

"What did he want?"

"I don't know; I told him to get stuffed."

"Must be something about the Susan Bean killing."

"If so, he's a little slow on the uptake, isn't he?"

"Yeah."

"Has he called you?"

"No."

"I think I'll just refer him to the precinct."

"No need to piss him off unnecessarily, Stone."

"Why not? He's pissed me off. You and I never pounded on people's doors at seven o'clock in the morning, did we?"

"Not unless we were arresting them. He'll probably come back with a SWAT team. By the way, Martin Brougham is the new chief deputy DA."

"I hadn't heard."

"It's being announced this afternoon. Rumor is, the old man is going to retire and is giving Brougham a head start on the election."

"I'll believe that when I see it," Stone said. "Only death will get the old man out of office. Maybe not even that."

"You want some dinner tonight?"

"Let me call you later in the day. Do you still have people on me?"

"I've got two cars on your block right now; one of them doesn't look like a cop car," Dino said. "If you're followed, that one will follow the follower."

"Thanks, Dino," Stone said. "I appreciate that. I don't want to get Sarah hurt. Can you have one of them stick with her for a few days?"

"Sure. After all, he seems to be going after people close to us, not you and me. I'll have Anderson and Kelly stick with her."

"Thanks."

"I gotta go. Call me later about dinner."

"Will do." Stone got up and dragged himself into a shower, while Sarah slept on. He shaved, got dressed, and went down to the kitchen. He made himself some coffee, toasted a bagel, and opened the *Times*. It was too soon for them to report the events of the night before, but there were accurate, if incomplete articles on the killings of Susan Bean and his neighbor, Miranda Hirsch. There were obituaries on both, as well.

The doorbell rang, and Stone punched the intercom. "Yes?"

"This is Thomas Deacon. Is it late enough for you now?"

"Walk around the railing to my office entrance," Stone said. "I'll meet you there." He hung up, grabbed his coffee, and headed downstairs, wondering what the hell the man wanted.

16

STONE LET DEACON AND ANOTHER MAN IN THROUGH the street-level entrance, led them to his office, and pointed at two chairs. "Okay," he said, sitting down. "What do you want?"

"This is Detective Simmons," Deacon said. "We're investigating the murder of Susan Bean."

"I believe that's being handled at the Nineteenth Precinct," Stone said.

"Our investigation supersedes theirs," Deacon replied.

"Lieutenant Bacchetti will be very surprised to hear that."

"I don't much care what surprises Bacchetti," Deacon said. "I have some questions for you, and you'd better give me straight answers."

"Listen, Deacon," Stone said. "If you want my cooperation, you're going about it in the wrong way. First, you wake me up at the crack of dawn, then you come into my house and encroach on a police investigation while behaving like the Gestapo. If you want to talk to me about *anything*, you'd better start acquiring some social graces."

The two men stared at each other across the desk for a long moment. Finally, Deacon spoke.

"Mr. Barrington, I apologize for our intrusion at such an early hour this morning. An important official in the District Attorney's Office has been murdered, and we would be very grateful if you would answer some questions for us in order to give us a clearer idea of what happened that evening."

Stone threw a leg over the saddle and climbed down from his high horse. "I'd be happy to help in any way I can," he said.

"Thank you. Could you give us an account of your actions on the night in question from the time you left your home?"

"Of course. I left my house around eight-thirty that evening and took a cab to Elaine's, on Second Avenue between Eighty-eighth and Eighty-ninth Streets. I met Lieutenant Dino Bacchetti there for dinner. Later in the evening, sometime after ten-thirty, I believe, Lieutenant Bacchetti suggested that we attend a party at the home of Martin Brougham. We arrived there around ten-forty-five, I believe. After being introduced to our hosts, I took a drink into the library and there found Susan Bean. We conversed for a few minutes, then we agreed to go out for a late supper. Since most of the neighborhood restaurants seemed to be closed or closing, Ms. Bean suggested that we go to her house and order Chinese food to be delivered. On telephoning the restaurant, we learned that delivery was unavailable, and Ms. Bean asked if I would go there and pick up the food. I did so. When I returned, I found Ms. Bean lying on the kitchen floor; she was dead. I called nine-one-one and reported the murder, then waited for the police to arrive."

Simmons was taking notes furiously.

"You said you met Lieutenant Bacchetti for dinner, is that right?"

"Yes."

"But then, a couple of hours later, you were going to have Chinese food with Ms. Bean?"

"I wasn't very hungry when I met Lieutenant Bacchetti at Elaine's, and I only had a salad."

"I see," Deacon said, as if he didn't see at all. He nodded to Simmons to take note of this discrepancy.

Stone rolled his eyes and sighed.

"When and where did you first become acquainted with Susan Bean?" Deacon asked.

"On that evening, at the home of Martin Brougham."

"Had you ever met her before that?"

"No."

"Had you ever heard of her?"

"Not that I can recall."

"As an attorney, you sometimes try cases in criminal court?"

"I do."

"Have you never dealt with Ms. Bean in your capacity as an attorney?"

"No."

"Some years ago, shortly after you left the police force and began practicing law, you represented a man named Marvin Herbert Van Fleet."

"I did."

"Do you recall who the opposing counsel was?"

"I believe it was Paul Haverty."

"Do you recall who his second chair was?"

"No. I mean, it was a young woman; I don't recall her name." Stone blinked. "Was that Susan Bean?"

"You remember now?"

"I remember a rather plump, plain young woman who rarely spoke, at least, to me."

"That was Susan Bean."

"Really? She'd changed a lot by the time I met her at Brougham's house."

"So you *were* acquainted with Ms. Bean?"

"I was introduced to her, I suppose."

"On how many occasions did you see her socially after meeting her in court?"

"None."

"I ask you again, Mr. Barrington: on how many occasions?"

"None whatever."

"You are an habitué of Elaine's restaurant, are you not?"

"I'm in there a couple of times a week."

"For how long?"

"For many years."

"Have you forgotten that Susan Bean was also an habitué of Elaine's?"

"I was never aware of that."

"You have no recollection of seeing her there?"

"None." Stone began to wonder where this was going.

"On at least one occasion, you picked her up at the bar at Elaine's, took her home, and had sex with her, did you not?"

Stone was brought up short by the question. He racked his brain for any memory of such an incident. He had, he knew, met women at Elaine's, and sometimes those meetings had resulted in sex, but that had not happened for a long time, not since he had left the police force. "I have no recollection of such an incident," Stone said.

"Would it surprise you to learn that Susan Bean remembered such an incident?"

"It certainly would. When was this supposed to have occurred?"

"Do you have any recollection of meeting a woman named Jean Martinelli at Elaine's?"

"The name doesn't ring a bell."

"Ms. Martinelli also works for the District Attorney's Office, and she was also a habitué of Elaine's, often in the company of Susan Bean. She recalls meeting you there on several occasions. She recalls your leaving the restaurant in the company of Ms. Bean, and she recalls being told by Ms. Bean the following day that the two of you had gone to her apartment and had sex. Do you deny that this occurred?"

"I have no recollection of any of this," Stone said. "How long ago was this supposed to have happened?"

"That's not relevant," Deacon said.

"Relevant to what?"

"Relevant to the murder of Susan Bean."

"I should think it would be *very* relevant," Stone replied.

"Let's say that the incident in question occurred before the Van Fleet legal matter."

"Then you're talking of more than six years ago?"

"Approximately."

"And how does this alleged incident relate to the murder of Susan Bean?"

"If it's not relevant, Mr. Barrington, why have you been lying to us?"

"I haven't lied to you," Stone replied, with some heat. "You've made an allegation that I had some prior relationship with Susan Bean, however brief, some years ago. I've told you that I have no recollection of such a relationship, and that's the truth."

"When you began speaking with Ms. Bean in Martin Brougham's library, you were renewing an old acquaintance, weren't you, Mr. Barrington?"

"I had no reason to think so."

"In fact, when you introduced yourself to Susan Bean, she told you that you had met before, didn't she?"

"She did not. She indicated nothing of the sort."

"Describe your conversation with her."

Stone tried to remember. "She was reading something when I sat down; we talked about that, I think. We talked about her name, Bean, I remember. She told me that she had assisted Martin Brougham on the Dante trial, and I congratulated her on the verdict. That's about all I recall."

"And what did you talk about on the way to her apartment?"

"It was just idle conversation; it didn't seem to have any particular point."

"Did you talk about her work?"

"I suppose so, in passing."

"Did she tell you anything about her work?"

"I remember getting the impression that she was thinking of leaving her job."

"What did she say that gave you that impression?"

"I don't remember, exactly; she seemed tired of the work, I thought. She didn't seem elated about the Dante verdict."

"You're aware that she went to a party celebrating that verdict?"

"Yes."

"And you say she wasn't happy about the verdict?"

"I recall that, at the party, she was alone in another room, reading, rather than taking part in a celebration. And I didn't say she was unhappy about the verdict, merely that she was not elated."

"Something I don't understand, Mr. Barrington."

"What's that?"

"Why would you want to murder a woman you say you hadn't seen for more than five years?"

Stone sat up straight. "I did not murder Susan Bean, and I had no motive to do so." He looked at Simmons, who was still taking notes. "Write that down, please."

"I'm writing it down," Simmons replied.

Stone stood up. "I think that will be all," he said to Deacon.

"I'm sorry you're reluctant to answer my questions, Mr. Barrington," Deacon said.

"On the contrary," Stone replied, "I want it noted for the record that I have answered all your questions. For further information about the events surrounding the death of Susan Bean, I refer you to the detective squad at the Nineteenth Precinct. I have given a full statement to them. As for any further questions to me, I refer you to my attorney, William Eggers, of Woodman and Weld. Good day."

Deacon got to his feet. "Woodman and Weld? Very elegant firm. I don't suppose they're going to be pleased about being involved in this mess."

"I said good day," Stone replied, opening the door and letting them out. He had to resist the impulse to plant his foot in Thomas Deacon's ass as he departed.

17

STONE LEFT HIS HOUSE AND WALKED UP THE BLOCK TO where an unmarked police car was parked. He got in. "Are Anderson and Kelly in another car around here?"

"Yeah," the driver replied.

"Can you reach them without using the radio?"

"I can call them on their cell phone," the cop said.

"Please."

The cop dialed the number, then handed the phone to Stone.

"Anderson," a voice said.

"Andy, it's Stone. I'm in the other car now."

"I saw you."

"We're going to drive away; after we've been gone two minutes, please ring my doorbell three times. Miss Buckminster will come out, and you can drive her to Elaine's. You know where that is?"

"I used to drive Lieutenant Bacchetti," Anderson replied.

"Make sure you're not followed."

"Right."

Stone broke the connection, then handed the phone back to the cop. "All right, we're headed for Second Avenue between Eighty-eighth and Eighty-ninth. Don't go direct; I'll watch our tail."

"Right," the cop said, putting the car into gear. "You want me to use the light?"

"Let's be inconspicuous," Stone said.

They drove down to Third Avenue and turned uptown, while Stone watched every car behind them. "Go over to Park, then back to Third," he told the detective.

"Whatever you say," the bored detective replied.

They spent half an hour reaching Elaine's. Just before they arrived, Stone called Anderson again.

"Anderson."

"Andy, when you've dropped off Miss Buckminster, please come into the restaurant and take up a position at the bar, near the window. You know what the perp looks like, don't you?"

"I didn't get much of a look at him last night," Anderson replied, "but I've got the description."

"Keep an eye peeled for him."

"Will do."

The car stopped. "You guys watch the block for a guy matching the description," Stone said.

"Right," the detectives replied.

Stone got out and went inside. He gave Elaine a kiss, then joined Dino at their usual table.

"Sarah coming?" Dino asked.

"She'll be here in a minute; Anderson is bringing her. Anything happen today?"

"We checked with the Hamburg police for the whereabouts of Mitteldorfer's nephew, Ernst Hausman. They checked his home address and the cigarette factory; he was at work today. Hasn't had a day off in more than a month."

"What about the check of Mitteldorfer's old neighborhood? Turn up anything?"

"Half a dozen of the older residents remembered Mitteldorfer, but they didn't know anything about relatives. As far as they knew, Herbie and his wife were childless."

"Did they talk to Herbie's correspondent? What was her name?"

"Eloise Enzberg. Yeah, this morning. Frightened her, it seems. She didn't know anything; she just writes to Herbie once a week and visits him once a month. Takes him strudel."

"How *gemütlich*."

"If you say so. You know, Germantown isn't what it used to be."

"What is?"

"I mean, there's not so many Germans anymore, just some old people. I guess their kids moved away. You remember the Gay Vienna restaurant?"

"Sure, the one with the *kalbshax*."

"The veal shank that looked like a giant drumstick."

"Yeah, that's the one."

"And they had a zither player. I liked the zither music. Where was that place, exactly?"

"You're sitting in it," Dino said.

"It was *here*?"

"It finally closed, then Elaine bought the building and opened up."

"I'll be damned; I never connected the two."

"I guess all the *kalbshax* lovers died or moved away." Dino sighed.

Elaine came and sat down. "How's it going?"

"Not bad," Stone replied. "Say, do you think you could put *kalbshax* on the menu?"

"What're you, some kind of Kraut?" Elaine asked.

Sarah bustled in, followed closely by Andy Anderson, who took up his position at the bar.

Dino grabbed a waiter. "See the tall guy at the bar by the window? Tell the bartender to give him one scotch, no refills." The waiter went off to do Dino's bidding.

Stone and Dino stood up to welcome Sarah; she rewarded Dino with a kiss on the cheek. "Elaine," Stone said, "you remember Sarah Buckminster, don't you?"

"Sure; long time," Elaine said. She turned to Dino. "I heard about last night," she said.

"How the hell did you hear about that?" Dino demanded. "It hasn't been in the papers."

"I got my sources," Elaine replied.

"Yeah, you probably know more about the case than I do."

"I probably do."

"Maybe you can tell me where to find the perp?"

Elaine leaned over, and whispered conspiratorially, "Try Central Park."

"I had a visit from one Tom Deacon today," Stone said.

"What the fuck did *he* want?" Dino asked.

"He's apparently taking over your case."

"He should live so long," Dino snorted.

"He questioned me at some length, while his partner took notes, then he accused me of murdering Susan Bean."

"Who's Susan Bean?" Sarah asked.

"A dead person," Elaine explained.

"Why did you murder her?" Sarah asked Stone.

"Oh, just for the hell of it," Stone said. "I murder two or three women a month, if I'm not too busy."

Sarah turned to Elaine. "You think I should move out?"

"I didn't know you'd moved *in*," Elaine replied. "It's nice that Stone can get laid again."

Sarah burst out laughing. "Has it been a while?"

"Oh, yeah," Elaine said. "I can't tell you what a pain in the ass he's been."

"I have *not*," Stone protested.

"He's kinda got that glow again, you know?" Elaine said to Dino.

"Yeah," Dino replied, "he's all pink in the cheeks again."

"I'd like to think I'm the only person here who's seen his cheeks," Sarah said, "and they're really quite a lovely shade of pink."

"So are yours," Stone said, clinking her glass with his.

"Why do you think Deacon is poking his nose in?" Dino asked.

"Wouldn't you think Martin Brougham was behind it? After all, Susan was one of their own."

"That's not a good enough excuse," Dino said.

"He told me that Susan used to be a regular here, at the bar. Did you know her, Elaine?"

Elaine shrugged. "Who can keep track of all those people at the bar? They come, they go, they get murdered."

"She was friends with a woman named Jean Martinelli."

"*Her* I know," Elaine said. "I threw her out of here when she used to get drunk and start annoying people at the tables."

"She apparently works at the DA's Office, too," Stone said. "Deacon seems convinced that I knew Susan before the other night, that I'd seen a lot of her in here. I told him I had no memory of her."

"She used to be fat," Dino said.

"You knew her before, then?"

"I testified in trials that she was prosecuting—two or three times, I think. She lost a hell of a lot of weight and started doing things to herself, you know? Maybe that's why you don't remember her."

"Remember Van Fleet?" Stone asked.

"I believe I shot him dead," Dino said. "How could I forget?"

"Well, I defended Van Fleet on some minor charge, once, and Deacon said Susan was assisting the prosecutor, a guy named Haverty."

"Could be," Dino said. "I think she was in the DA's Office since she got out of law school."

"You think you could give Brougham a ring and tell him I didn't murder Susan?"

"Well, I guess if I were completely convinced of that, I could."

"Do it tomorrow, Dino; I don't want those people to start leaking to the press that I'm a suspect."

"Maybe I'll do it right now," Dino said, nodding toward the door.

Stone turned to see Martin and Dana Brougham coming through the front door.

18

STONE WATCHED AS ELAINE MADE HER WAY THROUGH the crowd to meet Martin and Dana Brougham. They were obviously asking for a table, but the place was jammed. Then Elaine was pointing at Stone's table.

"Dino, I think Elaine is suggesting they join us," Stone said.

"Be interesting to see their reaction," Dino said.

Their reaction was to nod yes.

"What the hell," Dino said. "Now is as good a time as any."

"Why would they want to sit with us if Brougham thinks I murdered Susan?"

"I guess we'll find out," Dino said, as the couple made their way to the table.

Sarah turned to Stone. "Later, I hope you'll take the time to explain to me what the fuck is going on."

"I will," Stone said, as he got to his feet.

"Hi, Dino," Martin Brougham said. "Hi, Stone. You remember Dana?"

"Of course," Stone said. "This is Sarah Buckminster; won't you join us?"

The Broughams sat down and ordered a drink. "Have you eaten yet?" Brougham asked.

"Not yet," Stone said.

"Then dinner's on me; we're celebrating."

"I heard; congratulations. Any truth to the rumor that the old man is going to retire and anoint you?"

Brougham laughed aloud. "Not while there's a breath left in his body."

They looked at menus and ordered dinner. Stone could not understand Brougham's behavior, so he decided to charge in head-first. "Your man Deacon came to see me this morning."

"He did? What about?"

"Don't you keep track of the guy?" Dino asked.

"Usually," Brougham replied. He looked back and forth between Dino and Stone. "Something going on here that I don't know about?"

"Deacon seems to think he's taking over the investigation into Susan Bean's murder," Dino said.

"Oh, nothing like that, I assure you, Dino. He asked me if he could look into it, and, of course, I told him he could. After all, she was one of us, and we want to see this cleared up."

Stone said, "Deacon seems to think that I murdered Susan."

Brougham nearly choked on his drink. He looked at Dino. "Do you have any evidence to support such a notion?"

"None whatever," Dino said.

"Because, if you do, I shouldn't be sitting at this table."

"Relax, Martin," Dino said. "We cleared Stone of any involvement within half an hour of her death. He had gone out for Chinese when it happened."

"I've heard the timeline," Brougham said. "It made sense to me. Besides, what possible motive could Stone have had?"

"Exactly," Dino replied.

"You can talk directly to me, Martin," Stone said. "If you have any questions, I'd be glad to answer them."

"You mean, off the record?"

"I answered all of Deacon's question *on* the record, right up to the point he accused me of murder, then I told him to call my attorney, and I threw him out. But as a courtesy, I'll be happy to answer any questions you have, right here, right now, in front of witnesses."

Brougham thought about this for a moment. "Did you know Susan before our party?"

"Deacon says I did. He says she assisted Haverty in prosecuting a client of mine. I met Haverty's second chair, but I don't remember anything about her. Deacon also says she was a regular here, at the bar, and that I took her home one night and slept with her. I don't remember that, either, and I think I would, if it had happened."

"You don't remember meeting her at the bar? Not at all?"

"No," Stone replied. "For what it's worth, Elaine doesn't remember her, either, and she's in here a lot more than I am."

"I suppose so."

"Elaine remembers Jean Martinelli, remembers throwing her out of here one night, drunk. Apparently, Martinelli is the source of Deacon's conjecture."

"Martinelli hasn't worked for me for nearly a year," Brougham said, "but it doesn't surprise me that she talked to Tom; they were something of an item for a while. I expect she called him."

"What else would you like to know?" Stone asked.

Brougham shrugged.

"Come on, Martin," he said. "I want to lay this to rest now."

"Who do you think did it?" Brougham asked.

Dino butted in. "We think it's somebody Stone and I busted a long time ago, but we don't know who, yet. There've been two other murders, one of them Stone's secretary, Alma, the same night as Susan Bean, and the other a woman who lives behind Stone's house in Turtle Bay, the following night."

"I know about those," Brougham said. "You think they're connected to Susan's death?"

"Only by the murderer," Dino said. "The night Susan was killed, we think somebody followed Stone from his house here that night, then to your house, then followed Stone and Susan to her place. When he saw Stone leave to get the Chinese, he went in. We think he was still in the building when Stone got back. He was gone when the patrol car arrived. I got there five minutes later. It was Stone who called nine-one-one."

"That, I knew," Brougham said.

"Any other questions for me, Martin?" Stone said, trying not to sound too confrontational.

"None that I can think of at the moment."

"I'll be happy to come down to your office with my lawyer and answer any others you may think of," Stone said.

"I appreciate the offer."

"But," Stone said, "if I start reading in the papers that I'm a suspect, I'll know it came from Deacon, and I'll go straight to the old man. I've known him a long time." This was true, up to a point.

"I don't think that will be necessary," Brougham said. "But, you understand, if Deacon starts poking holes in your story, we'll be talking again."

"There aren't any holes in my story," Stone said, "because it's the truth."

Dinner arrived, saving everyone the embarrassment of continuing the conversation. Dana Brougham changed the subject.

"Aren't you the painter who's about to have a show at the Bergman Gallery?" she asked Sarah.

"Yes, that's right," Sarah replied. "The opening is next week; may I send you an invitation?"

Dana produced a card from her purse. "I've seen some of your early things, and I'd love to see your more recent work. Can you give me a hint?"

"It's a Tuscan show," Sarah replied. "I've lived there for the past six years, so it's a combination of landscapes, still lifes, and portraits of people in the Chianti district."

"Oh, I love that part of Italy."

A waiter came and whispered something in Dino's ear, and he left the table. Stone watched him take a phone call, but his face betrayed nothing. He came back and sat down.

Everyone looked at him.

"That was the precinct," Dino said. "We had a suspect, but his alibi is holding."

"I'm sorry to hear it," Brougham said. "Who is it?"

"A guy named Mitteldorfer; Stone and I nailed him twelve years ago for the murder of his wife."

"What made you suspect him?"

"Stone and I saw the murder of the woman who lived behind his house. The perp looked the way Mitteldorfer looked twelve years ago. But he doesn't look that way anymore."

"Peculiar," Brougham said.

"We thought so, too. We've been looking for a relative who might have been involved, but there isn't anybody—not so far, anyway. The precinct was just confirming the questioning of some peripheral people. Mitteldorfer appears to be clean."

"Is he out of prison?"

"No, but he's up for parole soon."

"You want me to toss a grenade into his hearing?"

Dino shook his head. "I don't like the guy, but I don't have a thing on him. If he gets out and then we get some evidence, it'll be simple enough to get his parole revoked."

Brougham put down his fork. "You think he might get out, then start killing again?"

Dino shrugged. "No way to predict that. He adds up as a one-time perp—killed his wife in the heat of the moment when he found out she was running around on him. She seems to have been his only enemy."

"Except you and Stone," Brougham said.

19

STONE WAS DRESSING THE FOLLOWING MORNING WHEN Sarah stuck her head out of the bathroom. "Why don't you take me to the country this weekend?"

"What country?" Stone asked.

"Any country," she replied. "You forget that I'm English—an English rose, as it were." She batted her eyes. "And I need frequent communing with trees and grass to keep my corpuscles together. A nice country inn does wonders for them, too."

"I'll rent a car."

"Stone, you told me you just got this big fee, right."

"Yes."

"*Buy* a car."

Stone shrugged. "Okay."

"A nice one, please."

"Yes, ma'am."

"What a good boy are you."

"I am, am I not?"

"Didn't I just say so?"

She came out of the bathroom naked, and Stone stopped dressing, ogling her shamelessly.

"None of that, now," she said. "I've got to get to the gallery to start hanging pictures, and your two very nice policemen are waiting in the garage. Well, one nice policeman."

Stone started dressing again. "Yeah, Kelly's not exactly good company, is he?"

"He's a proper little shit," she replied, slipping into jeans and a sweater, no bra.

"You want me to ask Dino for another cop?"

"Don't make waves," she said. "Dino's already doing us a very big favor. I can live with Kelly."

Stone put his arms around her. "You can live with me," he said.

She grabbed his wrists and held his arms at his sides. "We'll talk about that when I don't *have* to live with you anymore," she said, "and on some nice, neutral ground, that doesn't have a bed so close at hand."

"Okay," he replied, stealing a kiss.

"Go buy a car," she said.

Stone got out of the police car on Park Avenue in front of the Mercedes-Benz dealership, but not before looking up and down the street once more. "I'll be a while," he said to the two cops up front.

"Yessir," one of them replied, saluting smartly. "We're at your disposal."

"Krakauer," Stone said, "I'll dispose of you at the earliest possible moment." He turned and walked into the showroom. Half a dozen cars were on display: a new SLK, the little sports car with the retractable hard top—cute, but tiny. There was an S600 sedan—big, powerful, and extremely expensive, maybe too much of all those things. And sitting in a prime spot, an E320, the middle Mercedes, in a nice, tan metallic color.

A man materialized at his elbow. "May I show you something?" he asked.

"I'm interested in the V8 version of that one," Stone said, pointing at the E320.

"The E430? Wonderful automobile. I can get you one in about four months, if you'd like to order now."

"I was thinking about this afternoon."

"Can't be done, I'm afraid. The demand has just been too great."

Stone was annoyed. He'd rented an E430 in Los Angeles a few months before and loved it. He strolled toward the big V12 sedan. "How much?"

"A hundred and thirty-seven thousand, plus various taxes."

Stone held up a hand. "Stop. Don't tell me what the taxes are."

"You're very wise," the man replied. "I can get you an S500, the V8 version of this one, almost immediately."

"How long is 'almost immediately'?"

"I've got one coming in in about two weeks."

"You really know how to take the pleasure out of impulse buying," Stone said.

"I'm sorry, but we're dealing with a lot of demand and not enough cars."

Stone looked out the side window of the showroom. A car-carrier truck had pulled up and unloaded something black. Now a double door had been opened, and four men were pushing a car onto the sales floor. "What is *that*?" he asked.

"Ah, now there's something special," the salesman said. "It's called the E55; it's an E430 that has been specially modified by AMG, the German tuning shop that does a lot of work on various Mercedes models. It's in obsidian black with parchment-leather upholstery."

The car was a lot like the E320 on display, but seemed lower and meaner-looking. "Just what, exactly, has AMG done to that car?"

The man went to his desk and removed a folder from a drawer. "This is very out of the ordinary," he said, reading from the folder. "The car has a five-and-a-half-liter V8 that's more powerful than the one in the S500, at three hundred fifty-four horsepower, and with the S500 transmission. The body is lowered, and the suspension has upgraded shock absorbers, antiroll bars, and springs. It's got eighteen-inch wheels, Z-rated tires, and the brakes from the SL600."

Stone sucked in a breath.

"The windows are tinted darkly enough to make the occupants unrecognizable, and, after it arrived in this country, we sent it to a specialist to be lightly armored."

"What, exactly, does 'lightly armored' mean?"

The salesman opened a door, pressed a button, and a window rolled down halfway. "As you can see, the glass is a lot thicker than standard—half an inch thick, in fact—and the roof, all the door panels, and the floorpan have been reinforced with lightweight, but very tough materials like Kevlar. The car will repel small-weapons fire, even heavy machine-gun fire, but it won't, of course, stop a bazooka or a land mine. You'd need the fully armored version for that level of protection."

Stone got into the car and looked around.

"You've got sport seats and special trim; there's also a concealed radar scrambler on board," he said, looking around to see that no one was listening. "It detects, then makes police radar useless; it's legal in most states."

"It's very nice," Stone said. "How much?"

"It doesn't belong to us, actually," the salesman replied. "It's the property of the widow of a former client, a South American gentleman."

"And why is she a widow?"

"The car was delivered a couple of days too late to serve the purpose the gentleman had intended."

"You mean he was in another car when . . ."

"When he needed the extra protection that this car affords."

"How much does the widow want for it?"

"Something in the region of . . ." He named a figure. "But I believe she is a highly motivated seller."

"I see," Stone said, feeling to be sure he had his checkbook with him.

"The car has only eighty-one miles on it, and it has every option ordinarily available on the S600," the salesman said, "including the portable telephone and the separate rear-seat air-conditioning. Even with the extra weight of the options and the armoring, the car will do zero to sixty in six seconds flat," the salesman said, "and the top speed is no longer limited to the standard, electronically controlled one hundred thirty miles per hour."

"What *is* the top speed?" Stone asked, trying to breathe deeply and slowly.

"Nobody knows," the salesman replied.

"Ask the widow if she will accept an offer of . . ." Stone named a number. "And please tell her it will be my only offer."

"Let me make a call," the salesman said. He went to his desk and picked up the phone.

Stone walked around the car, looked in the trunk, then raised the hood. He gave a little gasp. The engine was the most beautiful mechanical object he had ever seen, ingeniously crammed into a car allegedly too small for it and beautifully polished wherever possible. He closed the hood and looked at the wheels. He reckoned they were two inches larger than standard; the rear wheels were wider than the front, and the tires were low profile.

The salesman returned. "The widow accepts your offer," he said. A film of perspiration covered his face. "Will that be cash, or would you like to finance it?"

"It will be cash," Stone said, pulling out his checkbook. "How soon can I drive it away?"

"The car's already been prepped; you can be on your way in half an hour."

"Can you get me a number for the car phone in that time?"

"You better believe it," the salesman said, trying not to pant.

20

STONE DROVE MADDENINGLY SLOWLY THROUGH THE crosstown traffic, two detectives in a car behind him. Sarah was reading through the instruction book that came as a supplement to the owner's manual.

"It says here that the electric, rear-seat sunscreen is made of a material that is designed to stop any incoming . . ." She stopped. "Incoming what?"

"Just incoming. It means bullets or shrapnel."

"Any incoming that penetrates the rear glass." She found the button under the armrest and watched as the fabric sunscreen went up and down. "Cute," she said. "Does it have built-in machine guns like James Bond's car?"

"Of course not. I shouldn't have told you about the armor."

"Oh, I'm very glad to hear about the armor," she said. "Gives one a cozy warm feeling inside. Where are you taking me?"

"It's a surprise."

"How long a surprise?"

"Normally less than two hours, but I want to make a brief stop along the way."

"A brief stop where?"

"Ossining, New York."

"Yuk; sounds like an awful place."

"Many of the people who reside there think so."

"Why are we stopping there?"

"I want to ask a man some questions." Stone pulled onto the West Side Highway and left the thick traffic behind. He put his foot down and felt himself pressed into his seat as the car accelerated.

"My goodness," Sarah said.

"Yes, indeed." Stone looked into the rearview mirror at the small dot that was the detectives' car. He punched a programmed button on the car telephone.

"Krakauer," a voice said.

"Thanks, Krakauer," Stone said. "I'll take it from here. You can tell Lieutenant Bacchetti that you got me out of town alive."

"Right," Krakauer replied. "Try not to come back."

Stone punched off the call, flipped on the radar scrambler, and concentrated on driving and watching for cops. In what seemed like half the usual time they were on the Saw Mill River Parkway, headed north. He crossed the Hudson on the Tappan Zee Bridge and picked up the New York State Thruway.

"There's a little wind noise around this window," Sarah said. "I would have thought that at, what, seventy miles an hour we wouldn't hear that."

"We're doing a hundred and ten," Stone replied.

"Oh. Are we going to be arrested?"

"Probably not." He spotted a state trooper going in the opposite direction and slowed down, watching the car make a U-turn across the meridian. By the time the trooper was up to speed, Stone was at sixty-five. He could see the man fiddling with something on his dashboard, looking confused. A moment later, the trooper made another U-turn and drove off to the south. "Zap," Stone said aloud.

"What?" Sarah asked.

"I just zapped his radar."

"I thought his radar was supposed to zap you."

"That's the way it used to be."

A little later Stone pulled into the visitor parking lot at Sing Sing and approached the guardhouse.

"Can I help you?" the guard asked.

"I'd like to speak to Captain Warkowski."

"Just a minute." The guard picked up a phone, said something into it, then handed it to Stone. "He's on the line."

"Hello, Captain," Stone said. "This is Stone Barrington; I was up here with Lieutenant Bacchetti."

"How could I forget?" Warkowski replied. "What can I do for you?"

"I'd like to see Herbert Mitteldorfer again; just a few questions."

"I'm afraid you've missed him."

"Missed him? Is he in town, running errands?"

"Herbie got out yesterday."

"I see." This didn't come as a complete surprise. "Can I have his release address?"

"I'm afraid I don't know his new address."

"May I have the name of his parole officer, then?"

"He doesn't have a parole officer."

"I beg your pardon?"

"He got an unconditional release."

"He was released *unconditionally*? From a sentence for murder? I've never heard of such a thing."

"It's rare, but it happens. Herbie was an outstanding prisoner, very helpful to the warden and me, and his psychiatric examination showed no likelihood of a repeat offense."

"So you just cut him loose, and you're hoping for the best?"

"That's about it."

"And you have no address for Mitteldorfer?"

"None at all; he's as free as an eagle."

"Thanks; sorry to trouble you."

"No trouble at all," Warkowski replied.

Stone could hear him laughing as he hung up. He returned to the car.

"Business all done?"

"Almost," Stone said. He drove away from the prison and into the town, looking for something. It didn't take him long to find it, and he drove into a parking place.

"I've got to run in here for a minute," Stone said.

"Stone, darling, do you really feel an urgent need for stationery right *now*?"

"I won't be a minute." He got out and went into the store; the sign over the door read, WILHELM'S STATIONERS. A young woman was behind a counter near the door. "Good afternoon," Stone said. "I wonder if I could speak to Mr. Wilhelm?"

"I'm afraid he's out for a couple of hours, delivering," the young woman said.

"Oh." Stone turned to go, then stopped. "Did a man named Herbert Mitteldorfer used to buy supplies here for the prison?"

"Herbie? Oh, yes. He was one of our better customers. He and Mr. Wilhelm used to speak German to each other."

"How often was he in here?" Stone asked.

"Oh, practically every single day, even when there was a lock-down at the prison."

"He bought office supplies *every day*?"

"Oh, no, not really. At first, he'd come in to see Mr. Wilhelm, then he started working here."

"He worked for Mr. Wilhelm?"

"Well, not *for* Mr. Wilhelm; Mr. Wilhelm rented him office space. He had a computer and everything."

Stone blinked as he tried to get his mind around this. "Did you know he was released yesterday?"

"Oh, yes. Herbie came by to get his stuff and to say goodbye."

"Did he have a lot of stuff?"

"A couple of filing cabinets and his computer and printer; that was about all."

"Do you think I could have a look at where Herbie worked?"

"Are you a friend of his?"

"I came up to see him today, but I didn't know he'd been released until I got to the prison."

"Sure, I guess you could see it; follow me."

Stone followed the young woman through aisles of stationery and office equipment to a door on the other side of the store.

She opened the door and stood back. "This is where he worked," she said.

Stone looked into a room furnished only with a desk, a chair, and a small leather sofa. "Do you have any idea what Herbie did in here?" he asked.

"Well, I know he traded stocks," she replied. "I don't know what else he did."

Stone stared at her. "On the stock market, you mean?"

"Oh, yes; he was a very active trader; he spent every afternoon on the computer and on the telephone, talking to his broker. He gave me and Mr. Wilhelm a number of good tips; we made out real well. I was sorry to see Herbie go."

"Thanks," Stone said.

"Come see us again. Shall I tell Mr. Wilhelm you stopped in?"

"No, that won't be necessary. By the way, do you have Herbie's new address?"

"I'm sorry, I don't; neither does Mr. Wilhelm. He did say that he was headed west."

"How far west?"

"I don't know, really; he did say that he'd let us know when he was settled."

"I see. Tell me, how did Herbie take his computer and his file cabinets away?"

"He had a man with a van; I guess somebody he hired."

"Was there a name on the van?"

"Nope, just a plain, black van."

"Can you describe the man who drove the van?"

"I'm sorry, I just didn't pay that much attention; I was helping customers."

"Thanks again for your help," Stone said. He walked back to his car, wondering why the hell Sing Sing would let a prisoner spend his afternoons in Ossining, trading stocks.

"All done?" Sarah asked, as he got into the car.

"Completely done," Stone replied. He had no idea what to do next.

21

THEY CROSSED INTO CONNECTICUT ON I-84, AND STONE soon turned off the interstate at Southbury and headed north. The car behaved like a living thing, clinging to curves and accelerating in the straights.

"When do I get to know where we're going?" Sarah asked.

"When we get there, not before," Stone replied. "Just enjoy the countryside; it restores your corpuscles, remember?"

"I can feel them pumping even now."

In Woodbury, Stone turned left on Highway 47, and a few minutes later they entered Washington Township.

"Oh, Washington!" Sarah enthused. "I spent a weekend here a few years ago; what a lovely place!"

"I'm glad you think so," Stone said, making a right turn at a sign that read, MAYFLOWER INN. They drove around a pond and up a steep hill, pulling up outside a handsome, shingled building.

"This is lovely," Sarah said. "How did you find it?"

"It wasn't hard," Stone said. "It was voted the best country inn in America last year in some magazine. I clipped the article."

"Well clipped," she replied.

Someone took their bags upstairs and let them into a handsomely decorated suite overlooking the rear gardens.

"Have you reserved a dinner table, sir?" the young bellman asked.

"No. Could you do that for me, at eight o'clock?"

"Certainly. You'll need a jacket, but not necessarily a tie."

"Thank you." Stone tipped him generously, and he let himself out of the room. "Well," Stone said, "we've got two hours until dinner; how shall we amuse ourselves?"

Sarah walked into his arms. "I'll need an hour to bathe and dress. That leaves a whole hour of free, unsupervised time."

Stone kissed her. "Unsupervised?"

"Well, not entirely," she said, working on his buttons. "I'll do the supervising."

At seven-thirty they walked downstairs, now showered, changed, and entirely relaxed, and entered the handsome bar, taking a table near a window.

"I could live here," Sarah said. "All I'd need would be this table and the bed upstairs."

"I've heard worse ideas," Stone agreed.

A young woman appeared. "Would you like a drink, Mr. Barrington?"

Stone nodded at Sarah.

"A vodka gimlet, straight up, shaken very cold, slightly sweet," she said.

"Two," Stone replied.

Shortly they were sipping the clear, green-tinted liquid. The waitress returned. "Mr. Barrington, there's a phone call for you at the front desk."

"Excuse me," Stone said to Sarah, taking his drink with him. He went into the front hall and was shown to a phone booth. "Hello?"

"It's Dino; I hear you're driving something alarming."

"Entirely so; I'll show you the first of the week."

"Okay; how'd it go with Mitteldorfer?"

"It didn't."

"Warkowski wouldn't let you see him?"

"He wasn't there to see."

"I don't get it."

"He's out."

"Paroled?"

"Unconditionally released."

There was a long silence before Dino spoke again. "Well, the little shit. He must have spent the last twelve years bending over for Warkowski."

"I wouldn't be surprised. I went by the stationery store where he bought supplies and found out that Mitteldorfer was keeping an office there."

"An *office*? What the hell for?"

"That was pretty much my reaction. The lady in charge said he had a computer in there and that he was trading stocks."

"Holy shit, and I bet I know who for."

"Warkowski."

"Damn right, and I wouldn't be surprised if it wasn't for the warden, too."

"The lady said he gave her and the store's owner a few hot tips."

· "You ever hear of anything like this?"

"Never."

"So where's Mitteldorfer now?"

"Nobody knows, or, at least, nobody's saying. The lady in the store said he said he was going west."

"Jesus, I hope so," Dino said. "I never want to see the little bastard again."

"Somebody came up with a black van and took his computer and his files away."

"So he's not without friends."

"Not while Warkowski's alive. I wouldn't be surprised if the captain helped him move. What have you got to report?"

"I've had two detectives going through every case we worked as partners, and I'm damned if there's anything that looks good. Just about everybody we sent up for anything serious is still inside."

"You had any new experiences that would indicate that our guy is still out there?"

"Nah. I think he's licking the wounds that Mary Ann gave him. He'd be pretty noticeable with a big bandage on his ear."

"Nobody followed us out of town that I could see."

"That's what Krakauer said."

"And once I was on the West Side Highway, nobody could have kept up."

"What *are* you driving?"

"You'll have to wait and see."

"How's the inn?"

"Perfect, except that I'm talking to you when I should be talking to Sarah."

"Bye-bye."

"Bye." Stone hung up and returned to the bar.

"That was Dino, wasn't it?" she asked.

"It was."

"Dino knows before I do where I'm spending the weekend?"

"I wasn't surprising Dino."

"Good point."

"You hungry?"

"You bet."

"Miss, could I have a menu and a wine list, please?"

They polished off a dinner of smoked salmon and roast pheasant and a bottle of very good cabernet, then, sated, went back upstairs.

Later, after they had made love again, Stone said, "I like having you around. I'd like to have you around all the time."

"I hope to God that's not a proposal," she said, lifting her head from his shoulder.

"Not yet."

"Not for a long while," she said.

"As you wish, but I would like to point out that you are, technically, at least, homeless."

"And whose fault is that?"

"Mine, entirely mine. And I want to make up for it by offering you a bed . . . home, rather."

"And a very nice home it is," Sarah said. "Your house was a shambles when I left for Italy."

"Do you think you could feel at home in it?"

"I think I could feel at home with you."

"Then there's nothing more to say."

"Yes, there is."

"What?"

"I told you before, I'm a country girl; I need a place outside the city."

"Where would you like to have a place?"

"Not the Hamptons; I've had too much of that crowd."

"Where, then?"

"Maybe here."

"I don't think I could swing the inn, even with a mortgage."

"A house, silly, and not a big house; a cottage, perhaps."

"Sounds good," he said. "Why don't we find a real-estate agent tomorrow morning?"

"Do you mean it, Stone?"

"Do you think I'm saying this just because you got me into bed?"

"Yes."

"Then you're a rotten judge of character."

"We'll see in the morning," she said, snuggling her naked body against his.

Stone fell asleep wondering where Herbert Mitteldorfer was.

22

STONE SAT IN THE FRONT PASSENGER SEAT OF A BLACK Range Rover and tried not to fall asleep. The car was being driven by a real-estate agent named Carolyn Klemm, and she had already shown them half a dozen houses, all charming, but not quite right. Sarah dozed in the rear seat. The car stopped, jarring Stone fully awake.

"What do you think of that?" the agent asked.

Stone focused on a very large, very beautiful shingle-style house in the medium distance.

"I've got the key in my pocket," Carolyn said.

"Carolyn, I don't want a house tour," Stone grumbled. "I want to see houses I can afford."

"Not *that*," Carolyn said. She pointed. "That."

Stone turned his head to the right. There, much closer, was a very much smaller relative of the large house.

"The big place is called The Rocks," Carolyn said. "The little place was originally the gatehouse."

Sarah spoke up. "Let's see it."

Carolyn pulled into the driveway, past a row of evergreens that partly shielded the little house from the road. It was a Victorian, or perhaps a Queen Anne, style, shingled, with a turret taking up half the front facade. "Two bedrooms, two and a half baths, garage, and in back, a very nice little pool." She got out of the car, led them up the front path, and opened the front door.

Stone and Sarah stepped into a larger room than he had expected. A new-looking kitchen occupied a rear corner, and the wooden floors looked recently refinished.

"It was built in 1889, at the same time as the house," Carolyn was saying. "When the original owner left, he sold it separately from The Rocks, and it's changed hands two or three times since."

"Let's see the upstairs," Sarah said.

They followed the agent up a handsome staircase and were shown a large master bedroom with a new bath and a second, smaller bedroom, with only a shower. They poked into closets and looked out windows. The bedrooms overlooked The Rocks, and the front windows took in the Gunnery School, across the street. They went back downstairs.

"This whole area is called The Green," Carolyn was saying. "It's the oldest part of town and the most sought-after."

"What are they asking for the house?" Stone asked.

"You could get lucky here," Carolyn replied. "The couple who own it are divorcing, and they're highly motivated sellers. They want to get their money out and divide it." She named a figure.

Stone looked at Sarah inquiringly; she responded with an almost imperceptible nod. Stone turned to Carolyn and quoted a figure twenty percent lower than the asking price.

"Let me use the upstairs phone," Carolyn said.

When she had gone Sarah grabbed Stone by the lapels. "If you hadn't made the offer *I* would have! It's absolutely beautiful, and it's just been renovated."

"There are still a few things that need doing, but I could do them myself," Stone said.

"And there's a lovely little garden out back. Do you know what that means to an Englishwoman?"

"I can imagine. The garden's all yours."

Carolyn came back down the stairs. "Did you plan to pay cash or finance it?"

"I can pay cash," Stone replied.

"Good; here's the deal. Increase your offer ten percent and agree to close in two weeks, and the place is yours."

"Done," Stone said.

"Let's go to my office and type up an offer," Carolyn said, marching them out to the Range Rover. "And you'll have to come to dinner the next time you're up from the city. I'll introduce you to a lot of people."

Two hours later, the sellers had faxed back a signed contract, and Stone left with it in his pocket, having left a large check as deposit.

"Did that really happen so quickly?" Sarah asked.

"It certainly did."

"Why were you so ready to buy it?"

"Weren't you?"

"Of course, but . . ."

"I was way ahead of you. I'd been thinking about a country place for a while, and I spent a weekend up here a couple of years ago with . . . an acquaintance."

"And who might that have been?" Sarah asked archly.

"A woman named Amanda Dart."

"The gossip columnist? The one who was murdered outside the Plaza Hotel?"

"One and the same."

"Did they ever figure out who killed her?"

"No arrest was ever made."

"But they know?"

Stone shrugged. "Maybe, but it won't ever be solved."

"Why not?"

"Because the people who arranged it don't make a practice of committing murders that can be solved."

"Stone, tell me the house you just bought wasn't Amanda Dart's."

"It wasn't. I'm not even sure exactly where Amanda's place is. I was only there a couple of times, and it was on some back road or other."

"You didn't tell me you'd been to Washington before."

"You didn't ask."

"Am I ever going to get to know all the nooks and crannies of your devious mind?" she asked.

"God, I hope not."

"I'm going to have to start looking for furniture and fabrics."

"Listen, Sarah," he said, "we still have to be very careful."

"With money?"

"With your safety."

"Why? Hasn't your suspect flown the coop?"

"Yes, but we don't know where he's flown to. You can't tell anybody about this place for the time being, and maybe not for a long time."

"But I want to tell *everybody*."

"I'll tell you when it's okay. As far as decorating goes, I think we should buy a bed and some other necessities in the city, then furnish the place from the shops and antique shops around here. There are a lot of them."

"Sounds good to me."

"Something else."

"What?"

"I'm worried about your show. I know it would be difficult, but do you think you could cancel, or at least, postpone it?"

"Are you *insane*? Bergman has sent out a thousand invitations, at the very least."

"I drove past the gallery yesterday; it's very exposed, opening right onto Madison Avenue. I'd feel better if it were on a side street."

"Stone," she said, "understand me clearly: I am *not* going to have my life ruled by some maniac who wants to harm us. I'll tell you a story: I lived in London at the height of the IRA bombings a while

117

back. I was having dinner with my parents at a little restaurant in Chelsea, when someone set off a car bomb next door. We all hit the floor, of course, but when the smoke had cleared, my father ordered another cup of coffee to replace the one that had blown away, and he sat there and finished it. 'Never,' he said, 'never let people like that cause you to alter your existence in the slightest.' Since that time, I never have, and I never will. I wouldn't have left my friends' apartment if I hadn't been so anxious to get into bed with you."

"Well, that was an awfully good reason," Stone said.

"So you understand that I will not cancel my show."

"I understand. I hope you understand that I'm going to do whatever I can to make it as safe a show as possible."

"I'll be happy to introduce you to Bergman; the two of you can discuss that."

"I'll be happy to meet him."

They reached the inn and went upstairs to dress for dinner.

"It was an awfully nice day," Sarah said, as she ran her bath.

"I suppose there are worse ways to see a place than with a real-estate agent who knows her stuff."

She got into the tub. "Join me?"

"You betcha." He climbed into the tub with her, but his mind was on the Bergman Gallery.

23

MR. AND MRS. HOWARD MENZIES ARRIVED AT THEIR Park Avenue apartment building for the first time and got out of a taxi. Mrs. Menzies was an attractive woman in her early fifties, dressed in a Chanel suit and very good shoes, her graying hair carefully coifed. Mr. Menzies was perhaps two or three years older than his new wife and was dressed in a gray, pin-striped suit that was, though of good quality, a little out of fashion.

"Oh, I'm so nervous," Mrs. Menzies said. "I hope you're going to like it."

"My dear," Mr. Menzies replied, "put your mind at rest. I have the utmost confidence in your taste and judgment."

The doorman greeted Mrs. Menzies warmly.

"Oh, Jeff," she said, "I want you to meet Mr. Menzies; he was abroad when we bought the apartment, and he's seeing it today for the first time."

"How do you do, Mr. Menzies," Jeff said, shaking hands. "I'm sure you're going to love the building."

"I'm sure I will, too, Jeff," Mr. Menzies replied, rewarding the doorman with a smile.

"Please let me know if there is anything I can do for you," Jeff said.

"Darling," Mrs. Menzies half whispered, "Jeff has been *very* help-ful with our moving in."

"Thank you so much for helping my wife, Jeff," Mr. Menzies said warmly, slipping a hundred-dollar bill into the doorman's hand.

They took the elevator to a high floor and got out. Mrs. Menzies slipped a key into her husband's hand. "You open the door," she said nervously.

"Of course, my dear." Menzies unlocked the door, pushed it open, and allowed his wife to precede him into the apartment. He was immediately struck by the warmth, comfort, and beauty that his wife had brought to the decorating of the apartment. He followed her from room to room, admiring what she had chosen and occa-sionally spotting an old, familiar piece of furniture or a picture that he had chosen years before. The apartment was only six rooms, but perfect for a childless, middle-aged couple. They had views across Park Avenue to the park and down the avenue. "It must be beautiful at Christmas," he said, "with all the trees lining the avenue."

"I'm told it is," she replied. "We'll have to wait a few months to find out."

He took both her hands in his. "My dear, I can't tell you how grateful I am for the way you have put the place together. It feels as if we have always lived here." He kissed her lightly.

"It was my great pleasure to do this for you," Mrs. Menzies said. "I've done all the other things you asked me to do, as well. Shall I fix you a drink, and we'll talk about them?"

"What a very good idea," Menzies replied. "May I have martini? I haven't had a martini for such a long time." He took a seat on the living-room sofa and relaxed, while his wife puttered at the wet bar.

She returned with a tray containing two martinis and some canapés that she had prepared earlier, in anticipation of her hus-band's homecoming. She set her drink on the coffee table, then brought an accordion file to the sofa, before taking a sip. "Here are the legal documents," she said, "all in perfect order. Here are the ownership papers for the apartment; and here are the bank and brokerage statements, arranged by date. And here are your passport and driver's license applications. Your appointment for the driving test is tomorrow at three."

Menzies looked quickly through the documents. "You are a wonder!" he exclaimed. "Everything is exactly as I wished it to be. Now, my dear," he said, taking her hands in his, "what about your personal arrangements?"

"I did everything exactly as you asked. I brought nothing from my old apartment here—not so much as a teacup."

"And everything at your old apartment is in perfect order?"

"Absolutely perfect. There is nothing new there; only my old things. I intend to give everything to the Salvation Army."

"Now tell me this, dear, and this is most important. Have you told anyone of your move here?"

"Not a soul."

"Have you done anything to alert any of your friends or neighbors that you were about to move?"

"Nothing. No one knows."

He patted her cheek and kissed her again. "Good girl." He polished off his martini. "Now, if you will forgive me, I must do some work in my study for a while."

"I'll start cooking dinner, then," she said.

"Oh, no; I've already made a reservation at a very good restaurant for dinner. It will be my surprise; can you be ready at eight?"

"Of course! I look forward to it. Now, you go and do your work. My soap opera is on now, and I never miss it."

"Good, good." Menzies gathered up the papers and went to his study, a handsome, book-lined room—books that he had collected for many years. He closed the door behind him, set the papers on his desk, sat down behind it, picked up a phone, and dialed a number. "I'm here," he said to the man who answered. "Yes, all is well. Be downstairs in"—he looked at his watch—"three-quarters of an hour, exactly." He hung up the phone and went to work, examining each of the legal documents in minute detail. It was perfect. He looked over

121

the copy of his combined credit report, stretching back the usual seven years. Every payment on every account had been made on time. He leafed through the stock-account statements, though he was already very familiar with them. The balances, at the end of the previous month, totaled just over fifteen million dollars, and the market had gone up since then. He felt a wave of contentment at the thought of his wealth.

A copy of that day's *Wall Street Journal* sat on the desk. He folded it and opened a desk drawer, looking for an envelope and finding it exactly where he had asked her to put it. *She really is a good organizer,* he thought. He stuffed the newspaper into the envelope, sealed it, and wrote in large letters on its outside "Mr. Smith" and an address. He glanced at his watch, then returned to the living room. "My dear," he said, "there is one more matter to which I must ask you to attend, if you don't mind."

"Oh, no, Herbie," she said. "I don't mind at all."

"Ach!" he exclaimed, raising a forefinger.

"Oh, I'm so sorry—*Howard.*"

"That's better; you must never forget. Now come, we'll go downstairs, and I'll explain on the way." He led her out of the apartment and onto the elevator. "Take this envelope," he said, handing it to her.

She accepted the envelope. "Mr. Smith," she said.

"Yes, and the address in Long Island City is also there. I've arranged a car and driver for you, and I want you to deliver this envelope to this gentleman and get a receipt. That's very important, the receipt."

"What sort of receipt?" she asked.

"It should read, 'received of Mrs. Menzies, one envelope of documents,' and be signed with his full name, which is Franklin P. Smith."

"I understand," she said, as they reached the lobby.

"Would you like a cab, Mr. Menzies?" the doorman asked.

"No, thank you, Jeff, I believe a car is waiting . . . there he is!" He waved, and a black Lincoln Town Car, like thousands of others in the city, pulled up. The driver wore a bandage on his left ear. Menzies opened the door for his wife, and she got in. "The driver has the address," Menzies said, "and he will escort you into the building when you arrive. I'll see you in an hour or so, my dear."

"Of course, my darling," she replied, waving as the car pulled away.

Mitteldorfer, now Menzies, turned and walked back into the building. As the elevator rose, he sighed deeply. Now that that little detail was taken care of, he felt free. Now he could take care of a few other little details, then begin his new life. His first order of business was to inflict pain.

24

O N MONDAY MORNING, STONE BEGAN BY CALLING BILL
Eggers at Woodman & Weld. "Good morning, Bill; could one
of your associates close a real-estate transaction for me?"

"Sure, Stone; commercial or residential?"

"Residential. I've bought a house in Connecticut."

"You? The quintessential city boy?"

"I like a little grass between my toes from time to time."

"I smell a woman."

"You have a very good nose."

"I want to meet her."

"You will, soon enough. I've agreed to close within two weeks."

"You want me to get you a mortgage?"

"I'm paying cash."

"There goes that big fee from the Allison Manning case last
year."

"Some of it."

"I'll assign Barry Mendel to close it for you. He'll call you, and
you can give him the seller's lawyer's name, and he can take it from
there."

"Thanks very much, Bill."

"Lunch?"

"Not this week, I'm afraid; I've got a lot on my plate. I'll call you." He hung up. *But not until this business is over,* he thought. *No need endangering any more of my friends.*

Stone walked into the Bergman Gallery on Madison Avenue and asked the receptionist for Edgar Bergman. The gallery owner came out of his office immediately, a short, distinguished-looking man in a beautifully cut suit.

"Mr. Barrington?"

"Yes," Stone replied. "I believe Sarah Buckminster called you about me."

"Indeed she did. I believe you have some security concerns?"

"Yes. There was an attempt to harm her recently, and I prefer to take it seriously until I'm sure there's to be no repeat of the episode."

"I understand, of course," Bergman said, as if he really didn't understand at all. "I should tell you that, as a gallery which frequently houses millions of dollars in art, our security precautions are quite extensive. Our insurance people insist."

"Could you give me a brief tour?" Stone asked. "I'm interested in Sarah's personal safety rather than in any possible theft, of course."

"Of course. First of all, let me show your our rear entrance," Bergman said, signaling Stone to follow. He walked to the rear of the gallery, opened a door, and led Stone down a hallway, emerging into the side street. "Sarah can enter and leave through this entrance," he said. "It runs behind the boutique next door, and both the street door and the one to the interior of the gallery are steel and ballistic glass."

"That's good to know," Stone said. "We'll certainly take advantage of the entrance, and there'll be a policeman on guard there. You should make a list of anyone else who is likely to use that entrance on the night."

"Right."

"May we look at the main entrance to the gallery?"

"Of course, follow me." Bergman led the way back into the gallery and to its front. "There you are," he said, gesturing at the front door.

Stone noted that it was made of stainless steel. "What about the plate-glass window?" he asked.

"It's the best armored glass I could find in such a large size," Bergman said. "I was concerned with smash-and-grab artists taking a painting or a piece of sculpture."

"Is there any kind of coating?"

"No, I don't believe so. In fact, I'm not quite sure what you mean."

"There is a coating available that can be applied like wallpaper. It's perfectly clear, but it greatly reinforces large areas of glass and, of course, prevents shattering. I can give you the name of a man who installs it, if you like."

"Based on what I was told when I had the glass installed, I'm perfectly satisfied that, as it is, it will offer excellent protection."

"As you wish," Stone said, fingering the thick curtains that lined the window. "What are these made of?"

"Just ordinary wool. I pull them sometimes when we're doing installations, and the gallery looks messy."

"I see. Sarah said you've sent out a large number of invitations."

"Yes, indeed; to my A-list."

"Are you keeping a record of acceptances?"

"Yes, but you should understand that people will often show up without having responded to the invitation."

"In that case, could you let the officer on the door have your mailing list, so that he can check off arrivals?"

Bergman frowned. "I wouldn't like to do anything that will delay the entrance of guests; I wouldn't want them lined up down the block while someone searches a list of twelve hundred people for names. What if it rains?"

"I see. Tell me, do you have an employee who would recognize most of your list on sight?"

"I have my wife," Bergman said. "I, of course, must move around the crowd, but she could stand near the door early on, while guests are still arriving. If there is a strange face, she could make a signal to the policeman, I suppose, but I wouldn't want her there all evening."

"I think that's a good idea," Stone said. "The policeman will have a sketch of our suspect, but we can't be sure how accurate that is."

"I'll speak to my wife," Bergman said. "I assume that someone will be with Sarah the whole time."

"I will be with her," Stone said.

"Are you a policeman, Mr. Barrington? You certainly don't look like one."

"No, but I used to be. I'm an attorney, now; my interest in Sarah is personal. What's upstairs?"

"Accounting, shipping, and clerical," Bergman replied. "The fire exit and all the windows are heavily reinforced against outside entry."

Stone's cell phone vibrated in his pocket. He held out a hand to the gallery owner. "Thank you, Mr. Bergman," he said. "I won't take up any more of your time."

"Not at all," Bergman replied, shaking his hand. "We have a mutual interest in Sarah's safety. Good day."

"Good day." Stone turned toward the door, reaching in his pocket for the phone. "Hello?"

"It's Dino. We need to talk."

"How about lunch? I'm just down the street from La Gouloue."

"Ten minutes," Dino said, then hung up.

Stone put the phone back in his pocket, walked outside, and headed uptown.

25

L A GOULOUE WAS A FASHIONABLE MADISON AVENUE restaurant with a clientele of beautiful people and people who wished to be seen in the same restaurant with beautiful people. Stone wasn't a regular, but he got a decent table. Dino arrived a minute later. When they had ordered drinks and lunch, Stone looked at his friend, who seemed concerned.

"What's up, Dino?"

Dino sipped his mineral water. "You remember Eloise Enzberg?"

"Who?"

"Mitteldorfer's regular correspondent, a woman he used to work with."

"Oh, yes; you had her checked out after our meeting at Sing Sing, didn't you?"

"Yeah; she told us nothing, and neither did her neighbors."

"What's up with her?"

"Nothing, anymore."

"What?"

"They pulled her body out of the East River this morning. She was once a government employee, so her prints were available."

"Any suspects?"

"Just the one."

"Why would he kill her?" Stone asked.

"Maybe he used her, then dumped her."

"Used her for what? He was in prison, remember?"

"Yeah, I know, and I don't have an answer to your question."

"How did she die?"

"Her throat was cut."

"That sounds familiar, doesn't it?"

"All too familiar. There's something else."

"What?"

"She was wearing a Chanel suit."

"Maybe she was a wealthy lady?"

Dino shook his head. "She apparently took early retirement from her job last year, and she lived on her pension. I don't see how it could have been very much."

"So a Chanel suit would have been out of the question?"

"Yes, unless she got lucky in a secondhand shop."

"Who's to say she didn't do just that? I'm sorry, but it just doesn't make sense for Mitteldorfer to kill a woman who had been kind to him for years. And if you're right about her income, money couldn't have been a motive."

Their lunch arrived, and they ate the food in silence, each lost in his own thoughts.

"So, tell me about this new car," Dino said finally.

Stone related his buying experience.

Dino laughed. "I've never known you to own a car, and right out of the gate, you buy *that*?"

Stone shrugged. "Sarah said to get something nice."

"A fucking *armored car*?"

"Lightly armored. And anyway, right now seems a pretty good time to have an armored car, wouldn't you say?"

"You got a point," Dino admitted.

Stone put down his fork. "Have you been to Eloise Enzberg's place?"

"No, the detectives who caught the homicide have, though; they say it's unremarkable, just what you'd expect."

"Let's go take a look at it," Stone said.

"The key is in my pocket," Dino replied, signaling for a check.

The building was an undistinguished row house in the East Eighties, near York Avenue, in what used to be Germantown. Eloise Enzberg had lived in a second-floor, rear apartment. Dino removed the crime-scene tape and let them into the place.

Stone looked around. It was fairly plain, with a lot of heavy Germanic furniture—respectable, with a kind of seedy elegance. Stone went to a small desk in the living room and began opening drawers. "Here's her checkbook," he said, removing it from a drawer and opening it on the desktop. He began leafing through the stubs. There was nothing out of the ordinary—checks for utilities, rent, groceries, liquor, and household repairs. "Nothing here," he said. He looked through the old bills. "She apparently had only one credit card, and the balance was less than five hundred dollars."

Dino was going through the bedroom drawers. "Very neat," he called, "but nothing from Victoria's Secret."

Stone walked into the bedroom and opened the closet. "Suitcases still here," he said. "She didn't seem to be going anywhere." The closet was full of clothes, not expensive and very nearly dowdy.

"Not much in the way of family pictures," Dino said, pointing to the top of a dresser, where two framed photographs sat. One was an old photograph of a woman, apparently in her thirties, wearing severe black clothes; the other was of the same woman, holding a baby wearing a lace communion dress. "My guess is, it's Ms. Enzberg in her mother's arms."

Stone nodded. "The clothes and shoes are nothing special," he said. "Any jewelry?"

Dino took a padded box from a dresser drawer. "Here we go." He opened the box. "Nothing expensive; looks European."

"Probably her mother's. Have you located her next of kin?"

"A nephew," Dino said, "lives in Jersey. We found some correspondence with him. He came in late this morning; didn't know anything; hadn't seen her for months."

"Let's check the kitchen," Stone said. The kitchen was well stocked with pots, pans, knives, and implements. "She was a pretty serious cook," Stone said. He bent over and opened a cabinet door. As he did, half a dozen neatly folded shopping bags slid off a shelf to the floor. "Look at this," he said, placing the bags on a countertop. "Chanel, Saks, Bergdorf's, Ferragamo. They clash with the lifestyle, wouldn't you say?"

"I'd say so," Dino agreed. "Were there any payments to any of those stored in her checkbook or credit-card receipts?"

"No, nothing."

"Then she'd have been paying with cash."

"Or someone was paying for her."

"Mitteldorfer? What would a prisoner in Sing Sing be doing with that kind of money?"

"Good question. Where did Mitteldorfer work? You remember?"

Dino took out his notebook and flipped through some pages. "Ginzberg and O'Sullivan, accountants, on West Forty-seventh Street."

"Let's talk to them."

Dino picked up a phone and, consulting his notebook, dialed a number. "Hello, may I speak to Mr. Ginzberg? Yes? How about Mr. O'Sullivan? I see. I'm looking for information on someone who worked there more than a dozen years ago; is there anyone in who's been around that long? I see. This is Lieutenant Bacchetti of the New York City Police Department; could I have his home address and number?" He scribbled it down and hung up. "The original partners sold out a few years ago and retired. O'Sullivan is still alive; he lives in the East Seventies; let's go see him."

Daniel O'Sullivan was a big, bluff Irish-American in his late seventies, with snow-white hair and a florid complexion, who still wore his weight well. He seemed glad to have visitors. He showed them into a spacious, beautifully furnished apartment that took up a whole floor of a brownstone, offered them a drink, and, when they declined, fixed one for himself.

"It's not often I get visited by the police," he said, settling in a big armchair. "What can I do for you?"

"Mr. O'Sullivan," Dino said, "do you remember Herbert Mitteldorfer?"

"Herbie? How could I forget him? He was the only one of my employees—that I know of—who ever murdered somebody."

"Can you tell us what Mitteldorfer's job was in your firm?"

"Sure; he was my top accountant."

"Could you describe his duties? Did he do corporate work?"

O'Sullivan shook his big head. "No, no; we weren't an ordinary accounting firm. We were personal managers to theater people—actors, producers, set designers—people at the top of their fields. We paid their bills, invested their money, got them bank loans and mortgages, sometimes loaned them money, when they had lean years."

"And what part did Mitteldorfer take in the business?"

"Herbie did a little of everything. He started with us as a simple bookkeeper; but he was so good, so bright, that soon he was taking an active part in managing our clients' accounts. By the time of the, ah, unfortunate incident, he was practically running the firm. My partner and I were thinking of retirement by then, and we'd expected to sell out to him. As it was, after he was arrested, we had to put our plans on hold. It took several years before we got two other men trained to do what Herbie did, and, finally, we sold out to them."

Stone spoke up. "Did Mitteldorfer have any personal wealth?"

"His wife did," O'Sullivan replied. "She was from a meat-packing family out of Chicago—not filthy rich, but she had some assets, which Herbie managed brilliantly. At the time of her death, I believe, together they may have had two, three million in assets, or so Herbie told me. The lawyers would have made a pretty good dent in that, but

I'm sure that when he went to jail, he still had some money put away. Plus, there was a very nice apartment on lower Park Avenue that her family gave them as a wedding present. I believe that was sold."

"But," Stone said, "having murdered his wife, he wouldn't have been able to inherit her wealth."

"It had all been in Herbie's name for years," O'Sullivan said. "He made sure of that."

"Do you remember another employee named Eloise Enzberg?"

"Sure, I do. Eloise was with us for better than twenty years, longer than Herbie. She was our office manager, the best-organized person you ever saw. Day in, day out, she made the place work. If you gave her a job to do, she'd handle it better than anybody, and she *never* dropped the ball, not once in all the years I knew her. I mean, if you said to Eloise, 'I'm going to London for a week,' inside an hour she'd made hotel and restaurant reservations and booked a car and driver to meet you at the airport. When you got to your hotel, you were in your usual suite, with extra towels and a bottle of wine waiting."

"Do you know what sort of relationship Mitteldorfer and Enzberg had?" Stone asked.

"Well," O'Sullivan said, smiling, "she was sweet on Herbie, she really was. When he was charged with his wife's murder, she refused to believe it. She was in court every day, took him things in jail— books, fruit. But you have to understand, women *loved* Herbie Mitteldorfer. I mean, he wasn't good-looking, but he was a snappy dresser, had charm and wit, never forgot any woman's birthday. He had quite a beautiful wife. I was astonished when he killed her; we all were."

"Mitteldorfer was released from prison a few days ago," Dino said, "and this morning, Eloise Enzberg's body was found in the East River, her throat cut."

O'Sullivan's face fell. "Well, I'm really sorry to hear that. She was a very nice lady." He thought for a moment. "And Herbie's out? Do you think there's a connection?"

"Do you think Herbert Mitteldorfer could have killed Eloise Enzberg, Mr. O'Sullivan?" Stone asked.

"Of course not," O'Sullivan scoffed. "That could never have happened. Herbie wouldn't have done that." He looked thoughtful. "Of course," he said, "that's what we all said when Herbie murdered his wife."

26

HOWARD MENZIES LEFT HIS APARTMENT BUILDING AT the stroke of 9:00 A.M., dressed in his most conservative suit, unconsciously fingering his rather recently grown Van Dyke beard.

The doorman greeted him warmly, "And how are you and Mrs. Menzies today?" he asked.

"I'm very well, Jeff, but I'm afraid Mrs. Menzies was taken ill last night while visiting a friend, and she spent the night over there. I'm just on my way to see her now."

"I hope she's better," Jeff said. "Would you like a taxi?"

"No, I think I'll walk," Menzies replied. "Oh, by the way, some men will deliver some boxes this morning and will be doing some installations. Please let them into my apartment."

"Of course, sir."

He strolled over to Fifth Avenue and walked briskly down the west side of the street, taking in Central Park. At Fifty-ninth Street, he walked into the Plaza Hotel, was given a table by the window in the Edwardian Room, and ate an enormous breakfast. Thus fortified, he crossed Fifth Avenue and entered the Bergdorf Goodman Men's Store, just as it opened, marveling at the handsome new shops, which had not existed when he had last been in the city. He stopped in the Charvet shop and bought a dozen shirts and neck-ties, taking one of each with him and sending the others. He took the elevator upstairs and after touring the clothing shops, walked into the Oxxford shop and bought four suits, noting with pleasure that a size thirty-eight still fit him perfectly. Only the trouser lengths needed altering. He requested that one suit be made ready to wear immediately, then walked around the store for half an hour while the work was done, making other purchases. When he returned to the Oxxford shop, he went into a changing room and got into his new suit, shirt, tie, and shoes, instructing that his old clothing be discarded. Finally, he bought a new hat and, on the way out, his eye was caught by an antique ebony walking stick with a silver handle.

Swinging his new stick, he crossed Fifth Avenue and, feeling quite the boulevardier, strolled west on Fifty-seventh Street until he came to the address his researches on the internet had provided. He took the elevator to the top floor and emerged into a comfortable, if anonymous waiting room. He gave his name to the receptionist and was conducted to another room, where he was seated in a barber's chair.

Two hours later he emerged, having been fitted with a small, very becoming hairpiece—one that matched his gray hair perfectly and cleverly showed a lot of forehead, making it seem all the more real. Now fully equipped, he found a photography shop and had two passport photos taken. Finally, he visited a service that specialized in the quick obtaining of visas and passports and left them with his photos, his completed passport application, his name-change docu-ments, and a fee. He was promised his new passport the following day.

He walked back to Fifth Avenue, then downtown, and entered the Cartier store, where, after a careful viewing of their merchan-dise, he bought a gold Tank Francais wristwatch with the matching bracelet. Wearing his new jewelry, he continued his jaunt, shopping as he went. He bought new luggage at T. Anthony on Park Avenue and pajamas at Sulka; he bought soap and toiletries at Caswell-Massey on Lexington and ordered stationery and calling cards from Dempsey & Carroll. He finished up at the Mercedes-Benz dealership on Park Avenue.

He stood for a moment and gazed at a silver S600 sedan, revolving slowly on a turntable.

"May I help you, sir?" a salesman asked, covertly noting the customer's fine clothing.

"I believe," Menzies said, pointing with his stick, "that is the car with the V-12 engine, is it not?"

"It is, indeed, sir. The world's finest automobile, in fact."

"And how much is it?"

The salesman quoted the price. "Plus sales tax, gas-guzzler tax, and luxury tax," he said.

"I'll take it," Menzies said.

The salesman tried not to hyperventilate. This was his second truly breathtaking sale inside of a week; his Christmas bonus was growing quickly.

"Please have a seat at my desk, sir," the salesman said, "and we'll complete the paperwork and registration."

Menzies sat down, answered the man's questions, and wrote him a check.

Later, on his way back to the Park Avenue apartment, he allowed the joy of freedom and wealth to wash over him. Certainly, years before, he had not planned to commit an act that would send him to prison, but, having lost control of himself on that fateful day, he had planned this outcome for twelve years. It had taken him less than a month to demonstrate his value in the prison offices; it had taken him the mandatory two years to win a small measure of freedom as a trusty; and it had taken him little longer to win the financial trust of Captain Warkowski, the warden, and a number of other prison administrators. He had, in fact, won their devotion by advising them to get out of the stock market shortly before the 1987 Reagan crash. That coup, combined with the bull market of the nineties, had allowed him to increase his wealth tenfold and that of his new clients, as well. Seven years before, with the kind help of Eloise Enzberg, he had had his name legally changed. By the time the governor, on the recommendation of the grateful warden and the parole board, had approved his unconditional release, Mitteldorfer had become the most popular man in Sing Sing.

As he neared his apartment building, he realized that his elation had overwhelmed his good sense. He could not afford to be seen by the doorman wearing brand-new clothing on the day of his wife's grave illness. He waited around the corner until Jeff had to walk up Park half a block to find a taxi on a cross street for a resident, then he ducked into the building and went up to his apartment.

There he found his computer, which had been delivered and installed in his absence, and his files and records. He went through them carefully, weeding out anything with the name Mitteldorfer on it, shredding the documents before stuffing them into garbage bags. Then he fired up his computer and visited his investments. The market was holding up nicely, he was pleased to see.

He had some lunch, then answered the house phone.

"Mr. Menzies, it's Jeff, at the front door. A gentleman is here with your car."

"Yes, Jeff; tell him I'll meet him in the garage."

"Yes, sir."

Menzies rode the elevator down to the basement, where the salesman went through all the Mercedes's features and controls. He wanted badly to drive the car, but that would have to wait until his driver's license had been issued. He did not wish to allow even the possibility of a brush with the law. He thanked the man and returned to his apartment.

He rang Jeff on the house phone. "There will be some parcels delivered later today," he told the doorman. "Things I bought earlier in the week."

"Of course, sir; I'll bring them right up when they arrive. And how is Mrs. Menzies doing?"

"I'm afraid she has had a stroke," he replied. "I'm very concerned about her, and I'll be leaving in just a few minutes to be with her."

"I'll remember her in my prayers," Jeff said.

"You do that, Jeff," Menzies replied. He hung up the phone with a smile on his face.

27

DINO WALKED AROUND THE MERCEDES, CONSIDERING it carefully. "Jesus, it's a sinister-looking thing, isn't it?"

"The only exterior differences from the standard E Class are the side moldings and the front air dam," Stone replied, opening the car door. "And the black, rear-seat glass. Of course, under the hood it's a whole new ball game."

"Let me drive," Dino said.

"You've got to be kidding," Stone said. "You always drive as if you've just stolen the car; the only way you'll ever get your hands on this car is on a track, if you want to go to that much trouble."

"You're a real pain in the ass, Stone," Dino said, sliding into the passenger seat. "You know that?"

"I know," Stone said. "I'll get us to the Brooklyn Bridge, and you'll have to direct me after that. I've never been farther into Brooklyn than the River Café."

"And that's not very far," Dino said. "Drive. I'll watch our ass; I don't want anybody tailing us to the Bianchi place."

Stone pulled away from Dino's apartment house. "This is going to be an interesting dinner," he said. "I've never met your father-in-law."

"You're a lucky man," Dino said. "He's a poisonous old son of a bitch. Don't let him offer you any work; he'll own you before you know it. He's never let me forget how we got the apartment."

"How old a man is he?"

"He won't tell anybody, but he's got to be seventy. You'd think a lifetime of crime would show up in his face, but there's no justice. By the way, assume that anything you say is going to be overheard by representatives of one or more branches of the federal government."

"He's wired?"

"Probably not, but he never really knows. That little anxiety is probably the only punishment he's ever going to receive in this lifetime."

"Surely the feds are going to get him one of these days; they get them all, eventually."

"Don't count on it, pal. An FBI man told me a few weeks ago that they're still not even sure that he's Mob. I mean, he's got a mini-conglomerate of legitimate businesses that never break a law or fail to pay taxes, so he can explain his lifestyle. He does business with the city and the state, and he never tries to bribe anybody. Every conceivable law-enforcement agency has been through every company with a fine-toothed comb, and they've never found a thing. Last time the IRS audited one of his businesses, he got a half-million-dollar refund."

Stone laughed aloud. "He sounds like a real piece of work."

"Listen, he's made enough legit bucks to live like a goddamned Florentine prince. He's got a palazzo in Venice, which ain't exactly Mafia country; he's got an oceanfront house in Vero Beach, Florida, where no mobster has ever shown his face. I don't think he's ever even been to Sicily, where his people come from."

"If he's done so well legitimately, then why does he stay mobbed up?"

"I've got my theories about that: to begin with, his first money came from his father, who was one of the originals, right out of Prohibition. Eduardo, though, went to Columbia and got both a law and an accounting degree. What he was learning, I figure, was how to hide the sources of the money, and this was during the Hoover years, when there wasn't even supposed to be a Mafia, according to that jerk, J. Edgar. Eduardo, when he got out of college, never went near anything that could be identified with the Mob, except his father, who died at sixty, when Eduardo was in his late twenties. By the time the FBI started paying attention, he was so far removed from anything crooked and the past was buried so deep that they were never able to get anything on him."

"Then how does he run the family?"

"When he wants something done, he whispers into somebody's ear, and that guy whispers into another ear, and so on, until the source of the order is obscured."

"Why hasn't anybody ever given him up?"

"The young goombahs are so stupid that they can't connect him with the family any better than the FBI. When one of them gets turned and testifies, he knows nothing to tell. I mean, they know, but they don't know."

"And why haven't some of the guys closer to him had him capped?"

"He's too smart; he makes them so much money they've got nothing to complain about. And my guess is he's already got the succession worked out, so that there won't be any big-time squabble when he finally dies, if he ever does."

"Why do you think he invited me to dinner?"

"Who knows? I guess he's heard about you from Mary Ann since she's been staying out there. Anyway, he knows your name from when we were partners, and all that. I mean, he reads the papers, and you're in them often enough."

They crossed the bridge, and Dino started giving directions.

"Anything new on Mitteldorfer?" Stone asked.

"Yeah, he's vanished off the face of the goddamned earth," Dino said. "That's what's new."

"Why would he do that?" Stone asked. "He's got his unconditional release; he's clean; and, apparently, he's got some money. Why would he need to disappear?"

"Well, I guess he might have thought we might like a chat with him after Eloise Enzberg was murdered."

"If he did her, surely he's smart enough to see that her body wouldn't be found in the East River, wearing a Chanel suit."

"Maybe, but also, maybe whoever's helping him isn't as smart as he is, and we know he's getting help, don't we?"

"He has to be," Stone agreed. "Maybe somebody he knew in Sing Sing?"

"We've run down the names of everybody who served with him who's been released in the past two years, and we can't connect any of them. Where's Sarah tonight, at home?"

"She's at the gallery, hanging her work. Anderson and Kelly are with her. The opening is tomorrow night, remember?"

"Oh, yeah."

"You and Mary Ann are coming, aren't you?"

"I am; I'm not letting Mary Ann out of her father's house until this is over, if it ever is. Listen, Stone, after tomorrow night, I'm not going to be able to justify keeping a team on you and Sarah."

"It's too soon to stop, Dino."

"Look, I report to people, you know? Nobody in the department is really convinced that these murders are connected to you and me. They think I'm crazy."

"What about the attack on Mary Ann?"

"They're saying that it was just a mugging attempt."

"Even when she described the same guy that we saw do the woman behind my house?"

"They think I somehow influenced the description. Anyway, it's been a while since anything happened, and they're bored with the investigation. It's been all I could do to keep them interested this long. After tomorrow night, pal, you and I are on our own. You'd better give some thought to how you're going to protect Sarah."

"I've hardly thought about anything else."

"I know it's tough. I mean, Mary Ann and Ben are okay at the old man's place, and I can watch my own back, but I don't envy you, trying to keep a lid on Sarah. She's not the type to like it."

"You've got a very good point there, Dino. I've talked with her about visiting her folks in England for a while, but she's been out of New York for so long that I think she missed it, and she doesn't want to leave."

"I think England is a great idea," Dino said. "You want me to talk to her about it? Will that help?"

"I doubt it; she'll just think we're ganging up on her, and she'll resist all the more."

"Women," Dino sighed.

"Yeah,"

"Here we are." Dino pointed to a set of wrought-iron gates on the left. The ocean was on their right.

Stone pulled into the drive and stopped at a security box.

"Ring the bell, and tell them who you are," Dino said.

Stone did as he was told, and the gates swung silently open.

28

STONE HAD BEEN EXPECTING SOMETHING LIKE DON Corleone's house in *The Godfather*—discreet, anonymous, hidden, even. What lay before him now was a perfect Palladian mansion behind five acres of closely mown lawn. "I don't think we're in Brooklyn anymore," he said to Dino.

"Just barely," Dino replied. "There's all kinds of Brooklyn."

Stone drove up the winding driveway and stopped at the front door in a circle of crunchy gravel. As they got out of the car the splashing of water from a stone fountain in the middle of the circle reached Stone's ears. Before they could ring the bell, the front door was opened by a small, gray man in a black suit.

"Good evening, Mr. Bacchetti," the man said, in Italian-accented English.

"Howyadoin', Pete?"

He shot a rebuking glance at Dino. "Good evening, Mr. Barrington," the man said. "I am Pietro. Please come this way."

Stone and Dino followed Pietro through a marble-floored entrance hall and through a large, elegantly furnished drawing room into a small sitting room, paneled in antique pine. A cheerful fire burned in a corner fireplace. The pictures on the wall were of imaginary, ruined palazzos in the Italian countryside.

"May I get you something to drink, gentlemen?" Pietro asked.

"Scotch," Dino said. "The good stuff, Pete."

"You know very well we have no other kind, Mr. Bacchetti. Mr. Barrington?"

"A Strega, on ice, please," Stone replied.

Pietro beamed his approval and left the room.

Stone started to take a seat next to the fire.

"Not there," Dino said. "That's the old man's perch. He'd have Pete cut your throat on the way out."

Stone chose another chair. "The man obviously doesn't like to be called Pete, Dino; why do you do that?"

Dino sat down. "Twenty years ago, he was Little Pete Drago, a button man for the boys on Mulberry Street. He's probably got twenty notches on his piece, and I don't want him to forget it."

"Twenty years? You certainly know how to hold a grudge, Dino."

"I'm Italian; it's what we do."

Pietro returned with the drinks. "Mrs. Bacchetti is dressing; Mr. Bianchi is in the garden with Ben and will join you shortly," he said.

"Thanks, Pete," Dino replied, sipping his scotch.

Pietro left the room and closed the door behind him.

"Be sure you don't make any sudden moves in Eduardo's direction," Dino said to Stone, "or Pete'll slip a dagger between your ribs before you know what's happening."

"I'll keep that in mind."

The door opened, and two women entered the room. First, came Mary Ann, and she was followed by a woman so beautiful that Stone was transfixed. It took him a moment to get to his feet.

Mary Ann came over and planted a kiss on Stone's cheek. "Hey, baby," she whispered, then she turned and indicated her companion. "Stone, this is my sister Rosaria; in the family we call her Dolce. Sweetie, this is our friend Stone Barrington."

Dolce Bianchi glided across the room and placed her hand in

Stone's. She was half a head taller than Mary Ann and clad in a perfectly cut black dress that accentuated her full breasts and her narrow hips. "Hello, Stone," she said in a husky voice.

Stone was nearly unable to speak. "Hello," he finally managed to mumble. The woman looked like a Sicilian princess, he thought. Her hair fell in black waves to her shoulders, and she wore a single piece of jewelry, a diamond necklace that looked like something out of Harry Winston's window.

Before anyone could say anything else, Eduardo Bianchi entered the room. He came in so silently, almost stealthily, that Stone did not at first notice him. When he did, he was being greeted by a tall, handsome man, apparently around fifty years of age, with iron gray hair, white at the temples, and wearing a double-breasted, chalk-striped suit that had never known a wrinkle.

"How do you do, Mr. Barrington? I am Eduardo Bianchi." The voice was well modulated, cultured, accentless.

"How do you do, Mr. Bianchi?" Stone thought that the man could host *Masterpiece Theater*.

"Dino," Bianchi said, "you may wish to say good night to Ben; he's in his room."

Dino left the room.

Bianchi signaled for them all to sit. He took his own seat and accepted a Strega from a silver tray held by Pietro.

Stone was glad of his own choice of the drink, and even more glad that Dino had kept him from taking his host's usual chair. Bianchi exuded a royal presence, and Stone felt very much on his best behavior.

"I hope you had a pleasant drive here," Bianchi said.

"Yes, indeed," Stone said. "I was not aware of this part of Brooklyn."

"My family has slowly developed this part of Brooklyn over many years," he replied. "My father wished to have a pleasant neighborhood in which to build a house. Unfortunately, he died before he was able to do so. It was left to me to build this place on land he had reserved."

"The house is very beautiful," Stone said. "You are to be complimented."

"Thank you," Bianchi replied with a small nod. "It is good to have a guest who appreciates it."

Stone felt confused. Could this man be the ogre of a father-in-law that Dino had for years disparaged at every opportunity?

Dino returned silently to the room and sat down.

"My daughter's husband has never been susceptible to its charms," Bianchi said, with regret in his voice. "Dino prefers . . . *Manhattan*." He spoke the word as if the island were a prison colony off the coast of Long Island.

Dino, uncharacteristically, said nothing.

Stone and Bianchi chatted amiably for half an hour, while the others merely listened. Finally, Pietro appeared at the door and gave a little bow.

"Ah, yes," Bianchi said, rising. "Dinner is served. I believe we are in the small dining room, Pietro?"

"Yes, sir," Pietro replied.

Bianchi led the way to a lovely little room and placed his guests at an antique round table set with Italian silver, English china, and French crystal.

Stone found himself seated next to the lovely Dolce, who had not said a word since her father had appeared.

Now she spoke. "I believe that you are in the practice of law, Mr. Barrington."

"I am," Stone replied.

"Do you specialize?"

"I specialize in what my clients require," Stone said.

"Oh, good," she breathed. "Lawyers too often forget that they are servants of their clients and not the other way around."

"I admit I have known such lawyers," Stone said.

"So have I," Dolce replied.

Stone, who had been only vaguely aware that Mary Ann had a sister, would have agreed with anything this creature had said.

Bianchi spoke up. "My younger daughter would not be so familiar with lawyers if she had more often heeded her father's advice."

"Yes, Papa," Dolce said meekly.

Stone felt that she was rarely meek. A risotto of porcini mushrooms was set before him. Careful to choose the correct fork, he tasted it and was transported to a country he had never visited.

"Have you visited Italy, Mr. Barrington?" Bianchi asked, as if he were reading Stone's mind.

"I'm sorry to say that I haven't," Stone replied. "I have a friend who has just returned from several years in Tuscany and speaks highly of it."

"That would be Miss Buckminster, the painter, would it not?"

"Yes," Stone replied, surprised.

"I knew her work when she lived in New York," Bianchi said. "I thought she had great promise, though I felt she needed maturing as an artist. I understand that her recent work is much elevated in its perceptions."

"She is an excellent painter," Stone said.

"And you would know, would you not? Coming from a mother who was such an illustrious artist."

"Thank you," Stone said. "Perhaps I inherited an appreciation of good painting from my mother, but none of her talent, I fear."

"I have tried on a couple of occasions to buy a Matilda Stone, but I have always been outbid."

Stone was astonished that Bianchi had ever been outbid for anything. "You must keep trying," he said.

"Oh, I will," Bianchi replied. "I will not long be denied."

Stone's empty plate was removed and replaced with a main course of osso bucco.

"We are dining in the fashion of Milano this evening," Bianchi said. "Milanese dishes are among my favorites."

"Everything is delicious," Stone said.

"I will tell my sister you said so. She does all the cooking for the house."

"Please give her my compliments."

"You will have an opportunity to do so yourself," Bianchi said.

Suddenly, Stone felt an unaccustomed sensation. Something was climbing up his right calf. He froze, his wineglass in midair.

Bianchi stared at him. "Is the wine not to your satisfaction?"

Stone took a sip and swallowed hard. "It's superb," he said. He now realized that what was climbing his calf was a foot belonging to Dolce Bianchi.

"It is grown in my own vineyard in Veneto," Eduardo Bianchi said.

"Absolutely superb," Stone said, trying to keep his voice from trembling. Dolce's stockinged toes had reached the top of his sock and were drawing it down around his ankle. He felt as though he was being undressed by an expert.

"It is an Amerone," Bianchi was saying. "The grapes are dried in the sun before they are pressed. It concentrates the flavor."

"Just wonderful," Stone said, trying not to giggle. She was tickling his leg now. Carefully, he drew his foot away from hers. From a corner of his eyes, he saw her make a moue.

"Dolce," Bianchi said to his daughter, "you are unusually quiet; you must entertain our guest."

"Yes, Papa," she said, sliding a glance in Stone's direction.

When they had finished dining, Bianchi stood. "All of you, please return to the little sitting room, where Pietro will serve coffee." They all rose and filed out. Bianchi turned to Stone. "Mr. Barrington, perhaps you will join me for a glass of something?"

Before Stone could reply, Bianchi had turned and departed through another door. Stone hurried to catch up.

29

EDUARDO BIANCHI LED THE WAY INTO A RICHLY PAN-
eled study, all walnut and leather. The shelves were filled with
gorgeously bound books, and the paintings on the walls were newer
than those in the rest of the house, but very good.

"Will you join me in a glass of port?" Bianchi asked.

"Thank you, yes," Stone replied.

Bianchi went to a butler's tray across the room and read the
label on a bottle from which the cork had been drawn.

Stone took the opportunity to pull up his sock.

"Pietro has decanted a Quinto do Noval Nacionale '63 for us," he
said, setting down the empty bottle, picking up a beautifully blown
Georgian decanter, and pouring two glasses. He handed one to
Stone, indicated that he should sit in one of a pair of wing chairs,
side by side, then sat down beside him. He raised his glass. "To the
future," he said. "May it be less uncertain."

Stone wondered what his host meant by that. He sipped the
wine, which filled his mouth with the most wonderful flavors. "It's
superb," he said.

Bianchi nodded. "The Nacionale vineyard at Quinto do Noval is
very small, containing the last of their oldest vines that have not yet

been attacked by the phylloxera pest that wiped out most European vineyards in the last century. We will not always have this wine to drink."

Stone sipped it gratefully.

"I have heard a great deal about you over the years," Bianchi said. "From Dino and Anna Maria—she prefers a more American version of her name. And, of course, I have heard of you from others."

"Others?" Stone could not prevent himself from asking.

"We have acquaintances in common."

"We do?" Stone bit his tongue. He must stop responding like a trained bird.

"I am occasionally represented in some matters by Woodman and Weld, with whom, I believe, you are associated."

Stone nearly choked on his port. Woodman & Weld was representing a Mafioso?

"Perhaps this surprises you?"

"Well, no," Stone lied.

"I understand that most, perhaps all of what you know of me is from Dino."

"Well . . ."

"My daughter's husband and I subscribe to, shall we say, different philosophies of life. And Dino is not so tolerant as I when judging others; therefore, something of a gulf exists between us, one that I fear may never be bridged."

"I'm sorry."

"So am I. I have the greatest respect for the intelligence and integrity that my son-in-law brings to his work. His manners are another matter."

"Dino is, sometimes, a bit too frank."

Bianchi laughed for the first time, revealing magnificent dental work. "One could say that. He is not, you understand, disrespectful—not to my face, at least. But as a modern Italian-American, he does not fully grasp the meaning of my family's history. Dino is from a northern Italian family, whereas we are Sicilian. Our customs are very old, and they still shape our daily lives in ways that Dino cannot fully appreciate."

"I see."

"Perhaps you do; perhaps not. It is paradoxical that honor is so important to both Dino and me, and yet, we take very different paths to the upholding of honor. Dino does not yet understand that I approved of his marriage to Anna Maria."

Stone could not resist. "Approved? It was my understanding that you *insisted* on it."

Bianchi laughed again. "Well, yes, I suppose I did. A wedding in the presence of a shotgun is not unknown in my family. In fact, there was one present at my own marriage. And my wife and I had a richly rewarding marriage for forty-one years, before her death last year."

"I believe Dino and Mary Ann have such a marriage," Stone said.

"I hope you are right," Bianchi said. "What I know of the marriage tends to come from Anna Maria, and sometimes I am not sure whether she is more motivated by loyalty than by love."

"I assure you, she is not."

"Thank you, Mr. Barrington; you have made an old man feel better." Then his face clouded. "A man's daughters are important to him," he said, hesitantly. "And when I heard that an attempt had been made on Anna Maria's life, I was very angry."

"I can understand that."

"Since I have no sons, my grandson is extremely important to me, and now he cannot even attend his school."

"I know."

"But I have held my temper. I understand that it is Dino's place—both by dint of his place in her life and by his work—to correct this situation. It is only right that he should have that opportunity. However, to date, his best efforts have been insufficient."

"It is a difficult case," Stone said. "In a situation like this, Dino is at a very great disadvantage."

"Revenge is always difficult, even tedious, when it must be

accomplished within the framework of the laws of this country," Bianchi said.

"You do understand, though, that the only way Dino can deal with this is within the law?"

"I do understand, and that is why I have been so patient. However, my patience is not inexhaustible, and I am not required to operate under the same constraints as Dino." He gazed at Stone. "Neither, for that matter, are you."

Stone did not reply to that.

"I understand that you, too, were once a policeman, and that now you are a lawyer, and that your background and inclinations may cause you also to feel constrained."

"Yes," Stone said.

"But, perhaps, not so much as Dino."

Stone was wary, now, and said nothing.

Bianchi crossed his legs and sipped his port. "I am aware that you spent some days in California last year."

"Yes, I did." What was the man getting at?

"And word has reached me that, when you felt wronged by another man, you took the extraordinary step of sinking his very large and very expensive yacht."

Stone was astonished. "Did you hear this from Dino?"

Bianchi shook his head slowly. "I was, shall we say, indirectly acquainted with the yacht's owner."

"I see."

Bianchi raised a hand. "Only in the most legitimate sense, you understand. I have interests on the West Coast, and they sometimes coincided with the interests of the gentleman in question. He did, after all, run a large banking business—in addition to his *other* interests, of course."

"Of course."

"What impressed me about this incident was the very carefully crafted nature of your vengeance."

Stone wondered for a moment if this conversation was being

overheard by some federal representative, but then he remembered that the feds were very aware of the incident. "I wasn't thinking very carefully at the time," he said.

"Then your instincts speak well of you. Somehow, you looked at this man and knew that little else could hurt him as much as the loss of his beloved status symbol."

"I suppose there's some truth to that."

"I'm glad you and I understand each other, Mr. Barrington."

We do? Stone thought.

"You see, just as you were protecting a cherished woman at that time, you are now protecting yet another woman important to you."

"Yes," Stone agreed.

"As am I," Bianchi said. "Do you understand?"

"Up to a point," Stone replied.

"You understand that I would like to help bring an end to this business?"

"Of course."

"And that I cannot tread on Dino's toes, as it were."

"Yes."

"Then perhaps it might be possible for me to help you, instead of Dino."

"You must understand, Mr. Bianchi, that Dino is my closest friend, that I owe him my life, quite literally."

"Of course. I know all about that, and I understand completely. I am not suggesting that you should do anything to violate that friendship."

"Good."

"I am merely saying that there may arise information that Dino would not wish to be privy to, and that our sometimes awkward relationship prevents me from offering him."

"What sort of information?"

"Then you will accept this from me?"

Stone was uncomfortable. "I'm not certain what I would be accepting."

"I understand that this Mitteldorfer, on being released from prison, has disappeared."

"That is correct."

"Perhaps I can help you find him."

"How can you do that?"

Bianchi shrugged. "Let us just say that I have . . . acquaintances who have acquaintances who have friends who might be able to help. If I should request it."

"I must tell you, I am uncomfortable with this."

Bianchi held up a hand. "I understand completely." He reached into the ticket pocket in his jacket, produced a card, and handed it to Stone.

Stone examined it. It contained only a Manhattan telephone number.

"If you should feel you need my . . . advice, please telephone this number and leave a recorded message. Someone representing me will be in touch."

Stone pocketed the card and gave Bianchi his own, which seemed only courteous, in the circumstances.

"I will wait to hear from you before making inquiries," Bianchi said. "Shall we join the others?" He replenished their glasses, and they walked slowly toward the door. "Perhaps, if you will permit me, I will just speak a name to you. The name is Judson Palmer."

"It doesn't ring a bell," Stone said.

"Mr. Palmer is a minor theatrical producer," Bianchi said, taking Stone's arm.

"I'm afraid I don't understand."

"It was he who was having an affair with Mitteldorfer's wife when she was murdered."

"Does Mitteldorfer know who he is?"

"That is uncertain."

"Thank you."

Bianchi stopped walking. "Stone—may I call you Stone?"

"Of course."

"And please call me Eduardo."

"Thank you."

"I have very much enjoyed our evening together. I don't go out much since my wife's death, but it would please me if you would accept another invitation to dinner here."

"Thank you, Eduardo; I'd be very pleased to come."

The two men walked back to the small sitting room and joined the others. A large woman in an old-fashioned black dress had joined the group.

"Allow me to introduce my sister, Rosaria," Bianchi said.

Stone took her hand. "Dinner was a wonderful experience," he said. The woman blushed. Bianchi sat next to her.

Stone chose a seat as far as possible from Dolce Bianchi.

30

Dino SLAMMED THE CAR DOOR. "ALL RIGHT, WHAT WENT on in that room? You came back arm in arm with him; I've seen that before, and it means he wants something from you. What did he want? What did you give him?"

"Dino," Stone said, starting the car and driving away, "I don't know what you're talking about."

"What did *Eduardo* talk about? That's what I want to know."

Stone shrugged. "He seemed to want to get to know me a little. Maybe that's why he invited me to dinner."

"Eduardo *never* has reasons as simple as that for doing *anything*. In all the time I've known him, you're the first person I've ever seen sit at that table who wasn't family."

"Speaking of family, why did you never tell me that Mary Ann had such a beautiful sister?"

"You knew she had a sister."

"But I never had an inkling that she was so . . ."

"Yeah, she is, isn't she? Stay away from her; she's dangerous."

"Why?"

"Well, for a start, she has a real snake for an ex-husband."

"Who is he?"

"His name is Johnny Donato."

"That has a familiar ring."

"It should; he was a capo under Big Paul Castellano, before Gotti had him capped. Word is, he was supposed to be driving the Paul that night, which means he would have got it, too, but Paul sent him on some errand or other, so he survived. He disappeared after that and didn't turn up again until Gotti and Sammy Gravano were in jail. Now he's running a supposedly legit concrete business, taking up where Sammy left off."

"And how did a girl as elegant as Dolce end up with a guy like that?"

"Pretty much the same way Mary Ann ended up with me. He was a guy from the neighborhood, working for a bookie and running his own little protection racket on the side. He tried to get a weekly paycheck out of my old man for not burning down his candy store, but when I heard about it I took him aside and discussed it with him."

"You mean, you beat the shit out of him?"

"Something like that."

"So why didn't he and his friends retaliate?"

"I made sure I got him alone, made it personal; nobody saw it, so he didn't have to salvage his pride. Besides, by that time I was a cop, so he didn't want to mess with me."

"Dolce looks too smart to get mixed up with somebody like that, let alone marry him."

"She *is* smart, but she was eighteen, nineteen, and for a while, she was stupid. He was a very slick item, drove a convertible, dressed well, flashed money around. Eduardo had her on a tight leash, and she didn't like it. By the time he got a handle on the situation, they were in Miami on their honeymoon."

"So Eduardo brought her back?"

Dino shook his head. "That's not his style. He gave her some rope, and Donato hung himself. They hadn't been married a month before he was fucking around. She got smart and went home."

"What's she doing now?"

"She's Eduardo's right-hand man, and I use the gender advisedly. She's got more balls than any four guys I know."

"An Italian of Eduardo's generation makes a business associate out of a daughter?"

"What's he gonna do? He's got no sons, and it's fifteen years before Ben could step up to the plate."

"You think he wants to bring Ben into his business?"

Dino shrugged. "He'll try like hell, but the kid has an independent streak. Anyway, it might not be a bad thing, if he wanted it. Eduardo will have the whole thing scrubbed clean before then. It's a generational thing: Eduardo's grandfather was an out-and-out, leg-breaking extortionist and pimp; his father was up-to-his-ears Mob, but he had a legitimate fruit business, and he was a good family man. Now Eduardo is a trustee of Columbia, he's on the board of the Metropolitan Museum, he's a papal knight, and he's got a portfolio of businesses that would turn Warren Buffet's head. You think anybody cares where the money came from?"

"Except you."

"Except me, but I'm a cop."

"The police commissioner doesn't care, but you do."

"Call me crazy, but yeah. I just can't cozy up to Eduardo."

"I think he likes you, Dino."

"Huh?"

"He told me he has the greatest respect for your intelligence and integrity as a police officer. Those were his very words."

"You're kidding."

"He also told me that he approved of Mary Ann's marrying you."

Dino snorted. "He gave you some of that Quinto de something-orother port, didn't he? It makes you hear crazy things."

"I think you've underestimated Eduardo, Dino."

"That, I would *never* do."

"I mean as a man, as a father. He's growing old; he wants to see his family happy . . . and safe."

"And he thinks I can't protect them? The son of a bitch!"

"Has he interfered in your investigation in any way?"

"Not yet, but just watch him!"

"Maybe he can help you."

"I don't want his help. He's not gonna make me dirty."

Stone sighed.

"That's what your little talk was about, wasn't it?"

"He made it clear he wants to help, but he doesn't want to get in your way. He just said to call him if we need help."

"I told you, I don't want his help."

"He might have sources that aren't available to us."

"If he knows something, he can call the precinct and report it."

"Somehow, I don't think he's accustomed to doing things that way, do you?"

"He wants to be the hidden hand, the way he's always been, but this time, he wants to manipulate *me*; he wants to pull the strings with the law. I *hate* that."

"Dino, you would use any pusher or pimp on the street as a snitch, but you won't accept out-of-channel information from your own father-in-law?"

"Stone, I know what you're saying is perfectly logical, but I can't go against my own best instincts on this. If I accept his help, then I'm no better than he is. That's the way I feel about it, and that's an end to it, all right?"

"All right." Stone drove along in silence for a few minutes. "You know," he said, finally, "Dolce was playing footsie with me under the table."

Dino's mouth dropped open. "Right there, in front of Eduardo? No kidding?"

"No kidding."

Dino burst out laughing. "Did I tell you she has balls? She's some piece of work, isn't she?"

"She certainly seems to be."

"Stone, don't call her; don't get involved."

"Well, I . . ."

"I'm not kidding you. Eduardo is Satan, and Dolce is his hand-maiden."

"Dino, you're getting *very* Italian on me."

"You want Johnny Donato on your back? He tells everybody they're still married."

"So why hasn't Eduardo dealt with him? Why isn't Donato—to put it in your own graceful and expressive manner—'at the bottom of Sheepshead Bay with a concrete block up his ass'?"

"It'll happen, don't worry. But when it does, it'll be done in such a way that nobody will even think of connecting it with Eduardo or Dolce. That's how Eduardo works."

"It'll be interesting to wait and watch."

"And in the meantime, you stay away from Dolce; she's poison."

"Dino, I've got Sarah, remember?"

"I remember. Just don't *you* forget."

31

STONE AND SARAH SAT UP IN BED, EATING BAGELS AND cream cheese, the *Times* spread out before them. "Oh, look!" she cried, thrusting the paper at him, "a really nice write-up about tonight!"

Stone read the piece, smiling. "I'm happy for you; this should make your opening even more successful. There's nothing like a little validation from the *Times* art critic."

"Edgar says he's had over two hundred acceptances, and this will put us way over the top. And Edgar has already sold two of the most expensive pictures."

"Before the opening? To whom?"

"He won't tell me; he just says it's an important collector, somebody on the board of the Metropolitan! Can you imagine?"

"When did this happen?"

"Yesterday. The man called him and requested a private showing, even though the work wasn't hung yet."

"I think I had dinner with him last night."

"Who? Edgar? He was hanging the work with me."

"No, the buyer."

"Who is he?"

"My guess is he's Dino's father-in-law; his name is Eduardo Bianchi."

"Didn't you tell me that Dino's father-in-law is some sort of Mafia guy?"

"Maybe I did, but believe me, after meeting him, I can tell you he's no run-of-the-mill gangster. He has a very fine collection. He mentioned you, in fact, but he didn't tell me he had bought two pictures. He knew your work from before you left for Italy."

"Well, I don't care if he's Al Capone reincarnated if he had the good judgment to like my work. Anyway, that's nearly twenty thousand dollars in my pocket, after Edgar's commission!" She threw off the covers. "Let's go shopping!"

"Shopping for what?"

"We've got a gatehouse in Connecticut to furnish, haven't we?"

"You're not paying for that with the first money you've earned in years."

"Well, I'll buy you a very nice housewarming present, then. Come on!"

Half an hour later Stone was backing the car out of the garage, when he noticed a black van parked across the street.

"What are you looking at?" Sarah asked, turning so she could see out the rear window.

"A van I haven't seen before in the block."

"What about it?"

"The feds are famous for using vans for stakeouts and electronic surveillance, and that one has a couple of extra antennas."

"I'll bet it's some of Dino's people," she said.

"Could be; the feds don't have a monopoly on vans." He turned downtown on Second Avenue.

"Stone, after tonight, I don't want any more cops around. Anderson is all right, but that guy Kelly gives me a serious case of the willies. I'm sick of him."

"Don't worry about cops; after tonight, Dino has to pull his people off, anyway. He can't justify it to the department any longer."

"I'm beginning to think these murders and attacks are just a string of coincidences."

"Maybe you're right," Stone replied, "but in my experience, when you get too many coincidences, it's called fate."

"Now *you're* giving me the willies!"

"I'm sorry, but this is a serious business, and I don't want you to start letting your guard down. Not until we've located this guy Mitteldorfer and done something about him."

"But he's been in prison for all these years; how could it have been him?"

"I don't know, but both Dino and I have the very strong feeling that it is him. I didn't tell you this, but a friend of Mitteldorfer, a woman who corresponded with him in prison, was murdered a couple of days ago."

"So, he would get out of prison and, right away, murder a woman who would write to him? Why would he do that?"

"I don't know, but it's one more coincidence, isn't it?"

She was quiet for a minute. "Stone, is there any reason in the world why the two of us couldn't go to England tomorrow? I mean, after the opening tonight, my obligations to the Bergman Gallery are finished; there's nothing to keep me here. How about you?"

"I don't like to run off and leave Dino with this thing hanging over him."

"What thing? Nothing has happened for a while, now. Take some time off."

Stone thought about it. "Open the glove compartment; there's an address book inside."

She did as he asked.

"Look up the number for the American Express Platinum Travel Service. Call them on the car phone; book us two first-class seats to London tomorrow morning."

She grabbed the phone. "You bet I will!"

Stone felt as if a burden had been lifted from him. She was right; he needed to get away. He found a garage on Broadway, and they walked around the corner to the ABC Furniture store. During the next two hours, they bought a bed, sheets and towels, a sofa, two chairs, some rugs, lamps, a dining table, and occasional furniture. Stone had everything shipped to Connecticut for delivery after the closing on the house, with a note for the driver to call at the Klemm Real Estate office for the key. Then they found a housewares store and bought pots and pans, silverware, a coffeepot, dishes, glasses, and everything else they could think of.

When they went back to the garage for the car, Stone noticed a black van parked across the street. It was not the same one that had been outside his house.

"You're getting black-van fever, aren't you?" Sarah asked, as they drove away.

"I'm not making them up, am I?"

"Just don't make too much of them. The world is full of black vans."

"You're right," Stone said, taking a deep breath and letting it out. "Tomorrow we're out of this city, and when we come back we'll have a house and a lot of furnishings waiting for us in Connecticut. I'd better call Bob Eggers and arrange to have the closing papers for the house sent to England. Where will we be?"

"Probably at my parents' country house, in Hampshire, but they have a town house, too. I'll call them when we get home and find out where to send the papers."

Stone drove home, happily thinking of his first trip abroad, but his eyes constantly flicked to the rearview mirror.

32

STONE AND SARAH WERE DRESSING FOR HER OPENING. "I spoke to Mother this afternoon," Sarah said, "and she suggested we come straight to the country house. I think that's best, don't you? We can just relax and do some sailing."

"Sounds good to me," Stone replied, pulling his black bow tie snug. He slipped into his dinner jacket. "What sort of sailing?"

"The house is on the Solent, the strip of water that separates the Isle of Wight from the rest of England. Daddy keeps a cruising boat nearby, in the Beaulieu River. Do you sail?"

"I did some sailing as a kid, at a summer house on Martha's Vineyard, belonging to the parents of a friend. I've chartered in the Caribbean, too, but the last time, I didn't get much sailing done."

"This is going to be wonderful, Stone," she said, turning so he could zip up her dress. "I haven't been home for three years, and I do so love it in Hampshire. I'm happiest on the water, I think."

"I'm looking forward to it."

"How do I look?" she asked, turning for inspection.

"You look absolutely beautiful," he replied. "The dress is spectacular, too."

"And you, sir, look like a prince," she said, straightening his tie. "I've never seen you in a dinner jacket, you know."

"I didn't even own a dinner jacket before you went to Italy."

"You should wear it all the time; it makes you even more hand-some."

Stone took her arm and guided her downstairs. "We're being driven this evening," he said.

"You've hired a chauffeur?"

"Sort of a chauffeur; he's an ex-cop named Bob Berman, who does various investigative jobs for me now and then."

"I suppose he'll be armed," she said with a trace of disgust.

"I think that's best."

"What other measures have you taken?"

"Anderson and Kelly will be in a car in the street; Bob will watch the back door, where we'll enter the gallery, and Dino will be inside with us."

"I really think all this is unnecessary, Stone."

"You won't have to think about it anymore after tonight."

"Good."

They arrived in the garage, and Stone introduced Sarah to Bob Berman, a short, well-built man in his late forties. They got into the backseat, and Bob took the wheel and backed out of the garage.

"Bob, I've built in some extra time; take a circuitous route, so the cops behind us can be sure we're not being tailed."

"Right, Stone," Berman said. "Are you packing?"

"Ah, no," Stone replied.

"Whatever you say."

They drove back and forth across town, working their way slowly uptown. Half an hour passed before they arrived at the rear door of the gallery, precisely on time. Berman got out of the car, walked a few steps away, and checked up and down the block. He came back to the car and opened the door.

"Looks okay," he said to Stone.

Stone hustled Sarah across the sidewalk and through the door, which Edgar Bergman was holding open. Berman removed a traffic cone from a reserved space, parked the car, and took up his position at the rear door of the gallery.

"Anything unusual happen today?" Stone asked Bergman.

Bergman shook his head. "No, except we got a lot of acceptances after the *Times* piece appeared."

"Did you know them all?"

"Most of them were people to whom invitations had been sent; a few were other dealers. I suppose half a dozen of them were people I didn't know or had never heard of."

"We'll want to pay particular attention to those, as they enter."

"I'll speak to the receptionist," Bergman replied.

They entered the gallery, which was empty of guests, so far. "Everything looks wonderful, Sarah," Stone said. "Will you excuse me for just a moment? I'd like to talk with Edgar and his receptionist."

They walked to the desk at the front door, and Stone was introduced to the young woman who sat behind it and to Bergman's wife.

"Here's how I plan to work it," Bergman said. "My wife and I will be near the door, greeting the guests as they enter. If someone comes in whom I don't know, I'll simply turn and look at you and nod. Is that all right?"

"That's very good," Stone said. "I won't be far away."

"This is already nerve-wracking," Bergman said.

"I'm sure everything will be all right; there are two policemen in the street and my man at the back door." Stone looked toward the display of paintings, walked over, and examined one he particularly liked. He came back to Bergman. "How much is number thirty-six?" he asked.

Bergman consulted the catalogue. "That's six thousand dollars; it's one of the smaller pieces."

"Please mark it sold," Stone said, handing a credit card to the receptionist.

"I'd be delighted."

"Which two did Mr. Bianchi buy?"

"Why, number . . ." Bergman looked startled. "How did you know that? The transaction was done under the strictest confidence. He would be very upset if he thought I had told anyone."

"It was just a guess; I had dinner with him last night, and he mentioned Sarah's work."

"I see," Bergman said, looking relieved. "He bought numbers six—over there by the flowers—and number fourteen, the big one in the center of the north wall."

"He has a keen eye," Stone said, looking at the paintings.

"Yes, he does, and I hope you'll hold that transaction in the strictest confidence. He's been a good customer for a long time, and I have no wish to alienate him."

"Of course," Stone replied. He looked up and saw Dino coming through the door in a tuxedo. "Don't you look dapper?" he said.

"Yeah, yeah," Dino replied. "I talked to Anderson and Kelly outside. Is anybody on the back door?"

"Bob Berman; he's driving us."

"Okay."

Stone explained the procedure for identifying guests the Bergmans didn't know.

"I guess we've got it covered," Dino said. "You nervous?"

"Yes."

"So am I; I wish this weren't happening. That piece in the *Times* worries me."

"Me, too. We've done everything we can; let's try to relax and enjoy the party."

"You relax," Dino said. "I'll be nervous."

Guests began to arrive, first in a trickle, then in large numbers. Stone watched the Bergmans as the people came in and, occasionally, he got a nod from Edgar or his wife. Dino did everything but search the strangers, but everybody behaved well.

At the peak of the party, Stone turned to Dino. "You got it covered here? I want to take a look outside."

"Yeah, sure."

Stone slipped outside and looked up and down the street. Everything seemed normal. He could see Anderson and Kelly sitting in their car, parked across the street. Then he noticed the van.

It wasn't black; instead, it was an anonymous gray, with no markings. He looked into the front seat; there was a map of the city on the passenger seat, but nothing else in sight. There were no side windows, and the small windows in the rear door had been soaped over. Stone stepped back and made a note of the license number, then walked across the street and rapped on the window of the police car. Kelly rolled down the window a couple of inches.

"Yeah?"

Stone tore off the sheet from his notebook and handed it through the window. "Run this plate," he said.

"What's it from?"

"The gray van in front of the gallery."

"That was there when we got here," Kelly said. "I don't see a problem."

"Just run the plate, Kelly."

Anderson took the slip of paper from Kelly and got on the radio. A minute later, he got out of the car and spoke to Stone across the car's roof. "The plate belongs to a 1996 Buick Century, stolen in Queens this afternoon."

"Call the bomb squad," Stone said, and started across the street. The light changed, and a raft of traffic forced him back. Impatient, he dodged through the stream of cars and walked quickly into the gallery. Bergman and his wife had abandoned their post by the door, and the receptionist was dealing with payment for pictures. "Excuse me," Stone said to the receptionist, "we're going to have to move you."

"I don't understand," the young woman said, looking around for her boss. "Mr. Bergman didn't say anything . . ."

"Just do it," Stone said, with urgency in his voice. He spotted Dino and waved him over.

"What's up?"

"There's a van with a stolen plate parked directly in front of the gallery; we're going to have to get these people out the back door right now."

Dino nodded. "Let's do it quietly." He walked over to a group of people and spoke to them, pointing the way to the rear of the gallery.

Stone was about to join him, when he saw that the receptionist and her customers were still at their business. Stone took the man by the elbow. "Sir, I'm sorry to disturb you, but everyone is going to have to leave the gallery through the rear door. Would you and your wife please walk back that way." He could hear sirens coming up Madison Avenue.

"I don't understand," the man said, annoyed at being interrupted. "I wouldn't want somebody else to get my picture."

"Please don't worry about that; this is just a security precaution."

The man reluctantly took his wife's arm and steered her toward the rear of the room.

Bergman walked up, looking panicky. "What's going on?"

"A suspicious van outside; please help Dino get all these people out the back door."

"Right in the middle of an opening? Are you crazy?"

"Mr. Bergman, this is very serious. Don't waste another second, and get this woman out of here," he said, indicating the receptionist. Bergman did as he was asked.

Sarah came over. "Stone, what's happening?"

"Possibility of a bomb outside," he whispered. "A crew is on the way to deal with it, now let me get you out of here." He started to move away from the front of the gallery, then, as an afterthought, he went back to the front window and drew the heavy wool curtains. "Let's go," he said to Sarah, taking her arm.

At that moment there was a huge noise, and the front-window curtains billowed as the plate glass behind them exploded inward.

33

STONE WAS THROWN THROUGH THE AIR, TAKING SARAH with him, landing hard on the gallery's marble floor. He lay, dazed, on top of her, and then he realized she was struggling to get out from under him. He rolled over. "Are you all right?" he asked, groggily.

Sarah said nothing, but scrambled up and began running toward the back of the gallery, screaming.

Stone got unsteadily to his feet as Dino arrived and slipped an arm around him. He looked back at the window: the window frame was empty, and fragments of broken glass were everywhere. The heavy wool curtains had disappeared, leaving only fragments clinging to the rod. Outside, where the van had once been, there was only a shallow crater in the asphalt. The cars on either side of the crater were on fire. The noise was incredible. Men and women were screaming inside the gallery and fighting to get out the rear door, as the approaching sirens got louder and louder.

Dino got out a handkerchief and held it to the back of Stone's head. "You're bleeding, pal; hold this against your head."

"I'm okay, Dino; find Sarah for me, will you? And get her to my car; it's the safest place right now."

"Okay, but don't go out front; there might be somebody out there to take a shot at you."

Stone stood, holding the handkerchief against the back of his head, and surveyed the damage. There seemed to be surprisingly little. Many of the paintings were still on the walls, and only one or two seemed to be badly damaged. He looked back at the window and realized what he had not before: the window did not occupy the entire front of the building. Instead, there was a border of masonry around it a good three feet wide. The blast had been funneled through the window opening, but the masonry still stood.

Forgetting Dino's advice, Stone walked out the front door, which had merely been blown open, its glass still intact. On the way, he picked up a piece of the broken window and looked at it. The edges were not sharp to the touch. This puzzled him.

Andy Anderson ran up to him. "Stone, are you all right?"

"I'm okay, I think," Stone replied. "Did you see what happened?"

"After I called the bomb squad, we moved the car up to the end of the block, to be out of the way. We were about to go back and stop traffic when the bomb went off. The light was red, and that had stopped the Madison traffic, so no cars were in front of the gallery when it blew, just the ones parked there. Nobody on the street was hurt that we can find; what about inside?"

"Go around to the back entrance and check for injuries; direct the ambulances there when they arrive."

"Right."

"Where's Kelly?"

"I don't know; I lost him."

Stone looked around the street. Some shop windows across Madison were broken, and some parked cars had shattered windows, but he saw little else in the way of damage. He turned and walked back into the gallery, which was now empty. He walked to the rear hallway and out the door, onto the street. Dino was standing with his arms around Sarah, who was sobbing; the scene was repeated up and down the block, but he didn't see any bodies, or even anyone who was not standing up or leaning against a car. Dino saw him and waved him over.

He took Sarah and held her at arm's length. "Are you hurt anywhere?" he asked.

She seemed to get control of herself. "I don't think so," she said.

"You've got some cuts on your legs," Dino said. "Come on, we're going to get you both to a hospital."

Bob Berman ran over to them. "Anybody hurt? That was a big bang."

"Not badly," Dino said. "Get Stone and Sarah over to the emergency room at Lenox Hill Hospital."

"Can we take anyone else?" Stone asked.

"I think you're hurt worse than anybody else; you were closest to the blast, and Sarah was behind you," Dino said. "Was it you who pulled the curtains?"

"Yeah, I think I did."

"I think that had a damping effect and took a lot of the glass. You may have saved some lives, including your own. Come on, get in the car."

Berman already had it started. They got in, and Berman backed down the street to Fifth Avenue, his emergency blinkers on. "Hang on," he said. "I'm going the wrong way on Fifth." He turned uptown, dodging oncoming cars, and, two blocks north, turned east.

"Smart move, Bob," Stone said. "You wouldn't have been able to get across Madison if you'd gone downtown. The explosion will have traffic backed up for fifty blocks."

Sarah had stopped crying and was sitting rigidly, clasping Stone's free hand tightly, saying nothing.

"Sarah, are you sure you're all right?" Stone asked.

"I'm all right," she replied in a low voice.

At Lenox Hill, Stone's jacket and shirt were stripped off, and he was laid facedown on a gurney. Somebody gave him a local anesthetic and began picking glass out of his scalp and back.

"You're not badly hurt, sir," a young resident said. "We've got more people arriving with similar injuries; what happened?"

"A bomb," Stone said. Somebody was shaving patches of his hair off, and he put a hand back to feel his head.

"Don't worry, beautiful," a nurse said. "I won't take any more hair than necessary. You'll still be gorgeous."

"I've got a headache," Stone said. "Can I have some aspirin?"

"In a minute, after we've cleaned these wounds. You're going to need a stitch here and there, too."

Stone tried to lie quietly and let them do their work. Finally, they sat him up, and the nurse handed him a white lab coat. "Better put this on to keep out the night," she said. "Your jacket and shirt aren't in such good shape." She handed him the tattered garments. "You can go, now; let's get you into a wheelchair; hospital policy."

"Where's Sarah Buckminster?"

"The lady with you? We patched some small cuts on her legs; she's in the car with the man who brought you in." She stopped at the door.

Stone stood up. "Thanks; how long have I been here?"

"I don't know exactly; something over an hour."

Stone walked out to the car and got in. "Take us home, Bob."

The car moved out, and, shortly, they pulled into the garage. Stone held Sarah in the car until the garage door closed. Just before it did, Dino ducked under it.

"Hey, I like the white coat," he said. "Suits you better than the tuxedo. You okay?"

"I've got a headache," Stone said. "They forgot to give me some aspirin."

"Let's get you upstairs," Dino said, taking his arm.

"Oh, come on, Dino, I'm not hurt; I can walk." They went up to the master suite.

Sarah went straight to the bathroom. "I'm taking a pill," she said. "If anybody wants to speak to me while I'm conscious, he'd better do it now."

Stone got her tucked into bed; then he took four aspirin, and he and Dino went into his study, where Dino poured them a drink. "What was the final count on the damage?" Stone asked.

"A few cars," Dino said, "a few shop windows, a few hysterical people, a few pictures; that's about it. The bomb guys said it was just a bundle of dynamite tossed into the back of the van—no direction to it, no nails or other shrapnel, except the pieces of the van. None of that hit anybody inside the gallery. It blew in every direction. The van took the worst of it, the window, then the armored-glass window slowed it down some more, and the curtains damped some of that. The glass was designed to hold up to a point, then shatter into dull fragments. By the time the bomb blew we had nearly everybody in the back part of the gallery. We were real lucky; it could have been a slaughterhouse. Anderson and Kelly should have run every license plate on the block, but nobody told them to—I blame myself for that—and they weren't expecting anything like a bomb."

"I was expecting *something*," Stone said, "but not that."

"It's a bad business; but at least this will keep my investigation open. This will be all over the news tonight and the papers tomorrow. Why don't you and Sarah get out of town?"

"We're already booked on a London flight tomorrow morning," Stone said. "Think you can handle this without me?"

Dino shot him a withering glance. "Gee, I'll do my best."

34

THE HEADACHE WAS STILL THERE WHEN STONE WOKE up. Sarah was up and in the shower, and her suitcases were spread over her side of the bed. She came back into the bedroom, clad only in a towel.

She held up a hand. "Don't you look at me that way," she said. "We've got a plane to catch, and there's no time for hanky-panky."

Stone sat up in bed and put his feet on the floor. "You're in no danger from me, not with the headache I've still got."

"You want something stronger than aspirin? I'm a walking pharmacy."

"You prescribe, I'll imbibe."

She went to the bathroom and came back with a pill and a glass of water. "Don't have any wine for breakfast; the two together will put you under the table."

Stone took the pill. "What time is it?"

"It's seven-thirty, and our flight is at ten. You'd better get packed; what with the security measures at the airport, we don't even have time for breakfast. They'll have something for us in the first-class lounge—pastries or something."

"Right, right," Stone said. He took a shower, and by the time he was out, his headache was gone, though he felt a little fuzzy around the edges. He got packed, then put their luggage on the elevator, which he rarely used, and sent it to the basement. "Dino's going to drive us to the airport, just to see that we get off safely."

"Sounds good to me," Sarah said, getting into her coat. "Let's get out of here."

They rode in Dino's police car, with a young detective for a driver. Not much was said, but finally, Stone had time to think, and he was not happy. When they arrived at the airport, Sarah handed him the tickets and her passport. "Will you get us checked in?" she asked. "I've got to go to the loo, and it can't wait."

Dino sent the young detective to escort her, and Stone got a porter and sent their luggage inside. He shook Dino's hand. "Thanks for ferrying us out here," he said.

"Don't worry about what's going on here," Dino said. "I'll take care of it."

"You should get the feds in on the bombing; they might come up with something."

"Already done; what's left of the van is in their garage now."

"Listen, Dino, I don't know if you've thought about this, but with Mary Ann and Ben in Brooklyn, and with Sarah and me out of the country, you're all that's left for these people to go after. You're going to have to watch your ass."

"I always do," Dino said. "You relax and have a good time. Call me, and I'll update you on what's happening."

"I'll do that," Stone replied. They hugged, and Stone followed the porter into the terminal. There was no line at the first-class counter, so check-in was quick. Stone set Sarah's luggage on the scales. He was thinking hard.

"Is this everything?" the woman at the counter asked. "Don't you have any luggage?"

He made up his mind. "There'll just be one traveling. Do you mind if I leave my bags here for a few minutes? I'll come back for them when I've seen my friend off."

The woman handed back the tickets and the passports. "Sure, I'll keep an eye on them." Stone stuck the tickets into his pocket, just as Sarah arrived.

"Are we all set?" she asked.

"Yep; let's go find the first-class lounge."

They sat quietly and had coffee and pastries while Stone had a look at the *Times*. "Well, we made the front page," he said.

"I don't want to hear about it," she said. "I'm putting it out of my mind—and for God's sake, don't mention it to my parents. They'll go bonkers."

"All right."

Their flight was called, and they walked silently to the gate. Stone waited until they were about to enter the airplane, then he took Sarah aside. "I can't go," he said. "I can't leave Dino in the middle of all this; if I do, he'll be their only target."

"Dino can take care of himself," Sarah replied.

"If these people got to him, I'd never forgive myself."

She looked at him for a moment. "Stone, I'm not coming back to New York."

"Look, this will be over, eventually. Stay with your folks until we've cleared it up, then come back."

"No, I've had it with this city. I left the first time because I was unhappy here; now it's trying to kill me. I'm sorry, but I won't be back."

"What about your attitude toward being pushed around by terrorists?" he asked.

"I've reconsidered my position."

"You know I can't live anywhere else but New York."

180

"I know." She put her arms around him. "You're the sweetest man I know, but, as you said, when there are enough coincidences lined up, it's fate. The fates are against us."

"I'm sorry," he said.

She kissed him. "So am I."

He gave her her ticket and passport, and she disappeared down the ramp and into the airplane.

Stone trudged back to the ticket counter, returned his ticket for credit, and picked up his bags. To his surprise, Dino's car was still sitting at the curb. Stone tossed his bags into the backseat and got in. "I'm back from England," he said.

"How come?" Dino asked.

"I didn't like the weather."

"You let that girl go?"

"I'm afraid so."

"Will she come back when this is over?"

"No. Take me to a hotel, Dino; if somebody watched me go, I don't want him to know I'm back."

Dino motioned for his driver to move on. "That was some girl," he said.

"I know."

"You incredible schmuck."

"I know."

35

STONE CHECKED INTO THE CARLYLE HOTEL AND instructed the desk that they were not to acknowledge his presence there unless the caller asked for Elijah Stone, which was his maternal grandfather's name.

"Of course, Mr. Stone," the desk clerk said.

Once in his room he called his answering machine. There was only one message, from Bill Eggers. He returned the call, and Eggers came on the line.

"It's Stone."

"You all right? I read the *Times*."

"I'm all right."

"You came off as something of a hero."

"Don't believe it. What's up?"

"We're all ready to close on your Connecticut house."

"Oh, okay. Today?"

"Yep. The seller has already signed off on everything. All we need is your signature, notarized, a couple of dozen times, and a cashier's check for the purchase price and closing costs; or you can give me a personal check and we'll pay it out of our trust account." He gave Stone the exact amount.

"I'll wire it to your trust account today, and you can issue the check." He wrote down the law firm's account number.

"Sure; you want to come over today?"

"Listen, Bill, I'm holed up at the Carlyle, and I don't want to go out today. Could you come over here?"

"Sure, what time?"

"Come at noon; I'll buy you a room-service lunch."

"Okay, I'll be there."

"I'm in Room 1550, registered under the name of Elijah Stone."

"See you at noon." Eggers hung up.

Stone called his broker and asked him to wire-transfer funds from his money market account to the trust account of Woodman & Weld, then he called ABC Furniture and asked them to go ahead and deliver his purchases to the Connecticut house.

"We've got a truck going up that way tomorrow," the woman said.

"That's great," Stone replied. He called the housewares store and asked for overnight delivery on his purchases, then he called Bob Berman.

"I thought you were on your way to England," Berman said.

"Change of plans. I didn't want to go back to the house, so I'm at the Carlyle Hotel. I wonder if you'd do me a big favor?"

"Name it."

"Would you go over to the house tonight—and I mean in the *dead* of night—make sure the house isn't being watched, then let yourself in. You've still got a key?"

"Yeah, not that I need one; I installed your security system, remember?"

"I remember. Go up to my study; there's a gun safe in a cabinet under one of the bookcases. Can you pick the lock?"

"Is the pope Polish?"

"Get the little Walther .765 automatic and its shoulder holster, and a spare clip. Then get the car out and take it to the Carlyle garage—it's open twenty-four hours—and tell the attendant it's for

Mr. Stone in 1550. Lock the gun in the glove compartment."

"I can do that," Berman said.

"Thanks, Bob, I owe you one."

"Only one?"

"All right, a couple of dozen."

"That's more like it. Good luck on staying alive." Berman hung up.

That done, he called the Klemm office in Washington, Connecticut, and got the numbers of the local utilities and the phone company. By the time Bill Eggers rang the doorbell, he'd arranged for water and electricity, and he had phone numbers for the house.

Bill Eggers came in, followed by Joan Robertson, who had earlier offered to help with Stone's secretarial work. She greeted him cheerfully, as if he had not nearly gotten her involved in his current dangerous mess.

"Why don't we order lunch now, and then we can close while they're preparing it?" Stone suggested. "Joan, will you join us?"

"Thanks, but I have a lunch date; my mother is in town."

They found a menu, and Stone and Eggers ordered, then they got down to business. Eggers handed Stone a series of documents, Stone signed them, and Joan notarized them. The whole business took three-quarters of an hour. Finally, Eggers handed Stone a completed document. "Here's your deed; you want us to file it for you?"

"Please, and put it in your safety deposit box for the time being," Stone replied.

"Congratulations, you now own a house in the country. I'll get the completed documents and the check to the seller this afternoon."

The doorbell rang, and a waiter wheeled in a cart bearing their lunch.

"I must run," Joan said. "I'll deliver the documents to the seller's law firm on the way to lunch, if you like."

"Thank you, Joan," Stone said, "and when all this is over, I'll take you up on your offer of help."

She left, and Stone and Eggers sat down to lunch. "I want her, Bill," Stone said.

"Don't you have enough women?"

"I want her for a secretary; I'm giving you fair warning."

"Then you'll have to make her an offer she can't refuse."

"I'll do that. By the way, I hear you have a client who makes offers like that, from time to time."

"I don't know what you mean."

"You never told me you represented Eduardo Bianchi."

Eggers stopped buttering his bread. "And where did you hear that?"

"From the horse's mouth."

"Which horse?"

"Bianchi, himself."

"You *know* Bianchi?"

"I know lots of people."

"You know Bianchi, *personally*?"

"I had dinner with him the night before last." Stone was enjoying this.

"Bianchi doesn't go out since his wife died."

"I had dinner at his home."

"Let's get this straight; we do *not* represent Eduardo Bianchi; we represent his charitable foundation."

"Ah, that keeps the hands clean, does it?"

"It's perfectly legal. We do it pro bono."

"Let me get this straight," Stone said, slipping the needle in a little deeper. "You represent a Mafia chieftain *pro bono*?"

"It's not only legal, it's downright *noble*."

Stone laughed aloud.

"And how did you come to be acquainted with Bianchi?" Eggers asked.

"Why? Have you never met him?"

"Many times, since he came to us about the foundation. Well, he *sort* of came to us. I got a call from somebody who'd gotten a call from somebody who'd gotten a call. Apparently, Bianchi is very sensitive about being rebuffed because of his family's reputation. He always feels out situations before presenting himself. Saves embarrassment on both sides, I guess."

"Yes, he does seem to be a cautious fellow."

"Finally, he came into the office, and we set up the foundation for him, with his daughter as its president. Tell you the truth, I was very impressed with him. With his daughter, too," Eggers said, wiggling his eyebrows.

"Yes, she's quite something, isn't she?"

"We've got a couple of associates down at the firm who would do Mob hits on the side just to sniff her underwear."

"She comes into the office a lot?"

"The foundation's offices are one floor up from us. We got them the space."

"And what sort of giving does the foundation do?"

Eggers put down his fork. "This goes no further, right?"

"Right."

"I mean, Bianchi is a bear about discretion, and he's not the sort of guy you want to cross."

"I will be the soul of discretion."

"They do arts grants. He's supporting a dozen young painters. Also, the foundation owns his art collection, and they lend to museums. Mostly old masters."

"What's the organization's name?"

"The Briarwood Foundation."

"I've seen that name on public television, as a sponsor of various stuff."

"They do that, too. Basically, they give to whatever interests the old man. Okay, your turn. How did you meet Bianchi?"

"He's Dino Bacchetti's father-in-law."

"What?"

"I kid you not. The older daughter; they've been married, seven, eight years."

Eggers shook his head. "Now I've heard everything."

"And that goes no further."

"As you wish."

They finished their coffee, and Eggers looked at his watch. "I've got a deposition; gotta go."

"Thanks for coming over here."

"Not at all. When do we get to see the Connecticut place?"

"Give me some time to get it sorted out. By the way . . ." Stone wrote some numbers on his card and handed it to Eggers. "Here are the phone and fax numbers. They should be working by tomorrow night, but keep them to yourself for the time being."

"Okay, see you soon." They shook hands, and Eggers left.

Stone pushed the tray into the hall, then sat down and picked up the *Times*. He read the paper thoroughly, as he always did, and in the Arts section a theater listing caught his eye. It read, "Judson Palmer presents, *A Poke in the Eye with a Sharp Stick*, a revue."

The name registered, and it brought Stone back to the problem at hand. *What the hell*, he thought, *I'm not getting anywhere on my own*. He fished Eduardo Bianchi's card from his wallet and dialed a phone number. The ringing stopped, and he heard a beep, no message.

"This is Stone Barrington," he said. "I can be reached at the Carlyle Hotel, 744-1600. I'm registered as Elijah Stone, Room 1550." He hung up. Was this the first step on the road to perdition?

36

NOW STONE HAD NOTHING TO DO WITH HIS DAY. HE couldn't go home safely, and the Connecticut house still had no furniture. He'd already read the *Times*; the *Wall Street Journal* bored him; he wasn't about to watch soap operas; and there were no good movies on TV. He got up and walked around; he was stiff and sore from his experience of the night before. He picked up the phone and dialed the concierge.

"Yes, Mr. Stone?"

"I wonder if you could arrange a massage for me in my suite?"

"Of course; what time?"

"As soon as possible."

"Male or female?"

"Female."

"Swedish or Japanese?"

"Swedish."

"Please hold for a moment; I'll check availability." He came back after a moment. "Sheila will be with you in an hour."

"Thank you." Stone hung up, watched two episodes of *This Old House* on television, then went to the bedroom, got undressed, and put on a robe. Shortly, there was a knock on the door, and a pretty girl came into the suite and set up a massage table in the bedroom.

"Let's start you facedown," she said.

Stone slipped out of the robe and lay on the table; she draped a small towel over his buttocks.

"Oh, you've got some cuts on your back," she said.

"An accident; can you work around them?"

"Sure; let me know if I hurt you."

She began kneading his back, and Stone gave himself to the experience. Soon, he was in a light sleep. Then the doorbell rang. "Would you get that, please?" he asked. "It's probably the maid; I forgot to put out the DO NOT DISTURB sign."

"Sure; I'll be right back." She left the bedroom.

Stone heard the door open and some whispering; then the door closed, and she came back. "Did you put out the sign?"

"Uh-huh," she said, then began rubbing his back.

He fell back into a doze, waking only long enough to turn over at her request. She put some sort of bean bag over his eyes as he turned, then he resettled the towel in the appropriate place and began to doze again. She rubbed his neck and his face, then began working her way down his body. She lingered over his nipples, which he thought was a little odd, but he was too comfortable to protest. Then he felt her remove the towel. *Oh, well,* he thought, *if she doesn't mind, I don't.*

She rubbed his belly, then his upper thighs, and, occasionally, her hand would touch his penis, as if by accident. Then it began to be clear that it was no accident. *What kind of service is the hotel running?* He heard her squirt some lotion on her hands and rub them vigorously together, then she touched him in a very deliberate way. In a moment, she was massaging more than he had counted on.

He opened his eyes, but the bean bag still covered them, and he closed them again. She went at her work gently, but firmly, and in seconds he was fully erect. His instinct was to reach out for her; he resisted that, but nothing else. Within a couple of minutes she brought him to a climax, then caressed him gently as his breathing returned to normal. Then she wiped him dry and kissed him gently on the lips.

"I'm going to wash my hands," she whispered. "You relax, and I'll be back in a minute.

He heard her close the bathroom door. He sat up and slipped into his robe. What was going on here? He'd never experienced anything quite like this. He supposed she would expect a *very* generous tip, and it seemed the least he could do. He got down from the table to get his wallet; then the bathroom door opened, and she came out.

His jaw dropped, and he was unable to say anything. Dolce Bianchi stood there, smiling at him.

"Did you enjoy your massage, sir?" she asked.

"I . . . I . . ."

"Oh, I believe you did," she said. "I'd like a drink; may I fix you something?"

"In the kitchenette," he said. "Whatever you're having."

She walked back into the living room as he tried to get his brain in gear, and he followed her. She returned with half a bottle of champagne and two flutes.

"Sit down and relax," she said, setting down the glasses and drawing the cork from the bottle. "You shouldn't exert yourself too soon after a massage."

Stone sat down, and she handed him a flute of champagne. "How did you . . . ?"

"I got your message, and I came right over," she said. "I didn't bother with the desk, just came right up, and when the masseuse came to the door, a couple of hundred persuaded her to leave early."

He was recovering, now, and he raised his glass. "To unexpected pleasures," he said.

She laughed. "Those are the best kinds." She sipped the champagne.

"You are certainly full of surprises," he said, because he couldn't think of anything else to say.

"Oh, I am," she agreed. "You must always remember that about me. I'm very forward, too. I don't hesitate when I want something."

"I don't have any trouble believing that," he said. "But how did you know I wouldn't jump up from the table, shocked?"

"I'm psychic about these things," she said.

"I'm a little psychic, myself," he said. "Would you like a reading?"

"Why not?"

He set down their glasses, then took both her hands and held them palm up, gazing at the lines. "I can see that you have very talented hands," he said.

She laughed aloud. "That's not very psychic," she said.

"You were foolish when you were young, but you're smarter, now."

"Dino told you about my marriage, no doubt."

"I see that you do useful work," he said. "That you are a giving person. That you give in your work."

She looked at him oddly. "Go on."

"Your work is somehow connected with the arts," he said. "But you are not an artist, exactly. No, but you help an artist—more than one, I see. Money is involved, to allow them to do their work."

Her black eyes narrowed; she seemed puzzled. "Dino couldn't have told you that," she said.

"There are paintings, many paintings; they are displayed in different settings—museums, perhaps. And there is a connection with television, perhaps art on television."

She tried to pull her hands away, but he held on to them. "I get an impression of thorns," he said. "A name that has something to do with thorns or briars."

She snatched her hands away. "Stop it, this is spooky."

Stone shrugged. "Merely a gift. Nothing to be superstitious about."

"How did you know all that?"

"I sensed it," he said.

She laughed. "For a moment, you had me believing you." She

sipped her champagne again, leaned toward him, and kissed him. "I believe you are in my debt," she said.

"I suppose I am, at that," he replied.

"I am not accustomed to waiting to be paid; and I always insist on interest."

"That seems only fair."

She stood up, reached behind her, and unzipped her dress. It fell at her feet, and she stepped out of it. She was wearing no bra, only stockings and a garter belt, with panties over them. She shucked off the panties and walked toward him.

He began to get up, but she pushed him back into a sitting position and straddled him. She pulled his head forward, and her scent filled his nostrils.

"First installment," she said huskily.

Stone paid up. For a moment, he wondered what he was getting himself into. Then he stopped worrying about it.

37

THE ROOM-SERVICE WAITER SET UP THE TABLE, OPENED the two bottles of wine, and left. "Dinner's ready," Stone called toward the bathroom, where Dolce was repairing her makeup.

She came out of the bathroom, still having not dressed, and sat down at the table.

Stone tasted the wine, then poured it. "I believe," he said, "this is the first time I've ever dined with a woman who was wearing only stockings, a garter belt, and high heels."

She raised her glass to him. "To the first of many new experiences to come."

"I'll drink to that," Stone replied, raising his glass. They began their dinner with a first course of pasta with a lobster sauce. "You are an extraordinarily beautiful woman," he said.

"I know," she replied. "I don't mean to sound arrogant, but I've been told that often enough to know that it's true. Perhaps it won't always be, but . . ."

"Yes, it will," Stone said. "When you finally get around to aging, many years from now, you will do it well."

"Why don't you take off the robe?" she asked. "I enjoy seeing you naked."

"I'm afraid I'll spill the pasta sauce," he said. "It's hot."

"Coward."

"Absolutely, where hot food and tender areas are concerned."

"I suppose you're right; I wouldn't want you wounded."

"Why do you want me any way at all?" he asked. "I'm not fishing for compliments; I'm just curious."

"To begin with," she said, "you are as beautiful as I am, in your way. Beautiful men are not exactly scarce, but beautiful, interesting men are. Why did you want me?"

"I didn't know I had a choice."

She laughed, a pleasant sound. "I suppose you didn't. Are you put off by my assertiveness?"

"Did I seem put off?"

She laughed again. "No, not in the *least*. To continue, I liked what I've heard about you from Mary Ann over the years. Dino wouldn't talk much, and he definitely wouldn't introduce us."

"I think Dino wanted to avoid complications."

"It is un-Italian to avoid complications," she said. "No, he just likes to keep his life, and his friends, as far from my father and me as possible. He disapproves of us."

"A difference in philosophies, as your father put it."

"Papa liked you," she said.

"He made me believe he did. I liked him, too."

"It is impossible not to like Papa, if he wants you to."

"A family trait."

"What are your ethnic origins?" she asked.

"English on both sides, if you can call that ethnic."

"Ah, yes, Barrington sounds very English." She cocked her head. "I find it difficult to believe that you were ever a cop."

"The NYPD found it difficult to believe, too. I didn't exactly fit in. Dino once told me that the NYPD was a fraternal lodge, and I never joined."

"Tell me about your family history."

"Both sides of my family, the Barringtons and the Stones, came from English Midlands to Massachusetts, in the early eighteenth century and established themselves in the weaving trade. In the nineteenth century, that grew into the textiles business. They were quite prosperous. My father had no wish to enter the family business; he loved woodworking, and it was all he wanted to do. His father, however, insisted that he go to Yale. My mother was sent to Mount Holyoke, to study art. When the stock market crash came, in twenty-nine, both families pretty well crashed with it. My father left Yale and moved to New York, where he met my mother, who was living in Greenwich Village, painting.

"They had known each other as children, and when they met again, they fell in love. My father began going house to house with his tools, looking for handyman's work. Eventually, he was able to open a small woodworking shop, and over the years he established a reputation as a maker of fine furniture. They had many left-wing friends, and my father actually joined the Communist Party during the Depression."

"I'm doing the math; they must have been quite late in life when you were born."

"Yes; I came as something of a surprise."

"Whatever happened to the family in Massachusetts?"

"It petered out, I suppose. My father was disowned for being a Communist; my mother was disowned for marrying my father. The only family member I ever had any real contact with was a great-aunt, on my mother's side, who, when she died, was kind enough to leave me her house in Turtle Bay."

"This is an honorable background," she said, "except for that business about Communism. But many good people were hoodwinked into joining in the thirties, I suppose."

"He never regretted holding Communist views. He regretted what the Party turned out to be." Stone looked at her narrowly. "Why do I get the feeling that I'm being interviewed for some position?"

"Perhaps you are, but not the one you are thinking of. I am a Catholic, and my father is a *devout* Catholic; I'm allowed only one husband."

"Somehow, I can't imagine you with a husband."

"Neither could my husband, after we'd been married a while."

"So what position am I being interviewed for?"

"I haven't decided," she said. "Why haven't you asked me any questions about my family?"

"I told you, I'm psychic; I already know what I need to."

"You mustn't joke about such things with an Italian girl; we take them seriously."

"I will always know more about you than you will want me to know," Stone said, and he hoped she would believe it, even if it weren't true. He thought he saw a tiny flicker of fear in her eyes.

"Please," she said.

They finished their first course, and Stone took their entrée, a crown roast of lamb, from the hot box under the table. Stone tasted the red wine and poured it.

"It's not Italian," she said, sniffing her glass.

"It's a California wine, perhaps made by Italians; it's called Far Niente."

"*Dolce far niente*," she said. "Sweet nothings." She sipped it. "It's delicious, and it's not even Italian."

"Does everything have to be Italian?"

"Not everything, but Papa believes that Italy is the most important country in the world, even though we have been here for four generations. He tends to think of anything not Italian as slight, of little weight."

"Do you feel the same way?"

"I am more American, but I understand his feelings."

"There is nothing Italian about me; what does your father think about that?"

"You are not wine or food or art or architecture."

"I'm not Catholic, either."

"He is not so concerned about that. In a strange way, he feels the family is protected by my divorce."

"Widowhood would free you, would it not?"

She smiled a little. "You are clever. The only reason my former husband is still alive is that my father does not want me to be free to marry again."

"I see."

"Why did you telephone today?"

"Your father gave me the number, in case I needed his help."

"And now you do?"

"Yes."

"Does Dino know?"

"Dino doesn't want to know."

"Your call was precipitated by the incident of last evening?"

"Yes."

"And where is the beautiful painter?"

"She has returned to her native England. She will not be back."

"Are you sad?"

"Less so than I was this morning."

"What help do you want from my father?"

"You know that this Mitteldorfer has disappeared?"

She nodded. "Papa has told me what he knows."

"Dino had a little flap with the captain of the guard at Sing Sing; because of that, I am unable to get any information from the prison that might help me find him. That, and the fact that Mitteldorfer managed the financial assets of the captain and the warden, and they are, shall we say, kindly disposed toward him."

"You want information from the prison?"

"Yes. There must have been prisoners who were close to Mitteldorfer; he was there for twelve years. Perhaps one or more of them might know something about his plans after he left prison."

"This can be done," she said. "It will take a few days, perhaps a week. Do you think you can stay alive that long?"

"I'll do my best."

"We seem to have finished our business and our dinner," she said. "Can we go back to bed, now?"

"We haven't had dessert."

"I'll give you dessert," she said.

38

STONE WOKE AROUND SEVEN, HAVING NOT HAD MUCH sleep, and found Dolce gone. There was a note on the dresser: "Thank you for an interesting evening. Let me know when you need more information, or another interesting evening. Dolce." Her phone numbers, office and home, were below.

Stone ordered some breakfast and read the *Times*. Again, he saw the theatrical advertisement by Judson Palmer. He cut it out and put it in his money clip. He checked out of the hotel at nine and ordered his car from the garage, checking the glove compartment to be sure the pistol was there, before relocking it. He consulted the theatrical ad; Palmer's theater was on West Forty-fourth Street, west of Sixth Avenue. He parked in the Hippodrome Garage at Forty-fourth and Sixth and walked to the theater. A janitor was sweeping out the lobby.

"Good morning," Stone said. "Can you tell me where to find Judson Palmer? Where his offices are?"

"They're right up there," the janitor said, pointing upward. He indicated a door. "Through there and up the stairs one flight."

Stone walked upstairs and emerged into a shabby waiting room, where a young woman was sitting at a desk, eating a Danish and drinking coffee. "Good morning," he said.

She had to swallow before she could speak. "Hi. What can I do for you?"

"I'd like to see Mr. Palmer."

"Are you an actor? We're already cast; we open this weekend."

"No, it's a matter of personal business."

"Does he owe you money?"

"No, nothing like that."

Stone heard footsteps coming up the stairs, and he turned to see a man in his fifties wearing a bush jacket walk into the room, carrying a brown bag. He was overweight and looked hungover. "Mr. Palmer?" he said.

"We're already cast," Palmer said, opening the door to his office. "Leave your picture and résumé with the girl; I'll consider you for the next show."

"I'm not an actor," Stone said. "My name is Stone Barrington."

"Sounds like an actor," Palmer said, pausing in the doorway. "What do you want?"

"It's in connection with a man named Mitteldorfer."

Palmer winced. "Are you a reporter?"

"No, and I think you should hear what I have to tell you."

"All right, come on in," Palmer said.

Stone followed him into the room, which was decorated with posters from Palmer's previous shows. The place had a temporary look; Stone thought that Palmer must move his office from theater to theater, with his shows.

Palmer indicated a chair, then he took coffee and a bagel from his brown bag. "That's a name I haven't heard for a long time," he said. "What's that guy got to do with me?"

Stone sat down. "I'm aware that you had an affair with his wife some years back, and that, as a result, Mitteldorfer murdered her."

"I won't confirm or deny that," Palmer said. "Are you a lawyer?"

"Yes, but I'm not here in a legal capacity. I used to be a police officer; I arrested Herbert Mitteldorfer for his wife's murder. At the time, we didn't know with whom she'd been having an affair, so we didn't talk to you."

"Why now? Mitteldorfer's in prison, isn't he?"

"No."

Palmer stopped chewing the bagel. "Then he must be dead."

"No. He was released from prison recently."

"Jesus Christ," Palmer said. "I thought he went away for life."

"At the time, life didn't necessarily mean life; there was no life sentence without the possibility of parole."

Palmer put down the bagel and sipped his coffee; he looked worried.

"Tell me, Mr. Palmer, did Herbert Mitteldorfer know with whom his wife was having the affair?"

Palmer swallowed hard. "I don't know, for sure," he said. "Arlene thought he was onto us, though. She didn't know if he knew who I was. I was a client of the firm where he worked; I met her when she came into the office one day. It was the only time he saw us together, that I know of, and that was very casual. In fact, Herbie introduced us. Something passed between Arlene and me, though, and I waited outside for her. When she came down, I asked her out for a drink."

"How long did it go on?"

"Four or five months, I guess; right up until she . . . died."

"Did you ever write her any letters?"

"No."

"Might she have had your business card?"

"No. If you're screwing somebody else's wife, you don't give her things like that; you're more careful."

"Just how careful were you?"

"Very. I never went to her place, and she never came to mine. I had an office in the Schubert Building at the time, and she used to come up there. I had a little bedroom and a shower; I was living in Scarsdale, married, and I'd stay in town two or three nights a week."

"Were you in love with her?"

"Not really. I liked her a lot, though; she was a nice girl in a bad marriage."

"Was she in love with you?"

"She was in love with the idea of getting out of her marriage," Palmer replied. "She knew I was married, but she knew mine was rocky, too, that I wanted out."

"So she looked upon you as a way out?"

"Maybe, but I tried to discourage that. I knew that if I got a divorce, it was going to cost me most of what I had. I was right about that."

"Did she talk about her marriage much?"

"Some; you know what women are like in those circumstances, don't you?"

"Not really; tell me."

"She'd complain about him, about how finicky he was about everything—their apartment, his clothes, *her* clothes. Apparently, he was very good with money, but she complained that she had no control over the money she'd brought to the marriage, which was considerable, I think. She was afraid that if she divorced him, she wouldn't be able to get the money back, and it was all she had. Her parents were dead. That's about all she ever told me about him."

"Did she see a lawyer?"

"Yeah, just a day or so before she was killed."

"Do you know his name?"

Palmer wrinkled his brow. "I used to know it; he was a well-known divorce lawyer at the time—even bigger, now. I see his name in the papers now and then."

"It would help if you could remember it."

Palmer looked at Stone. "Help who? What's your interest in this?"

"Mitteldorfer disappeared after he got out of prison. I'm trying to find him."

"Why?"

"I want to put him back in prison."

"Goldsmith," Palmer said.

"Bruce Goldsmith?"

"That's the one. He's a big-time divorce lawyer, isn't he?"

"Yes, he is." Stone had gone to law school with him.

"Look, tell me what's going on, will you?"

"It looks as though Mitteldorfer is taking revenge on people he thinks have wronged him."

Palmer rested his face in his hands. "Oh, Jesus. I can't get involved in this. Investors are hard enough to find; if my name turns up in the papers . . ."

"Mitteldorfer may already be responsible for the deaths of half a dozen people, including a police officer who happened to get in the way. He seems to be attacking people he thinks of as enemies and . . . people close to them. Did you see the story in the *Times* about the bombing at a gallery opening on Wednesday?"

"Oh, shit, yes. And I've got an opening tomorrow night."

Stone wrote down Dino's name and number on the back of his card and handed the paper to Palmer. "This is the detective in charge of the investigation; he was my partner in the murder investigation. I'd suggest that you get in touch with him, tell him about your past association with Mitteldorfer's wife, and ask for his help."

"But what if Mitteldorfer doesn't know who I am?"

"Then you should have nothing to worry about."

"But if he does . . . ?"

"Then, in addition to calling Lieutenant Bacchetti, I'd hire some private security for your opening."

"Oh, God." Palmer moaned, resting his head on his arms.

"My number's on the card, too; I'd appreciate a call if you think of anything else that might help me find Mitteldorfer. Good luck with your opening."

Palmer said nothing. Stone left his office.

"Maybe you should be an actor," the young woman at the reception desk said. "You're good-looking enough."

Stone smiled at her. "You, too," he said.

39

STONE DROVE OUT OF THE GARAGE AND CALLED INFOR-
mation for Bruce Goldsmith's number, using the hands-free
phone. He remembered that he and Goldsmith had once been rivals
for a girl, and that Goldsmith had lost. He dialed the number.

"Goldsmith, Craven, and Moyle," a woman said.

"Bruce Goldsmith, please. My name is Stone Barrington."

"Are you a client, Mr. Barrington?"

"No. An old acquaintance. Tell Mr. Goldsmith that it's important
that I speak to him right away."

"Just a moment."

There was a very long delay, time enough for Stone to get onto
the West Side Highway, before Goldsmith came on the line.

"Hello, Stone, what can I do for you?" he asked, sounding in a hurry.

Stone remembered that Bruce Goldsmith had always been in a
hurry. "Hello, Bruce; how have you been all these years?"

"I can't complain. What can I do for you?"

"I can't complain, either."

"Stone, I don't have much time; what is it?"

"You remember, about twelve years ago, a woman named Arlene
Mitteldorfer came to see you about a divorce?"

There was a long silence.

"Bruce, you still there?"

"What's this about, Stone?"

"I take it you remember her. You may also remember that she was murdered a day or two after you saw her."

"How do you know about this?"

"I ask a lot of questions. What I want to know is, what did she say about her husband in that meeting?"

"I remember that you were the arresting officer. You know very well I can't discuss that with you; the conversation was privileged; otherwise, I'd have called you at the time."

"She's been dead for twelve years, Bruce; privilege shouldn't be a problem."

"My notes from those days are in storage in Queens. It would take weeks to find them."

"I don't want your notes, Bruce; I just want to know what you remember about that meeting. Mitteldorfer is out of prison, and I'm trying to find him. I'm hoping you can tell me something that might help."

"I don't remember much."

"She was a beautiful woman, Bruce. I'm sure you remember the meeting very well."

"I don't see why I should violate a confidence to help you, Stone."

"Let me give you a reason, Bruce: it appears that Herbert Mitteldorfer is going around New York City, killing people who have annoyed him in the past, and, sometimes, their friends. We're at six bodies, and counting. If you gave her advice that might have been to his disadvantage, and I'm sure you did, then he might very well be annoyed with *you*."

There was only a brief silence, and then Goldsmith was talking. "I took her to lunch; she was gorgeous, and I didn't mind being seen with her. She told me her husband had appropriated the money her father had left her, and that she wanted to divorce him and get the money back. She wanted to know if that was possible, and I told her it certainly was. My recollection is that we were talking about something in the range of three or four million dollars, plus an apartment her father had given them when they got married. She was worried that he might become violent. I advised her to move out of the house immediately and file for divorce. I told her I could get her the apartment back very quickly, and she'd be able to move back in during the proceedings. She said she'd get back to me. I never heard from her again."

"Did you sleep with her, Bruce?"

"That's hardly relevant to this conversation."

"It is, if she told her husband about it. Spouses tend to spit out these things in the middle of domestic quarrels."

"Yeah, all right, I fucked her. We had lunch at a little hotel in the Sixties; I kept a room there, at the time."

"Was there anything else she said about her marriage, anything at all?"

Goldsmith thought for a moment. "Yeah, there was: she said she thought her husband had another wife, that he was a bigamist."

"Did she say who or where the other wife was?"

"No; we were . . . getting involved about that time, and we didn't get back to that. I would have asked her, of course, if she had called me back."

"Of course."

"Stone?"

"Yeah?"

"Should I watch my back?"

"Bruce, if I were you, I'd leave town; that's what I'm doing."

"Hang on," Goldsmith said. "Millie, tell Moyle that I'll do the deposition in San Francisco, and get his plane ticket changed to my name. He's on the two o'clock flight, isn't he? I don't care what he says, just do it." He came back to Stone. "Thanks, pal, I appreciate the warning."

"And I appreciate your recollections," Stone said, feeling slightly soiled from having received them. He hung up and called Dino. He was headed north on the Saw Mill River Parkway.

"Bacchetti," Dino said.

"It's Stone. You may get a call from a guy named Palmer, who . . ."

"I just did."

"So, you're on top of that?"

"You bet I am. Anything else come up?"

"Yes. Arlene Mitteldorfer saw a divorce lawyer right before she was murdered. He told me that she said she thought Herbie had another wife."

"Before her?"

"*During* her."

"Herbie was a bigamist?"

"Could be. I don't know if the marriage records were computerized that long ago, but it might be worth doing a search; I'd sure like to talk to the other Mrs. Mitteldorfer. Maybe she's hiding him."

"I'm on it," Dino said.

"I'm on the way to Connecticut, now; let me give you the numbers up there; they'll be working later today." Stone gave him the numbers and his new car-phone number. "I'll be in the car for another hour and a half if you need to reach me."

Stone continued up the Saw Mill, through a bright, spring day, with new, green leaves on the trees. It was a winding road and fun to drive on.

He called his own number and tapped in the code for the answering machine. The mechanical voice said, *You have two messages. One:*

"Hi, it's Dolce. The Carlyle said you'd checked out. I don't know if you have any plans for the weekend; if not, call me, and we'll do something interesting."

Two:

"Stone, it's Vance Calder; I hope you're well. Arrington and I are in the East this weekend, and we'd like you to join us for dinner, if you're free. We'd both love to see you, and, of course, you haven't seen the baby yet, and we'd like you to. Please call me." He left a number.

Stone found the breath momentarily sucked out of him. He had known that this would happen, eventually, but he hadn't expected them to turn up in town this soon. He wasn't sure he could handle this, and he was going to be in the country, anyway, so he had an excuse not to see them. He dialed the number.

Transferring your call, a recorded voice said. There were some beeps, then the phone rang. A woman, not Arrington, answered.

"Hello?"

"May I speak to Vance Calder, please?"

"Who's calling?"

"My name is Stone Barrington; I'm returning his call."

"Just a moment."

A few seconds later, Vance came on the phone. "Stone, how are you?" he asked, sounding enthusiastic.

Stone tried to match his tone. "I'm very well, Vance; how are you and Arrington and the baby?"

"We're just wonderful, all of us. Do you think we might get together for dinner this weekend?"

"I'd love to, Vance, I really would, but as we speak, I'm on my way to the country."

"Where in the country?"

"I've bought a little house in Washington, Connecticut."

"Well, there's a coincidence; we're at my place in Roxbury right now, and that's the village next door to Washington."

Stone hadn't been aware that Vance had a place in Connecticut. "Gosh, Vance, I'm just moving in today, and . . ."

"Well, then, by tomorrow night, you're going to need a break and a hot dinner. Give me your new address, and I'll send my car for you."

"I can drive over, I guess. Give me some directions." He juggled his notebook while driving and wrote down the address.

"About seven, then?"

"All right, about seven."

"It'll be very casual, and by all means, bring somebody, if you'd like."

"Thanks, Vance; see you then." He hung up. *Well, all right,* he thought; *we're all civilized people; we can get through this.* Then it occurred to him that he'd rather not get through it alone. He dialed Dolce's office number and was put through to her immediately.

"Hello, there," she purred.

"Hi, I got your message."

"Any plans for the weekend?"

"Actually, yes, but why don't you join me? I would have asked you this morning, but you had gone when I woke up."

"What did you have in mind?"

"I've just bought a place in Connecticut, and I'm moving in this afternoon. By tomorrow night I should have been able to make some sense of it, so why don't you drive up tomorrow? Oh, there's dinner with a movie star, tomorrow night, too."

"Which movie star?"

"That'll be a surprise. Get a pencil, and I'll give you some very precise directions."

She wrote them down. "How long will it take me?"

"Under two hours, from midtown."

"I should be able to leave here by two."

"See you around four, then." They hung up.

Suddenly, he felt very much better about the following evening.

40

BRUCE GOLDSMITH STARTED PACKING HIS BRIEFCASE. "Millie, get in here!" he shouted. His secretary came in with a pad. "Where was Moyle staying?"

"At the Ritz-Carlton; he's got a club-level room reserved."

"Change it to a suite, a big one; the client can afford it, and have a car meet me at the airport—a Mercedes, not a Lincoln."

"Right," she said, making notes rapidly.

Goldsmith's partner, Lester Moyle, walked into the office. "What the hell is going on?" he asked.

"I'm taking the San Francisco deposition," Goldsmith said.

"The hell you are; that's *my* client."

"And who gave her to you?"

"Listen, Bruce, I don't know what's going on, here, but this is very high-handed, and I'm not going to put up with it."

"Les, shut up and give Millie your notes; I don't give a shit whether you like it or not; I'm doing the deposition."

"That tears it for me, Bruce," Moyle said. "I'm sick of your prima donna act. You want to buy me out of the firm?"

"That's fine by me, you little prick," Goldsmith rejoined. "You know the formula by heart, I expect; figure out what your share is

209

worth and draw up the agreement. Fax it to me in San Francisco, and I'll sign."

"I'm taking my clients," Moyle said.

"The hell you are; read our contract. You walk out of here, you do it alone. If you try to take a single client with you, I'll lock you up in a lawsuit that'll set you back years, and you know I can do it. Now get out of my office."

Moyle stalked out of the room, swearing.

"Anything else?" Millie asked.

"Yeah, what was that woman's name—I did her divorce from the winery owner a couple of years ago? She took her maiden name back."

"Madeleine Cochran."

"Right. Get her on the phone for me."

Millie went back to her desk; a moment later the phone in Goldsmith's office buzzed. "She's on the line," Millie said.

Goldsmith picked up the phone. "Maddy? How the hell are you?"

"I'm all right, Bruce; what a surprise to hear from you."

"Well, I haven't been west for a while, but I've suddenly gotten yanked into a deposition in San Francisco, and I'll be there tonight. Why don't you and I have dinner, and we'll catch up."

"Uh, Bruce, you're still married, aren't you?"

"Barely; I'm filing for divorce as soon as I get back. It's been hell; I'll tell you about it tonight."

"I don't want to poach another woman's game, Bruce. I still feel guilty about that one time during my divorce."

"I'm telling you, Maddy, it's over, and I really, really need to see you."

"Oh, all right; where and what time?"

"Seven-thirty at the Ritz-Carlton?"

"Which restaurant?"

"I'll have a suite; we'll order in."

"You're very naughty, Bruce."

"Just ask at the desk; see you then, babe." Goldsmith hung up, chuckling. "Millie, get me my wife." A moment later, his phone buzzed. "Ellen? It's me. Listen, we've just had a big blowup here; Les Moyle has just walked out of the firm, leaving me with a critical deposition to do."

"Oh, Bruce, you're not going to fink out on this dinner party tonight," his wife said, horrified. "I arranged this for your benefit, not mine."

"Sweetie, I know, and I'm really sorry, but Les has left me up the creek, with nobody else to handle this but me."

"Surely, you can spare a couple of hours for your guests."

"Sweetheart, by dinnertime, I'll be in San Francisco."

"Oh, Jesus; for how long?"

"At least a week, maybe more; this is a big one, major money."

"Bruce, we've got the Willards coming to Easthampton this weekend! You're supposed to be entertaining them."

"Call them and explain, will you? I'll be working straight through the weekend with the client; I've got a lot of catching up to do on this case. Damn Moyle for doing this to us!"

"Oh, God, how am I going to face these people tonight?"

"You'll manage, sweetie; you're the greatest hostess in New York, you know."

"You will be back for the school play, won't you? Helen is starring, and she's so counting on you."

"I'll move heaven and earth, if I can. Listen, pack me a bag, will you? The works, dinner jacket, too."

"*Dinner jacket*? I thought this was a deposition!"

"The client wants me to meet some important people next week. Could be great for business."

"I hate you for this," she said.

"Baby, I know how you feel, and I promise, I'll make it up to you. How about Tuscany this summer? And listen, will you just leave my suitcases with the doorman? I'm rushing to the airport, and I don't even have time to come upstairs."

"Oh, all right!" She slammed down the phone.

Goldsmith buzzed his secretary. "Millie, call Pebble Beach and get me a two o'clock tee time tomorrow, and book me into the Inn, a nice suite, ocean view. Talk to the manager, if you have to; tell him it's for me. And call the car and tell Mike to be sure my clubs are in the trunk; if they're not, tell Pebble Beach to keep a set of Callaways for me—the tungsten-titanium irons, nothing else."

"I've got your deposition case packed. Anything else?"

"I think that'll do it." Goldsmith hung up and dialed his urologist's number, then got his secretary on the line. "Hey, sweetheart, how are you?"

"Fine, Mr. Goldsmith."

"Listen, big favor; my wife and I are off to San Francisco this afternoon, kind of a second honeymoon. Will you call the Ritz-Carlton out there, get the name of a drugstore, and phone in a Viagra prescription for me?"

"Sure, how many?"

"Oh, a couple of dozen ought to do it—ho, ho, ho! Ask them to deliver them to my suite."

"I'll take care of it; you and Mrs. Goldsmith have a wonderful time."

"Don't you worry, with your help we will. See ya." Goldsmith closed his briefcase, grabbed his jacket, and headed for the door. "Is Mike downstairs with the car?"

"Yes, and your golf clubs are in the trunk."

"Okay, I'm going to be gone a week, maybe two; cancel anything that can wait or that I can't handle with a phone and a fax machine, and get Craven to take care of the rest. Tell him about Moyle's leaving, and by the way, as soon as Les goes to lunch, clean out any files in his desk and briefcase, padlock his filing cabinets, and put his Rolodex in my safe, got it?" Without waiting for an answer, he grabbed his deposition case and left the office.

"Got it, you complete and total shit," Millie muttered under her breath.

Goldsmith rode down in the elevator, feeling nothing but elation.

In one fell swoop, he had rid himself of a law partner who had always put too much emphasis on ethics, gotten out of a boring dinner party and an awful weekend, built a two-week vacation for himself in his favorite city and at Pebble Beach, and lined up a spectacular piece of ass that he had never had enough of. He felt *very* pleased with himself.

Mike was waiting at the curb with the rear door of the BMW 750i already open. Goldsmith handed him the two briefcases to be put into the trunk and slid into the rear seat. Mike closed the door after him and walked to the rear of the car.

Goldsmith looked to his right and saw a black Lincoln Town Car standing shockingly close—no more than an inch from his new BMW. He punched the window button and screamed at the driver of the Lincoln, whose face was only inches from his. "Goddamnit! You put one fucking scratch on this car, and I'll have your ass in court!"

The driver turned calmly toward him and raised something that looked, from Goldsmith's perspective, like a short length of black pipe. He didn't even have time to flinch; the *pfffft!* noise was the last thing he heard.

41

STONE DROPPED BY THE KLEMM REAL ESTATE OFFICE in Washington Depot, which was the business district, a mile from Washington Green, and picked up the keys to his new house.

Carolyn Klemm greeted him with enthusiasm and presented him with a cold bottle of good champagne and a list of tradesmen, repairmen, gardeners, and other necessary help for any homeowner.

He stopped at the Washington Market and picked up some groceries for the weekend, then at the local liquor shop, where he bought a mixed case of wines, half a dozen bottles of spirits, and some mixers. Finally, very excited, he drove up the hill, turned left at the church, and, a couple of hundred yards later, rolled past the fringe of evergreen trees and into his own driveway. It was the first house he had ever bought.

He got out of the car, unlocked the front door, and walked inside. The place was cavernously empty and spotlessly clean. He unloaded his groceries and booze, put the perishables and white wines into the fridge, then carried his suitcases upstairs and unpacked, placing his things in the smaller of the two master closets, both of which contained drawers and shelves.

He walked back downstairs to find the UPS deliveryman on his doorstep, and the man trundled half a dozen large boxes into the kitchen, got a signature, and left. Stone began unpacking the dishes, pots and pans, and other housewares he and Sarah had bought, but before he got very far, the ABC Furniture van arrived, and most of the next hour was spent distributing furniture around the house. When the deliverymen had left, he went back to work in the kitchen, and in another hour he had it organized.

He was upstairs putting the new sheets on his new bed when the phone man arrived. Stone put him to work, then went back to his own tasks. He had just finished putting the bedroom and bath in order when the phone man pronounced himself finished. Stone tried the various extensions around the house, heard a dial tone at each, thanked the man, and signed off on the installation. He did some straightening of the new furniture, lamented the lack of pictures and other ornaments in the place, then treated himself to a beer. He had just sat down when the phone rang.

"Hello?"

"It's Dino; I've been trying to reach you."

"The phone just got turned on; what's up?"

"You said you spoke to Arlene Mitteldorfer's divorce lawyer earlier today?"

"That's right."

"Was his name Bruce Goldsmith?"

"Yes, and what do you mean, 'was'?"

"He got popped at lunchtime, less than an hour after you and I spoke."

"How did it happen?"

"He was leaving his office for a trip to San Francisco. He got into his car, a black Town Car pulled alongside, and somebody put one round into his head at point-blank range. No noise, probably a silencer. Got the backseat of a nice, new BMW all messy."

"Jesus; I warned him to get out of town; I guess he didn't go fast enough."

"I guess not."

"Don't tell anybody where I am, okay, Dino?"

"Who else knows?"

"Just a girl, who's coming up tomorrow, Bill Eggers, and Vance Calder and Arrington."

"They're in town?"

"No, they're up here; Vance has a house less than five miles from mine. I'm having dinner with them tomorrow night."

Dino gave a long chuckle. "She can't stay away from you, can she?"

"Nothing like that; Vance wants us all to be friends. Come to think of it, she said something to that effect in the last conversation I had with her, last year."

"You're a braver man than I am, Stone, going to their house all by yourself."

"I'm not going by myself; I'll be well armed with a beautiful woman."

"Anybody I know?"

"Nah; a new lady." He half expected Dino to call him on the lie.

"This is all too civilized for me," Dino said.

"What are you doing about Palmer's opening on tomorrow night?"

"Maximum effort; the department finally believes me about this business."

"It's about time. Have you put out an APB on Mitteldorfer?"

"I'm not at that point, yet; we don't really have any hard evidence on him, nothing to tie him to these crimes but our suppositions and a lot of bodies."

"I think you ought to get his most recent prison photograph into the Sunday papers, along with the artist's drawing of the hit man. You can say that Mitteldorfer may be in danger, and you want to talk with him. At least, that'll get his face out there, and you might get a tip from a citizen."

"Good idea; I don't think I'll ask the brass; I know a guy at the *Times*. How's the house?"

"The stuff Sarah and I bought all arrived, and I've spent the afternoon making it habitable. Still needs a lot of pictures and lamps and other things."

"Have a good weekend; when you coming back?"

"I don't know; I may not come back at all; at least, not until Mitteldorfer has popped you, and I have to look for him, myself."

"Don't hold your breath, kid; he's not going to get a crack at Dino. The department has lent me a special car, not unlike your own."

"A Mercedes?"

"No, just a Crown Victoria that could take a hit from a tank. They've been using it to transport VIPs to and from the UN."

"That's good news."

"You bet it is. I gotta go."

"Keep me posted."

Dino hung up, and so did Stone. Immediately, the phone rang again.

"Hello?"

"Stone? It's Carolyn Klemm; how are you coming with the house?"

"It's in pretty good shape for the first day, I think."

"My husband, David, and I are going to grab a bite at our local joint, the George Washington Tavern; why don't you join us? It's real casual, and a lot of the weekend crowd will be there."

"Thanks, I think I'd like that," Stone replied.

"Want us to pick you up?"

"Just give me directions; I'll meet you."

"Go back down the hill to the Depot, cross the river, then a right at the intersection, and you'll see it on your right. About seven?"

"See you there." Stone hung up, relieved not to have to spend his first evening in Connecticut alone.

Pity about Bruce Goldsmith, he thought. *But not much of a pity.*

42

STONE ARRIVED AT THE RESTAURANT AND FOUND THE parking lot nearly full. He found a spot and went inside. Carolyn Klemm spotted him from a seat near the fireplace and waved him over.

"This is my husband, David," she said.

Stone shook David Klemm's hand.

"Welcome to Washington," David said. "You're going to love it."

They ordered drinks and got a menu. Stone was facing the restaurant's entrance, and he looked up to see Captain Warkowski, from Sing Sing, enter the room, in company with a middle-aged woman. Warkowski saw him and nodded; Stone nodded back. The couple were taken to a booth in the back room.

"Somebody you know?" Carolyn asked.

"Not very well; I met him in passing, once."

"A local?"

"No, he's from New York State, I think; that's where I met him, anyway."

"We saw the story in the *Times* about the bombing of Sarah's opening—a terrible business," Carolyn said. "Is she all right?"

"Yes, she is."

"When can we expect to see her here?"

"Sarah's gone back to England; she's planning to live there."

"Oh, I'm sorry; somehow I thought you would be sharing the cottage."

"That was the plan, but the incident at the gallery changed her mind, I think."

"Well, we'll have to have a few single women to dinner," Carolyn said. "There aren't many around, but there are a couple of very nice divorcées."

"Oh, don't bother," Stone said.

"No, we'd like to have you to dinner; we entertain a lot. Leave it to me."

They ordered dinner, and a procession of arriving diners stopped by their table. The Klemms introduced Stone to a dozen people in a matter of minutes, giving a running account of who they were. Most of them were New Yorkers, up for the weekend, like Stone.

"Do you know anyone at all up here?" Carolyn asked.

"Just some people from California who have a house in Roxbury."

"That would be the Calders."

"Why, yes; how did you know?"

"I sold Vance the house about four years ago. Of course, he's pulled it apart and put it back together since then. He's a charming man, isn't he?"

"Yes, he is."

"How do you know them?"

"A mutual friend introduced me to them a couple of years ago at a dinner party. Then I saw something of them in LA last year and got to know Vance a little better."

"Oh, I haven't met Mrs. Calder yet; her name is Arrington, isn't it?"

"That's right."

Dinner was served, and they began to eat.

"I hear she's lovely; she was a writer before they married, wasn't she?"

"Yes, she wrote for several magazines."

"And I read in the paper that they have a new baby."

"Right, again. You don't miss much, Carolyn."

David spoke up. "You might say that Carolyn is the unofficial historian of Litchfield County."

"You're going to love Vance's house," Carolyn said. "It's really something."

"I can't wait to see it," Stone replied. They finished their first course. Stone looked into the back room and saw Warkowski's companion leave the table, apparently for the ladies' room. Stone stood up. "Will you excuse me for a moment? I'll be right back."

He walked into the back room and stopped at Warkowski's table. "Good evening," he said. "Do you mind if I sit down for a moment?"

Warkowski looked up at him. "Suit yourself."

Stone slid into the booth opposite him. "You live around here?"

Warkowski shook his head. "Just a weekend outing with the wife."

"I'm sorry I didn't get to see you the last time I was at the prison."

"I was pretty busy at the time," Warkowski said.

"Look, I know that Dino got off on the wrong foot with you, but there's something really serious going on, and we need your help."

"We?"

"Dino and I are both involved."

"What is it?"

"We need to find Herbert Mitteldorfer, and quickly."

"I've no idea where he is," Warkowski replied. "He didn't leave a forwarding address."

"Is there anyone you know who might have a way of contacting him?"

Warkowski shook his head. "Nope."

"I'm surprised that you would so quickly lose contact with him. After all, you were pretty close, weren't you?"

"Not really; in my work, you don't get close to prisoners."

"That's what I would have thought, but it's my information that Mitteldorfer handled all your financial affairs for several years."

Warkowski looked at him sharply. "Where the hell did you hear that?"

"Look, Captain, we think that Mitteldorfer has been involved in half a dozen murders since he got out."

Warkowski burst out laughing. "You've gotta be kidding! Herbie Mitteldorfer wouldn't hurt a fly!"

"He murdered his wife, didn't he?"

"That was a kind of temporary insanity; you can hardly blame the guy, in the circumstances."

"What circumstances?"

"His wife was screwing half the men in New York."

"Anybody in particular?"

"I don't know the details," Warkowski replied.

"Look, Captain, this is a very serious matter. It wouldn't look good for it to get into the papers that a serial killer performed personal services for officials at the prison."

"Are you threatening me?" Warkowski asked. "Because if you are, you'd better be able to back it up."

"I'm not threatening you; I'm just saying that we need your help in finding Mitteldorfer."

"What's this 'we' stuff? You're not a cop, and Bacchetti hasn't asked for my help. If I get an official request from the NYPD, I'll respond to it. I've got nothing at all to say to you, except that I have no knowledge of Mitteldorfer's whereabouts. I will give you a piece of advice though: Herbert Mitteldorfer is a sweet guy, a decent man who deserves to be able to live out his life with some privacy. I don't believe he could ever be involved in killing anybody, and I'll testify to that in court, if necessary."

Stone looked up and saw Mrs. Warkowski returning. He got up. "I'm sorry to have bothered you, Captain. I hope you don't end up with blood on your hands." He walked back to his own table.

The main course had been served, and Stone sat down.

"Another minute, and your food would have been cold," Carolyn said.

"Looks good," Stone said, digging in.

"Is everything all right?" Carolyn asked. "You look a little depressed."

"I'm fine," Stone said. "I was just thinking about something back in New York. This is delicious food."

"Do you play golf?" David asked.

"No, golf is difficult if you live in Manhattan."

"We've got a beautiful nine-hole course here. If you'd like to play sometime, let me know."

"Thanks, perhaps I will." Stone looked up to see Warkowski and his wife leaving the restaurant.

"Your friends didn't seem to be here long enough for dinner," Carolyn said.

"I guess he lost his appetite," Stone replied.

43

STONE SLEPT WELL BUT WOKE UP DISORIENTED. HE SAT up and blinked, wondering where he was, but after a few seconds it came to him. He was in his new cottage, in Connecticut, and he needed pictures on the walls.

He got up, showered, and made breakfast, missing the morning *Times*. He looked at Carolyn Klemm's list and found the delivery service. He'd have to arrange that and also subscribe to the local paper, the *Litchfield County Times*. Then Warkowski came back into his mind. He picked up the phone and called Dino.

"Yeah?" Dino said sleepily.

"Come on, Dino, it's nearly nine o'clock; wake up."

"I'm awake," Dino said. "You are one stupid son of a bitch, do you know that?"

"What, I get up too early for you?"

"I'm talking about Dolce."

"What about her?"

"I warned you about her, but you just had to go and . . ."

"Oh, come on, Dino; she seems like a nice enough girl."

"You're *way* out of your depth there, pal, I'm telling you."

"Dino, she's a beautiful, bright woman."

"She's coming up there today, isn't she?"

"How do you know all this stuff?"

"She has a sister; she talks to her."

"Oh." He hadn't, after all, asked her not to tell Mary Ann. "Listen, I ran into Warkowski at dinner last night."

"*Père* or *fils*?"

"*Père*."

"You had dinner at Sing Sing?"

"No, Warkowski and his wife were over here on what he called a weekend outing—the Mayflower Inn makes it a popular destination. We happened to be in the same restaurant."

"Great. What did he have for dinner?"

"Dino, listen; you need to make an official request of Warkowski for information as to Mitteldorfer's whereabouts."

"I'm not going to ask that bastard for anything. And what makes you think he would help?"

"Even if he ignores you, the request will be on the record; you'll have covered your ass."

"And it's worth covering. You're right; I'll fax him. You talked to the guy?"

"Yes, I asked him if he knew where Mitteldorfer was, and he said no. He was unhelpful, but he said if you sent him an official request, he'd respond."

"Yeah, I know what his response will be. What else did you tell him?"

"That I knew Mitteldorfer had done his investing for him."

"Did he deny it?"

"No, but he didn't confirm it, either."

"Well, let's see what you accomplished, then: first, now Warkowski knows everything we know, right? Second, in the event that Warkowski does know where Mitteldorfer is and is communicating with him, now Mitteldorfer knows we're looking for him."

"He'll know that when the *Times* story comes out. But you're right; I shouldn't have told Warkowski that we knew about the investing. I thought it might help his memory, but it didn't."

"Something else, kiddo: if he does talk to Mitteldorfer, he's going to tell him that you're in Washington, Connecticut, and I thought you didn't want him to know that."

Stone winced. "Okay, I was stupid."

"I believe I mentioned that earlier in our conversation."

"Don't rub it in."

"Mitteldorfer is going to rub it in, if he finds out where you are. You'd better watch your ass."

"I will, but Warkowski doesn't know I have a house here; for all he knows, I'm just visiting for the weekend, as he is."

"I hope you're right, pal. And I hope you survive the weekend with Dolce."

"Is there anything else I need to know about her?"

"I told you all you had to know to avoid trouble; the rest, you're just going to have to learn for yourself."

"Okay, Dino; I'll talk to you later."

"Good luck, Stone; you're going to need it."

Stone called about the newspapers, then got dressed and drove down to the Depot. He went into the Washington Supply, the hardware store, and bought a toolbox and an assortment of tools for the house.

"Guess you're Stone Barrington," the man at the counter said.

"That's right," Stone replied, surprised.

"Guess you'll be needing a charge account."

"Don't mind if I do; can I have an application?"

"Don't need an application."

"How about my address?"

"Know your address."

Stone picked up a map of the area, signed for the tools, and went back to his car, figuring that he had a lot to learn about small, New England towns.

He spread out the map and recognized a familiar name: New Preston. He'd heard something about antiques there. Following the map, he drove up a hill, down another, crossed a highway, and came to an attractive village. An hour later, he'd bought two lamps, three pictures, all local landscapes, and a shopping bag full of small items.

He continued along the road and came to a large lake—Lake Waramaug, the map said. He followed the winding road around the lake, enjoying the sun on the water and the views of the hills, and ended up back where he started. He drove back to Washington and had lunch at the Pantry, a restaurant and kitchen supply shop, where he bought a few more things for his kitchen, plus a couple of cheeses from a large display.

Back at the house he hung the pictures, plugged in the lamps, and started looking for things to fix with his new tools. He didn't find much. The place was newly renovated, and everything appeared to have been taken care of.

He fixed himself a lunch of bread and cheese, then stretched out for a nap on the living-room sofa, to await the arrival of the reputedly evil Dolce.

44

STONE WAS AWAKENED BY A NOISE RESEMBLING THE
start of the Indianapolis 500. He sat up, rubbing his eyes, wondering what the hell was going on. The noise died, and he heard a
car door slam; by the time he got to the front door, Dolce was standing there, her arms full of things. A bright red Ferrari was parked
next to Stone's car.

"Is this the Barrington mansion?" she asked, peeking inside.

"It is," Stone replied. "Won't you step inside, madam?"

"Try mademoiselle," she said, coming into the house, "or better
yet, signorina."

Stone took her packages inside, while she went back to the car.
She returned with an armful of flowers and a large vase. "I suspected
the place would need brightening," she said, handing him the vase.
"Fill that two-thirds with tepid water."

Stone did as instructed, and she quickly arranged the flowers
and set them on the living-room coffee table. "There; makes all the
difference, doesn't it?"

"It certainly does. What's in the packages?"

"Housewarming gifts," she replied. "Open."

Stone opened the packages and found two beautiful oils, a

Venetian scene and a landscape he didn't recognize, with a Roman ruin prominently featured.

"They're beautiful," he said, kissing her. "Where's the landscape?"

"Sicily, where else?"

"They're both wonderful. I'll get some tools, and you can hang them for me."

Soon both paintings were displayed to good effect. Stone thought that with the walls no longer entirely bare and the lamps in place, it was looking a good deal more like home.

Dolce walked around the place, looking at details. "I like it," she said. "It's very Connecticut, and in some ways, it's very you."

"You'll have to come often," Stone said.

"I intend to," she replied. "Will you get my bag from the car and show me the upstairs?"

Stone went out to the Ferrari and found a surprisingly small bag on the front seat. There was hardly anyplace else to put it in the car. He brought it inside and led her upstairs.

"Oh," she said, "*lots* to do here. Nice closet space, though. We'll have to find you some good wallpaper." She unpacked her bag and hung up a dress. "That won't need ironing," she said.

"Our host says it's very casual."

"Yeah, sure." Dolce laughed. "For men, maybe."

Stone slipped his arms around her and pulled her close.

"My goodness," she said, batting her eyelashes, "you're ready, aren't you?"

"You betcha."

She broke away. "Well, you're just going to have to wait; I have a lot of questions." She led him downstairs, and when they had settled on the sofa, she began. "All right, now; a girl doesn't like surprises; who's the movie star?"

"Vance Calder."

She nodded as if she had dinner with movie stars every evening. "And his wife is Arrington."

Stone blinked. "You're way ahead of me."

"Get used to it," she replied.

"Ah, yes, I forgot about Mary Ann."

"A girl's best friend is her sister; remember that."

"Believe me, I will."

"Now, who are the other guests?"

"I'm not aware that there are any, but there could be."

"A girl likes to know what the competition will be like."

"Competition?"

"The other women. But since you're ignorant of these things, just tell me how Arrington is likely to dress."

"Jesus, how would I know that?"

"Well, how did she dress for casual dinner parties when she was living with you?"

"For casual parties? Well, simply, but elegantly, I suppose."

"You're a gigantic help. I'll just have to go middle of the road, I guess. Does she wear a lot of jewelry?"

"Not a lot, as I recall."

"Yes, but she wasn't married to Vance Calder then, was she?"

"Well, no."

"Her jewelry box will be much better stocked by now. Did she get her figure back after the baby?"

"I don't know; I haven't seen her since the baby."

"Well, she's a Beverly Hills wife, now; I'll assume the worst."

"That she's fat?"

"That's she's svelte and in top shape. What about her hair and nails?"

"She has hair and nails."

"How much hair, dummy, and does she lacquer her nails?"

"About as much hair as you, last time I saw her; she kept her nails long, but she seemed to paint them only on special occasions."

"Then they will be painted tonight," Dolce said. "Excuse me a minute, will you?" She went out to the car and came back with a train case.

Stone couldn't imagine where she had stored it in the car.

"There is a small trunk," she said, reading his mind. "What time are we due there?"

"At seven."

She glanced at her watch. "I'd better get started," she said, heading up the stairs.

"It's only five o'clock," Stone said. "Wouldn't you like a drink or something?"

"No time," she said, disappearing up the stairs.

After a moment, he heard the tub running.

She came halfway back down the stairs. "You can have the bathroom at six-thirty," she said. "I don't want to see you up here before then."

"Yes, ma'am," he said.

"*What?*"

"Yes, signorina."

"You're learning," she said, vanishing up the stairs.

45

A T SIX-THIRTY, STONE WENT UPSTAIRS AND WALKED into the bedroom. The bath was empty, and Dolce was, apparently, in her dressing room. Stone shaved, showered, and dried his hair, and when he came out, Dolce had left the room. He dressed in cream trousers, a brown-plaid shirt, a light tweed jacket, and tan alligator loafers, then went downstairs.

Dolce was standing in front of the living room's curved windows, her hands behind her back. She was wearing a simple, black-silk dress, moderately high heels, and a slender diamond necklace. A red cashmere sweater was thrown casually over her shoulders, matching her nail polish; her jet-black hair fell softly against the sweater. "Good evening," she said.

Stone was stopped in his tracks at the sight of her; he thought he had never seen such a beautiful woman. Her makeup was slight, almost nonexistent, and her eyes seemed even larger than usual. "Good evening, signorina," he said. "You are very beautiful."

"And you are very observant," she replied.

"Would you like a drink before we go?"

"It's seven o'clock; let's have one at our hosts'. People dine earlier in the country."

He gave her his arm, installed her in the Mercedes, and drove away.

"It's very beautiful here," she said, as they turned past the spired white church on the Green.

"Yes, it is."

"How did you happen to buy a house here?"

"I came up for a weekend at the Mayflower Inn, which we're just passing now—it's up the hill, out of view—and it seemed like a good idea."

"Was it yours or Miss Buckminster's?"

"I believe Sarah first mentioned it, but the thought had crossed my mind before. Nobody I know, except Dino, spends the weekend in the city anymore."

"Quite right."

They drove down a winding road slowly, taking in the trees and flowers. Following Vance's directions, they eventually came to an unmarked driveway with a closed gate. Stone reached out the window and rang the bell.

"Yes?" a voice said.

"My name is Barrington."

The gates swung open, and Stone proceeded up the winding drive, which was beautifully planted on both sides. They rounded a bend and, beyond a green lawn, sat a gray, shingled house with white trim and shutters. Stone parked near the front door, and they walked up the steps, across a broad porch featuring rocking chairs, and rang the bell. A man in a white jacket answered the door and led them into a living room furnished with big sofas and lovely antiques. Vance Calder stood before the fireplace, a drink in his hand, wearing a blue blazer, white trousers, and a silk shirt, with an ascot tied at the neck. Stone was about to offer his hand, when Vance, ignoring him, walked toward his date.

"Dolce!" he cried, taking her in his arms and hugging her. "What a delicious surprise! I had no idea you and Stone knew each other."

"We didn't until recently," Dolce replied. "How are you, Vance?"

"Just wonderful! And how's Eduardo?"

"In good form."

Finally, Vance turned to Stone and shook his hand. "Stone, how good to see you; it's been too long."

"It's good to see you, too, Vance," he managed to say through his surprise. "I had no idea *you* and Dolce knew each other."

Dolce spoke up. "Oh, Vance was my date at my sweet sixteen party," she said. "And the best dancer there."

"I've known her father for a very long time," Vance said. "We've done some business over the years. Arrington is putting the baby to bed; she'll be down in a moment. Can we get you a drink?"

The butler took their orders and came back with the drinks.

At that moment, Arrington appeared on the stairs, carrying the baby. Somehow, Stone had not expected the infant, and he was a bit thrown by the sight of mother and child. Arrington came slowly down the stairs; she was wearing a white-silk dress, and with her blond hair, she was the visual antithesis of Dolce. She handed the baby to Vance and embraced Stone more warmly than he had anticipated.

He caught a glimpse of Dolce's face as they hugged; the eyes were daggers. "How are you, Arrington?" he whispered in her ear.

"I'm all right," she whispered back, then they broke their embrace.

"Arrington," Vance said, "I'd like you to meet Dolce Bianchi; she is the daughter of my old friend Eduardo Bianchi; you've heard me mention him."

"Of course," Arrington said coolly, taking Dolce's hand. "Welcome to our home, Dolce; it's always good to see Vance's old friends."

"Thank you, it's good to be here," Dolce replied.

The two were looking each other up and down. Stone noticed that Arrington's nails were, indeed, lacquered, and she was wearing a discreet necklace of diamonds and rubies.

"And this is Peter," Arrington said.

Stone now met the baby who might have been his son. The boy was a quiet, grave infant, who was the image of Vance. If Stone had

had any doubts about the blood tests, he no longer did. Dolce made the right noises at the baby, then a young nanny materialized and took the boy away.

The butler brought Arrington a martini on a silver tray. "Why don't we go out onto the terrace," she said. "It's such a lovely evening."

"Yes, it is," Dolce agreed.

Vance led the way to a patio filled with cushioned white furniture, and they took seats. The evening was pleasantly cool, and the crickets kept them company. "Betty asked me to give you her most affectionate regards," he said to Stone.

Betty was Vance's secretary, with whom Stone had had a brief liaison in LA the year before. Stone saw Dolce shoot a glance his way at the mention of a woman's name. "Please give her mine," Stone said.

"She's holding down the fort at the office, of course. Oh, you remember Lou Regenstein, the chairman of Centurion Studios?"

"Of course I do."

"He'll be with us for dinner." Vance glanced at his watch. "I've sent a car to Oxford Airport for them; they should be here any moment. It's only a few miles away, and it has a runway long enough for the Centurion G-IV."

"It'll be nice to see Lou," Stone said.

They chatted idly for a while, then Lou Regenstein arrived in the company of a lovely redhead, thirty years his junior.

"Dolce!" Lou cried, hugging her. "What a surprise!"

Nobody was more surprised than Stone; the world was getting smaller by the minute. He and Lou shook hands, and Stone was presented to the redhead, whose name was Lola.

"Would you like to freshen up?" Arrington asked.

"No, we changed for dinner on the airplane," Lou replied.

Stone remembered from his one ride on the airplane that the Gulfstream had a shower. He was relieved that another couple would be with them for dinner; it eased the strain, a little. As they chatted, he cast an occasional surreptitious glance at Arrington.

Dolce had been right; she was slim and taut. He strained to catch the sound of her voice when she was speaking to someone else.

Lou sat next to Stone. "I'm astonished that you and Dolce know each other."

"Yes," Vance said. "How did you meet?"

"My former partner, Dino Bacchetti, on the police force, is married to Dolce's sister, Mary Ann."

"And how is Mary Ann?" Both Vance and Lou asked simultaneously.

"She's very well," Dolce said.

As the conversation continued, Lou leaned over to Stone. "After Oney Ippolito went to jail last year, Eduardo bought his Centurion stock. It was a great relief to me to have someone of his caliber as an investor; it lends stability."

Incest, Stone thought. *All these people are in bed together.* It occurred to him that his thought was something more than a metaphor.

Then they were called in to dinner.

46

THEY DINED AT A ROUND, BURLED-WALNUT TABLE IN A lovely room with a bay window overlooking the gardens, which were illuminated in the twilight. An unnecessary, but cheerful fire glowed in the fireplace. Stone suddenly had an overwhelming sense of déjà vu.

"Vance," he said, "when I was at Centurion during your shooting of a film last year, wasn't I in this room?"

"You're very observant, Stone," Vance replied. "Much of the design of the cottage set was based on photographs of this house. Then, when I saw how they had done the dining room, I bought the furnishings and sent them here. I suppose it's a bit 'through the looking glass,' isn't it?"

"Just a little disorienting." Stone was seated on his hostess's right, between her and the scrumptious Lola. It occurred to him that he had never been at table with such gorgeous women. Dolce was opposite him, between Vance and Lou, charming them both. Nobody was playing footsie with Stone.

"Stone," Vance said, "I saw the piece in the *Times* about the explosion at the art gallery. Tell us about that, will you?"

Stone was immediately uncomfortable; he didn't want to get into this. "Fortunately, nobody was seriously hurt. The feds are working on the bomb and the van, and Dino is in charge of the local investigation."

"I understand you saved some lives," Arrington said.

"I was lucky enough to notice the van before the explosion, so everybody was well away from the windows."

"Except Stone," Dolce said. "You should see the cuts on his back." She shot a glance at Arrington.

"It really was nothing," Stone said quickly.

"But what's behind it?" Lou asked.

"The police don't know, yet."

"Stone, you're too modest," Dolce said. "Someone Stone arrested for murder years ago is out of prison, and bad things are happening to the people who helped put him there—and to the people close to them." She let that sink in.

Everybody stopped eating.

"Stone's secretary was murdered, and there has been an attack on my sister, who is now holed up at my father's house with her child."

"Alma is dead?" Arrington asked, aghast.

"I'm afraid so," Stone replied.

"Plus, one of Stone's neighbors is dead, and the doorman in his friend's building, and a policeman who was there."

"Dolce," Stone said, "this is an unpleasant subject."

"What are you and Dino doing to catch this man?" Arrington asked.

"Everything we can; he's been elusive, but his photograph will be in tomorrow's *Times*, and we hope that will produce some leads."

"This man killed a lawyer in New York yesterday," Dolce said.

"How do you know about that connection?" Stone asked, astonished. "I only heard about it late yesterday afternoon, and the connection with the other murders is not public."

"I have my sources," Dolce said.

"Mary Ann again," Stone said.

Dolce shrugged.

Lola spoke for the first time, in a surprisingly small voice. "Does this mean that *we're* all in danger?"

"Certainly not," Stone said. "If I thought that for a moment, I wouldn't be here."

"I'm relieved to hear it," Vance said.

"Very few people know that I bought a house here," Stone said, glancing at Dolce. "Although some of them are very talkative."

Dolce gave him a wry smile.

Dinner resumed, but the conversation was more subdued.

"You certainly lead an interesting existence, Stone," Lou said. "I'm beginning to think that your mixing in our little contretemps of last year was only a minor episode in your life."

"Lou," Arrington said, "you might keep in mind that the mess we drew Stone into was our doing, and not his, and that we all owe him a great deal."

"Of course, of course," Lou said, backpedaling rapidly. "And I, for one, am very grateful to him."

"That's the first time I've heard you express it," Arrington said.

Lola spoke up again. "What mess?"

"I'll tell you later, my dear," Lou said quickly.

There was a long silence.

"Tell us about your new house, Stone," Arrington said.

Stone was grateful for the change in subject. "It was once the gatehouse for the property next door, a place called The Rocks."

"Oh, I know that house," Vance said. "Carolyn Klemm showed it to me when I was house-hunting here."

"And what is your gatehouse like?" Arrington asked.

"Two bedrooms, two baths, a powder room, living room, dining area, and kitchen. It's shingled, like the main house, and has a turret in front."

"It sounds charming," Arrington said. "I'd love to see it."

"Wait until I get it properly put together, then you and Vance must come to dinner."

"We'd love to," Vance said. "Do you know who bought The Rocks?"

"No, I haven't met them yet."

"You will, if Carolyn Klemm has anything to say about it. Carolyn is the social engine around here; she puts people together in amazing ways."

"She's been kind enough to ask me to dinner," Stone said.

"Then you're on your way; soon you'll know everybody."

There was another long silence.

"You've done a beautiful job with this place, Arrington," Stone said, finally.

"Oh, this is my first visit to the house," Arrington replied.

Stone winced.

Arrington jumped in to save him. "Vance has the most amazing taste and judgment about furnishings and antiques. When I walked into the house I felt as if I'd arrived home."

"Vance," Lou said, "how did a vicar's son from the south of England come by such a gift for design?"

Vance shrugged. "By watching my elders and betters, I suppose. My mother was always good at making the vicarages we lived in very homey, and that wasn't always easy. We lived in everything from a run-down thatched cottage to a large, but very seedy Georgian house. I learned a lot by going to the movies, too; the movies were my second home and my university."

Stone listened gratefully as Vance spun out the story of his childhood in England, happy to have the attention of the group off him.

Finally, the party broke up. Lou and Lola said good night and disappeared upstairs, Dolce went to the powder room, and Vance went to dismiss the cook and butler for the night. Stone found himself alone with Arrington on the front porch.

"It was a lovely evening," he said.

"I'm so glad you could come," she replied. "Stone . . ."

"Yes?"

She seemed to he struggling to speak.

"Are you happy, Arrington?"

She nodded. "In my way. I want you to know that I would have been happier if . . ."

"Shall we go?" Dolce said, coming out the front door. "This country air is making me sleepy."

Vance joined them, and they made their goodbyes. Arrington held Stone for a moment longer than she should have, but her husband didn't seem to notice. Dolce, however, did.

On the way home, she said, "Well, that was nice, wasn't it? You got to see your inamorata again. Was it fun?"

"Dolce," Stone said, "you and I have known each other for only a few days, and it may surprise you to learn that I had a life before we met. I still have a life, and your place in it is tentative. You embarrassed me tonight, and you frightened my friends. There was absolutely no need to go into my current problems."

"I'm sorry, Stone," Dolce said sheepishly. "I apologize; it won't happen again."

That night they slept without touching each other. Stone's mind was elsewhere.

47

STONE WAS HAVING AN EROTIC DREAM; THEN HE OPENED his eyes and found that he was not dreaming. Sunlight was streaming through the bedroom windows, and, lifting his head from the pillow, he found himself looking at the top of Dolce's head. His head fell back, and he emitted a small noise, taking her attention from her work.

She climbed on top of him, taking him inside her, and bent over to kiss him. The sunlight disappeared behind her falling hair, and he gave himself to the moment, which turned out to be longer than a moment. They had christened the house.

Stone lay on his back, sweating, breathing hard, while Dolce went into the bathroom and came back with a warm face cloth and tended to him.

"Good morning," she said.

"Yes, indeed," he replied. "I think I'm ruined for the day; I'll never get out of bed."

"You rest, and I'll fix us some breakfast," she said, then went away.

Stone lay staring at the ceiling, then drifted off. He was awakened by Dolce getting back into bed and by wonderful smells. He sat up and built a backrest of pillows, and Dolce set a tray in his lap. He stared down at scrambled eggs, sausages, English muffins, orange juice, and a thermos of coffee. The Sunday *New York Times* was on the bed beside him.

"I could get used to this," he said, buttering a muffin. He looked over, and Dolce was having melon and coffee. "You fattening me up for something?" The eggs were delicious.

"You don't gain weight," she said. "I know all about you; you eat and eat, and stay the same size. How do you do that?"

"I chose my parents well; they were both slim all their lives."

"If I ate everything my aunt Rosaria put in front of me, I would weigh four hundred pounds," she said.

"Are you named for her?"

"Yes."

"Is she your only other relative?"

"Most of my relatives are dead; Mama died last year, and Papa's two older brothers died a long time ago, when they were in their twenties."

"In their twenties? Of what?"

"Of being in the wrong place at the wrong time."

"Oh."

"Papa wasn't even allowed to go to the funeral; his father shipped him off to Columbia Law School and told everybody he was in Europe, studying. He wasn't allowed to come to Brooklyn for three years. He was the only student in law school who went to class armed."

"It's hard to think of your father doing anything as crude as firing a weapon."

"He never had to, as it turned out, but Papa is a survivor; he would have done whatever was necessary." She gazed at him. "It's a family trait."

"Did you know your grandfather?"

"No, he died a long time before I was born. Papa was still in his twenties, so he had a heavy burden to bear. He didn't marry for a long time, for fear of making his wife a widow. It took him years of work to stabilize the situation he inherited. It was a mess."

"But no longer?"

"No longer. Papa has devoted his life to making the family respectable; that was why he was so upset when I married Johnny."

"Why did you marry him?"

She laughed. "I was a virgin. With Papa watching over me, it was the only way I could get laid."

"There must have been more to it than that."

She laughed again. "Not really. When I went out, I was always watched by somebody Papa sent. If I had let a boy make a wrong move, he would have gotten hurt, and I couldn't have that on my conscience."

"I'm glad to know you have a conscience."

"Of course, I have a conscience!" she nearly yelled. "You think I'm like my grandfather?"

"I have very little idea of what you're like, except in bed, and there you are spectacular."

"A native talent," she said, "like singing."

"I believe you." Stone set aside his breakfast tray and began leafing through the *Times*. He found it in the Metro section. "Here it is," he said, showing Dolce the paper.

"*That's* Mitteldorfer?"

"Yep."

"He looks like such a little twerp."

"He is, but he's a dangerous one."

"Where do you think he is?"

"My guess? Manhattan, somewhere on the East Side, living well. That's why I'm hoping one of his new neighbors will recognize the picture."

"Who's the one in this drawing? He looks like Mitteldorfer."

"That's the drawing done from Mary Ann's description of the man who attacked her. They really do look a lot alike, don't they?" Stone stared at the two pictures. "Holy shit!"

"What?"

Stone picked up the bedside phone and called Dino.

"Hello?"

"I'm looking at the *Times*. You notice anything about Mitteldorfer's photograph and the police sketch?"

"Sure, they look alike. Remember the guy who cut your neighbor's throat? He looked like Mitteldorfer with hair. That's why we checked to see if he had any kids, and we drew a blank; just a nephew, and he's living in Germany."

"Dino, if Mitteldorfer has another wife, as Arlene said he did, maybe he's got a kid by her."

"Ah, good point."

"You have any luck on the marriage records?"

"Not yet. The computer records only go back a few years, but I've got a couple of rookies going through the old files, on microfilm."

"That's it, I know it is. If we can find the first Mrs. Mitteldorfer, then we can find her son, and then we'll find Mitteldorfer. Why don't you check everybody by that name in the state? Hell, in the country; it can't be that common a name."

"I'll get my people on it first thing tomorrow morning. How was your dinner last night?"

"I'll tell you later; call me if anything comes up. Oh, I almost forgot: how'd it go at the theater opening last night?"

"Zilch; nothing happened."

"Maybe Mitteldorfer doesn't know Palmer's name."

"That's my guess. When are you coming back to town?"

"I'm not sure; I can't go back to the house."

"Okay, talk to you later."

Stone hung up. "I don't suppose you've had any results yet from your inquiries at Sing Sing?"

"Let me make a call," she said, picking up the phone on her side of the bed. She dialed a number. "You know who this is? What have you got?" She signaled Stone for paper and pen, and Stone got out of bed to get it. "Yeah. Spell it. You got an address? What's the parole officer's name? Thanks." She hung up and handed Stone the pad. Three names were written on it. "The first two were in with Mitteldorfer; the third name is the parole officer for both of them; they were both released before Mitteldorfer was. My man couldn't get an address, but he says they were both tight with your man."

"That's something to go on," Stone said. "But not before tomorrow. Come on, let's get dressed and out of the house. It's a beautiful spring day, and there's an auction up the road somewhere."

"An auction of what?"

"You know, a country auction—lots of stuff."

"What kind of stuff?"

"Antiques, furniture, pictures, bric-a-brac."

"Can't do it; I've got to get back to the city."

"But it's Sunday."

"I've got a board meeting tomorrow, and I've got to read over a hundred grant applications by then."

"Aw."

"Besides, there's too much oxygen up here for a city girl. You said you don't want to go back to your house?"

"Not yet."

"Why don't you stay with me?"

"In Brooklyn?"

"Of course not; I live in the East Sixties."

"Sure you've got room?"

"Sure; you don't take up much space."

"Maybe I'll come into the city tonight; that okay?"

"Sure." She wrote down her address. "Call me on your car phone when you're in the block, and I'll open the garage door for you."

"You and I must be the only people in the city with a garage."

"Could be." Dolce got up, threw her things in a bag, kissed him, and left the house.

A moment later, he heard the Ferrari's high-pitched roar. A moment after that, he was asleep again, exhausted.

48

STONE WAS JERKED AWAKE BY A LOUD RINGING. FOR A moment, he thought it had been a dream, then it rang again. It wasn't the phone; could it be the door? He had never heard his own doorbell. He got up, got into a cotton robe, and padded downstairs.

Arrington was standing on the porch.

"Good morning," he said sleepily. "Come in." She was wearing faded jeans, a chambray shirt knotted under her breasts, and no makeup. He thought she had never looked more beautiful.

She put her arms around his waist and leaned into his shoulder. "Good morning," she said.

"Would you like some coffee?"

"Yes, all right."

He moved away from her and into the kitchen, where he busied himself making coffee.

Arrington came and sat on a stool at the counter that separated the kitchen from the living room. "I take it I just missed Ms. Bianchi?"

"Yes."

"I saw her drive away."

Stone turned. "Did she see you?"

"No."

He breathed a sigh of relief.

"I like the cottage; it suits you."

"Thanks."

"Did you choose it with Ms. Bianchi?"

"No." He didn't elaborate on that.

"I like it even better, then."

"I'm glad; you'll have to bring Vance and Peter over."

She said nothing.

"What brings you out on a Sunday morning?"

"I thought I might go to a country auction, then I found myself driving by the green and thought I would rather see you."

"Oh." He poured them both a cup of coffee. "Have you had breakfast?"

"Yes. When you live with Vance Calder, there's always a servant at hand to grant your every wish." She didn't sound very happy about it.

"So, how's life in LA? Do you like it out there?"

"It's all right, when I'm not being kidnapped."

"I hope you haven't made a habit of it," he said.

"No; you were kind enough to put an end to that. I'll always be grateful." She put her hand on his.

"You're welcome," he said.

"I know you're not very comfortable with gratitude; but I had to say it, anyway. Vance feels the same way. He likes you very much, you know."

"And I like him."

"Let's sit in the living room," she said, taking her coffee and making her way to a sofa.

Stone followed and sat down next to her, leaving a respectable distance between them.

"How have you spent the time since we last saw each other?" Arrington asked.

The memory of their last time together flooded back. They had been in the bedroom of a Bel-Air Hotel suite, and Arrington had been naked. "Oh, the usual," he said. "A little work, a little play."

"How is Dino?" she asked.

"Very angry; he doesn't like his family being in danger."

She nodded. "And Elaine?"

"Exactly the same."

"Give them both my love, will you?"

"I will."

There was a long silence; Stone struggled to find something to say. "Are you writing?" he asked, finally.

"I started a novel, but after a couple of chapters I sort of gave up on it."

"Don't give up. You'd write a very fine novel; you have all the skills."

"I don't know that I'm cut out to be a novelist," she said.

"Why not?"

"I think that, in order to write a good novel, you have to be able to face reality, and I'm not very good at that."

"What is it about reality that you find so hard to face?"

"The reality is that I want to be with you."

That sucked the wind right out of Stone; he was unable to respond.

"I think about you all the time; about having dinner with you and Dino and Elaine; about living in your house; about making love to you; I think about that a lot."

Stone put down his coffee and massaged his temples. This was pretty much all *he* had thought about, until recently. Now she was here. What was he going to do about it?

"Do you think about me?"

"Yes."

She moved closer. "Do you think about making love to me?"

"Yes."

She sat up on her knees on the sofa and ran a hand through his hair. With her other hand, she pulled loose the tie of his robe and ran her hand inside.

Stone took her hand and put his on her shoulder, then took her into his arms and kissed her face. "Don't," he said. "It's too painful."

"I want the pain to stop," she said. "I want you."

"You know very well that I want you, too."

"Then I'm yours."

Stone took a deep breath. "No," he said, "you're not."

"I want to be yours again."

"I can't let myself want that."

"Why not? We can have each other."

"No, we can't." Stone could not believe he was saying this.

"I'll come back to New York; I'll get a divorce. I should never have married Vance."

"But you did."

"I made a stupid mistake," she said. "Do I have to pay for it the rest of my life?"

"We both do."

"I want to come back, Stone."

"You can't take Vance's son away from him; I won't be a party to that."

"Then I'll leave Peter with Vance. I can still see him."

"Arrington, I saw you with that baby last night; you love being his mother, and if I came between you, you'd end up hating me for it."

"I want you more."

"No, you don't."

She sat up and pulled his robe open. "Make love to me," she said. She ran her hands down his body and kissed him on the neck and shoulders. "Just this once; make love to me. Then, if you still want me to go, I will."

Stone took her shoulders and held her away from him. "Listen to me," he said. "I've done things in my life I'm not proud of, but I've never been an adulterer, and I'm not going to start now—not even with you, in spite of the fact that I've loved you more than any woman I've ever known. I just can't do it."

Tears spilled down her cheeks. "Stone, I love you."

"Arrington, some part of me will *always* love you."

"Then why can't we be together?"

"We both made choices that we're going to have to learn to live with."

"I was living with them until I saw you last night," Arrington said. "Really, I was."

"Then you can do it again." Stone stood up and pulled her to her feet. "You have to go home, now." He walked her slowly toward the door, his arm around her. She was still crying. On the way to the door, Stone grabbed a handful of tissues from a box on an end table.

At the open door, she turned and faced him. "Don't send me away; please don't do that."

"You have to go," he said.

"You don't really want me to go." She sobbed.

He dabbed at her eyes with the tissues. "What I want doesn't matter anymore."

She took the tissues and blew her nose loudly. "Kiss me good-bye?"

He took her face in his hands and kissed her lips lightly. "Good-bye, sweet girl," he said.

She turned and ran for the Range Rover parked in his drive. In a moment, she had driven away.

Stone walked back into the house and closed the door, trying hard to swallow the lump in his throat. Then he heard a car door slam outside. *Oh, God,* he thought, *she's come back, and I won't be able to send her away again.*

He went and opened the front door, ready to take her in his arms. Vance Calder stood on the little porch. "Hello, Stone," he said.

"Hello, Vance," Stone said weakly. "Will you come in?"

"No," Vance replied. "I just want to know if I have anything to worry about from you."

Stone shook his head. "No, Vance, you don't."

Vance took a deep breath. "Thank you for that," he said.

"Just try to find a way to make her happy."

Vance nodded, squeezed Stone's shoulder, went back to his car, and drove away.

Stone went back inside, hoping that every Sunday morning in Connecticut was not going to be as hard as this one.

49

STONE LOCKED UP THE HOUSE, GOT INTO HIS CAR, AND
drove away. He wasn't sure he'd done the right thing about
Arrington, and it was killing him. He kept thinking about what it
would be like to have her back again; then he would think about her
son and his father and come back to the same place. When he had
reached Pleasantville, he called Dino.

"Hello?"

"Hi, it's Stone."

"Where are you?"

"On the Saw Mill River Parkway. Can you meet me at P.J.
Clarke's in an hour?"

"What's up?"

"I've got a lead."

"From where?"

"Don't ask, just be there, and for Christ's sake, be sure you aren't
followed."

"Awright, in an hour at Clarke's."

He was in Yonkers when the car phone rang. "Hello?"

"Stone, it's Bill Eggers."

"Hi, Bill."

"We have to talk, and we can't do it on a car phone."

"What's up?"

"Let's meet somewhere; when are you due back in the city?"

"I'm meeting Dino at Clarke's in half and hour; you want to join me?"

"That's fine; this concerns him, too. I'll see you in half an hour." He hung up.

Stone punched the phone off. Now what?

Back in the city, he found a parking spot near Clarke's, then went inside. Dino was already halfway through a scotch.

"Hey," Dino said.

"How was your weekend?"

"Lousy; how was yours?"

"Don't ask," Stone replied.

"What's this about a lead?"

Stone took the paper from his pocket. "I've got two names that Mitteldorfer was friendly with in Sing Sing." He handed it to Dino. "They're both on parole, and they've got the same Manhattan parole officer. Tomorrow morning, will you give him a call and find out where they are? I'd like to talk to them with you."

"You bet your ass," Dino said. "It's about time we got somewhere with this."

"Here comes Bill Eggers," Stone said, nodding at the door. "He wants to talk to us about something; I don't know what."

Bill greeted the two men. "It's running onto dinnertime," he said. "Why don't we get a table?"

"Sure," Stone said.

They sat down and ordered steaks, home fries, and beer.

"So, what's up, Bill? You sounded depressed on the phone."

"I am," Bill said. "I got a call this afternoon from a friend in the DA's office; Marty Brougham is taking the Susan Bean murder to a grand jury this week."

"Then he must have a suspect," Stone said.

"He does. You. You're going to be subpoenaed."

"First I've heard about this," Dino said, "and the case is in my office. I smell something funny."

"Look," Stone said, "I don't mind being subpoenaed; I'll testify to what I know without a subpoena. In fact, I've already told Brougham I'd do so."

"Stone, you're a target; I can't let you testify before a grand jury."

"So, I should take the Fifth? How would that look?"

"It's how this is going to look that bothers me," Bill said.

"Sorry," Dino said, "I'm confused. I'm pretty well versed on this case, having arrived half an hour after the murder and having heard Stone give a statement to two of my detectives. What does Marty know that I don't know? Stone, is there something you haven't told me?"

"Absolutely not," Stone said. "I'm not holding anything back."

"Then he must have a witness," Bill said. "Otherwise, why would you be a target of the investigation?"

"A witness to what?" Stone said.

"Look," Dino said, "I'm happy to go down to the grand jury and tell them that my squad conducted a thorough investigation and that we cleared Stone."

"Then Marty will ask you about your relationship with Stone, and he'll discredit your testimony, because you're former partners and close friends. Anyway, he's not going to call you, because you wouldn't help his case."

"This just doesn't add up," Stone said. "Marty must know that he can't get an indictment of me."

"A good prosecutor can get anything he wants from a grand jury," Bill said.

"But he couldn't get a conviction, so why get an indictment?"

"There are two things here," Bill said. "One, he could have a witness to cast doubt on your story, or even to claim you murdered the girl."

"Then that would either be a perjurer or a frame-up," Dino said. "Or both."

"Right," Bill said. "The other thing is, suppose he thinks this case isn't going to be solved, so he wants to feed somebody to the press as the murderer. The day after your testimony, I can see a headline in the *News* that you're the chief suspect, but that they don't have enough evidence to indict you, *yet*."

"Oh, shit," Dino said.

"Well, Dino," Bill said, "at least *you're* getting the picture."

"But that won't wash," Stone said.

"It'll wash with enough people to ruin you in this town," Dino said.

"And," Eggers chipped in, "it would end your usefulness to Woodman and Weld. The firm couldn't be seen to employ—even on an occasional basis—the chief suspect in a gaudy murder."

Dino put down his glass. "You'd be the new O.J."

Stone sat and thought about this, ignoring his steak. "Martin Brougham doesn't strike me as that malicious," he said. "So who is?"

Dino's eyebrow's went up. "I smell Tom Deacon."

"Who's Tom Deacon?" Bill asked.

"He runs the DA's investigative division, under Marty, and he doesn't like Stone and me."

"Oh."

"Something else," Dino said. "Marty wants to be the next DA. He might like a flashy case to help imprint himself on the voters' frontal lobes."

"That all makes sense," Bill said. "You think this Deacon guy is just trying to make himself look good?"

"I think that fits right in with his character," Dino replied. "He knows a few reporters; he could make himself look good and Stone look bad. It would be easy."

Stone spoke up. "I've already told him that if he did something like that, I'd sue him for libel."

"It could come to that," Bill said. "How much faith do you think Brougham has in Tom Deacon?"

"A lot," Dino said. "If he's willing to put Stone through this on Deacon's say-so."

"We need other witnesses besides you, Dino, witnesses from the NYPD. Are you the actual investigating officer on the Susan Bean Murder?"

"No," Stone answered for him. "That would be Andy Anderson and Michael Kelly."

Dino shook his head slowly. "No, not Kelly; not anymore."

"What, did you kick him out of the precinct?" Stone asked.

"No, he left voluntarily."

"Congratulations," Stone said. "I don't expect you'll miss the little prick."

"He went to work for the investigative division of the DA's office," Dino said. "Starting tomorrow morning."

"So," Bill said, "we could have one of the investigative officers on the case testifying against Stone?"

"What could he possibly say?" Stone asked. "Anyway, Dino and Andy Anderson could refute any lies."

"I don't like any of this," Eggers said, "so what I'm going to try to do is to nip it in the bud."

"How?" Stone asked.

"I'm going to go see Marty Brougham tonight, at home, if he's in, and try to straighten this out. Can either of you think of anything else that might help me do that?"

Stone sipped his beer thoughtfully. "There was something that Susan Bean said to me. I didn't give it much thought at the time."

"What did she say?" Eggers asked.

"We were walking up Madison Avenue, just chatting, and I congratulated her on her team's getting a conviction in the Dante case."

"Is that the Mafia guy?"

"Right. She didn't seem all that thrilled to have won it, which surprised me; I would have thought she'd have been walking on air."

"What, exactly, did she say about it?"

"She said she was happy to have won, but she didn't like the way they'd won it."

"That's it?"

"That's it."

Eggers mulled this over. "So there might have been some sort of prosecutorial misconduct during the trial?"

"That could be what she meant."

"You have any idea what kind of misconduct?"

"No, but the very mention of it to Brougham might have some sort of effect."

"Maybe so," Eggers said. "It might give him pause about a subpoena if he thought you might testify about something like that. It's not much, but it might help as a bargaining chip."

"I wish I had more to tell you," Stone said. He turned to Dino. "There are cops on the DA's investigative staff, aren't there?"

"Sure; Deacon is a cop."

"You know anybody in Internal Affairs that you might interest in an investigation of the evidence in the Dante case?"

"I know some guys, but they would be reluctant to open that can of worms, especially after a successful conviction of a guy the department has been after for years."

"Do you know somebody in IA who hates Tom Deacon?"

"Now *that* might be a possibility; lots of people do. I'll give it a shot."

Eggers looked at his watch. "I'm going over to Marty Brougham's house now; you guys can fight over the check." He tossed his napkin on the table and stood up. "Stone, you might lay low for a day or two, until I've had a shot at sorting this out."

"Sure. I'll be at . . ."

Eggers cut him off. "I don't want to know where you are, if they ask me. Just call me in the morning, and if I'm not available, keep checking in. Don't leave a number."

"Okay."

Eggers shook both their hands and left.

Stone tossed a credit card on the table and waved for a waiter.

"So, where are you off to?" Dino asked.

"You don't want to know that. If you need me, try my car phone or my cell phone."

"I'll let you know if I have any luck with Internal Affairs," Dino said.

Stone signed the check, said good night, and got into his car. He'd had another thought on how to learn more about the Dante trial.

50

STONE TURNED INTO DOLCE'S BLOCK IN THE EAST Sixties and punched her phone number into his car phone. As the number rang, he squeezed past an elderly Mercedes 600 limousine that was double-parked in the street.

"Hello?"

"It's Stone; I'm in the block."

"I'll open the garage door; park next to my car and take the elevator to the second floor. And leave your luggage in the car," she said.

It sounded as though he would not be staying the night. Stone ended the call and looked for her house number. It turned out to belong to a large, handsome redbrick town house. He drove down a short ramp and through the open garage door; it closed behind him. He parked next to the Ferrari and took the elevator to the second floor. The door opened into a hallway; Dolce was waiting for him.

"This way," she said, beckoning him into a large study.

Stone walked into the room and found Eduardo Bianchi sitting in a chair beside the fireplace. He got up to greet Stone.

"How good to see you again," Bianchi said, offering his hand and indicating that Stone should sit opposite him.

Stone sat down, and Dolce brought him a drink, then perched on an ottoman.

"I understand you have bought a country house," Bianchi said.

"That's right; in Connecticut."

"It's a very good idea. One needs to get away from this city from time to time."

"Yes," Stone replied. He wondered if the man knew that his daughter had spent the night with him in that country house.

"I understand, too, that you are acquainted with my friends Leo Regenstein and Vance Calder."

He knew. "Yes, that's right. I spent some time in Los Angeles last year, and Vance arranged for me to fly out there with Leo on his studio's airplane."

Bianchi nodded. "I think that airplane is a dreadful extravagance, but Leo says he couldn't hold up his head in Hollywood if he didn't have it. I suppose such things mean something in that place." He spread his hands. "What would I know about it?"

Stone didn't buy that.

"Has the information Dolce obtained for you been of any help?"

"I won't know until tomorrow," Stone said, "but I'm very grateful for any leads in finding Mitteldorfer."

"If there is anything else I can do to help, please let me know."

"Actually, there may be," Stone said.

"Tell me."

"You may recall that the district attorney recently got a conviction of a man named Dante."

"Salvatore Dante? I've heard the name, I believe."

Stone thought he caught a hint of irony in the statement. "A prosecutor, Susan Bean, who worked on the trial was murdered, and before her death she hinted to me that there may have been some irregularity in the way Dante was prosecuted, possibly some prosecutorial misconduct."

Bianchi's eyebrows went up. "Oh?"

Stone thought he looked *very* interested. "I've just had dinner with Bill Eggers, from Woodman and Weld, and Bill tells me that the lead prosecutor on the Dante case may be making me a target of the investigation of Susan Bean's murder, even though the police have cleared me of any involvement. He's not concerned that I could be convicted, but he is concerned that such a move on the DA's part could be very damaging to my reputation."

"Which would not be good for Woodman and Weld," Bianchi said, nodding.

"Nor would it be good for my ability to function as a lawyer," Stone said.

"I see your problem. And you think that if you knew what was, shall we say, fishy, about the Dante prosecution, it might improve your bargaining position with the District Attorney's Office?"

"Yes. It occurs to me that if, for instance, evidence had been fabricated, Dante would certainly know that, and so would his attorneys."

"A reasonable supposition," Bianchi said. "Dolce, why don't you take Stone into the kitchen and give him something to eat?"

"Yes, Papa," she said, rising and taking Stone's hand. She led him into the kitchen. "Papa wants to telephone," she said. "You said you'd eaten; would you like some dessert?"

"Yes," Stone said.

"How about a nice piece of Italian cheesecake?"

Stone wiggled his eyebrows. "Yes, please."

Dolce laughed and removed a cheesecake from the refrigerator and cut a slice, handing it to him. "You can have the other Italian cheesecake later."

Stone ate his cheesecake, drank some coffee, and chatted with Dolce for three-quarters of an hour, then Eduardo Bianchi came into the kitchen.

"Was the cheesecake good?" he asked.

"Absolutely delicious," Stone said.

"Rosaria makes a wonderful cheesecake. Now. I have spoken to . . . certain parties and, I believe, have made some progress. It seems that the prosecution of Mr. Dante turned on what was said on some surveillance tapes made by the district attorney's investigative division. The odd thing is that, in spite of the evidence, which was played in court for the jury, Dante denies ever having spoken the words on the tape."

"So the tapes were doctored?"

"Mr. Dante's lawyers, of course, had the tapes examined by experts, but they were unable to find any evidence of their being tampered with. They will have them examined again, by other experts. The parts in question, although they comprised hardly more than a minute of the tapes, were crucial to the conviction of Mr. Dante, and he still insists that he never spoke those words. Since he did not testify in his own defense, he was unable to make the denial in court, not that it would have helped."

Stone nodded. "May I use a telephone?"

"Please use the one in the study," Bianchi said. "I think I will have a little cheesecake."

Stone went into the study, hoping against hope that Martin Brougham's telephone number was not unlisted. It was not. He called the number, and when a woman answered, asked to speak to Bill Eggers, hoping he was still there. He was.

"Hello?"

"Bill, it's Stone; listen carefully: the tapes that Marty used to convict Dante were somehow falsified by Deacon, or somebody in his division. I have this on very good authority."

"Thank you," Bill said. "That's very interesting."

"How's it going?"

"Call me tomorrow." He hung up.

Stone hung up and went back to the kitchen.

"This information was helpful?" Bianchi asked.

"I believe so; I won't know for sure until tomorrow."

"I would very much like to know the outcome of this," Bianchi said.

"I will certainly let you know."

"It is terrible to see such abuses of power by public officials," Bianchi said. "To think that a man like Brougham could destroy another's livelihood for nothing more than his own political benefit. He wants to be district attorney, of course, when the present occupant of that office finally vacates."

"I've heard that."

"Perhaps it would be a public service if that could be prevented," Bianchi said.

"Perhaps so."

"I will give it some thought." Bianchi looked at his watch. "Well, it is getting late; I must go. I will leave you young people to your evening." He shook hands with Stone, and Dolce walked him to the front door.

Stone had another cup of coffee and waited for her to return.

She came in. "Now you can bring your bags up," she said, kissing him.

Stone went to the garage for his luggage and returned.

"Your father knows we were together in Connecticut," he said.

"He talked to Leo this morning, so that cat is out of the bag. Still, I didn't think he would like to see you arrive with luggage." She kissed him again. "Now, how about another slice of Italian cheesecake?"

"I'm starving," Stone said.

Half an hour later, Dolce stroked Stone's face. "What's the matter?" she asked.

"I don't know; just tired, I guess." He had discovered that he could not think of Arrington and make love to Dolce at the same time.

"You'll get over her," Dolce whispered into his ear.

Stone pretended to fall asleep.

51

DINO'S DRIVER DOUBLE-PARKED THE CAR AND PUT down the visor with the police badge. "There's the shop," Dino said. "You want to take the back or the front?"

"He's not going to run, Dino," Stone replied. "He's a legit parolee with no violations."

Dino looked at the paper again. "Eliot Darcy," he said. "Murdered his wife, like Mitteldorfer, but nearly twenty years ago."

"Let's go," Stone said, getting out of the car.

It was a shoe-repair shop, larger than most, with seats for customers to try on their shoes or get them shined. Two men worked at machinery behind their counter.

"Mr. Darcy?" Dino asked the older of the two.

Darcy looked at both Dino and Stone before switching off the machine. "That's right," he replied. "What can I do for you?"

Dino showed him a badge. "Is there someplace we can talk?"

Darcy lifted a panel and beckoned them behind the counter. He led the way to an office so small that Stone had to lean against the door while Dino took the only chair. "Okay, what's it about?" Darcy asked.

"So," Dino said, "how's it going since you got out? How long has it been?"

"Nine months, and it's going okay," Darcy said. "I didn't know the NYPD did follow-ups to see if parolees are happy."

"Oh, we're a very compassionate organization," Dino said.

"And I rate a visit from a lieutenant?"

"We wouldn't send out a patrolman to talk to a distinguished small businessman," Dino said. He waved a hand. "This is your place?"

"It is."

"Tell me, how'd you swing the capital to open up? This is a pretty good location."

"I wasn't broke when I went in," Darcy said. "I pleaded to the charge, so the lawyers didn't take everything."

"How much did you have when you went in?" Dino asked.

"Not a whole lot; a few thousand dollars and some personal property—car, furniture, like that. I sold all my stuff."

"And the money grew while you were inside?"

"Yes."

"And Herbie Mitteldorfer was your investment advisor?"

"He was helpful, yes."

"How did you meet Mitteldorfer?" Dino asked.

"We had the same work assignment—same department, that is."

"What department?"

"The prison office. Later, I ran the shoe shop; Herbie got me transferred."

"Herbie could do that?"

"He wanted somebody with computer experience."

"*He* wanted?"

"Herbie sort of ran the office."

"Where's Herbie now?"

"I don't have the slightest idea. I saw his picture in the paper; I don't believe a word of it. Herbie would never hurt anybody."

"He killed his wife."

Darcy shrugged. "So did I, but I wouldn't hurt anybody, either. You don't know how crazy a wife can make you."

"When was the last time you talked to Mitteldorfer?" Stone asked.

"The day I was released from prison."

"Darcy," Dino said, "do you want to go back to Sing Sing? I can arrange it."

"I haven't done anything to get sent back," Darcy said.

"I could arrange for you to do something."

"All right, I understand that you can do anything you want, but I'm telling you, I don't have any information at all about Mitteldorfer. Herbie would never contact me, anyway."

"Why not?" Stone asked.

"He considers me his social inferior," Darcy said. "After all, I'm only a cobbler. Herbie would never mix with me; he's a terrible snob."

"Then why did he help you invest your money?" Stone asked.

"Because I paid him a percentage of my profits," Darcy replied. "So did the others."

"Which others?"

"There were half a dozen prisoners who had some money outside, that I knew about."

"Who were they?"

Darcy counted them off on his fingers. "Middleton, Schwartz, Alesio, Warren, and me."

"That's only five."

"Okay, *about* half a dozen. Plus the prison staff, of course."

"Of course. How many of them were there?"

"Half a dozen, or so."

"Who's out besides you and Alesio?" Stone asked.

"Alesio's out? I didn't know. I guess we're the only ones; the rest are still inside."

"You in touch with any of them?"

"I've had a couple letters from Schwartz; he wants to go into business with me when he gets out next year."

"What has he said about Mitteldorfer?"

"Only that he hasn't heard a word from him since Herbie got out. According to Schwartz, Herbie went around and said goodbye to them and told each one that he wouldn't be hearing from him again, that they were on their own. He told them they'd have to find a broker."

"Who had Mitteldorfer used for a broker?"

"I'm not even sure he had one. He had some way of trading on the computer, I think; he could do it right from the prison office, but then he started working outside the pen. When I got out, he had my assets transferred to my local bank. I don't even know how he did it. He kept twenty-five percent of my profits for his fee."

"Who else was he friendly with inside?" Stone asked.

"Friendly? He wasn't friendly with *anybody*. I told you, he was a snob. I mean, he was polite, in his way, but he didn't suffer fools gladly, not even Warkowski. He even had a cell to himself, the only guy I knew who did."

Back in the car, Dino gave his driver another address. "All right, let's go see Alesio," he said.

"I have the feeling he's not going to be any more help than Darcy was," Stone said. "Mitteldorfer is far too smart to stay in touch with anybody he was in jail with. Anyway, I think Darcy's comment about his being a snob is right on the money. He wouldn't associate with ex-cons."

"We've got to try," Dino said.

Alesio turned out to be an elderly man, nearly seventy, Stone thought. They tried his apartment house and were referred to a senior citizens day center, where they found their man playing chess. He looked up at them and laughed.

"I've been expecting you," he said.

"Oh? How's that?" Dino replied.

"Ever since I saw Herbie's picture in the paper. You're never going to find him."

"And why not?"

"Because he's not stupid, that's why. I think—and this is only a guess; I don't have any real knowledge of it—that Herbie already had himself set up as somebody else, even before he got out."

"If you don't have any knowledge of it, why do you think that?" Stone asked.

Alesio shrugged. "Herbie was like a good chess player," he said. "He always thought several moves ahead. You could see it in the way he handled the prison staff. If he asked for something and didn't get it, he'd have another request ready, and if he didn't get that, he'd want something else, until finally, they gave him that. After a while, they just gave him whatever he wanted. After all, he was making money for them."

They got back into the car.

"The precinct wants you," Dino's driver said to him.

Dino got on the phone. "When? Where?" He turned to Stone. "We've got him." He went back to the phone. "Nobody, but *nobody* talks to him until I get there, which will be in twenty minutes." He hung up.

"Mitteldorfer?" Stone asked.

"No, the other guy. The picture in the paper worked; somebody called it in from a dry cleaner's on Third Avenue." Dino grinned. "He's missing part of an ear."

52

STONE AND DINO HURRIED INTO THE PRECINCT AND UP the stairs to where the detective squad worked. Andy Anderson was using a computer terminal at a desk in the center of the room.

"Okay, Andy, tell me," Dino said.

"The guy went to take some dry cleaning to a place on Third Avenue in the Seventies, and the manager recognized him from the picture in the *Times* and called it in. There was a black and white half a block away, and the two patrolmen jumped him as he left the place. He was carrying a 9mm automatic and a large switchblade, so we can hold him on weapons charges no matter what."

"Where is he?"

"Cooling his heels in the lockup."

"Set up interrogation one for video and audio," Dino said.

"Already done."

"Anybody read him his rights?"

"The two patrolmen."

"Okay, you go in, read him his rights again, and tell him the interview is being recorded."

"Uh, Lieutenant," Anderson said hesitantly.

"What?"

269

"There may be a problem; he hasn't spoken a word since he was picked up."

"Is he a mute?"

"I don't know."

"Go do what I told you," Dino said.

"Dino," Stone said, "we need a lineup first."

"I'll get Mary Ann in here, and we'll do that," Dino replied.

"No, we need a lineup now, before we see the guy. We need that for court; we're both witnesses to one of the murders."

"Oh, right," Dino said. "Thanks, Stone. Andy, get a lineup together; use other prisoners or other people Stone and I won't recognize. This has to be good for court; I don't want any mistakes."

Anderson went to do as he was told.

"This had to be how it would end," Stone said. "Somebody would just call in, and it's over."

"It won't be over until we have Mitteldorfer in a cell and a solid case against him," Dino replied.

Dino went into the lineup first, then left by another door. When Stone came into the little room, he made the man immediately, then went out to find Dino waiting for him.

"Any doubts?" Dino asked.

"None; it's him."

"Come on, let's take a closer look at him before we go in."

Stone followed Dino into the viewing room next door to interrogation room one. The two were separated by a one-way sheet of plate glass, with a mirror on the interrogation side. Anderson sat in the room alone with the man, who made smoking motions. Anderson shook his head slowly.

"Mary Ann was right," Dino said with some satisfaction. "She clipped his ear."

"He looks remarkably like the younger Mitteldorfer," Stone said. "Got to be a relative."

270

"Okay, I'm going in," Dino said. "You'll have to observe from here; I don't want to do *anything* that a lawyer could pounce on."

"I want to question him, too, Dino. What grounds would a lawyer have to object?"

Dino thought about it. "Okay, but don't say anything unless you think I've forgotten something. Leave it to Andy and me."

"All right." Stone followed Dino into the room, then pulled a chair behind the man and to his left, out of his direct line of sight. Dino took a chair beside Anderson, across the table from the suspect.

"Okay," Dino said to Anderson, "have you read this gentleman his rights?"

"Yes."

"Does he know this interview is being recorded?"

"I've told him; I don't know if he understood me."

Dino turned to the man. "Can you hear me?"

The man nodded.

"Do you understand English?"

He nodded.

"What's your name?"

The man sat impassively, not moving.

"You run his prints, yet?" Dino asked Anderson.

"Yes; no results yet."

"You know," Dino said to the suspect, "we'll know who you are as soon as your fingerprints come back."

The man motioned for something to write with.

Anderson shoved a legal pad and a ballpoint across the table.

"You'd rather write your answers?" Dino asked.

The man nodded.

"Okay, what's your name and address?"

The man sat motionless.

"I'll go check on the prints," Anderson said, then left the room.

Dino sat, looking at his suspect. "Why did you kill those people?" he asked suddenly.

The man began to write. He turned the pad so that Dino could read it.

"It seemed a good idea at the time?"

The man nodded vigorously.

Anderson came back and sat down. When Dino looked at him, he shook his head.

"Nothing?" Dino asked.

Anderson shook his head again.

Dino turned back to his suspect. "Write down the names of the people you killed."

The man began writing, then turned the pad around.

Dino read aloud. "Three women, doorman, cop, lawyer."

"How did you kill the three women?" Dino asked.

The man made a motion as if to hit himself on the head, then drew a finger across his throat.

Stone held up four fingers, behind the man, so that he wouldn't see.

"There were four women," Dino said. "How'd you kill the other one?"

The man made the hitting-on-the-head motion again.

Dino shook his head.

Stone suddenly had an idea. "*Herr ober!*" he said sharply.

The man's head snapped around in Stone's direction.

"We know about your German accent," Stone said. "There's no reason not to speak."

The man thought about that for a moment. "*Ach,*" he said softly.

53

THEY ALL SAT STILL, SAYING NOTHING FOR A LONG moment. Then Dino seemed to realize that the man was speaking, and that, moreover, he was talking.

Stone got out the first question. "Herr Mitteldorfer?" he said.

The man looked at him and laughed. *"Nein,"* he replied. *"Sprechen Sie Deutsch?"*

"Not really," Stone said. "Your name is Mitteldorfer, though, isn't it?"

"No," the man replied.

"Then what is your name?"

"You are not needing to know," he said. His accent was thickly German.

"But you are his son, aren't you?"

The man smiled but said nothing.

Dino took charge; he shoved the pad back to the suspect. "Write down the *names* of the people you killed."

"I am not knowing all these names."

"Write down the ones you know."

The man began writing, then stopped and read aloud from the pad. "The secretary—I am not knowing the name; the Hirsch lady, naked with the machine—ah, the cleaner."

273

"The vacuum cleaner," Dino said.

"*Ja*. Yes." He continued. "Fräulein Enzberg; the man of the door on Fifth Avenue and the policeman; and the lawyer, Herr Goldschmidt."

"Goldsmith."

"Yes."

"Why did you kill Fräulein Enzberg?"

The man shrugged.

"Surely, she was Mitteldorfer's friend; why would he want her dead?"

"Who is this Mitteldorfer you keep saying?" the man asked, smiling a little.

"You know perfectly well who he is," Dino said.

"He's your father," Stone interjected.

"I am orphan," the man said, smiling.

There was another German name Stone could try, but he couldn't remember it.

Andy Anderson spoke up. "Why did you kill Susan Bean?" he asked.

The man looked genuinely puzzled. "Bean? This is a person?"

"The woman in the penthouse apartment in the East Sixties," Anderson said. "You followed Mr. Barrington there and killed her when he went out. Why did you kill her?"

"I am not knowing about this," the man said.

Stone remembered the name. "Herr Hausman," he said, "are you telling us you don't know who Susan Bean is?"

The man turned and looked at Stone, exasperated. "I am not knowing . . ."

He stopped.

"Hausman *is* your name, isn't it?" Stone asked.

The man shrugged.

"Your Christian name is Ernst, isn't it?"

The man laughed.

"I got it," Dino said. "The nephew in Hamburg, the one who works at the cigarette factory."

The suspect shook his head. "No," he said. "Ernst is being in Hamburg still."

"And your mother is still in Hamburg, isn't she?" Stone asked.

The man turned and glared at Stone but said nothing.

"Let's get back to Susan Bean," Anderson said. He read out her address from his notebook. "You were at this address?"

"No," the man said. "I am not knowing this place."

Stone took the legal pad from the table, tore off a sheet of paper, and wrote on it. "Check to see if Ernst Hausman is still in Hamburg. Find out his address and his mother's name. Find out if there are any siblings." He handed it to Dino, who looked at it, then handed it to Anderson. Anderson left the room.

"I don't understand," Dino said. "You've admitted killing all these people, but you deny killing Susan Bean. Why?"

"You must be listening better," the man replied. "I am not knowing this lady."

Anderson returned to the room. "It's being done," he said, handing Dino a note.

Dino read it and handed it to Stone.

Stone read it aloud. "No fingerprint record in this country. Have sent request to Interpol."

"How long have you been in this country?" Dino asked.

The man shrugged. "Few weeks, I think."

"Did you enter the country legally?"

"Oh, yes," the man said. "I am being very legal always."

"Except when you are killing people."

"Except at this time." He smiled.

"You're enjoying yourself, aren't you?" Dino asked.

The man shrugged.

"Let me acquaint you with a point of the law in the state of New York," Dino said. "We have the death penalty here. You understand the death penalty?"

The man shrugged and said nothing.

"They take a needle," Dino said, pointing at his arm, "and put it here, in the vein. That's all; lights out; *kaput*."

"In Deutschland is being no death," the man said. "Deutschland is being civilized."

"Well, here, we're still barbarians, I guess," Dino replied. "Here we still put murderers to death, and you are a murderer. You have confessed to killing seven people."

"Six only," the man said. "Not this lady Bean."

"Bad news," Dino said. "Six is enough for the death penalty, the needle. Of course, before that happens, you'll spend many years in a small cell, talking to nobody. We have prisons like that in this country. Dangerous people like you are put into special cells where they see nobody, talk to nobody for twenty-three hours a day. One hour a day, you get to exercise alone. Once a week, you get to shower. Then, after a few years, when you're already crazy from being alone, they take you to a little room and they put the needle in your arm, you understand?"

The man said nothing, but his face had become grim.

"Now," Dino said, "maybe there is a way for you to live. You see, we know that you did these murders because Mitteldorfer wanted you to. You had nothing against these people, right? Maybe Mitteldorfer made you kill them. If you tell us about that, if you testify to that in court, then maybe we can ask the district attorney not to go for the death penalty."

"But I am being in the place alone?" the man said. "I am not speaking to any person? I am not seeing any person?"

"Maybe," Dino said. "If you're *real* helpful, maybe we can make that better, too."

"I am not believing you," the man said. "You will be putting me in this room all the time."

"I'm offering you a deal," Dino said. "You understand deal?"

"No."

"You help me, I help you."

"How am I helping you?"

"You tell me where to find Mitteldorfer. You tell me why Mitteldorfer wanted these people dead. You say this in a court of law."

The man shook his head. "If you are not killing me, *he* is killing me."

"No," Dino said. "We will protect you from Mitteldorfer."

To Stone's astonishment, the man began to cry.

Dino gaped at him, startled.

The man stood up. "I must have toilet," he said.

"Later," Dino replied.

The man began unzipping his fly.

"All right, all right," Dino said. He handcuffed the man with his hands in front of him, so that he could use the toilet. "Let's go," he said.

Stone followed the two into the hallway outside the interrogation room. It was a narrow hallway, and momentarily crowded. Dino held the man against the wall to allow two police officers to pass.

Stone saw it coming and opened his mouth to yell, but too late. The man reached out and plucked the pistol from an officer's belt, elbowed Dino out of the way, and pointed the weapon at Stone.

"Gun!" Stone yelled, diving for the floor. From behind him he heard two shots, and he looked up to see the suspect fall to the floor beside him. A good part of his head was missing. Stone looked back down the hallway. Andy Anderson was still in a combat crouch, with his weapon pointed at the dead man.

"Oh, shit!" Dino said.

54

ALL HELL BROKE LOOSE IN THE HALLWAY. HALF A DOZEN cops had their weapons out, pointing them in every direction. Andy Anderson was leaning against the wall, vomiting. The cop whose gun had been taken was screaming, over and over, "It's not my fault, it's not my fault!"

Dino, who was lying on top of the dead man, got to his feet. "Nobody shoot!" he yelled. "Everybody shut up!" Gradually, the noise died down. "The perp is dead," Dino said. "Everybody holster your weapons right now."

Stone took Andy's pistol and handed it to Dino, then got Andy headed toward the locker room. "Go in there and splash some cold water on your face," he said to the young cop.

"All right," Dino said, pointing at various cops, "you call the medical examiner and get him over here; you get a blanket and cover the body; everybody go and write down exactly what you saw, and do it now, before it gets cold." The hallway emptied of policemen. "Jesus Christ, did I fuck this up," Dino said. "We had the guy."

"It's okay, Dino," Stone said. "He wasn't going to give us Mitteldorfer, anyway. He was going to jerk us around for the fun of it, that's all."

"At least, we got a confession on tape," Dino said. "That's something, anyway."

Shortly, the ME arrived, did his work, and had the body removed. The precinct janitor arrived with a mop and cleaned up the bloody mess on the hallway floor. Dino and Stone repaired to Dino's glassed-in office, and Dino pulled the blinds.

"Now we're back where we started," Dino said.

"No, we're not. The guy who was doing the killings is gone, so we don't have to watch our backs anymore. Somehow, I don't think Mitteldorfer is up to doing his own killing."

"You think this guy was his son?"

"Apparently, he had two—Ernst, who works at the cigarette factory, and this one. Remind me to thank Andy Anderson," he said. "He was very quick; the guy didn't even have a chance to get off a round."

"I'll get him decorated for that," Dino said.

"If you need an affidavit, let me know."

Andy Anderson knocked on the door, came in, and set some papers on Dino's desk. "There's my account of what happened, Lieutenant," he said.

"Andy," Stone said, "thanks for being so quick. You saved my ass."

"I'm glad I could help," Andy said. "What can I do now?"

"I don't guess you've heard anything from Hamburg yet," Dino said.

"Not yet; I'll call again."

Stone spoke up. "Andy, when you brought the guy in, you emptied his pockets, didn't you?"

"Yes; everything's deposited with the desk sergeant."

"Get the envelope; let's see what he had on him," Dino said.

Andy disappeared.

"What's our next move?" Dino asked Stone.

"Let's start at the dry cleaner's and work outward, distributing the guy's picture," Stone said. "If we can find out where he lives, maybe he has some stuff there that will tell us something."

"Good idca; I'll get Andy on it."

Andy returned with a brown envelope and handed it to Dino.

Dino tore open the envelope and dumped the contents onto his desk, and the three men gathered around.

"A little over a hundred bucks in U.S. currency and a bunch of German marks," Dino said. "No wallet; a key ring with two keys."

"Outside and inside doors," Stone said. He opened a folded piece of paper. "And a rent receipt made out to Erwin Hausman." He read out the address.

"That's around the corner from the dry cleaner's," Andy said.

"That's a break," Stone said.

"Yeah," Dino said, "let's get over there. He turned to Andy. "Make sure that this doesn't get into the press yet; I don't want Mitteldorfer to read about it and run."

"Uh, Lieutenant," Andy said, "I'm afraid we got unlucky there."

"Tell me."

"There was a camera crew from Channel Four in the neighborhood when the patrolmen arrested the guy. They got the whole thing on tape."

"Do they know who he is?" Stone asked.

"I don't know."

Dino looked at his watch. "We've got until the five o'clock news," he said.

"If they don't do a bulletin at the top of the hour."

"Andy, you get on the phone to Channel Four; see if you can get them to hold the story for twenty-four hours. Offer them an exclusive, if you have to."

"Lieutenant," Andy replied, "they've already got an exclusive."

"Tell them I'll do an interview if they'll hold it for twenty-four hours."

"I'll be lucky if I can get them to hold it until eleven o'clock," Andy said.

"Do the best you can. Come on, Stone."

*   *   *

The building was a run-down pile of bricks with a fire escape hung on the front. There was no Hausman on any of the mailboxes, but one of the keys opened the front door. Dino banged on the super's door. A small, Hispanic man emerged.

"Yes?" he asked.

Dino showed him a badge. "You have a tenant named Hausman," he said. "What's his apartment number?"

"I don't know nothing," the man said.

Dino showed him the rent receipt. "What's his goddamned apartment number?"

"They are in 3D," the man admitted.

"They? Who's they?"

"Mr. Hausman and his friend."

"Male or female friend?"

"Male."

"What does he look like?"

The super shrugged. "Kind of like Mr. Hausman, but with real short hair."

"Is the friend in the apartment now?"

"I don't know. They come and go a lot."

"Fine; you go back inside your apartment and stay there until I call you."

The man went inside and closed the door.

Dino turned to Stone. "Are you armed?"

Stone produced his 7.65mm automatic.

Dino whipped out his cell phone and called for backup. "Let's go," he said.

They walked quietly up the stairs and found apartment 3D. Dino put his ear to the door. "TV is on," he whispered.

They took up positions on either side of the door.

Dino knocked firmly. "Hello?" he said, imitating the super's accent. "It's the super here."

Nothing.

Stone listened to the door but heard nothing but the TV.

Dino knocked again, this time louder. No reply. He inserted the key in the lock and turned it as quietly as he could. As the door opened, the TV got louder. "Hello?" he called. "It's the super here; I've got the plumber with me to check the plumbing."

No reply.

Dino nodded at Stone and, as they had done a hundred times before, they went in, guns out ahead of them. They went from room to room, which didn't take long, since there were only three of them.

"We've got two different shoe sizes here," Stone called from the bedroom, "and a lot of empty hangers in the closet."

Dino came into the bedroom. "What else?"

"Top drawer of the dresser is empty and open."

"You think the other guy ran?"

They walked back into the living room, just as the TV station cut to the news desk.

"We've got more on that arrest on Third Avenue this afternoon," the newscaster said. "Let's go back to the scene and Maria Jones."

The station cut to a young woman with a microphone, standing outside a dry cleaner's. "Thanks, Bob. I've been able to confirm with the shop owner that the man who was arrested outside this dry cleaner's shop earlier today is a dead ringer for a drawing that the police ran in Sunday's *New York Times*. He is apparently connected with a Herbert Mitteldorfer, an ex-convict being sought by police for questioning in at least five murders and the bombing of an art gallery last week. I'm going over to the precinct now and talk with the police. Back to you, Bob."

"Well, if that was the second report, I guess our guy saw the first one and lit out."

"And the first thing he would have done is call Mitteldorfer," Dino said.

Stone looked around. "There's no phone here."

"Shit," Dino said.

They could hear cops pounding up the stairs. Andy Anderson was the first through the door.

"Andy, tape this place off, then get a team in here and turn it over very carefully. There was a second occupant besides Erwin Hausman; look for anything that could tell us who the other guy is, and anything that might tell us where to find Mitteldorfer."

"Yes, sir," Andy replied.

"Anything from Hamburg, yet?"

"No, sir, and nothing from Interpol, either."

"Keep on them," Dino said.

"Dino," Stone said, "we need to talk. In the car."

55

J EFF BANION, THE PARK AVENUE DOORMAN, WAS ON DUTY
when a taxi pulled up to his awning. He hurried to get the door,
but as it opened, he saw that the cab's occupant, who was paying the
fare, was not likely destined for Jeff's building. He stepped back to
the front door and let the man deal alone with closing the cab's door.

Then, to Jeff's surprise, the young man came toward him. He
was short, his hair was cut so closely as to make him nearly bald,
and he was roughly dressed in baggy clothes and heavy boots. He
was carrying a nylon duffel. "Can I help you, sir?" Jeff asked, not
moving away from the door.

"I am seeing somebody in this building," the man said with a
thick accent.

"And who would that be, sir?"

"Mr. Howard Menzies."

This did not add up at all to Jeff. "And what business would you
have with Mr. Menzies?"

"I am having *private* business," the young man said.

"Your name?"

"Peter Hausman."

Jeff looked him up and down. "Wait right here, please," he said.

Jeff went inside and spoke to Ralph, the new desk man. "I've got a suspicious character out here who wants to see Mr. Menzies. Is he in?"

Ralph consulted a list of the building's occupants. "Yes, unless he went out through the garage."

"Get him on the house phone; I want to speak to him."

Ralph dialed the number and listened. "Mr. Menzies? Jeff, the doorman, would like to speak with you." He handed the phone to Jeff.

"Hello, Mr. Menzies?" Jeff said.

"Yes, Jeff, what is it?"

"There's someone down here wanting to see you, but I wanted to speak to you before I let him in."

"Who is it?"

"He says his name is Hausman, Peter Hausman."

There was a long moment's silence on the line, then Menzies spoke. "Oh, yes, that's my nephew. He was in town for my wife's funeral last week. Please send him up."

"Excuse me, Mr. Menzies, but could you describe your nephew, please? I want to be sure it's the right person."

"He is about my height, has very short hair, and dresses rather oddly," Menzies replied.

"Does he have an accent?" Jeff asked.

"Yes, he does."

"I'll send him right up," Jeff said. He walked back to the front door and opened it. "Come in," he said to the young man. "Take the elevator to the sixteenth floor; Mr. Menzies is expecting you."

Hausman said nothing but went straight to the elevator and pressed the button.

Jeff felt he had covered himself, but he didn't like having someone like that in the building. The other apartment owners wouldn't like it, either, he knew.

"Jeff," Ralph said.

"Yeah?"

"Carlos called in sick, and it's recycling day. Would you please put the cans and newspapers out?"

"Sure, Ralph," Jeff said. He didn't like doing this very much, but there was no one else. He took the other elevator to the garage level, where the bags of recycling material and bound newspapers waited in a corner. He hung his uniform jacket and cap on a hook, pressed the button to open the garage door, and went to work. He humped the bags up to the street, four at a time, then turned to the heavy newspaper bundles. The people in his building sure read a lot of newspapers, he thought. He had never seen the attraction, himself. He sometimes watched the local TV news, but the news, in general, seemed to have little to do with him.

He broke a sweat with the newspapers, and as he piled the last bundle on top of the others, something caught his eye. On the front of Sunday's Metro section was a drawing of a man, and he looked alarmingly like the young man he had just let into the building. There was also a photograph of another, older man.

Jeff eased the section from the bundle and read the story accompanying the pictures. The young man in the drawing had bushy hair, but otherwise was a ringer for this Peter Hausman. He turned his attention to the photograph of the older man. There seemed to be a familial resemblance between the two, and the older man looked a little like Howard Menzies, except that Mr. Menzies had a little beard and, of course, hair. The man in the picture was bald on top, so he couldn't be Mr. Menzies.

He tore the story from the paper, folded it, put it in his pocket, then returned the Metro section to the bundle of newspapers. As he did so, he heard a car start in the garage, and, a moment later, Mr. Menzies's Mercedes came up the ramp with Hausman at the wheel and Menzies in the front passenger seat. Menzies gave him a smile and a wave, and Jeff returned it.

Jeff went back into the garage, closed the door, put on his coat and cap, and went back upstairs in time to help a lady with her packages. When he had a moment, he took out the clipping and read the story again. Seven murders. He shuddered.

He reflected that, if he had not been personally acquainted with

Howard Menzies, he might have called the police number in the story, but a gentleman like Mr. Menzies could never be involved with something like this. He wasn't so sure about the nephew, though. He'd have to think about that.

Jeff put the clipping back into his pocket and went to get the door for someone.

56

BACK IN DINO'S OFFICE, STONE ASKED TO USE THE phone and called Bill Eggers at Woodman & Weld. He'd called earlier, but Eggers had been late coming in.

"Hello?"

"Bill, it's Stone."

"Good morning."

"How'd it go with Martin Brougham last night?"

"I didn't make much progress; I think he still plans to subpoena you."

"Did you mention the business about the doctored tape in the Dante trial?"

"I didn't get a chance. I was on my way out when his wife called me to the phone, and by the time I hung up, Marty was in his bath. I've got a call in to him now. I saw on TV that you caught the guy you've been looking for. He's your suspect for the Susan Bean murder, isn't he? That should go a long way toward stopping Marty in his tracks."

"Bad news there, Bill; the guy, whose name was Hausman, confessed to six killings, but he denied all knowledge of the Bean murder. I'm not sure what to think about it."

"Well, you need to work on him some more. If he's in a confessing mood, he can clear you completely."

"I'm afraid he's not in any kind of mood; he's dead. He made a grab for an officer's gun at the precinct, and another officer shot him."

"Oops."

"Yeah."

"Look, Stone, I've got an idea. Are you still determined to testify if he subpoenas you?"

"Yes, I am. I'm not going to do anything to make myself look guilty."

"Then let's go down to the courthouse tomorrow morning; just show up outside the grand-jury room and demand for you to be allowed to testify."

Stone thought about this. "I like it; it might rattle him."

"There'll be some press there, too, and we can make a point of your showing up. That'll make the evening news."

"I'll tell Marty about what we know of the Dante business, too; he can worry about that while he's questioning you, and if he makes us mad, we can mention it to the press after you've testified."

"All right," Stone said.

"Meet me down there at nine sharp tomorrow morning, and don't tell me where you plan to be in the meantime. If they try to subpoena you, I can deny knowledge of your whereabouts."

"See you at nine in the morning," Stone said. He hung up.

"What's up?" Dino asked.

Stone explained the situation to him.

"I wish we could wrap this up before you have to testify," Dino said.

"So do I."

There was a knock on the door, and Andy Anderson came in.

"Sit down, Andy, and tell me what's happening," Dino said.

Anderson took a seat and got out his notebook. "Okay," he said, "first, the apartment. We took it apart, but there wasn't much there, except one more rent receipt in Erwin Hausman's name—no IDs, no notes of any kind, only two sets of fingerprints, Erwin's and one more."

"Nothing at all that would help us find Mitteldorfer?"

"Nothing. If there had been a phone, we could have checked the records for numbers called."

"That's why there was no phone," Stone said. "Mitteldorfer is very smart."

"Now, on fingerprints," Andy said. "Interpol got a match for Erwin. He had been arrested half a dozen times, all over Europe, for participation in violence at international soccer matches. He's one of a lot of repeat offenders. The Hamburg police confirm this, and, more important, they confirm that he has a younger brother who has also been arrested a number of times for the same thing, name of Peter Hausman. I'm running the other set of prints with Interpol now, on the supposition that they belong to Peter. The only other sibling is Ernst, who works at the cigarette factory and who is, apparently, a solid citizen. The boys' mother is named Helga, and she refused to speak more than a few words with the police. She wouldn't answer any questions about the boys' father, who, apparently, doesn't live in the house with them."

"Bingo," Dino said. "Now we're getting somewhere."

"Where are we getting?" Stone asked. "What have we learned that will help us find Mitteldorfer, or Hausman, or whatever his name is?"

"I checked the Hausman name against utility records," Andy said. "There are only two Hausmans in New York City: one is an elderly, retired machinist who lives in Queens, and the other has been a cab driver for the past sixteen years."

"Then we're back to the pictures in the paper," Stone said, "and we've had only the one report."

"And it was on Hausman, not Mitteldorfer," Dino said. "Andy, talk to the local TV stations and get both the photograph of Mitteldorfer and the sketch of Hausman on the air tonight, but have the Hausman sketch altered to show very short hair."

"Right," Andy said. "Anything else?"

"Concentrate on getting that done; we're short of time."

"Actually, Lieutenant, there's something else I want to tell you."

"Shoot."

"It's about the Bean murder; it didn't seem important until now, and, well, Mick Kelly asked me not to bring it up. There didn't seem to be any reason to, so I didn't."

"What is it?" Dino asked.

"When the three killings—Bean, Stone's secretary, and the Hirsch woman—happened so close together, I thought they were all connected."

"We all did," Dino said.

"Well, now I don't think Bean is connected to the other two. First of all, Hausman denied any knowledge of her, and he seems credible, in the light of his confessing to six other murders."

"Good point," Dino said. "You got another suspect?"

Stone spoke up. "Not me, I hope."

"Not you, Stone," Andy said. "Tell me, is there any reason why someone in the DA's office might want Susan Bean to be shut up?"

Stone sat up straight in his chair. "Very possibly," he said. "Why do you ask?"

"Well, you remember that Mick and I got to Bean's apartment pretty fast after you called it in?"

"Yes," Stone replied.

"That's because we were right around the corner when we got the call."

"Why?" Dino asked.

"Mick had wanted to meet somebody at a little bar on Lexington. I drove him there, and he got out and went in. He was in there, maybe, three minutes; I had a cramp in my leg, and I got out to walk it off. You know, there's a little window that's required for every bar; it was mandated a long time ago so that women looking for their husbands could see inside."

"Yeah, I know," Dino said.

"Well, I looked inside to see if Mick was about done, and I saw him talking to somebody."

"And who might that have been?" Stone asked, thinking he might know the answer to his own question.

"It was Tom Deacon, from the DA's Office," Andy said.

"And that's what, a thirty-second walk from the Bean apartment building?" Stone asked.

"Yeah," Andy said. "I'm really sorry I didn't bring this up before, Lieutenant, but it didn't seem pertinent at the time. I asked Mick what he was seeing Deacon about, and he said he was angling for a job in the DA's investigative division. He asked me not to mention it to anybody, because he didn't want you to know that, after a pretty short time in the precinct, he was looking to get out."

"Dino," Stone said, "when Susan and I were walking to her place that night, she told me she wasn't happy about how they had won the Dante case, and she was thinking of getting out."

"I remember your saying that," Dino said.

"I haven't had a chance to tell you, but I've learned from a source that Deacon may have fabricated or altered the surveillance-tape evidence that Marty Brougham used to get the Dante conviction."

"You think Brougham knew about it?"

"Maybe, maybe not," Stone said, "but I think I'll find out tomorrow morning."

Dino turned to Andy. "See if you can get a search warrant for Deacon's residence."

"What am I going to tell a judge we're looking for?"

"The murder weapon, or anything else you can think of. I know it's thin; try Judge Haverman; she's always been cooperative."

"I'm on it," Andy said.

"You'll never get the warrant," Stone said. "Why don't you just get Deacon in here and brace him? He doesn't know we know he was near the scene; maybe he'll make a mistake."

"At this point," Dino said, "I'm willing to try anything."

57

STONE WENT BACK TO DOLCE'S PLACE AND PACKED HIS things. He was out of clean clothing, and he figured, what with the death of Erwin Hausman, it might be safe to go back to his own house. He left a note for Dolce, but after a moment's thought, he kept the key she had given him.

Back in his own street he cruised the block a couple of times, looking for vans or other suspicious vehicles, but he saw nothing that alarmed him. He used his remote to open the garage door, drove inside, closed the door, took his things out of the trunk, and went upstairs.

The place was in good order. Helen had, apparently, with no instructions from him, continued to come in. It occurred to him that that might have put her in danger, and he winced at the thought that he had forgotten to tell her.

He threw his dirty clothing into a hamper and put away his cases. He was about to lock the 7.65 automatic in the gun safe, but he reflected that someone, probably Peter Hausman, was still out there, so he kept the pistol in its shoulder holster. He went down to his office and checked his machine for messages. There were a dozen or so, but none terribly urgent. Since settling his personal injury suit, there had been nothing much on his docket. There were three hangups recorded on the machine, and he wondered about that. He punched up the list of calls on his caller ID box and compared them to the messages. The three hangups were from a Brooklyn number that he didn't recognize. The thought that it might be Eduardo Bianchi crossed his mind, but Eduardo had probably known where he was. He shrugged it off; if it was important, the caller would try again.

The upstairs doorbell rang. Stone started to answer it through the phone system, but instead, he opened the street door to the office and peeked up at the front stoop. A slickly dressed man in his midthirties stood there, tapping his foot impatiently.

"Hello," Stone called out. "Can I help you?"

"You Stone Barrington?" the man asked.

"Yes."

The man came down the steps and walked to the office door. "I tried to call you a couple times, but you weren't answering the phone. My name is John Donato; does that mean anything to you?"

"I don't think so," Stone said, then, just as the man spoke again, he remembered.

"Funny, it ought to, since you been screwing my wife."

"Ah, yes," Stone said. "I know who you are, and you shouldn't jump to conclusions."

"I know Dolce," Donato said, "and I ain't jumping to any conclusions. You're screwing her, all right, and I thought I would warn you just once before I stick a gun in your ear and blow your brains out."

Stone snapped, throwing aside his lawyerly restraint. "Now, you listen to me, you dumb goombah," he said. "I know exactly who you are; you're the cheap, two-bit hood who *used* to be married to a girl who was way above you, and while you were married to her you spent most of your time screwing around with other women, so don't come around here bitching to me about your marital rights."

Donato took a step back, then he unbuttoned his jacket and

opened it so that Stone could see the pistol under his arm. "You see that?" he asked.

"Yeah, I see it," Stone said, unbuttoning his own jacket. "You see this?"

Donato blinked and stepped back again.

Stone took out his badge and flashed it. "And do you see this? It means that I can have half a dozen cops on your case with a single phone call. How would you like that? Or would you like to have the feds crawling all over your concrete business? I can arrange that, too. Are you beginning to get the picture?"

Donato looked a little shaken. He turned and walked back to the sidewalk. "You just remember that, as long as I'm around, Dolce is a married woman," he said. Then he crossed the street, got into a waiting car, and drove away.

Stone went back inside, slamming the door behind him. His residence phone was ringing, and he pushed that button on his desk phone. "Hello?" he said, irritably.

"Well, don't bite my head off," Dolce said.

"I'm sorry; I didn't mean to do that."

"I got your note, and I'm very sad; I wanted you here when I got home."

"Dolce, I really needed to get home. Good news: the man who has been trying to kill Dino and me and everyone we know, is dead. He was shot while in police custody."

"That *is* good news," she said. "Then it's all over?"

"No, we haven't got Mitteldorfer, and there appears to be one other man involved. Watch the six o'clock news."

"Can I come over there and watch it?" she asked, her voice low.

"Sweetheart, I need a night off. I've got a grand-jury appearance first thing in the morning, and I need to think about my testimony."

"Stone," she purred, "just because you had a problem last night doesn't mean you'll have one tonight. Why don't I come over and cook you something?"

At the mention of cooking, Stone weakened. "Okay, let me give you the address."

"I have the address," she said. "I'll bring groceries, you do the wine."

"What time?"

"Give me an hour or so."

"Take your time; I'm not going anywhere."

"I know you're not," she said.

Stone returned a few phone calls, then went to the cellar and chose some wines. That done, he went upstairs and changed into comfortable clothing, switching on the bedroom TV. The story was all over the tube, with the photograph of Mitteldorfer and a modified sketch of the second Hausman. He hoped to God they would get some more calls from that. The phone rang.

"Hello?"

"It's Dino; you're back in your own house?"

"Yeah, I figure with Erwin dead and Mitteldorfer's picture on TV, the bad guys are in disarray, so it's safe here."

"I'm glad to see you out of the witch's bed and back into your own."

"Dino, Dolce is on her way over here right now, and I want you to stop saying all these terrible things about her."

"I haven't said anything that wasn't true."

"I like her, Dino; I'll grant you, she can be a little overbearing at times, but I like her. I like her father, too. You may as well know that it was he who found out about the doctored tape used in the Dante trial, so we both owe him."

"I don't *want* to owe him," Dino said.

"Well, that's tough; you do, anyway, and I, for one, am glad to have all the help he can give us. I want my life back, you know?"

"Yeah, yeah, I know. I'm trying to figure out whether to bring Mary Ann and Ben home."

"Not yet; let's be cautious for a few more days. Maybe the TV news story will produce some calls."

"By the way, we got the warrant on Deacon's place; Andy's going to execute it tomorrow morning, as soon as he's out of his apartment."

"What do you expect to find?"

"Probably nothing; the guy's not stupid enough to take the knife home. But we've got to make the effort. The fact that he was around the corner when Susan was killed isn't enough."

"Why don't you brace Mick Kelly, too?"

"Good idea; I'll have him picked up at the same time as Deacon."

"Tomorrow morning, call me on my cell phone if you find out anything; I'd like to have as much ammunition as possible when I testify."

"Sure."

"Oh, by the way, Johnny Donato was here this afternoon."

"Oh, Jesus," Dino said. "You see what happens when you ignore my advice?"

"Tell me what you know about the guy, Dino."

"Well, he's not just a soldier, but he's not a capo, either, though the word is, he might be one of these days, if somebody doesn't pop him."

"Is he dangerous?"

"Who knows? He might call a hit on you, if he thought he could get away with it. In my judgment, he wouldn't have the guts to do the job himself."

"He showed me his gun, and I showed him mine."

Dino laughed. "That'll keep him off the block, anyway. Guys like Donato aren't used to dealing with people who are as well armed as they are. You ought to be grateful to the guy, Stone; he's a buffer between you and Dolce. As long as he's alive, she can't do anything permanent."

"What makes you think she'd want to do anything permanent with me?" Stone asked.

"I don't know, Stone. Eduardo apparently thinks highly of you, and he doesn't have a history of admiring Dolce's boyfriends."

"And where are you getting this?"

"From Mary Ann, where else?"

"Dino, you're making way too much of all this."

"Just make sure you don't shoot Donato; it wouldn't be in your best interests."

"Goodbye, Dino," Stone said, and hung up. A moment later, the front door buzzed. Stone picked up the phone. "Yes?"

"Your dinner has arrived," Dolce said.

58

DOLCE WALKED IN CARRYING TWO LARGE BAGS FILLED with groceries. She pecked him on the lips, handed him the bags, then walked around the living room, assessing the place. "This is nice," she said, finally. "A little gloomy, maybe; could use some color, but it has good bones."

"Let me show you the kitchen," Stone said, leading the way.

She liked the kitchen better. "A girl could do good work here," she said. "You got all the right appliances; how'd you know about that?"

"I cook a little," Stone replied, setting down the groceries. "Can I get you a drink?"

"A little Strega, maybe."

"Ah, I don't have any Strega, I'm afraid."

"Stone, you're seeing an Italian girl, now; stock up."

"I do have some very good olive oil."

"Never drink it; how about a good single-malt scotch? Is that whitebread enough for you?"

"I've got a Laphroaig," Stone said, looking through the kitchen liquor cabinet, "or a Glenlivet, or a Dalwhinney."

"The Laphroaig, please; no ice, just a little cold water."

Stone did as she asked.

She sipped the drink, then came into his arms. "Very good," she said, kissing him. "When do I see the bedroom?"

"First food, then love," Stone said, wondering why he had said "love" instead of "sex."

"Fair enough," she said, grabbing an apron from a hook and starting to unpack groceries. "By the way, you haven't heard anything from a Johnny Donato, have you?"

"Why do you ask?"

"He's been bothering me, but I think he's too smart to bother you. He's my husband."

"He bothered me this afternoon," Stone said. "He came to the house."

Dolce closed her eyes and clenched her teeth. She turned and looked at Stone, contrite. "I'll see that it doesn't happen again," she said.

"Don't worry about it," Stone said. "I think I scared him off with talk of the cops and the feds. I think he probably feels that he's out of his depth."

Dolce put some water on to boil and began chopping garlic. "Johnny has always been out of his depth," she said, "on this side of the East River. He's a Brooklyn boy, and he should never leave."

"He is handsome," Stone said. "I can see how your head might have been turned at nineteen."

"Trouble is, Johnny is *still* nineteen." She began chopping prosciutto. "He does crazy things, then wants to be forgiven. He's kind of a split personality—one moment, a sweet little boy, the next, a screaming maniac."

"How long did you actually live with him?"

"Less than a month. On our last day together, I hit him in the head with a cast-iron skillet and left him on the kitchen floor for dead. He had a harder head than I thought."

"Remind me never to make you angry," Stone said.

Dolce looked at him sweetly. "Never make me angry," she said. "Consider yourself reminded."

Stone opened a bottle of white wine and poured himself a glass, sniffing it first.

"Can I try it?" she asked.

He handed her the glass.

She swirled it, sniffed it, tasted it. "It's lovely; is it Italian?"

"It's a Mondavi Reserve Chardonnay '94. Not everything good is Italian."

"Mondavi is an Italian name," she said smugly. "By the way, speaking of Italians, Papa would like you to come to dinner in Brooklyn tomorrow night."

"I'd love to. Who else is coming?"

"Mary Ann will be there; I'm not sure about Dino. Pick me up at the house at six?"

"Sure."

"What is this grand-jury thing tomorrow? What are you testifying to?"

"I'm testifying that I didn't murder a young woman."

"Is that true?"

"Yes."

"Oh, good."

They dined on fettucini with a sauce of prosciutto, peas, and cream. Stone liked her cooking, and he was liking her more and more. There were times when she seemed steely hard, but here, in his kitchen, she was soft and funny and lovely. And God, could she cook!

"Would you like some of Aunt Rosaria's cheesecake?" she asked when they were finished with their pasta.

"Yes, if you could call for an ambulance first," Stone replied. "What with the pasta sauce and the dessert, I might as well just take the cholesterol straight into a vein."

*   *   *

301

After dinner he led her upstairs. She gave the bedroom the same inspection she had given the living room. "It's very masculine," she said.

"A person of the masculine persuasion lives here," Stone reminded her.

"I *am* aware of that," she said, unbuckling his belt and letting his trousers drop to the floor.

"I don't appear to be wearing any pants," he said.

She pulled his shorts down to his ankles, and he stepped out of them. "Just the way I like you," she replied.

"I don't think I'm going to have any, ah, problems tonight," he said, unbuttoning her blouse and kissing her breasts.

"I know," she said.

59

THE FOLLOWING MORNING, STONE MET BILL EGGERS on the courthouse steps, and together they walked to the corridor outside the grand-jury room. "We'll ambush Marty Brougham here," Eggers said. They took a seat on a bench in the hallway.

"You're sure this is the best way to do this?" Stone asked.

"He wouldn't take my phone call yesterday," Eggers replied, "so, as far as I'm concerned, it's the *only* way."

"Whatever you say."

"I had lunch with Eduardo Bianchi yesterday," Eggers said, "and he asked a lot of questions about you."

"Oh? What kind of questions?"

"The kind that might be construed as coming from a prospective father-in-law," Eggers said.

Stone didn't reply to that, but he felt a little queasy.

"He wanted to know about your upbringing and education; how you're doing financially; what your prospects are."

"And what did you tell him?"

"The truth, of course. He's not the sort of man you lie to."

"And how did he react?"

"It's funny, but I've known Eduardo for a while, and I've never heard him express a favorable opinion of anyone until yesterday. Of course, he's a very reserved man, and polite, and I've rarely heard him express an unfavorable opinion, either, but I have to say, I was surprised."

"That someone would have a favorable opinion of me?"

Eggers laughed. "Not someone; Eduardo. He's not easy to impress."

Stone was about to inquire further about this conversation when a hubbub arose down the hallway, and he looked around to see Martin Brougham walking slowly down the hallway, surrounded by half a dozen reporters. As he approached, Eggers stood up; Stone remained seated.

"Good morning, Marty," Eggers boomed, apparently oblivious to the press. He stuck out his hand, and Brougham was forced to shake it.

"Morning, Bill; if you'll excuse me . . ."

"Marty, I heard that you were interested in subpoenaing Stone Barrington, so I've saved you the trouble and brought Stone down here for you to question before the grand jury." He beckoned to Stone.

Stone stood up and offered his hand to Brougham. When the man took it, Stone hung on. "Good morning, Mr. Brougham," he said, loudly enough for microphones to pick up. "I've come down here voluntarily to answer any questions you may have about my relationship with Susan Bean and my actions on the night she was murdered. Do you think you could take me first this morning?"

Brougham was flustered but tried not to show it. "I'll, uh, see what I can do, Mr. Barrington," he said. "And I appreciate your volunteering to testify."

"I absolutely *insist* on testifying," Stone said, still hanging on to the man's hand. "You'll remember that I told you some time ago that I'd be glad to cooperate in any way I can."

"Yes, yes," Brougham said, wresting his hand from Stone's grasp. "If you'll just have a seat, Mr. Barrington, I'll try to get to you soon."

Eggers spoke up again. "Marty, could I speak to you privately for a moment? I have some information that might bear on this case, and I'd like to convey it to you before you convene the grand jury."

"Sorry, Bill, I don't have time right now; maybe later today." He turned and started into the jury room.

"I did try to reach you by phone yesterday," Eggers called after him. The door closed behind Brougham.

The reporters crowded around Eggers. "What information do you have for the DA, Mr. Eggers?" one of them asked.

"I think I'd better convey it to Mr. Brougham before I discuss it with you," Eggers said to the man. "Please excuse me." He sat down next to Stone. "He's going to have to call you to testify, now," he whispered. "If he doesn't, the press will practically assassinate him."

Stone sat quietly and waited. Other witnesses for the grand jury filed into the hallway and took seats. Stone exchanged greetings with a uniformed sergeant from the Nineteenth Precinct, Tim Ryan, whom he had known for years. As they were chatting, Stone's cell phone rang. "Excuse me, Tim," he said to the cop. He walked to the end of the corridor and took out the phone. "Hello?"

"It's Dino."

Stone could hear him grinning. "What's up?"

"We went into Tom Deacon's apartment an hour ago, and guess what we found?"

"The murder weapon, I hope."

"We weren't quite *that* lucky, but we did find Susan Bean's diary."

"Oh, *that's* good!" Stone said. "Have you read it?"

"You bet I have; it's telegraphic, but it lays out her knowledge of the doctored tapes in the Dante trial."

"Does the diary implicate Brougham?"

"Not directly, but it's hard to see how, if Bean knew about the tape, Marty didn't. Anyway, it's a first-rate motive for Deacon; the very fact that he had possession of the diary is incriminating. It makes him our number one suspect and Mick Kelly an accessory after the fact. At the very least, I can get Kelly bounced from the force for not reporting Deacon's presence near the scene of the murder."

"Have you picked up Deacon?"

"Not yet, but we're looking for him; Kelly, too. I haven't put out an APB yet; I don't want to spook either of them."

"That's great news, Dino, and it comes at a very good time for me."

"Have you testified, yet?"

"I'm waiting to go in, now."

"Give Brougham hell for me."

"You bet I will; can I use what you've told me?"

"Go right ahead. See you later."

"You coming to Bianchi's for dinner tonight?"

"I've been invited," Dino said.

"See you there." Stone hung up and returned to the bench.

"What's up?" Eggers asked.

"You're not going to believe . . ." Stone was interrupted as the door to the grand-jury room opened and a bailiff stuck his head out.

"Call Stone Barrington!" he yelled.

Stone stood up. "Right here."

The man opened the door and ushered Stone inside the grand-jury room.

Stone walked quickly to the stand and sat down. He was faced with the members of the grand jury, ordinary-looking people seated on raised tiers before him. Martin Brougham stood, looking confident, his hands folded before him. The bailiff swore in Stone.

"State your name and address for the record," Brougham said.

Stone did so. He added, "I would like to state for the record that I have not been subpoenaed but have volunteered to appear before this panel."

"Yes, yes," Brougham said irritably. "Mr. Barrington, how do you earn your living?"

"I'm an attorney-at-law," Stone replied.

"You were once a police officer, were you not?"

"I was. I served fourteen years with the NYPD, finishing as a detective second grade."

"And what were the circumstances of your leaving the department? Why didn't you serve until you could take retirement benefits?"

"I was wounded in the line of duty and, as a result, discharged from the department for medical reasons—with full pension and benefits." This seemed to bring Brougham up short. Apparently, Stone thought, he hadn't been prepared for this answer.

"I see," Brougham said, recovering himself. "Were you acquainted with a Susan Bean before her death?"

"I was," Stone replied. "I met her at your home." He gave the date.

Brougham grimaced; he clearly hadn't wanted that in the record. "And you knew her previous to that date, didn't you?"

"I once defended a client in whose prosecution she assisted, but I have very little memory of her from that time. When I met her in your home I had no recollection of ever having met her before; nor did she mention any previous meeting."

"Is it not a fact that, some years ago, you met Ms. Bean in a bar, picked her up, took her home, and seduced her?"

"I have already given you my entire recollection of my acquaintance with Ms. Bean. I have nothing to add to that."

"Did you seduce her?"

"Asked and answered."

Brougham turned his body so that he could face the grand jury while asking Stone his next question. "Is it not a fact, Mr. Barrington, that in a moment of blind rage, you murdered Susan Bean?"

"It is not a fact; I did not murder Susan Bean or harm her in any way," Stone replied calmly, addressing his answer to the jury.

Brougham took a deep breath, rose on his toes, and raised his voice. "Is it not a fact . . ."

"It is a fact," Stone said, interrupting Brougham, "that I was informed just a few minutes ago in a telephone conversation with Lieutenant Dino Bacchetti, who heads the detective squad at the Nineteenth Precinct, that there is a new prime suspect in the murder of Ms. Bean, and that he is now being sought by the police."

Brougham expelled a lungful of air in a strangled grunt. "What did . . . ?"

"Lieutenant Bacchetti tells me that the prime suspect is one Thomas Deacon, who heads the investigative division of the District Attorney's Office."

Now Brougham was speechless. He stood facing the grand jury, his mouth open, his face drained of color. He took another deep breath. "You are excused, Mr. Barrington."

"Wouldn't you like to know about the evidence against Deacon, Mr. Brougham?" Stone asked.

"*You are excused!*" Brougham practically shouted.

Stone got up and left the grand-jury room. Bill Eggers stood up and approached him.

"That was quick," he said. "How did it go?"

Stone was about to answer him when he looked past Eggers and saw Tom Deacon and Michael Kelly coming down the hallway toward them. "Excuse me a minute, Bill." He turned to Tim Ryan, who was standing nearby. "Tim," he said, "can I borrow your cuffs?"

Without a word, Ryan reached behind him and produced a pair of handcuffs.

"I'm about to make an arrest," Stone said to the cop. "You want to assist me?"

"Sure, Stone," Ryan replied.

"You know Deacon and Kelly there?"

"Yeah."

"I'll take Deacon; you make sure Kelly doesn't shoot me."

"Okay."

Stone, the handcuffs in his left hand, headed straight for Deacon, his right hand out. "Hello, Tom," he said.

Deacon looked puzzled, but reacted by reaching for Stone's hand.

Stone took hold of Deacon's hand and held it while he snapped a cuff onto his wrist. "You're under arrest for the murder of Susan

Bean," he said, and, before Deacon could react, Stone twisted Deacon's arm behind his back, pushed him against the wall and cuffed his hands behind him. Then he spun Deacon around, ripped the pistol from his shoulder holster and removed his police identification from his inside pocket. "You're not going to be needing this anymore," he said.

There was a thud behind Stone, and he turned to see Mick Kelly, spread-eagled on the marble floor with Tim Ryan's knee in his back, being handcuffed. "Take his gun *and* his badge, Tim," he said, "and read them both their rights. I'll call it in."

He shoved Deacon onto a bench, reached for his cell phone, and called Dino.

"Hello?"

"It's Stone. I've just made a citizen's arrest."

60

JEFF BANION WAS STANDING AT HIS POST IN FRONT OF the apartment building in the evening light, when he saw Howard Menzies's big Mercedes coming down the block, with two men in the front seat. As it pulled to a halt at the awning, Jeff watched as a familiar-looking man got out from behind the wheel and came toward him. It took him a moment to recognize Mr. Menzies's nephew, Peter Hausman, because Hausman had somehow acquired a very full head of hair.

"I am coming back after a moment," the young man said in his heavily accented English. "No need to announce; Mr. Menzies is expect me."

"Fine," Jeff replied. He looked up the block and saw a uniformed traffic officer coming down the block, writing tickets. He opened the door of the Mercedes and got in. "Excuse me, sir," he said to the other man, whom he did not recognize. "I have to move the car; there's a cop giving out tickets."

"Good idea," the man said. "Pretty nice car, huh?"

Jeff maneuvered the car to a space at the curb. "Sure is," he said. "Let me just wait until this cop passes."

"Like to buy it?" the man asked.

"Sure." Jeff laughed. "Just take it out of my paycheck."

"I don't understand this guy Menzies," the man said. "We only sold it to him less than two weeks ago, and now he's sold it back."

"Yeah?"

"Yeah. I'm just here to drive Menzies to Kennedy and then take the car. It cost him a year's depreciation on the car to sell it back like that."

Jeff saw the cop turn the corner and got out. "Well," he said to the man, "people do crazy things." He went back to his post, wondering why Menzies would sell his new car. The house phone rang. "This is Jeff," he said into the phone.

"Jeff, it's Howard Menzies; could you come upstairs and help me with some luggage, please?"

"Of course, Mr. Menzies; I'll be right up." Jeff stopped at the desk. "Ralph, watch the door, will you? I've got to give Mr. Menzies a hand." He rode up in the elevator to the sixteenth floor and found the Menzies door open. "Hello?" he called out.

"Come in, Jeff," Menzies called back. "I'm in the study."

Peter Hausman passed him, carrying bags, headed for the elevator.

Jeff went into the study. "There are some more bags in the bedroom," Menzies said.

"Going on a trip, Mr. Menzies?" Jeff asked.

"Just for a few days," Menzies replied, holding up a large briefcase. "Peter and I are taking my wife's ashes back to her homeland for burial. A sad task."

"Yes, it is; I'm very sorry about her death; I'll get the other bags." Jeff went into the master bedroom and found two cases on the bed. As he leaned over the bed to pick them up, his foot bumped against something, and he bent down to see what it was. He lifted the skirt of the bedspread and found an automatic pistol in a holster. Oh, well, he supposed some people were paranoid about living in New York City. He picked up the bags and took them to the elevator.

He rode down with Menzies and his nephew, both of whom said

nothing on the ride. He thought of asking about the sale of the Mercedes, but it was none of his business, so he didn't bring it up. When the elevator reached the lobby, he loaded the bags into the car's trunk, which was so full, he had to rearrange it to close the lid.

Menzies held out his hand. "Thank you for all your help, Jeff," he said. "I'll see you . . . ah, the middle of next week."

"Have a good trip, Mr. Menzies," Jeff replied. There were folded bills in Menzies's hand, and when Jeff had a chance to look he was surprised to find two hundred-dollar bills. He watched as the Mercedes drove down Fifth Avenue, then turned east.

Jeff walked back into the building, thinking about what had just occurred. It didn't add up: Hausman with hair; the resale of the Mercedes; the heavy tip. He had the very strong feeling that he wouldn't be seeing Howard Menzies again.

For the tenth time, he took the newspaper clipping from his pocket and read it. Seven murders, it said. He put the clipping back into his pocket and made a decision. "Ralph," he said to the desk man, "will you watch the door for a minute? I've got to use the phone in the package room."

Jeff had very mixed feelings about this, but he had to do it.

61

STONE WAS RECEIVED AT THE BIANCHI HOME BY Pietro, the butler, and taken straight through the house to a back terrace overlooking extensive gardens. Eduardo Bianchi was seated in a cushioned, wrought-iron chair, and he stood to receive his guest.

"Good evening, Stone," he said warmly, taking Stone's hand and guiding him to a companion chair. "While the women are talking, I thought we'd have an aperitif out here. It's such a lovely evening."

"What would you like, Mr. Barrington?" Pietro asked.

"May I have a Strega, please?"

Pietro beamed his approval and went for the drink.

"It really is a lovely evening," Stone said. The setting sun and the long shadows across the garden created a quilt of light and shadow. "Your garden is very beautiful."

"Thank you, Stone," Bianchi said. "I think it gives me more pleasure than any of my possessions. I am getting to be an old man, and it would comfort me to know that this house and its gardens would fall into appreciative hands when I am gone."

"I'm sure it will," Stone replied. "You seem to be in a reflective mood."

"I find I am reflective more and more often," Bianchi said. "It is the prerogative of old men, I suppose."

"You seem anything but old, sir."

Bianchi managed a small smile. "When you are my age you will find that old age is more than simply one's physical condition; it is a state of mind. Try as I might, I can no longer think like a young man, or even a middle-aged one. Lucidity in one's later years is a great gift from God; it gives one the opportunity for endless review: Have I done well in my life? Have I made others happy? Have my sins been forgiven?"

Stone said nothing.

"I had a long talk with Bill Eggers yesterday," he said, "mostly about you."

"Bill told me you had lunch," Stone said.

"I understand that your difficulties with the District Attorney's Office have been favorably resolved."

"Yes, that seems to be true. I haven't spoken to Dino since this morning; he's questioning Tom Deacon and a police officer about Susan Bean's murder, and I hope it's going well."

"Oh, I think it will go well," Bianchi said, as if he had certain knowledge of it. "And I think you will have no further problems with this Brougham person."

"I owe you a great debt," Stone said.

Bianchi waved a hand. "I do not wish to have my friends indebted to me; if I am able to do a friend a service, then that is its own reward. It should be enough for any man. Besides," he said, "I am not the sort of person to whom you should owe a debt. You must maintain your independence from all men, especially me."

Stone didn't know what to make of this.

"Bill Eggers told me many things about you," Bianchi said, "and from those things I was able to answer many questions for myself, to create a more complete picture of you as a man. I must say that what I heard fully agreed with my instinctive judgment of you."

Stone didn't speak.

"It pleases me to learn that you are an honest man, a loyal friend, and that you have a finely developed sense of justice. I believe that I can use a man like you in many of my business dealings."

"Eduardo," Stone said, "I'm grateful for your confidence, but I believe I would rather be your friend than your employee."

Bianchi smiled broadly, the first time Stone had seen him do so. "Then you continue to justify my confidence," he said. "You must know how important Dolce is to me."

"I can understand that," Stone said, wondering why the conversation was turning to Dolce.

"Her happiness, her *stability* are as important to me as anything else in my life. Other things—my grandson, for instance—are equally important, but Dolce holds a special place in my heart. She is so very like me; she understands so many things—the moral ambiguities of a rich life, the necessity of justice to success, the proper use of resources. I want very much for her to be a complete woman. Of course, for some time that has been impossible. Now . . ."

Stone's cell phone rang. Embarrassed, he dug into his pocket for the instrument. "Eduardo, I apologize, but only a couple of people have this number, and I should answer it."

"Of course," Bianchi said. "Please do so."

"Hello?"

"It's Dino; are you with Eduardo?"

"Yes."

"Good thing I called."

"What are you talking about?"

"I'll explain in a minute; that's how long it will take me to get to his front door. Meet me out front; you're going to miss dinner."

"Dino, what the hell is going on?"

"Mitteldorfer has surfaced."

"I'll be right there." Stone closed the phone and stood up. "Eduardo, I'm very sorry, but I'm not going to be able to stay for dinner. That was Dino, and the man we've been looking for, the one who

315

threatened Mary Ann and Ben, has turned up. Dino is coming for me now."

Bianchi stood up. "I understand, Stone. I'm very sorry our conversation was interrupted. I hope we can resume it very soon."

"Please make my apologies to Dolce and Mary Ann."

"Of course."

The two men shook hands, and Stone hurried toward the front door. As Pietro opened it, he heard the police siren growing closer.

62

THE CAR BARELY STOPPED MOVING FOR STONE TO GET in. He grappled with his seat belt as Dino spun the car to the left out of the driveway, spraying gravel. "Tell me about it, Dino," he said, when the car was stable again.

"A doorman at an apartment house on Park Avenue called," Dino said, roaring around another car, lights flashing, siren wailing. "He recognized Peter Hausman from the sketch in the papers, but it took him some time to get up the nerve to call. Mitteldorfer has been living in his building, under the name of Howard Menzies."

"He's sticking with his initials, then."

"Yeah; maybe he has monogrammed hankies. Anyway, Hausman showed up at the building after we busted his brother. Then, this evening, Mitteldorfer sells his brand-new Mercedes back to the dealer at a big loss, packs up, and heads for Kennedy. Said he was taking his wife's ashes back to her 'homeland.'"

"And the ashes would be Eloise Enzberg?"

"You guessed it. The doorman recognized her photograph when Andy Anderson showed it to him."

"So he's headed for Germany?"

"I'm not counting on it; there are flights leaving for London,

Paris, Rome, and half a dozen other cities, in addition to four destinations in Germany, and they're all going within the next hour. All the passenger lists are being checked for Menzies and Hausman. Andy's meeting us at the airport; we'll know more then." Dino swung right onto the shoulder to get around a truck.

"If we live that long," Stone said, gritting his teeth. Dino was a fast driver at the most relaxed of times, but an emergency brought out the Fanzio in him. "Did you crack Deacon?"

"Nope; couldn't get a word out of him; he's too smart for that."

"Shit!"

Dino grinned. "But I cracked Mick Kelly like an egg; cut him a deal."

"Can Kelly hang it on him?"

"You bet he can. Deacon had blood on his shirt cuffs when Kelly saw him after the murder. He blackmailed Deacon for a spot in the DA's Office. He's lucky Deacon didn't cut *his* throat."

"Good going, Dino! What about Brougham?"

"He had to know about the doctored tape, but we won't get him unless Deacon testifies against him. He's already resigned, though." Dino was cutting cross-country, avoiding the Long Island Expressway, cutting through residential neighborhoods and commercial districts.

Stone noted that their speed had never dropped below sixty, and at times was more than eighty. It was as fast as he'd ever traveled in an urban area.

"How did your conversation with Eduardo go?" Dino asked.

"Don't talk, drive," Stone said.

"I drive better when I talk," Dino said, jumping the curb and cutting across the lawn of a corner house to avoid a delivery truck. "What did he have to say?"

"He said he thought that Brougham would never be a problem again."

"Yeah, he would be happy about that, wouldn't he? Now Dante will get a new trial, and Eduardo can take credit for it with the goombahs."

"We couldn't have broken this without him," Stone said. "You might remember that."

"Yeah, it sort of takes the thrill away, you know?" Dino hit the six-lane approach to Kennedy, driving down the shoulder past heavy traffic. "Did Eduardo propose?"

"Propose what?"

"Marriage."

"What are you talking about, Dino?" Stone asked, closing his eyes tightly as they veered around a disabled car on the shoulder.

"You know what he's doing, don't you? He's arranging a marriage for Dolce."

"Dino, Dolce is already married."

"Oh, didn't I tell you? Somebody capped Johnny Donato this afternoon."

Stone froze. "You're kidding; tell me you're kidding."

"I'm not kidding."

"Who did it?"

"We'll probably never know, but I wouldn't have a heart attack if somebody told me it was Dolce herself. It was a straight mob hit, two rounds to the back of the head." Dino chuckled.

"It's not funny."

"Sure, it is," Dino said. He swung onto the drive to the international terminal and screeched to a halt. Andy Anderson came running to meet them.

"I've alerted airport security," he said. "Here comes their chief, now."

A man in a dark suit approached. "Lieutenant Bacchetti? I'm Sam Warren, head of airport security. Tell me what I can do to help."

"You've seen the pictures?"

Warren nodded. "They're being distributed to my people now, but from what I've heard of the timing, these two guys are already past security and into the departure area. We're talking about twenty-five gates, and there's at least one flight leaving from every one of them between now and midnight."

"Shut them down," Dino said.

"Beg pardon?"

"No flight leaves until we've searched it."

"Jesus, Lieutenant, I can't put a hold on twenty-five flights. Do you have any idea what that would do the system? People will be missing connecting flights all over Europe. It can't be done."

"Yeah, what happens when it snows?"

"Well, there are flight delays, of course."

Dino pointed to a window. "Man, look at that snow! It's a regular blizzard!"

"Lieutenant . . ."

"Listen, Sam, we've got two murderers on the loose in your airport, with six killings between them. Are you going to be responsible for letting them get out of the country?"

Warren said nothing; he was thinking about it.

"Andy," Dino said, "how many people we got here?"

"About a dozen; there are fifty more on the way, but the traffic . . ."

"Yeah, yeah, tell me about it. Let's do the flights to Germany first. Have you checked the reservations?"

"There's no Menzies or Hausman on any departing flight," Anderson said.

"So they've got backup passports; that makes it harder."

"Andy," Stone said, "check for the initials H.M.; start with the flights to Germany."

"Good idea," Dino said. "Do it, Andy. Call me when you've got an answer."

"All right," Warren said. "I'll do it." He spoke into a handheld radio. "Base, this is Warren."

"Yes, chief?"

"I want a code red on all departing international flights. Nothing moves from a gate until I say so."

"Roger, chief; what about taxiing aircraft?"

"Stop and hold everything international on my authority. I'll get back to you."

"Follow me," he said to Dino.

The four men began jogging toward the security gates.

Anderson peeled off and picked up an emergency phone.

"Where are the rest of my people?" Dino asked Warren.

"They're combing the departure lounges, trying to get a match on the pictures."

Warren got them through the security barriers, and they ran toward the departure areas.

"Let's go directly to the airplanes, Dino," Stone said.

"I've already got people at the security barriers," Warren said. "If they're in here, they can't get out, except on an airplane, and we've fixed that. The flights to Germany leave from the next four gates; if they haven't boarded yet, then we should check the lounges."

They entered the first lounge, where boarding was being announced. Warren took the microphone from a uniformed woman and announced that boarding would be delayed for five minutes.

"Dino," Stone said, "give me your backup piece."

Dino reached down to an ankle holster and handed Stone a snub-nosed .38 revolver; Stone tucked it into his belt. They began walking rapidly up and down the rows of waiting travelers. Stone looked at every male face, looked for short-haired young men, looked for Herbert Mitteldorfer.

Andy Anderson ran up to them, breathless. "Lieutenant," he said, "there's a Heinz Müller on the flight two gates down. He's the only male with those initials on a flight to Germany."

Dino grabbed Sam Warren and beckoned to Stone. "Let's go!" he yelled.

63

THE FOUR MEN RAN DOWN THE HALLWAY, SHOVING travelers out of the way, and burst into the second departure lounge. It was empty, except for a young woman at the ticket counter.

Warren ran up to her. "How long has the flight been gone?" he demanded, flashing a badge.

She looked at her watch. "Twenty minutes," she said.

"Oh, no." Stone groaned.

Warren grabbed a telephone and punched in a number. "Tower? This is Sam Warren, head of security; let me speak to a supervisor." He waited for a moment. "This is Sam Warren in security; I'm at Gate Eighteen; Flight 104 to Berlin taxied from the Gate Twenty minutes ago. Is it still on the ground?" He waited again. "Great! Have it return to the gate; tell the pilot to announce a mechanical problem that will take only a few minutes to fix; tell the passengers they'll have to get off the airplane, but they can leave their belongings." He hung up. "It's on the way back to the gate," he said to the group. "I'm going to have all the passengers deplane, and we can check them as they get off." He turned to the woman at the desk. "I want you to check them off the manifest as they leave the airplane. Don't let anybody get past you."

"Yes, sir," she replied.

The four men caught their breath while they waited for the airplane to return to the gate. Dino dispatched Andy Anderson to have his other men check the other German flights.

"I hope to God this is the flight," Dino said, pacing up and down the lounge.

"He's stuck with his initials so far; why should he change now?" Stone said.

More minutes passed. "Here comes the airplane," Sam Warren said, pointing out the window.

Anderson came back. "The other German flights are clean," he said. "If this isn't the one, then we'll have to search all the international flights."

Warren got on his radio. "Base, this is Warren; you can release all the flights to Germany, except 104; we're checking that now."

Other cops arrived and took up positions at the gate. Stone and Dino walked down the flexible ramp and were waiting at the aircraft door when it was opened from inside by a flight attendant.

Stone and Dino took up positions on each of the two aisles and searched the faces of the passengers making their way toward the exit.

Stone emptied his mind of all the faces except those of young men with very short hair and small middle-aged men. He had the feeling he was very close to Mitteldorfer, and he watched each passenger's face for signs of tension or recognition. Mostly, he saw fatigue and annoyance; then he locked eyes momentarily with a young man. He was short, stocky, wearing baggy black clothing, and, disappointingly, he had long hair. He looked away from Stone and continued up the aisle.

Stone had shifted his attention to passengers farther down the aisle when he heard a woman scream and a scuffle behind him. He was turning to see what the matter was when he experienced a hard blow to his left shoulder. His initial reaction was surprise at how much pain the blow was causing. He continued turning to find the young man in black with his fist raised above his head. He tried to raise his left arm to ward off the blow and, to his shock, could not. Everything was happening in slow motion.

He saw now that the young man held a small knife in his raised fist, and he was bringing it down toward Stone's face. As he did, the young man suddenly jerked and fell sideways, as if someone had yanked him. Blood spurted from his neck, and only then did Stone hear the gunshot. He turned to see Dino, his arm outstretched, a pistol in his hand.

Passengers were screaming; some threw themselves to the floor, others rushed past or over them, trying desperately to get off the airplane. Dino fought his way across the cabin, gun in hand, pointed down at the prostrate figure of the young man, who was twitching and grimacing. Beside him, in the aisle, Stone saw a bloody kitchen knife with a four-inch blade.

"Get these people out of here!" Dino shouted to Sam Warren. "I want the airplane cleared, and I want medical assistance here *now!*" As the last of the passengers rushed past them, Dino finally got to Stone. "Sit down," he said.

"What?"

"Sit down right here in this seat; you've been stabbed. Wait a minute; first get your coat off."

Stone got out of his jacket and was astonished to find the left sleeve soaked with blood. He'd had no sensation of the knife, just a blow to the shoulder.

"Where'd he get a knife?" Stone asked. "How'd he get it through the metal detectors?"

"From the galley," Dino said. "I saw him go for it, but I couldn't get a shot; there were too many people between him and me."

A flight attendant approached. "We've called for assistance," she said. "I'm sorry about the knife; I was slicing limes in the first-class galley, and . . ."

"It's all right," Stone said. "It's not your fault." He turned to Dino. "I saw the guy pass me, but the hair . . ."

Dino went to the young man and tugged at his hair; the wig came away in his hand. He felt for a pulse. "He's dead. Didn't I mention the wig?" Dino asked.

"No, you didn't."

"The doorman reported that Hausman had grown hair overnight. Sorry, I forgot to pass that on. I was driving."

"Forget it," Stone said. He was feeling a little weak.

The flight attendant brought a clean towel and pressed it against the back of Stone's shoulder. "Just lean back against the seat," she said. "That will hold the towel in place."

"You okay here?" Dino asked. "I want to search the rest of the airplane."

"I'm okay," Stone replied.

Dino beckoned to Sam Warren. They walked aft in the airplane, checking under seats and in the toilets. Shortly, Dino returned. "How you doing?"

"I'm fine, Dino; when can we get out of here?"

"You're going to have to go to the emergency room," Dino said.

"Well, I'm not going in an ambulance; you can drive me."

"All right," Dino said. "Miss?" he said to the flight attendant. "Can you get me a wheelchair?"

"I don't need a wheelchair," Stone said. "I can walk."

"I'm not going to have you walking through the airport, covered with blood, then passing out in front of everybody," Dino said.

"Did you get Mitteldorfer?" Stone asked.

"I didn't see him; Andy and his people are checking the lounge and the corridors now. He may have made it out during the excitement."

Two security people arrived with a stretcher and took Peter Hausman's body away, leaving Stone and Dino alone on the airplane.

"You just sit tight," Dino said. "I'm going to go find a wheelchair, then we'll get you out of here." He left Stone alone on the airplane.

Stone was feeling better after the shock of learning that he had been stabbed had passed. Twenty minutes had passed since the excitement, and he was even feeling a little drowsy. He pushed the recline button on his seat, which was at the rear of the first-class compartment, and tucked a pillow under his head. At least he could rest until they got him out of here.

Stone was nearly asleep when he heard the sound, which was very like snoring. He opened his eyes. How could he be snoring, when he wasn't even asleep, yet? The sound persisted. Stone pressed a button, and his seat returned to a sitting position. He could still hear the snoring, and it seemed to be coming from behind him somewhere.

He got to his feet, somewhat unsteadily, and began to make his way down the aisle toward the rear of the airplane, listening. The snoring grew louder. Well back into the tourist section of the airplane, he stopped and looked up and to his left. The large overhead bin was closed. He reached up and opened it, then took Dino's .38 from his belt and stepped back.

The snoring was coming from a raincoat stashed in the overhead bin. With the short gun barrel, Stone moved the coat out of the way. A middle-aged man with gray hair and a small beard lay on his back in the compartment, snoring loudly. At first, Stone didn't recognize him.

Dino came back aboard the airplane, pushing a wheelchair. "Hey!" he called to Stone. "What are you doing back there? You shouldn't be on your feet!"

"Come back here," Stone called to him, "and bring your cuffs."

Mitteldorfer jerked awake at the sound of Stone's voice. He turned and looked at Stone, and recognition distorted his face. "You!" he screamed.

"Me!" Stone shouted back at him.

64

I T WAS AFTER 1:00 A.M., AND IT HAD BEGUN RAINING when Dino's car stopped in front of Stone's house. The emergency room had been a zoo. They had given him a local anesthetic, stitched him up, given him a tetanus shot, some antibiotics, and a little bottle of painkillers. It had taken Stone some time to convince his doctor that he would be better off at home than in the hospital.

"Thanks," Stone said.

"It wasn't much out of my way," Dino replied.

"I mean for shooting Hausman. He was about to do more damage."

"I'm sorry I couldn't shoot him sooner."

"It's over, isn't it? Finally."

"Yeah, it's over."

"There's nobody out there trying to do us in?"

"You can sleep well tonight," Dino said. "Me, too, come to that. Mary Ann and Ben are already back at home."

"I'm glad; I know you've missed them."

"Yeah, I have. Being a bachelor isn't all it's cracked up to be."

"Oh, I don't know; it's not a bad life, when people aren't trying to kill you."

"What are you going to say to Eduardo?"

"I'll reason with him."

"It might work, if you can do it without annoying him. Sicilians perceive insults even where there are none."

"I'll reason with him very carefully."

"Good. You're my friend, Stone, but I can't say I want you for a brother-in-law."

"I'm hurt, Dino."

"You going to reason with Dolce, too?"

"I'm not sure she can be reasoned with."

"Now you're beginning to get the picture."

"I'm too tired to think about it right now," Stone said. "And the painkillers are starting to kick in. I hope I can get upstairs before I fall asleep."

"You want some help?"

"No, I'll make it." Stone opened the car door and stepped out into the rain. "Good night, Dino."

"Good night, Stone. I'll call you tomorrow and give you the latest on Mitteldorfer."

"You do that." Stone closed the car door and walked slowly up the front steps of his house. He let himself in and took the elevator upstairs, because he didn't feel like negotiating the stairs. He had a pretty good buzz from the painkillers.

There was a light on in the bedroom, which gave him a little start. He crept into the room and found Dolce asleep in his bed, naked, only partly covered by a sheet. The expression on her face was one of a somnolent child, all innocence and sweetness.

He slipped out of the sling that held his arm, got undressed as quietly as he could, switched off the light, and got into bed beside her. She stirred in her sleep and reached out for him, illuminated by the light of half a moon, coming through the clouds outside.

"You okay?" she asked, without really waking up.

"I'm okay. How'd you get in?"

Her brow wrinkled. "Remote control for the garage door. I brought your car back. What happened?"

She seemed to be waking up, now, and he didn't want that. He stroked her face, and she slept again. "I'll tell you tomorrow," he whispered, letting sleep come to him.

He had absolutely no idea what he would say to her tomorrow.

Acknowledgments

I am grateful to my editor, vice president and associate publisher Gladys Justin Carr, and her staff, associate editor Erin Cartwright and editorial associate Deirdre O'Brien, as well as all those at HarperCollins who have worked so hard for the success of my books.

I also want to express my gratitude to my agent, Morton L. Janklow, and his principal associate, Anne Sibbald, as well as to the staff of Janklow & Nesbit for their continuing efforts in the management of my writing career and for their warm friendship.

I am also very grateful to my wife, Chris, who is always the first subjected to my manuscripts, for plugging the holes therein and for the shoulder rubs that keep me working at the computer.

Author's Note

I am happy to hear from readers, but I should warn you that if you write to me in care of my publishers, three to six months will pass before I receive your letter, and when it finally arrives it will be one among many, and I will not be able to reply.

However, if you have access to the Internet you may visit my website at www.stuartwoods.com, where there is a facility for sending me e-mail. So far, I have been able to reply to all my e-mail.

If you have sent me an e-mail and not received a reply, it is because you are one among an alarming number of people who (a) don't know their e-mail return address; (b) can't spell their e-mail return address; or (c) don't have an e-mail address. If you are without a computer you may send e-mails from all sorts of places—libraries, copy shops, and from the computers of your children and friends.

Remember: e-mail, reply; snail mail, no reply.

Those who wish to point out typographical and editorial errors in the books should contact HarperCollins Publishers, 10 East 53rd Street, New York, NY 10022-5299.

Those requests concerning events should e-mail them to me or send them to: The Publicity Department, HarperCollins Publishers, 10 East 53rd Street, New York, NY 10022-5299.

Those ambitious folk who wish to buy film, dramatic, or television rights to my books should contact Matthew Snyder, Creative Artists Agency, 9830 Wilshire Boulevard, Beverly Hills, CA 90212–1825.

Those who wish to conduct business of a more literary nature should contact Anne Sibbald, Janklow & Nesbit, 598 Madison Avenue, New York, NY 10022.

If you wish me to do a book signing in your locality, you should ask your favorite bookseller to contact his HarperCollins representative and make the request.

If you wish to attend a book signing, the schedule for each book tour is posted on my website.

All my novels are still in print, in paperback, and can be ordered from any bookstore. If you wish to obtain hardcover copies of my earlier novels or my out-of-print non-fiction books, you should find a good used bookstore. Many of these can do a national search for the titles.